EXILE

EXILE

The Lunnaria Trilogy
Book I

by Luiza Dobrzyńska

EXILE

THE LUNNARIA TRILOGY

BOOK I

BY LUIZA DOBRZYNSKA

PAPERBACK ISBN: 978-1-7353456-0-4

EPUB ISBN: 978-1-3933694-5-5

***

WRITTEN BY LUIZA DOBRZYNSKA

PUBLISHED BY ROYAL HAWAIIAN PRESS

COVER ART BY TYRONE ROSHANTHA

TRANSLATED BY RAFAL STACHOWSKY

PUBLISHING ASSISTANCE: DOROTA RESZKE

***

FOR MORE WORKS BY THIS AUTHOR, PLEASE VISIT:

WWW.ROYALHAWAIIANPRESS.COM

***

VERSION NUMBER 1.00

Table of content

PROLOGUE

A scream.

Pain.

I am the one screaming. Please, no...

I'm dying, I have to stop defending myself, and it will be better that way...

The distinct touch of metal arms, the stabbing of needles, finally the pain subsides, I fall into some kind of a black abyss. I protest with the last remnants of my consciousness, but stop halfway. Don't listen to me, I want to live, live.... How long did it last? An hour, a day or two seconds? I don't know.

The world was returning to me slowly, unreal, with blurred colors and shapes, wavy and silent. I wake up and fall asleep. I don't feel any pain. I'm lying on a metal table, surrounding me are the smells of medications, melted plastic and hot metal. Above me, on the ceiling, I see an enormous mirror. I observed my naked body with amazement. From the outside you can see so little... maybe it's because I've never actually looked this good. I have the impression that they've improved my waist, the shape of my breasts, neck, and I don't think I've ever had such luxuriant hair. Did someone decide to remodel me like that on a whim? But who? Where are the doctors?

I want to ask them, find something out, but I can't get any sound out of my mouth, my lips are like someone's, not mine. I'm falling asleep. When the consciousness returns again, there are fuzzy figures dressed in white around me. I want to ask them a question, but instead I feel the pressure of a needleless syringe on my arm and the world is blending away again.

Same thing again.

I wake up and fall asleep.

I can barely feel anything.

Finally, the world comes back, stabilizes in expressive shapes, colors take on depth and sharpness. Where am I? I'm lying on an oblique table, the mirror which occupies half of the opposite wall is showing me a figure dressed in a clumsy overall, similar to those worn by porters. That's me.

"Congratulations, Miss Kaphool," I heard the mechanical voice of the coordinator, "your body responded positively to the connection. The damaged and lost parts have been successfully replaced by cybernetic implants. Their efficiency is guaranteed by the Corporation and no additional tests are required. Thank you for using the EPIPHANICS services."

Now the matter was partly explained. EPIPHANICS is a service company specializing not in typical plastic surgery, but in the reconstruction of the victims of the most serious accidents. For the sake of the patient's psychological comfort, they are kept in a pharmacological coma from the beginning of the procedure until the end. They are only fully awakened once they are able to leave the clinic and they are then serviced by remotely controlled robots – all so that the one cruelly mutilated doesn't have to look in the eyes of those who saw them in their worst condition and had to repair their body.

However, this was an unbelievably expensive center – so what am I doing here?

Slowly, uncertainly, I got off the table. The surviving nerves were receiving a new type of touch, somehow different from the old one. I'll have to get used to it, because from now on everything will be different. Although... what actually happened? I can't remember. I don't even know how I got here, I couldn't have done it on my own... I remember dying, my body was massacred, but how, by whom?

"Coordinator, who brought me here?" I ask loudly.

"Restricted information."

"Why?"

"Restricted information."

Somebody cares about me. Cares so much that they brought me here and began the expensive procedure. Could it have been one of the ones who did me in? Eh, unlikely, that's not why they tried to kill me. Then who? I don't recall anybody, anyone to whom I could be so dear. And then shreds of memories began flowing in. I already know that something happened... but the only thing I know is that it was something horrifying.

I'm walking like in a trance. My movements gained fluidity and lightness. I feel as if I will never be tired again, that I've lost this ability. The implants must be incredible and worth more than I could earn throughout my whole life. Suddenly, I became terrified that the one who paid for the repair of my body could now ask for compensation and would be entitled to it. Who could it be? What will they demand? I feel cornered, hounded...

But nobody was waiting for me outside. The surroundings were empty and quiet, dusk was falling. There was a single *vehicle parked in the driveway, a small, slim Suzuki car – one of those extremely expensive models from a limited series, metallic black, with silver accents. A folded sheet of silvery paper was stuck behind the windscreen wiper. My name was written on it in capital letters, it could be seen from afar. I walk over, take the piece of paper and unfold it. The paper has clean, printed text:*

"This car is yours. The key is in the ignition, the documents and further instructions in the compartment under the steering wheel."

There was no signature. Someone, who also paid for my implants, left for me this beautiful vehicle and now wants something in return. I hesitate. Something tells me that I'd be able to simply run away and forget about it all, but on the other hand it would be unfair and I always acted honestly. I've always paid my debts, and although this was not something that I've voluntarily gotten involved with, I still felt obliged.

Without enthusiasm, I open the door and enter the freshly smelling interior. In the compartment under the steering wheel I find the car's documents, issued in my name, a credit card and booking at the most expensive of hotels – Miraton, owned by Tenyson Corporation – with "Paid" stamped onto it. An apartment on the twenty-fifth floor.

I was never even able to afford an evening at Miraton, let alone accommodation, and the reservation is for an indefinite period. It isn't just strange, it's alarming. I don't get it. The more I think about it, the less I understand. Who could care about me this much? I'm all alone in the world, I have no influential friends or acquaintances, the last boyfriend who I was seeing left me a year ago and, what's more, he was poor and not interested in me that much. Even if he became rich, he wouldn't spend it on me. Chris? He left for that university of his and so far has written me only twice. Mabel? Sandra? There's no way.

I take a look in the mirror. My face is still my face, but it seems much more regular, and this hair... different, denser, alien, and redder. The ones I remember were of more brown color. I think they transplanted these for me too, I think they had to? Did someone scalp me? I fall into the springy seat and try desperately to remember anything specific.

***

"Get up, Chris! You'll be late for work!"

Every day is the same. I was already prepared to leave and make breakfast, while he's still asleep. I've managed to get used to it, I've had enough time for that.

We began living together after reaching adult age, when we were forced to leave the house. We were both orphans, but the social family allowed us to grow up in decent conditions. Of the six selected siblings, I was closest with Chris, so we decided to rent a shared flat to save on the costs of rent. He was a little younger than me, and maybe that's why he treated me like I really was his older sister and caretaker in one. One aspect of this was the sad fact that almost every day I had to wake him up like a child who doesn't want to go to school.

"Okay, okay," he murmured finally without opening his eyes, "I'm getting up."

I pulled the blanket off him and gave him a long slap to his bare bottom. This immediately sobered him up.

"Come on, Leeta!"

He jumped out of bed, covering himself with a small pillow, and fled to the bathroom. I went back to the table and started eating, waiting for Chris to finish his morning ablutions.

He finally left, buttoning up his shirt and went straight to his portion of cereal.

"So, are you going for the interview today?" he asked after a moment.

"Of course," I said, "it's a great opportunity for me. How many people of our category do you know who were offered work at the Medical Academy?"

"Uh," he muttered, swallowing quickly. "Something feels off about it to me. What does a plant technician have to do there?"

I shrugged my shoulders.

"I have no idea," I confessed, "that's what I'm going to find out. I doubt that it's a joke, it would be extremely stupid. What about you? You said that the test went well."

"I don't even know anymore. I think it did, but I don't want it to just go well. It has to be excellent. If I get first place, I will be able to study at my chosen department for the whole year. And if I make into the to top three, they'll allow me to continue my studies!"

I suppressed my sigh. This is the whole problem with Chris – he's always been a dreamer, always wandering in the clouds without paying attention to the reality in which he lived.

"Are you sure that's a good idea?" I asked with caution, "I don't want you to be disappointed. B3 isn't a civilian category for which they created the universities.

He placed his cheek to his hand and looked at me in the only way he could: as if he didn't see me at all, only his own, beautiful vision. During that time he looked like an inspired artist, and with his long blond hair and blue eyes, he resembled the image of a prince from a children's book. I always wondered, why he wasn't adopted by some rich family. He was such a beautiful kid, and in time grew up to be an extremely handsome man. Ones like him were usually able to find new parents without difficulty... unlike an uninteresting, hiding in the corners girl, who the babysitters at the orphanage referred to as 'The Bat' amongst each other.

And yet there were no volunteers and we ended up with the same family. I selfishly thought that it was a good thing. We were close to each other like real siblings and trusted each other indefinitely. Nonetheless, I wasn't so blinded with my love to my foster brother that I'd miss the obvious facts. The synaptic density, which was measured just after birth, combined with the classification of both of our parents placed us in the social category of B3, and so without any exciting opportunities.

Our IQ at birth was forecasted to be between 105 and 110 points. And although I didn't feel the need to see my measurable intelligence, Chris did and received 125 points on his first attempt. That's why he was admitted to the national tests, which were a bit like a lottery with the reward being a one-year reference to a high-class academy.

"Did you know that everyone used to be able to study, as long as they passed the exams?" Chris asked. I stirred my tea automatically. My cereal has completely cooled down and softened, and yet I still haven't touched it. I had no appetite.

"Now they can, too!" I murmured. "I mean, there aren't any rules that prohibit it."

"Yes only that from childhood they're always instructing us to not jump above the bar."

"Chris! You know that it makes sense. There are so many beautiful and interesting professions we can take on without exposing ourselves to bitter disappointments and obstacles that we cannot overcome. Do you really dislike your job that much?"

"I like it. I like it a lot. But I would like to try something completely different. It's not my fault that they classified me as B3, even though I deserve more."

I waved my hand and added some sweetener to my tea.

"Do what you want. Just don't come crying when something goes wrong, not as you planned."

"I definitely won't. Maybe it will go wrong. Either way, I would never forgive myself if I missed this opportunity."

I looked at him with pity, but gave up my persuasions. Chris was indeed extremely intelligent for our classification. I cheered him on with all my heart, but I hardly believed in any success. Although, on the other hand, why was that, exactly?

I was met with something unexpected myself. When I decided to change my current job to something better paid, I didn't expected them to send me such an offer from the distribution list. I surreptitiously took the folded computer foil out of my pocket and read through it again: *"The Medical Academy of Palm Springs has reported a need for a florist technician. The Rector will be waiting for Miss Julietta Kaphoolie at 11am on July 3rd inside the main building's office."*

I don't think there could've been a mistake, the foil showed my data, with the official hologram of the recruitment agency. This type of material wasn't used just to play a prank on someone. They're some strictly accountable foils, marked and impossible to forge. Who would feel like it, either way? Nobody was interested in me to that extent. There wasn't anything to be interested in.

***

Chris left for work and I was preparing for my interview. I thoroughly cleaned my nails, combed my hair and, after a bit of thinking, gave up on makeup. As for my clothes... that was more difficult. None of what I had in my closet fit for a prestigious university like the Medical University. Finally, I decided to pick my navy blue pants with a matching vest and a creamy blouse which I kept for special occasions. This will have to do, worst case scenario I'll have to simply purchase an outfit more suitable for work. Assuming of course that they even accept me...

I was so nervous that I left home early at ten. I arrived there fifteen minutes later, so I decided to go to a nearby park and cool down a bit. I've never been in this district before. It was very elegant, clean, but to my relief there were many B3 and even C1 walking around the streets – although admittedly the latter were just painting the fence of one of the houses, built in the style which was common more than two centuries ago. Some very rich people must live there since I saw two tiny spruces and a magnolia on their property. They must have cost a fortune. For a split second I wondered whether I should call them and ask if they need a florist, but I immediately gave up this idea. I didn't want to be anybody's maid, even for good payment.

The park was founded near the academic complex. It wasn't natural – nor did I expect it to be, only private parks sometimes were – but it was very well designed. Different species of trees, lawns, flower beds with realistically reconstructed flowers... and only sanded alleys the benches were real. There wasn't any way to distinguish where the polymer vegetation ends and the illusion begins.

Even though I knew that it was only a illusion, I paused and opened my mouth in amazement upon realizing that fluffy furry animals with bushy tails were jumping along the branches of the trees! It took me a moment to remember that these were squirrels, which used to live in places like these. They were recreated brilliantly, just like the large birds with rainbow-colored tails, walking lazily on the grass. I haven't seen them anywhere else, except in a holographic zoo. It was clear that first-class technicians were hired here, because everything looked so authentic that if it were not for the sign at the entrance which reads 'Videoplastic Park', I would have been deceived.

The illusion was intensified by sounds of the birds flowing from hidden speakers, as well as the smell of moss, grass and trees – the aromatic sprays must have been hidden somewhere, but I couldn't see them. Big boulders scattered here and there were probably brought from the mountains, judging by their color and shapes, and in the depths of the park a beautiful surprise awaited: a small, beautiful waterfall. A real one! I even put my hand under the falling curtain of water just to make sure that it was wet and cold. In the lake, to which the cascade fell, swam colorful fish but I didn't dare trying to check whether these were alive or just cybernetic creatures. I thought about how if I got a job here, I would be able to spend my break in this place and I felt that I really wanted that.

I've been to many similar places before, but it's my first one seeing one as beautiful as this. Living in a rich neighborhood was great after all. 'Our' park, although still pleasant and definitely not ugly, wasn't such a miracle. For a short time I sat on the bench by the waterfall, ate a portion of ice cream and drank some sparkling water with artificial juice. During this time of day the park was rather empty, I've only encountered a few people taking a lonely walk and two families with children, both A3 class.

I quickly got off the bench and apologized when one of the families approached.

"Please, don't get up," said the mother of the family, a platinum blonde in navy blue second skin-type clothes, which embraced her gorgeous figure like a glove. She smiled kindly at the sight of my confusion. "This is a public park, and you don't disturb us at all."

"I... I have to go. Have a nice day," I stammered incoherently and ran away. Although this lady was elegant and cultural, I felt awkward around her. In the Greenwood District, where I grew up, seeing a person of class A was a rare occurrence and we were taught to stay out of their way from a young age not because they could do something to us or the law required it. We knew class A consisted of the most important people, and those who work the hardest, which is why we had to respect them and help them as much as we could. That's what we were told at home and at school.

I wanted to be helpful, to be socially useful, but I still had no idea how. Until now I worked in a greenhouse belonging to a large florist studio and it was a nice job, but I had little contact with people. I wanted that to change with all my heart.

Since it was almost time, I began moving towards the buildings of the Medical Academy, feeling my throat tightening with each step. I was overwhelmed with the mere sight of these magnificent, ultra-modern buildings, I couldn't even imagine how I'll be able to gather the courage to cross one of their thresholds. Truth be told, I hesitated so much at the gate that a handsome guard in a black uniform noticed it and took pity on me.

"Do you have any business here, miss?" he asked. The diamond-shape caste mark between his eyebrows indicated C1 classification, and this fact gave me comfort. If he was hired here, then maybe I'll be accepted too.

"I'm here to talk to the rector about a job," I said, taking out my ID card.

He examined it carefully, then took a clean, rectangular visual registration plate from the desk drawer and put it in the marker. He entered my data and after a while the same plate slipped out, but already decorated with my photo and a hologram with the inscription: Juliette Kaphoolie, B3, and guest. The security guard quickly attached the pin, pinned the ID to my vest and handed the card back to me.

"Building A, first floor, corridor A, office number one," he said in a kind tone. "Good luck."

"Thank you."

I smiled at him gratefully and with a more confident step walked towards the building pointed out to me, located in the center and giving the impression that it was made of only glass. The academic year hasn't yet begun, so it was almost completely empty. I only came across two cleaning machine operators, one of whom was eating his second breakfast while the other was repairing something in on his remote-control console. None of them paid me any attention, so I went unhindered to the first floor and sought office one. On its door hung an old-fashioned plaque with the decorative inscription 'Rector's Office'. I knocked, timidly at first, then a little harder. A woman's voice came from the speaker on the wall:

"Come in!"

I touched the door. It opened, letting me into an elegant office, lined with a fitted carpet and decorated with framed graphs. They showed some charts and diagrams that I didn't understand. Behind a modern desk sat a young woman with an inverted V mark on her forehead – making her an A3. She wore a perfectly tailored deep purple costume with black insets, which made it look like it was taken from the exhibition of the most sophisticated kind of fashion house. My knees softened immediately, especially when she gave me a cool, professional, appraising look.

"What is your business here?" she asked. Her voice was complaisant, contrary to my fears, there was no shadow of dislike, disregard or superiority.

"I have an appointment with the rector which concerns work."

"Miss... Kaphoolie, directed by the assignment office?"

"Yes. Here is my referral and identification card."

I handed the documents to the secretary, who took them indifferently and placed them in a separate compartment in the binder on the desk. Then she got up and approached the wall. The door hidden inside it opened.

"Mr. Rector, Juliette Kaphoolie is here."

"Send her to me, Sandra," a male voice answered from inside, "and bring us two caffetinos."

"Yes, sir," this time I thought I heard a note of hesitation in the woman's voice, or maybe it was just my imagination. The idea of an A3 making caffetino for a representative of class B3 seemed completely surreal, and as I passed the secretary I gave her an apologetic look.

Behind the desk, which was stylized as a piece of furniture from the last century, sat a short thin old man. In front of him stood a brass plaque with the decorative inscription: Professor Harold Brotsky. The rector had a likeable, carefully shaven face decorated with a perked nose, a network of wrinkles around the eyes and almost completely gray hair. It surprised me a little. Nowadays, signs of old age are rarely seen in people before ninety. Apparently, Mr. Brotsky must have belonged to the small percentage of people allergic to the anti-age pill. He didn't seem concerned with that fact, however.

There was a stylized mark resembling an arrowhead on his forehead, which I expected anyway. Who else but an A1 could be the head of such a prestigious university? My intimidation doubled. I have never had the chance to talk with a representative of such a high social class and I didn't know how I should behave. The Rector must have sensed it because he smiled at me kindly.

"Please, take a seat," he said with such courtesy as if I belonged to class A. "Are you the florist technician recommended by the recruitment office?"

"Yes," I said, sitting up shyly on the chair, "I am a florist with a specialization in tropical plants, Professor."

He nodded in approval.

"I'm sure you're wondering what you're doing here," he said. "The thing is, our Academy has obtained, after many years of efforts, permission to create its own greenhouse. We're planning to give real flowers to outstanding students on the occasion of handing them their diplomas or to important guests, but first we must grow the flowers. You see, what we'd like to see is the special types, not ones that you can get at any floral studio."

"I understand," I was still trying to control my nervousness and raging heartbeat. I casually brushed my fingers against the desk. As I thought, it was real wood, not synthetic. The university must have been richer than I thought.

"Unfortunately, we were allocated only half the time for this task," the rector said. "So, we began looking for someone who could perform two functions at once. It isn't appropriate for our Academy to offer anyone a part-time job, it would lower our prestige. We chose you from the list sent to us by the office, because it is indicated in your data that you've also completed a librarian degree."

"Yes, that's correct. Our social mother insisted that we learn as much as possible. She claimed that in this way we would gain better life prospects. However, I've never worked in this profession before."

"I have no doubts that you'll manage either way..."

Sandra entered the office, carrying two cups of steaming caffetino, one of which she placed in front of me.

"Would you like some sugar or a sweetener?" she said without a shadow of resentment. She had amazing class, I don't know whether, being in her place, I would be able to be so kind to someone lower, not even by a layer, but a whole social level.

"No, thank you. Thank you very much," I replied, trying to make it known that I knew my place and wouldn't dare claim the right to such kindness towards my person. The secretary smiled slightly and left, and the door closed quietly behind her.

I took a sip with pleasure, because my lips were completely dried from emotions. The caffetino was delicious, much better quality than that I bought every day at the Fiona supermarket.

"As a librarian, it will be your responsibility to keep order in the database, assign numbers to new files, classify them properly, and help students find the literature they need," Brotsky summed up, taking a sip from his cup. "I hope you understand that giving someone access to our database is an expression of trust on the part of the university, especially since part of the library are antique books, printed on paper. They have great value. We expect responsibility and diligence in carrying out your tasks, as well as... discretion."

"Discretion?"

"Yes, Miss Kaphoolie. Our university is attended almost exclusively by representatives of class A, although sometimes there are extremely talented B1 students. From what I remember there were even two future medics from class C here, picked up by the investigators from the offices of IQ Investigation. Have you ever come across the IQI's activities?"

"Yes. My social brother was selected by them for the national test. He has a chance to study at the polytechnic, if he obtains the highest score..." with some difficulty, I suppressed the string of sentences that suddenly came over me. After all, my interlocutor didn't care about Chris or the private life of his employees.

"Exactly," he continued. "In that case, you must be aware that you will come across different kinds of people. You must never favor anyone, even if you happen to like them very much. The guardian of our library's records must follow the protocol no matter what. You cannot befriend the students. This is not discrimination," he added hastily. "This prohibition applies to all teaching staff and all employees of our Academy, even myself. There are other rules you must follow. For example, we must not allow someone from a lower grade to have an insight into the textbooks of higher courses. Also, no one from outside the university is allowed to use our collections – you will have to check the student's identity each time before granting access to the material. Either way, you will receive a detailed list of responsibilities and recommendations."

"Does this mean that I have the job?" I asked incredulously. The rector smiled.

"Of course. You are our best candidate. You can start at the beginning of next week. There will be some time left to prepare an accurate list of what is needed to set up the greenhouse, and we will prepare the appropriate contract. To start with, you'll get a thousand allocation points for each job."

"In other words, two thousand a month for both jobs?" I asked, opening my eyes wide. I wasn't hoping for anything more than a thousand, a thousand and two hundredths at best...

"For a start. After that there will be discretionary bonus and other extras. Why are you surprised? Our people must be properly rewarded, there is no other way."

I left the rector's office completely stunned. This job seemed like some sort of gift of capricious fortune and I wanted to pinch myself properly to see if I was dreaming. Sitting at her computer, Sandra looked at me and gave me a friendly smile.

"Is everything all right?" she asked.

"Yes, I was accepted," I answered. "I'm so happy. Thank you for the caffetino and I'm sorry for the trouble."

"Not a problem. I'm glad that you'll be working here. It will be nice to have a colleague of my age."

"How is that?" now I was completely cemented to the ground.

"Well, medical veterans are the ones who usually work here, in their sixties or better. I hope we will be good friends. It's boring eating lunch alone."

"But of course, if you don't mind..."

It was difficult to believe that this elegant lady would really offer me friendship. So far, I've only seen women like her on photos or on the television. I left the Academy building with cotton-soft legs, deeply confused by all that happened to me today, but even happier. I did it. I got the job.

***

I can't remember what exactly happened, and I don't think I want to remember. I felt like my eyes were shining much more than usual, but it may have been an illusion. I think it was this glow – although it could just be a matter of my imagination – or maybe even the realization that I have somebody else's hair on my head was causing me to examine the whole matter, find out who is behind it and what they want from me. With this resolution, I twisted the key and the Suzuki moved swiftly forward.

I have never sat behind the wheel of such a work of art. It reacted to my every movement as if it was an extension of my hands – it must have the latest the latest generation sensors built-in and you could definitely set it for voice control, but I don't have time to play around with that yet, I don't know how yet anyway. Somewhere in the car there was probably a navigation computer instruction manual. I decided to look for it a better time, but for now I have to reach the hotel and see whether this secret protector won't be there waiting for me, whoever they are.

I only know one thing about them so far, that they are very rich and influential. Money alone would not give them access to one of the exclusive EPIPHANICS centers and they wouldn't allow for a remote procedure to be carried out without its entire administrative layer. I mean, no one was writing down my data, I also didn't sign anything, no documents were requested from me – all of this came to my realization slowly and reluctantly, convincing me that it will best to explain all of it. An escape wouldn't solve anything, since someone who has this much influence would find me anyway. Who could it be? Someone from the government? From the secret police? Or maybe one of those anonymous rich people who manage the world's economy?

Yes, that's the most likely scenario. I wonder who exactly... These days, after crossing a certain income threshold a person becomes invisible to the rest of society, nobody knows the names or faces of those who live in the true luxury. You can't write about them, you can't talk about them, but they exist, and one of them paid for what saved my life.

My life up to this point was different. I've always been aware of the fact that I belong to a class of workers, not decision makers, but I didn't have to hide anything. I could do what I wanted, live in a house without protection, and openly bear my name. As a little girl, I've never even seen children from A classes, let alone play with them, as a teenager I finished school in the company of class B youth.

B1 often went to college, one of them even urged me to try to pass the initial test – I was remembering him now, a frail boy with a crooked nose, I think that he had a little crush on me. He claimed that I could make it in college that I could apply for a promissory note or even a scholarship but I never believed that it could work. My social mother also advised me against it, she claimed that there was no point in banging my head against the wall when there were so many good professions which would provide me with a livelihood. B3 was, after all, a fairly low civic category. My poor social mother... she wanted me to become a nurse, but I couldn't stand the sight of blood. I fainted even when I just cut my finger and I avoided places where there were fights. And it was me who must have experienced something terrifying... but I still can't remember what it was.

***

The new job turned out to be very absorbing. Most of all, it required a rather long drive by the public car, and thus, getting up early. I had to create the greenhouse practically from scratch, because what the technical department ordered was not suitable for the purposes set by the management of the Academy. For the first few days I didn't even go out for lunch, but after two weeks, when I dealt with all the most important issues, I allowed Sandra to persuade me for a meal.

Near the university there were several eateries with different standards. To my surprise, the rector's secretary was dining at the humblest of them all, called At Barney's.

"I don't earn much," she explained, "it's cheap here, and I like what they serve. My parents weren't rich and taught me how to economically manage what I have."

The At Barney's menu mainly consisted of substitutes, but it also included such delicacies as baked macaroni and cheese, rice balls with fruit, and even real wine. Of course, these dishes exceeded our financial capabilities, but we agreed that one day we would take something from the 'higher-shelf' and split the bill. For now, we ate what other regulars had and I had to admit that the chefs in this restaurant knew what they were doing. Someone who can conjure up such tasty dishes from meat and vegetable substitutes must be a genius.

Sandra turned out to be a cheerful and friendly girl, younger than I thought – barely twenty years old. At first, I was intimidated by the fact that she was an A3, but with time I stopped thinking about it and simply began to like her. When I left for the library after lunch, she often came there after work and we often returned together.

"I kept telling you, stop treating A-class citizens like demigods," Chris said rebuking when I told him about my new friendship. "They are people just like us, only that they have slightly higher synaptic density in the brains."

My brother was rebellious from an early age and as he grew older he was constantly looking for a way to break out of his social class. He dreamed of going to a university, and not just any of them. His ambition was space engineering, it was the only thing he talked about and bought used textbooks, eagerly exploring them later at night, which I honestly didn't understand.

"Because you don't have any higher aspirations beyond those plants of yours," he answered my questions with supremacy and returned to the books, stored in the memory of the best e-book reader he could get his hands on.

One day, around two months after I began working at the Academy, Chris returned home in a state of such excitement that at the sight of him I dropped my cup with juice. Not paying attention to anything else, he embraced me and danced with me wildly in the middle of our apartment.

"I did it! I got the highest amount of points!" he shouted. "I will get the index, dear sister!"

I have never seen him this happy. His eyes were glowing, his face was flushing, and I could almost hear the blood boiling through his veins. On one hand, I was happy for him, but on the other, I felt sudden sadness. If Chris was going to go to university, he had to move to Houston, because it was the Polytechnic there that organized this year's test. It meant that I would be alone. I did my best to not show my worries, trying to not spoil his extraordinary occasion. Chris deserved the best and there were many indications that he would be able to fight for it.

Maybe he was right, maybe I was not ambitious enough? I thought about it that day and the next, while helping him to pack, and later still, when I walked him to the station and returned to our apartment by myself. I had to look for a new, smaller one because the thought of living with a stranger was very unpleasant to me. I wrote to the central section of living quarters and the next day I received a dozen or so proposals, from which I chose a nice apartment in the Sunset Estate, located closer to the Silvergate district, where I worked. I called the facility's dispatcher and we decided that after work I could come and see the apartment, without any obligations for now.

"The Sunset Estate!" Sandra exclaimed when I told her about everything at lunch. "That's where I live! And in the building H, too! What a coincidence…"

"Is it some very exclusive place?" I asked, worried slightly.

"No way? Be reasonable, exclusive apartments don't get suggested on the main distribution board. I took what was cheaper, I told you that I have to save money."

I already knew why this was happening. She told me one evening that her parents once ran into some misfortunes concerning an important investment and were currently paying off a huge debt. Sandra, like the good daughter she was, helped them financially as much as she could, but since she earned only two thousand five hundred with an added bonus for a representative position, she didn't have much to spend on her own expenses.

"Well then, we'll be neighbors."

"I'm really happy about that. Building H is just beginning to be inhabited and I don't know anyone there."

Sandra's voice revealed genuine joy. She liked me, although I couldn't understand why. I could never match her social status, beauty or IQ index – honestly, I had no idea how it was possible that a person with her intelligence was working as a simple secretary. I didn't ask her, trying not to pry, but it seemed inappropriate to me.

I visited the apartment in the afternoon. It was small, but very functional, equipped with everything necessary. Bedroom, living room, bathroom, a small kitchen. The walls of the living room were decorated with holo-frames, the wallpaper opposite the bed, a remote control mounted in the bedside table.

"You can change the images on the holo-frames as you wish," said the dispatcher who was showing me around. "Each of them has in the memory a hundred and fifteen different motifs, from old masters of the brush to modern abstraction. If you prefer photos of nature, just insert the appropriate memory card into the reader. You can also change the color of the walls, although not at the level of a luxurious apartment and without decorations. On the panel you can select different shades, simply press the button. As for the television set, we have a local network, a flat fee, and five hundred programs to choose from. There is also a library and a video game and movie rental. A social center will also soon be opened in the estate. There's something for everyone.

"How much does it cost per month?" I asked, almost certain that I wouldn't be able to afford it.

"Six hundred allocation points together with all fees. What's your decision?"

Six hundred points? That's something I could afford. The former apartment which I rented together with Chris cost us almost a thousand, and we each paid half of it. Now I will be paying on my own, but it meant that I would spend only two hundred PP more than before.

"I'll take it," I answered firmly. "Can we finalize the contract now?"

"Of course, as long as you have all the necessary documents on your person. Let's go to the office."

I had all my documents. Another fifteen minutes and I was entered into the memory of the central controller as tenant number 227. The dispatcher took a print of my thumb, pattern of my retina and a sample of my DNA along with a voice recording, and then handed me the local identification card.

"Welcome to the Sunset Estate," he said with a smile.

I felt like someone from the upper classes.

That same afternoon I rented an autocar and a manbot from the transporting company to help me move. I had some communication problems – the orders given to manbots had to be short, clear and precise, and only words registered in their linguistic database should be used. I've never done this before, but after a few mistakes I managed to somehow get the hang of it and the manbot started listening to me. It moved my things to the autocar, and then, once we were there, brought them upstairs and arranged them as I wanted. There wasn't a lot of it, so it finished quickly and I could take it back to the company along with vehicle. I took the bail, signed where it was needed and came back unconscious from fatigue, about to spend my first night at the new place.

Before entering the building, I unexpectedly noticed Sean Lara, my social father. He was sitting on a bench, and next to him was placed a large box of colorful, openwork plastic. At the sight of me, Sean stood up and gave me a friendly smile.

"What are you doing here, Dad?" I asked, returning his kiss. "How did you know where to look for me?"

"Mira, your ex-neighbor, told me where you moved to," he replied. "I decided to bring you something special for your new apartment."

"What is that?"

"I figured you might feel lonely with Chris gone," Sean picked up the box and followed me to the elevator. "That boy really managed something great, don't you think?""

"He was always intelligent and stubborn. And above all, more hardworking than any of us. Do you remember how mother always chased after us to study?"

He laughed.

"Cynthia was a strict babysitter, but you have to admit that she was right. It's thanks to her that you all became something, because I was too soft."

"She wasn't that bad, dad. We loved her as our biological mother. In Milla's case even more."

Milla came from a truly pathological environment. She was used to domestic violence and hunger, and as a result of some legal turmoil, she wasn't placed in a social family until she was five years old. She remembered the terrible conditions and the biological parents who mistreated her very well, so it's not surprising that she became so attached to Sean and Cynthia.

"Yes, Milla... she's now a model at the professional Fashion House in Toronto. She writes and calls us often. Such a good girl."

We entered the apartment, and once inside Sean put the box on the floor.

"So, what's in there?" I asked. As if in response, the plastic container made a prolonged, pathetic sound. My father laughed at my surprised expression. He opened the lid and took out a fluffy, red-furred creature with very green eyes.

"It's a cat," he said. "Myrkheim started a breeding farm some time ago. He's been applying for permission for years. This little one doesn't have ancestry, because it was an extra, but you probably don't mind, right?"

I grabbed the kitten into my arms and it protested squeakily, slapping me with a clawed paw straight in the mouth.

"Dad, he must have cost a fortune...!"

"He didn't cost anything. Myrkheim became convinced that he owed me a debt of gratitude, because when we were still both single men, I lent him some money to start his first business. So he just gave him to me. His name is Sid and he belongs to you now."

A cat, a real cat! Only very rich people could afford such pets. Until now, I've seen such an animal merely twice, from a distance, and now I had one in my hands... he was warm, silky and after a while began to purr slightly.

"Oh, dad, I love you!"

He smiled in content. He was always like this, he loved to give us presents and see how happy we were. I kissed him warmly.

"All right, all right," he patted my back. "Will you make me something to eat? I'm starving. Cynthia has been on a business trip for two days and I'm a very poor cook."

"I remember that."

I quickly prepared a meal from a canned meat substitute and freeze-dried pasta. This simple dish had the advantage that it could be season in many different ways and was still always tasty. Besides, it cost mere pennies, and I was used to saving money. I've never had much. As a student I lived on a state scholarship and when I started earning my first money, out of habit I continued to buy the cheapest food and second-hand clothes. Apparently, poverty was primarily a state of mind, not of the wallet...

***

I felt some reluctance before entering Miraton. Contrary to all logic, I feared that somehow they would simply tell me to leave the moment they see my suit and the B3 sign on my forehead, but showing a reservation card with a hologram immediately opened the door for me. A young boy in a livery began parking my car, while another one leads me to an elevator and shows me the way to the apartment. He was so nice, and it was clear that someone paid him well. Someone – who? - invested so much in me that I felt my throat tighten at the thought of it. I will never be able to pay them back.

I'm only a florist technician and a guardian of the library collections at the Medical Academy, and sure, I may be earning well now, but I've never had any huge riches. And... I've never even seen an apartment like this. The whole wall was covered by a window through which you could see the panorama of the city. The second one had a three-dimensional screen with a full package of programs. A fluffy rug was spread on the floor. In the corner there was a huge distributor with free snacks, a great bed with an automatic vibrating massage, and a bathroom with all the possible conveniences...

A letter lied on the table. I pick it up with hesitation and unseal the envelope. Only a handful of words inside:

"I will speak to you soon. Please use anything you like without restrictions, but do not leave the hotel."

Well, that's something I didn't have to do. All Miratons have gyms, courts, a swimming pool, conservatories, and even a video plastic mini-zoo. You can live here all year and party like a king without getting bored for a minute. However, right now I don't feel like taking advantage of all these miracles.

First of all, I go to the bathroom. I take off the suit and stand in front of the mirror. I want to examine my body thoroughly in order to have some idea of what exactly they did to me. At first glance, there's nothing unusual to be seen, but a thorough inspection reveals a whole network of scars on my stomach and hips. It will take some time before they fully disappear. The left hand was cut and stitched back up as well. You couldn't see the implants of course, although... this bathroom is equipped with a simple scanner that can be used to determine the condition of the teeth or the type of minor injury. Top-class hotels offer such facilities in the luxury package.

I decide to use it. I begin to regret that soon after. The scanner screen reveals so many insertions that I almost drop the expensive device onto the floor. I didn't expect it to be that bad. The implants were literally everywhere – in my joints, bones, internal organs... some of my skin was also cybernetic. What actually happened? Was I skinned? I still can't remember the events that resulted in a visit to EPIPHANICS. I only vaguely remember that I was returning from work and the public autocar broke down on the way... since it wasn't far from home, I decided not to wait for the second one to arrive and return on foot instead. It was probably a grave mistake. Something happened and then I woke up in that terrifying center. That's right! You have to do something.

I put on the hotel dressing gown and return to the room. There, I make a connection to Sandra.

"Have some mercy, Leeta" she screams nearly the moment she hears my voice. "What's wrong with you?!"

"I can't tell you. Listen, take care of Sid. I don't know when I'll be back.

"You're horrible! Take care of Sid? The poor guy was meowing so badly that I took him back to my place. You can't leave him for that long, it's cruel!"

"Sandy, I can't explain anything yet, but it wasn't my fault. I'm glad I left you the code to the apartment.... make sure to lock it and look after the poor Sid until I get back. Then I'll tell you everything, but not until then."

"I don't know why I am even friends with you. You are so irresponsible."

"Sandy, honey, forgive me. Something really terrible has happened, but I can't talk about it right now. It's important that nothing happens to the cat, I'm the only one he has, and he's the only one I have after Chris left for the Polytechnic."

"How ungrateful. Am I nobody to you?"

She was right, Sandra has been my neighbor and friend almost from the very beginning, since I started working at the Academy. She's the only one I can count on. She has helped me more than once already, and honestly, I didn't owe her any favors. I know that she will look after the cat as well as I would until I get back for him. A cat is an expensive animal, much too expensive for me to afford, but I got it from my social father after all. Sid is big, red and has a gentle character. He's a great companion and I wouldn't want to part with him for anything in the world, although the special type of cat food consumes a large part of my income.

After calming down, I turn off the communicator and go to take a shower. Suddenly, I realize that I don't have my clothes here, I have nothing but that suit. I can't keep wearing it all the time, I would look ridiculous in this elegant hotel. I hesitate, but then I pick up my credit card and slide it into the ordering panel card-reader. The offer of the internal network of Miraton stores is displayed on the screen. I choose the clothing store number and order everything I need.

The sum on the card is displayed for a moment and I am left speechless – it was enormous. I wouldn't be able to earn that much within ten years. My secret guardian has invested in me as if I was at least a class A2 and as if he was hoping to gain a lot from it. Why? I'm only a florist technician and a librarian, I have no finished degrees and no beauty. I don't understand what I could be useful for, so much that I'm beginning to suspect that there has been a mistake here.

Yes, that is most likely. I was simply mistaken for somebody else and when the truth comes out, I can't be the one to blame. I comforted myself with this thought, then I finally take a shower and wipe myself with a very old-fashioned towel. I don't like the feeling of dryers or paper substitutes so I'm glad that they have real towels in Miraton. Then, wrapped in a bathrobe, I sit in front of the projector and switch the programs at random. I watch until the room service knocks on the door with my order.

***

The new apartment turned out to be a very comfortable matter, and not only because of its location. The Sunset Estate was designed for people with relatively low incomes, but with some ambitions. It was guarded, equipped with all the conveniences such as gyms, beauty salons and entertainment facilities. It's true that they were only of basic class, but still.

Living in such a place I could feel the taste of luxury reserved for the rich, or at least the illusion of this taste. An additional advantage was being neighbors with Sandra, and one more person – Mabel, my friend from high school. I met her only a month after moving into the estate and we fell into each other's arms. Only once we hugged and kissed for all times did we come back to my place, where we could talk peacefully.

"I thought you were at Vera Cruz," I said, making a caffetino for us, "your parents said you were doing really well there."

Mabel, who was just lying on the carpet playing with Sid, raised her face and grimaced at me slightly.

"I was, but I came back," she replied, "I realized that I don't want to spend my whole life at the drafter board."

"How is that? After all, the Professional Counseling Office has concluded that the job of an architect is your dream profession and that you have the necessary skills for it."

"Well, so what? That job bores and tires me."

"What do you want to do with your life then?"

"I decided to become a floress."

She said it so casually that I almost dropped the container with the sweetener.

"A floress? Give me a break..."

"What's wrong with that? It's a great job, well paid and interesting. You hang out in elegant company, travel..."

"And you have to satisfy the fantasies of some disgusting types."

She shrugged.

"One will be gross, another won't be, but all of them rich and important. They take you to banquets, to elegant premises, make sure you have beautiful clothes and jewelry, and pay for beauty salons and fitness clubs. You must be the most beautiful and effective because it raises their prestige. The agency pays you a salary regardless of what the client gives you, and some can be very generous. Life's good. You should try it yourself. I mean, when you go to the Dating Center, you don't know who you'll find either, not to mention, no one there will give you even a broken penny."

"Yes, but I can simply leave that place if I want to."

I shook my head. I was never attracted to this profession in particular, just thinking about what I'd have to do made my skin itch. Although it's true that I didn't have such physical conditions as Mabel, immaculately built and beautiful like from a picture, but they would probably still accept me for a floress course. It's another thing that I don't know if I'd even finish with a positive score. The course taught dance, appropriate manners, the art of conversation and many other things at which I have always been awful.

"Have you started yet?"

"No, I only just enrolled for lessons at a school of grace. I need to get the best results before I'm admitted for the official course organized by the Central Agency for Social Life. I'll manage, though, I know I will."

"You're probably on a diet, right?"

"Of course. And you're not? As far as I remember, you've always had the tendency to gain weight."

"How mean! After I missed you so much..."

I served her the caffetino and some diet cookies. It wasn't just floresses that had to take care of their figure, I was still doing it as well, because all it took was a month of neglect before I stopped fitting in my favorite pants. Fortunately, the local stores offered a wide selection of calorie-free snacks, because with my uncontrollable appetite I would definitely look like a barrel at this point. The downside of these delicacies with a 'c-f' marking is, unfortunately, the fact that consumed in excessive amounts they literally clog the intestines. Otherwise, I don't think anyone today would have problems with obesity.

"Beautiful pet, where did you get him from?" Mabel asked, helping herself with the cake.

"I got him from my father. And he got him from a breeder friend of his. I doubt you thought that I could afford one. I still can't believe Sid is here with me. He's more suited to some luxurious apartment in the district with villas."

"Once I have a floress certificate and permanent employment, I'll persuade some customer to buy one for me. He's cute. I'd just want to pet him for hours."

Sid, on the other hand, had nothing against such adorations, so he kept lying beside her and murmured intensely like a tiny motor. From time to time, he nudged Mabel on the nose, demanding further caresses.

Ever since that day, we often meet on Sunday for lunch or dinner. Sandra joined us sometimes too, and the three of us went to some place of entertainment. Those were some beautiful days. Working at the Medical Academy absorbed all my attention for most of the time, and Sid was waiting for me when I returned home. I met with friends, used social media, and went to social meetings and shows organized by the estate's administration.

Mabel kept to her resolve of becoming a floress. She completed the required course in a graceful school and was accepted into the official study sponsored by CAZT. She sometimes told me about the secrets of professional makeup and the art of choosing accessories for an outfit for every occasion. Her hair was now always combed by a professional hairdresser, she also regularly used the services of a beautician. She has always been beautiful, but now she also acquired a specific kind of style, as if she was born and raised in the salons of the highest class, which only the citizens of class A1 and A0 have access to.

If I didn't know that she's a B3 just like me, that's what I would probably think now, especially since floresses of both sexes have their classification symbols removed from their foreheads and replaced with the symbol of a flower. After completing the training, no one will be able to tell whether they come from the lower classes or from any of the upper classes of citizenship. Their manners are always impeccable along with their flawless elegance. Mabel turned into a real princess right before my eyes, but to my relief, on the inside she remained the same girl with whom I used to skip classes at the video-plastic park in high-school.

I was glad that, just like me, she lived in the Sunset Estate, although in a different building. We could see each other often thanks to this fact. I have to admit that, although I would not become a floress under any conditions, I sometimes envied Mabel for her elegance and charm. I am who I am and I couldn't be different...

***

Dressed in an elegant, brand-new outfit, I think I look decent enough to go to the restaurant and order one of the local dishes. Under normal conditions I wouldn't even be able to afford a starter at such a place, but I'm not under normal conditions, after all. Since it's the first time in my life that I have the opportunity to try a little bit of real luxury, I should hurry up, because that won't last long. Any moment now my protector will realize that he has made a mistake and then everything will end. I have to make use of it while I still can.

Almost nobody was here at this time, and that's a good thing too, because at the sight of the menu card I've become stupefied. If the photos of the dishes were not displayed next to the names, I would have no idea what they're serving here. Even the pictures don't give me full clarity, so finally I decide on what resembled the popular pittano resu which I ate at the bar next to the Medical Academy. However, what I receive is completely different from what I imagined. I look helplessly at the waiter.

He understands without words and hands me the correct cutlery, discreetly whispering to me how to begin. The complicated dish tastes completely different than anything I've eaten before, it's a little fibrous and has a strong smell, not resembling anything. I realize that it must be real meat, not some cheap synthetic. A rarity, but I have to admit that I don't like the taste at all. I eat it without enthusiasm, drink it down with some wine and leave. It's clear that exquisite dishes really aren't suitable for the palate of the lower castes. Disappointed, I return to my room.

There's nothing to do here. I don't know how to play tennis, I don't feel like swimming and I feel bad among all these rich people who are moving with the confident freedom of high-class citizens. So, I visit the zoo, I watch the videoplastic animals (most of them are species long-extinct) and return to my apartment. I can feel comfortable there since no one can see me and I don't have to be bored either. I have a TV with a full package of programs, internet access, individual gym equipment and a snack machine. As a last resort, I could order something for the room, but I decide that this wouldn't be anything fancy.

I lost my desire for luxurious dishes and all this elegance available here. I'm not a lady from the upper classes and I have to accept that, just as I've been accepting it my whole life. There's nothing wrong with the fact that you belong to a lower than some class, that's what I've always been taught – at home, at school, on courses – every social position has its concerns and joys, and the ambition to take a higher position than we're assigned usually ends badly. I've always had some doubts about whether this approach is right (under Chris's influence), but now I'm starting to think that universal indoctrination is right after all. Since I feel this bad amongst elegant company, it must mean that I'm not suited for it. My environment is people like me, petty officials, shopping center assistants, nurses, delivery truck drivers... there's nothing for me in these high societies and there cannot be anything.

On the third day, when I come back from the cosmetics store (in the end I decided to make a small purchase, although maybe not necessary, but still nice), there's someone in my room. A middle-aged man, extremely refined, with a completely bald head and face reminiscent of old statues from the library in which I worked: regular, serious, and at the same time imperious.

"Sit down," he says kindly. "We need to talk. You must have some idea as to who I am."

My heart is beating like crazy, as the moment which I was expecting and which I feared has come. I sit on the edge of a chair.

"You've mistaken me for someone else," I say, determined to immediately clarify this matter. "My name is Juliette Kaphoolie, a citizen of class B3. I work as a librarian and florist at the Medical Academy. I am not able to repay you for what you've done for me."

He waved his hand dismissively.

"You can call me Hakat, Citizen Hakat," he replied. "I'm one of the members of the Circle and I think you understand that I cannot give you my real name."

A member of the Circle, so I wasn't wrong. The circle, which is a group of people who decide everything and stealthily manage the activities of large corporations and even the government (some even say that they are the real government). Official politicians dare not oppose them. I froze, not knowing how to behave.

My mysterious savior continued speaking:

"You are wrong in thinking that in return for my help I'm expecting something which you would be capable of under

ordinary circumstances. They are not ordinary. There is something you've witnessed. You saw the robbery."

"You are mistaken," I deny, "I can't remember anything. Well, almost."

"That doesn't matter. It's all in your memory and there are methods to get there."

"You're scaring me."

He smiles gently, like a dad.

"There is nothing to be afraid of," he says reassuringly. "Tell me, please, has there ever been a time that you wished to rise above your social layer? Become a doctor, engineer or scientist?"

"That would've been unreasonable. Category B3 is not the class that doctors or scientists come from. And I never... thought about things like that."

"That's a mistake, Miss Kaphoolie. If someone is intelligent and stubborn enough, they can break through. There are ways to do it, but everyone must discover them for themselves."

"Why are you telling me this?" I ask. "I know that there are ways, my brother used one of them and he is currently at a university. I don't have enough enthusiasm or confidence to fight against windmills. I'm fine as it is. Well, I was until the robbery."

"I understand and feel sorry for you. I'll refer to you with your first name, okay? You are younger than me, Juliette, so it will be easier that way."

"Leeta. That's what everyone calls me."

"Okay then, Leeta. You yourself understand that everything has changed, and not by your fault or mine... but I'm involved just as you are. What happened then was not an

ordinary assault, but an assassination attempt of two of the most important people in the global government. Don't ask what they're doing here. Your appearance ruined the assassins' plans. They've failed to reach Number 1 or Number 2, though they killed most of their guards. The thing is, only you saw the bombers and only you can identify them."

Now I've become even more terrified. I've gotten myself involved in games which were at such a high level that I couldn't even understand them, and all because of the damned broken car. Suddenly, it comes to me that I will not be able to return to my peaceful life and I burst into tears. Hakat gets up, walks over and strokes my head. He has a hard, wide hand and makes me feel a little safer.

"Please, don't cry," he says kindly. "Tears won't change anything. An implantation procedure was needed in order to save your life. Because of that you are now very valuable, too valuable to remain within your caste, but that is a song of the future. For now, we must expose the conspirators. I've placed you here for your protection. Miratons have the best internal security systems, which is why I recommend you not to leave the hotel. I don't know whether the attackers know where to look for you or if they are even aware that you're alive, but I wouldn't take the risk."

"When do you want to search my memory?" I sniff helplessly, looking for a handkerchief.

"Have patience, Leeta. We will do it in a few days. It won't take long, we already have a lead. For now, please enjoy what the hotel has to offer without restrictions and don't worry about anything. Once everything is over, we will think about your future."

Somehow his words didn't calm me down. On the contrary, I am shaking and having a panic attack. I feel lost, without salvation, convinced that I will live only until the identification of the bombers, and then...

Hakat hands me a glass of water and sits down next to me.

"There's nothing to be afraid of," he says emphatically, "I know what you're thinking about right now. As I said, you are very valuable, not only because you can identify the bombers, but also because of the implants. Nobody in their right mind throws something so expensive out the window. You are under my special protection, and I assure I can protect you if you will listen to my instructions. Please, promise me that you will follow my instructions."

"I promise. I will listen to you blindly."

"That's the idea. Now, please, smile. You are pretty enough to take care of your appearance. Feel free to use the credit card. Miratons have some great make-up artists."

I've never been to a beauty salon before. I was able to afford some subordinate facility, at least a middle-class one, but I never felt the need to take care of my body more than was necessary. I only went to the hairdresser, who brightened and arranged my miserable hair. I touched my head.

"My hair was also transplanted, correct?"

"We had no choice. I see that the transplant was well received by your body, I can't even tell that something happened to you. Take care of yourself, eat and play regularly, but don't leave the hotel until I come back for you."

Hakat stands up touches my arm comfortingly. Despite his assurances, as soon as he leaves the room, I feel like a soldier on the battlefield, left to their fate by their companions."

***

I slowly begin to get used to life in the hotel. It's pleasant, although I still feel out of place here. The staff treats me with the same respect as the other guests. Although, this isn't that strange, considering the price of the apartment I occupy and the amount on the credit card. I am now elegantly dressed, my forehead is covered with a long fringe and, on Hakata's advice, I also used the services of a beauty and hair salon. I look so different that I can hardly recognize myself. Still, I can't wait for the day when it all ends.

Uncertainty tires me more than the sense of threat that I can't free myself from. I hope that those who organized the assassination attempt on Number 1 and Number 2 don't know about me, because after all – if they set their sights on the most important people on the continent, or even the planet – they wouldn't hesitate to eliminate some ordinary librarian, a B3 citizen at that. Even though Hakat assured me that I am safe in Miraton, I'm not completely convinced of that and every day before going to bed I put a few objects at the door that an unexpected guest would have to knock over, making a lot of noise.

I wish I could buy a gun or even a stun gun, but this is no longer possible even for higher classes – for anyone who doesn't work in the police or security. In that case, where did the attackers get their weapons? All available resources are strictly recorded, each gun, regardless of type, is operated by reading the user's genetic code, and unassigned ones are disabled. I read about it during my work at the library.

After separating military formations from the lives of civilians, it was easier to implement such a solution, and so they did, although the process lasted a long time and was painful, because for some time anyone who was unauthorized, and was caught with a gun in hand was killed on the spot. Thanks to that, however, we now live in a safer world... or that's what the book said, but I know that it's just an illusion. Co-operating gangs often rule the streets and it's better to avoid certain neighborhoods, especially at night. A bat could massacre someone as effectively as a bullet or a knife, and the villains are very ingenious.

That's why it's safe to move through the city by autocar or underground, not on foot. I've learned that in a very painful way. But the law is the law, so I can't have a gun, I have to rely on the hotel's security. But what if there's someone in the security who is supposed to eliminate the uncomfortable witness? Even though policemen and bodyguards are subject to appropriate conditioning, I no longer trust anyone.

In the middle of the night I'm woken up by a noise. I jump off the bed, ready to scream, but to my indescribable relief it turns out to be Hakat. It's a good thing that he came himself, otherwise I would sound an alarm for the entire Miraton.

"Put on some clothes please," he recommends. "It's time."

Rummaging through the room chaotically, I put on my blouse and pants, not caring about whether they look good together, and slip into some slippers. On the way to the parking lot, I comb my hair and wipe my face with a refreshing handkerchief. I have no time for makeup, and I have the feeling that where we're going no one's going to pay attention to my appearance. Only the contents of my brain matter.

Hakat helps me to enter the armored vehicle. Behind the wheel sits a stiff, gloomy man in bulletproof attire, in the back seat I see two guards armed with heavy weaponry. I sit between them, feeling like a prisoner accused of the most serious crime, although I am aware that they are here for my safety and only for that.

Hakat takes a seat next to the driver. This gives a clear message – right now I am more important than he is. Once I identify the attackers, the period of special protection will end. What will happen to me then? I decide not to think about it. Whatever happens, happens, I have no way to prevent it anyway. Right now, all I must think about is the identification. Who will I have to identify? After all, I still couldn't remember any details of the robbery. My protector reminded me that in the place they're taking me to they will stimulate my memory to bring out the details. That doesn't make me too enthusiastic, but I have no other choice. I have to go along with it, at least to repay Hakat for his care and what he's done for me. As I calculated, it must have been a real fortune and I will probably spend the rest of my life paying it back. That's all the more reasons for me to agree to everything.

The limousine moves us to the airport, from where the triangular mini-jet takes us into the air. It's the first time that I'm taking such a flight. The few times that I traveled to another city, I traveled by subway, after all I wasn't able to afford even the cheapest plane ticket. And even if I collected the right amount, I would feel sorry for that loss of points.

I have always imagined that flying must be something wonderful, but the reality turns out to be quite different. It's making me sick, I feel dizzy and terribly afraid, but luckily it doesn't last long. The jet lands in a place completely unknown to me – in a very modern complex, full of well-guarded buildings and armed patrols. I make a guess that this is a *government-owned property, a place where ordinary people are not allowed, where even the private soldier guards are A-class citizens.*

Instinctively, without thinking about what I'm doing, I grab Hakat's hand. He's the only one who isn't a complete stranger to me.

"Take it easy, Leeta," he says with a benevolent chuckle, "you are absolutely safe here. The Central Island is one of a kind. And please, don't forget that you are under my protection."

Our way is blocked by a young man in a fitted uniform.

"Secretary, please forgive me: I need your pass," he says.

Confused, I release Hakata's hand. Secretary? So he is the secretary? I didn't think that he was someone this high. In that case, what was he doing in my neighborhood?

"Here," Hakat reaches for a badge of rainbow metal. The guard scans it with the reader, then nods and hands it back. Then he knocks his heels and prepares to leave – it's at this point that I recognize him.

"Pablo!" escapes my lips. He looks at me, a little surprised. I have no doubt that it's him, Pablo, my high school friend, B2. He has a head pulled over his forehead, so I cannot see his mark, but it's him without a doubt. He must have recognized me, but for some reason he won't talk to me right now. Maybe he is ashamed of such a relationship?

"Excuse me, Mr. Secretary," he says stiffly and walks away.

"Please, don't look at me like that, Leeta," Hakat says to me, "I'm not some demigod, only a man who thanks to the will of the majority of those entitled holds a public position."

"*What about that guard? I know him, his name is Pablo Estevez...*"

"*And now he is constable Vernes... but we'll talk about that later. Come on, there's no reason to delay, they're waiting for us.*"

"*Of course, Your Excellency,*" *I mumble uncertainly.*

"*You don't have to be so official. Either way... I will have a certain proposition for you after the identification. If you agree, you will work for me and the honorifics won't be needed anymore. At a certain level, my dear librarian, they are no longer used.*

He smiles warmly, and I understand that I will not leave this island. Hakat is right, with all these implants I'm too valuable to just throw away, but my life now belongs to someone else, it's not my own. On one hand, it's very sad, but on the other – was my existence even that great? No, it was gray, monotonous and lonely. I had no obligations to anyone but the poor little cat, but Sandra took care of him. I know her well and I know that she won't hurt my furry friend. Maybe it wasn't nice on my part to put the responsibility on my friend, but I had no other choice. I will explain everything to her someday.

Hakat and the security guards lead me into one of the buildings, which was built concentrically – inside was a large assembly hall, with smaller rooms arranged in a circle. We enter one of them. It's something like an electronic workshop connected to a medical office – it gives the impression of hospital sterility and at the same time looks like an old watchmaker's workshop. There is a barely perceptible smell of chemical reagents and hot metal in the air.

50

Several men of different ages are working with some delicate devices. One of them stands up and approaches us.

"Hello, sir" *he begins speaking to Hakat.* "The ordered stimulator is ready. Is this the lady?"

"Juliette Kaphoolie," I introduced myself mechanically.

"Yes, that's her, doctor. Please sit down, Leeta, and no need to fear. The stimulator isn't painful."

That's not what I feared. I've always been rather pain-resistant, but what I'm terrified of is the fact that someone will be poking around in my brain. Hakat somehow senses it and doesn't let go of my hand. His paternal behavior makes me feel a little more confident, though not enough to erase this certain impression, an indescribable feeling, a note of falsehood that I can't identify. The guilt of this feeling is that I know a little too much about the world, more than I should. Even though I belong to class B3, I've always enjoyed studying and during long hours at the library I read everything I could get my hands on – fiction, medical textbooks and criminal records, as the Academy is connected with the Faculty of Law and students of both faculties use the same collection of books. Yes, I know too much and it isn't easy to fool me.

I meekly accept the injection in my arm and take the pills handed to me. The doctor approaches me with what looks like an electronic band, decorated on the sides with two modules. He puts it on my head and starts tuning, touching the buttons with an electronic stylus in order. At some point I feel a slight shock, and then as if a lightning bolt pierced through my brain. Hakat touches the pacemaker, fixing it slightly.

"Think about the robbery," his voice reaches me as if through a wall. "Find the last thing you remember and go from there. Focus on the faces, all of the faces that you've seen."

I listen to his words semi-consciously. Perhaps I wouldn't even need to. Suddenly I see an explosion, a series of shots, balls of fire rushing straight at me, a cacophony of screams in my ears, the memory of some terrible, excruciating pain tearing through my body. Faces... yes, for a split second I saw the faces of people with guns and two who were sitting in the car in the side street I was passing by. Then there was darkness. The next thing that reaches my consciousness is a prick in the arm – someone is giving me another injection.

"What's this?" I ask semi-consciously. I'm shaking like a leaf, Hakat is still holding my hand carefully, while the doctor hides the syringe. The headband is still on my head, I feel a slight tingling on my temples.

"Just some stimulant. You fainted. Tell me, did you see any faces?"

I nod meekly, still unable to control my chattering teeth. Hakat helps get on my feet.

"Let's go," he says, "we shouldn't delay a single minute."

Supine and devastated by what I witnessed in my memories I allow myself to be lead through the glass corridor all the way to the metal door. He opens it with an access card and suddenly I find myself in the government's assembly hall. I immediately know that the people gathered here are Supreme Citizens, although currently I wouldn't be able to explain why I know this. I shiver almost hysterically. Everyone is looking at me in surprise, silence falls. Hakat doesn't give me time to think, just pushes me towards the podium.

"Look at them," he says commandingly, quite differently from before. "Do you recognize anyone in this room?"

I look around, still unable to control my trembling knees. The men and women were silent, looking at Hakat and me, all *hellishly well dressed and different from the people I've lived amongst so far... Currently I can't describe what this difference is exactly – maybe the fact that everyone is so neat, so self-aware of their own values. I don't recognize any of them, though... although is that for sure? I slowly move my eyes over their faces and figures.*

"Them!" suddenly I shout out hysterically, pointing towards two middle-aged men standing to the right of the platform. "I've seen them!"

"Were they the ones who shot you?"

"No, those ones are not here. I'm certain. But these two were sitting in a car in a side street."

"Are you absolutely sure?"

"Definitely. I saw them, they were there!"

At this moment I become dizzy I lose consciousness again, so I don't witness the reaction to these words. And it must have been violent for sure...

I wake up in some office. I am lying on a sofa, next to it sits a young doctor – in the suit's flap he has a profession badge and barely visible diagnostic gloves on his hands. He looks kind and gentle, but his eyes are uncomfortably cold. Or maybe I'm just imagining that.

"Don't get up please, Miss Kaphoolie. I am doctor Tiaviani," he says, "your blood pressure is unstable. The memory stimulator doesn't work well with implants, and you have more of them than anyone I've known."

"I know. Right now I'm more of a cyborg than a woman. Has my body adapted to them yet?" I pose the question with effort.

"*I think it has. Although, this is never certain, not to mention that you come from a class in which there are different proportions of minerals in the food, so the results of our research may not be very reliable in relation to you.*"

In this gentle way he makes me understand that I'm not the same as their privileged group, but I don't care about that. I'm only thinking about what's going to happen to me now when I've clearly stopped being needed. It's true that

promised me protection, but I'm still afraid. The doctor examines me gently, carefully touching my neck, hand, stomach... I can't see what the indicator shows when it reacts to the sensors in the gloves, but Taviani seems to be pleased.

"*No signs of anything worrying,*" *he says finally.* "*Now please sit up and lean against me.*"

He helps me getting up from the sofa and go to the elevator. He takes us both into a room, not worse than the Miraton apartment. Something tells me that it's the lowest standard here.

"*You are to stay here for now. The secretary issued such instructions. You may order anything you'd like and go wherever a special access card is not required. For now you must rest and settle in a little. Whenever you feel unwell, please contact me at any time of the day or night.*"

He finishes his duty and leave me alone, sitting helplessly on the bed. I constantly feel like I did at a Christmas party a few years ago, when I got a little too drunk, but I'm slowly regaining full clarity of thinking. According to what I've seen, the situation was this: at the highest levels of power there was an attempt to take the position by force. The assassination attempt was unsuccessful, perhaps it was poorly prepared, and Hakat, the Secretary of Government and one of the few people who knew about Number 1 and Number 2, had learned about it. The attack must have been prepared by somebody equally well informed as him, and my protector must have known who that was. So why did he need me, an accidental victim?

I spend the next few days thinking and browsing the library files. Although admittedly I am not privileged to access them, but I've already circumvented such safeguards, downloading exam questions for students I was friends with. Yes, I know that I shouldn't and that it's illegal, but I was flattered by a kind of bond with some young people of class A1 and A2. I was pleased that they were turning to me, a B3, for help and that they did it in such a kind way, and my former friend from school, now a petty thief, taught me some methods. We were both teenagers at the time and we met in secret, since my social parents were against this relationship... now these tricks are useful.

After several dozen hours of work, I was able to create an entry to all the files and secure them so that I'm not detected. Now I'm able to browse them without any problems. In truth, I don't even know what I'm looking for, but I have a feeling that it's something important. In the puzzle which I received there is a very important piece missing. It seems like everything fits, but then something doesn't stick, and I don't know what it is. I write down everything that seems important, and then compare what I have and think about what it all means. I make sure that I'm not caught – whenever I hear even a rustle, I switch the computer to games or a show on demand. That turns out to be very useful when one day Hakat appears in my room without notice.

He is dressed differently than before. He's wearing a type of uniform made of ultra-durable nanite material and only after a moment do I notice the badge of the chief of uniformed services on his shoulder. So, he was promoted then.

"Are you feeling all right now?" he asks briefly. "That's great. From today you are my assistant with the codenamed Ankes. Forget about your old identity. As soon as today you'll begin a specialized training that will teach you how to make the most of these implants. It'll be useful in your new position."

"Thank you, sir."

"Please, don't thank me. It's what I owe you, and besides, I trust in your potential."

He looks around the room as if to see if anything is missing. I catch myself thinking that the uniform suits him, and that in general he is a very handsome man despite the lack of hair on his head. He must be liked by women.

"You must miss your cat, correct?" he asks with a smile. Does he know everything about me?

"Of course..." I murmur uncertainly.

"No need to worry. The animal is in good care. Miss Simpler sends her regards. One day we will give the animal back to you."

"What was Sandra told?"

"The truth. Well, almost. That you've been included in the Witness Protection Program and that you must remain in a guarded center for now. Please understand that there was very little we could actually say in order to avoid putting her or you in danger."

"Yes, I'm aware."

I was relieved at the thought that Sid would one day be with me again. He was a faithful and beloved companion and I was worried that I'd never see him again. Meanwhile Hakat is *looking at a computer screen on which two comedians are arguing and I could swear that he's smiling slightly.*

"Studying is great, but please remember of your health as well," he says as if instead of a light comedy he saw an open textbook. "You must use the gym and the regeneration salon. Either way, during today's training you'll learn what will be your duties and privileges. Now, please take this card."

He hands me a rectangle made of rainbow metal, stored in which is all the information about me.

"This is your access to the majority of the complex, except for a few highly protected objects which you may only enter with me. Of course, you may access my office and apartment at any time. You will live next door so that we can communicate with each other whenever the need arises. In two hours you will report to section D, green part. There you will meet with the rest of the training group and your instructors."

"Yes, Chief of Arms sir."

He smiles, this time more clearly. I understand that he must have been waiting for this title a long time and desired it more than anything in the world. Suddenly I realize that rummaging through the highly unavailable files there's one thing I haven't tried to find – who were the people who I indicated for identification. I didn't think about that.

When Hakat leaves, I throw myself at the computer. I still remember the faces of the men from the vehicle, all I have to do is recreate them with the graphic editor. I have two hours to do this.

It's going quickly, faster than I thought it would. The editor allows me to create a portrait of both men from memory, which I then put into the advanced search engine. The computer screen blinks and an identification program appears, followed by personal data. I bite my fingers. In truth, this is something I expected, but a confirmation of my unclear predictions is frightening. Suddenly all the pieces of the puzzle begin to fit, and perfectly at that.

I get up from my seat. I have a little over half an hour before the session begins, but I feel that I won't be able to focus on the training until I confirm this. Only then will I be able to decide whether I can live with this.

The office belonging to the Chief of Arms is located in the central section. My card doesn't yet allow me to enter this area, but after saying who I was, I was granted entry. It seems Hakat had issued such instructions before. A beautiful girl in the outfit of the support service, with the name 'Tanith' on her ID, is doing a cursory search, shows me the office and gives me a temporary passage. Her gaze is purely professional, but I feel like I sense some surprise – what could a B3 be doing in a government complex? In fact, that's a question I ask myself, too. The only explanation is that I'm held here on Hakat's whim, his half-irrational belief that he still owes me something.

The Chief of Arms receives me with his usual kind smile.

"Would you like to ask something before class?" he asks. I get my voice out with difficulty. I have to fight to be able to say what had to be said.

"Why do you keep me here? Is it because you are obliged to me, or is it to keep an eye on me?"

"What do you mean?"

"Mr. Hakat, or whatever is your name... I may be a B3, but I can think, and more importantly, I can associate the facts. You became the Chief of Weapons to replace Citizen Kelso, whom I identified in the assembly hall. I saw him in the vehicle... supposedly."

"Supposedly? The stimulator helped you recall images, do you not believe in them?"

"Oh, I believe that I saw the attack, the street, the car, but the faces in the car... I looked at the pictures available in the files. One of them was identical to my memories. Too identical, because even the details of the pattern on the collar of one of these men and the facial hair of the other matched. Please, don't take me for an idiot and tell me that this is a coincidence. There are programs that can be inputted into the stimulator's circuits using an ultrasound carrier and transfer images directly to the prefrontal cortex this way. Did you have a remote projector? Nobody searched you, you could have freely...."

I run out of breath and lose my voice, desperate and at the same time terrified of my own boldness. Hakat is silent for a moment, and in his eyes are sparks of amusement. What I said didn't, for whatever reason, frighten him or upset him as I thought it would. He isn't mad at me.

"You can see yourself, Leeta, that birth and official IQ tests don't mean anything," he finally speak. "Your intelligence is worthy of class A2, maybe even A1. So, what else would you like to know?"

"Why? Why did you do this to me?"

Hakat stands up, approaches me and places his hands on my shoulders.

"My child, you weren't supposed to be there," he says emphatically. "Because of your unexpected appearance you've complicated your life and gave me a weapon. I know that you have the right to expect the worst, but believe me, the attack was organized by Kelso and Santar. I was sure of this without any doubts, but I didn't have any real proof. I could've risked

accusing them, but that meant that I'd be getting on brittle ice, because they stood above me. Fate handed you to me."

"So that's why you paid for the procedure, the hotel and all these other things?"

"Correct. If there was no way for you to be useful to me, I'd leave you to die. I hope that you can appreciate my honesty. There is a certain pragmatic way of doing things in my world. I can't afford actions in the style of a lone rider."

I remain silent, devastated by all of this, frozen under his touch. So, I'm connected to a man for whom the moral principles that I've been taught are meaningless clichés. He isn't a bad person, but he is subject to completely different rules of life and is different from all the people I have met so far. Still, why didn't he get rid of me after the identification? A man in his position could get over the cost of implants and procedures. I ask him directly.

He shows me a warm and forgiving smile.

"You're right, of course," he says, "but your knowledge about me doesn't threaten me in any way, because you have no evidence to support your words. And I believe that people's talents should be made use of, not destroyed. I see great possibilities in you and I know that you will be useful to me in the game I am playing."

"What game?" I ask, stunned. "You've achieved what you wanted to achieve. You are the Chief of Arms, all those in uniformed services are under your comment..."

"Do you really believe that this is all that can be achieved in life?"

I'm speechless. I look at Hakat, unable to move or say a word. He returns my gaze with calm amusement, he emanates strength, intelligence and confidence.

"You want to become Number 1," I finally manage a whisper.

"Someday they will have to appoint a new one. I will be among the candidates. Why should I believe that victory won't be on my side?"

"You're scaring me."

"That will pass. You'll get used to your new life and new responsibilities. You'll have the opportunity to fully develop your mind and learn how to use the possibilities of your implants. Though of course, they won't turn you into a superwoman, so please don't delude yourself, but they will still be a great help. They improve your endurance, strength and speed. Now, you must attend the training, you'll be late."

I nod, apologize and leave.

At the section door, the same girl in a costume, Tanith, blocks my way.

"This way please, Mrs. Ankes," she says with anticipatory politeness. "It will only take a moment."

I feel sudden fear but I don't protest. If something is about to happen, let it happen as soon as possible. That will be for the best.

The girl leads me to a room on the side, where Dr. Taviani and his assistant are waiting for me. He has a small device in his hand, used to mark newborns after birth.

"Sit down and relax," he says. "I need to change your classification. An order from the top."

Startled, I sit on the indicated chair. The doctor's assistant holds my head, and Taviani touches my forehead with the marker, set for erasing. It burns a little.

"Hang in there, it'll be over soon. Now for a new symbol... and it's all done."

I get up and look in the mirror. Instead of the five-pointed star, which marks my social layer, now there is an inverted V, indicating class A3, between my eyebrows. I feel like I'm looking at a stranger. Different clothes that I've never worn, different hair, even a different attitude. And what isn't visible, but what I am painfully aware of, has been hidden from human sight. Still accompanying me, Tanith squeezes my hand lightly.

"Welcome in our ranks," she says with a smile. I smile back slightly. The feeling of unreality that overcame me after looking in the mirror doesn't disappear even after I leave the proprietary section and move to the training sector. There is no point in fighting it, I give into my fate. The poor, but proud and independent Juliette Kaphoolie, a citizen of class B3, no longer exists. The one walking the corridor is Ankes, class A3, government property, no voting rights, and no freedom of choice.

I

On that day, Citizen Hakat called for me in the early morning. I entered his office with my heart tightened slightly, because I still couldn't be rid of my fear of this man. Awareness of how powerful and resolute he is worked on me dishearteningly, while he in some way enjoyed it – at least I always felt that way when I looked at him. I don't think that I'm the only one who sees him that way. From what I've observed, overheard, and also learned during lunchtime conversations, the Chief of Arms was recognized on THE Central Island as a man extremely dangerous to his opponents and ruthlessly loyal to his allies, which, however, had a price. He destroyed traitors and losers without a twitch of the eyelids and everyone knew that.

Hakat was sitting behind the desk and writing something, but he raised his head at the sound of my footsteps.

"Hello, Leeta," he said warmly. I mumbled something in response, trying to control my nervousness.

"Sit down," he pointed to a chair. "I think it's time for your first mission."

I cringed involuntarily. They've been preparing me for this moment since receiving the regrouping, but I still didn't feel like any sort of 'agent'. The knowledge I've been taught, the fitness training, it all as if flowed down the core of my personality. I wasn't able to change my way of thinking. I wasn't interested in the world of great politics, the internal games in the agency frightened me deeply, and yet I had to remain in all this like a nail stuck in a tree. They are united but exist independently and will never be one.

"If that's your decision..."

"No need to be afraid. It won't be anything like in espionage movies. You won't be saving the world. To tell you the truth, I'm not even sure if anything is happening where I'm sending you to. I'm just concerned about certain aspects of the annual report..."

He ran his fingers over his computer's keyboard.

"Well, the matter is as follows: for some time now there have been unexplained deaths recorded among the employees of the Moon Mining Company. Interestingly enough, this doesn't apply to the miners, but to the administrative division. Seventeen of them died last year, and all due to the same causes. According to the pathologists, they were all healthy, but for some reason their brains lost the ability to enter the REM phase during sleep. This causes an obvious burnout and ends in death within a few weeks. The company denies the establishment of pathologists. In their opinion, someone wants to harm the interests of the entrepreneurs. Your task will be to review data from the company computers and note everything that seems suspicious to you. To do this, you'll have to travel to the moon. The company doesn't allow sending data in fear of industrial espionage. You know how it is, there is a constant struggle for influence over there, and all associations of entrepreneurs operating on Earth would gladly put their foot on the moon."

"I've heard that if the Company was allowed a greater degree of freedom, then they will declare independence of the Moon," I interrupted shyly.

Hakat smiled gently. He always reacted that way when I said something silly or inconsiderate.

"That would be reckless at best," he said. "The mining colony is almost completely dependent on supplies from Earth, and it would be easy to force them to surrender, even by hunger. Either way, everyone who works there has families on Earth. No, I can assure you that there are no such plans, it's just rumors. However, there are interpersonal and interfaculty games among others. The people of Lunnar have been doing filthy things to each other from the beginning, but if the death of the Company's employees is the result of intentional action, then the matter becomes very serious. Your task isn't about solving the secret. All you have to do is collect the data and pass it on to the detective who will contact you at the right time."

"I understand," I said, though I didn't understand anything. I was becoming dizzy. I've lived such a peaceful life until recently, and where did it all go? What am I doing here? I'm not fit to be a superhero from a cartoon. Right now I should be working at the greenhouse or handing out books to medical students, and then return to my quiet, warm apartment after work. This island wasn't my dream place to live.

"You will be living together with my niece," Hakat continued. "She is a professional virtualist. She's working with the Company as a specialist of network transfer exploration. I should warn you that Sue is, well, a little peculiar."

"Which means?"

"You know how virtualists are. It's often said that they'd rather live in a musty basement with a computer and a network access module than in a luxurious residence without these possibilities. Sue is very dedicated to her work and at the same time a little strange. She knows how to have fun, but she prefers working and doesn't know moderation when it comes to that. She doesn't leave her apartment at the colony for days at a time and you can expect it to be rather messy. Her last roommate, the engineer Corti, was sent back to Earth because of a nervous breakdown, and I'm guessing that Sue had something to do with it."

How nice!

"And wouldn't she be able to investigate the matter?"

"Oh, she certainly could, as long as it didn't require actions in the field. Sue doesn't like leaving her apartment, and her wandering around the colony would arouse suspicion. You're different. You're going there Juliette Ankes, inspector of the Central Health Office. With their pass you will have access everywhere, but you must remain vigilant. Even if you hear or notice anything unusual, don't let it show. They're supposed to take you for a clerk who got into the delegation in hopes for a bonus and doesn't care much about the job."

"Got it, boss. What else?" I asked suddenly.

"Keep in touch with me on a regular basis, but always through Sue. She will help you encode the signal so that it's not received by a third party. You don't have to worry about your flowers. If necessary, I will water them myself until your return."

"I see, what else?" I almost smiled.

Due to the fact that I was accommodated in the apartment right next to Mr. Hakat's, he visited me from time to time, mainly to check my progress or discuss some aspect of our work. Initially, I was afraid that his visits may be under a different basis, but nothing like that ever happened. The

Chief of Arms was kind to me, but in a completely asexual way. That worked well for me, not because I was disgusted by him. On the contrary, I've always thought that he was a very attractive man in his own way, but the thought of our relationship developing this way scared me – I'm not really sure why. This task seemed ordinary enough, but I had the impression that Citizen Hakat was trying to get rid of me from the Island.

"For now, it'll be better if you leave," he said, clearly guessing my thoughts. "It's getting heated over here. All I'll tell you is this: I made a little miscalculation. Not everything turned out as I hoped it would. It will be safer if you disappear, safer for you most of all."

"Do you care about that?"

He smiled slightly and touched my chin with his fingers.

"I've grown to be fond of you. And you remind me of someone. But now it's time for you to go and prepare for the journey."

"Can I talk to my brother first? He must be worried that I'm not answering the phone, not replying to his letters..."

I was expecting my protector to prohibit me from contacting Chris, but he nodded approvingly.

"I'll take care of that. But be careful of what you tell him. He mustn't know anything more than the fact that you have to leave to protect yourself from the revenge of the gangsters against whom you testified in court. You may only contact him through unassigned mail. Let him write back for the locket at the Distributive Center, number VNX 1072.

I packed up and went to the airstrip, where I was awaited by a light aircraft, piloted by a kind young man in an air force uniform. As I could already tell, the inhabitants of the

Central Island never used hydrofoils to get to the mainland, even though it would've been a simpler and cheaper solution. They always used the airborne method.

I suspected that it was supposed to be a sign of their status, but Mr. Hakat corrected my mistake: it was for security reasons. Attacks were more likely than I thought, even more so because right now they were happening more often than ever. I was still lost in all these political complexities, so I decided to listen to follow my boss's words in all cases, even if he ordered me to wear a pillow on my head in broad daylight. All the more reasons for me to agree to the light aircraft trip, although it still frightened me. It wasn't until I sat in the passenger seat and fastened my seat belt that it occurred to me that my fears were completely ridiculous. After all, in a few hours I was to be on my way to the moon.

I squeezed into the seat. How did it even come to this? I've never been that brave, how could the training on the island change that? There's no way it could, of course. I was terribly afraid, more and more with every moment, but refusing Hakat's orders was out of the question. I wouldn't dare doing that, and that meant I would have to spend some time in Lunnar, the city on the moon belonging to the Moon Company, as the Mining Corporation Association was called. My heart was pounding. I never thought I'd find myself there. Unlike Chris, I didn't dream of space travel and great adventures, I liked a stable life in a quiet place and the certainty that the next day will be the same as the previous one. That's what I needed and that's what was taken from me.

The pilot took me to the space port at the Canaveral Cape and bid me farewell there. I stayed alone and for a moment I felt like running away, returning to my apartment at the

Sunset Estate and forget about all of this. However, the next moment someone grabbed my elbow. Turning around, I saw a stewardess in uniform with a patch of the out of orbit communication.

"Miss Ankes?" she asked. "Please, follow me to the shuttle."

"Which one?" I asked helplessly.

"The one with the Moon Company's logo. Is this your first time in an out of orbit flight?"

"Yes. And I'm a little scared."

"There's nothing to fear. It's a short and safe journey, you'll see."

She smiled at me comfortingly. She was pretty and nicely shaped, although to my surprise she had a B3 class pentagram on her forehead, the same one I initially had. Which means, the range of professions available to people like me was wider than I once thought. I think that Chris was right when he said that you mustn't be guided by your social class, you just have to fight for your dreams. This stewardess took up the fight and won. And me? Although it's true that my class was changed and I was registered as a government employee, but this was not to my merit. It's only due to the circumstances I happened to find myself in. I wished that I could tell Chris about it, but thankfully my brother didn't notice that I was talking to him differently than usual. He was too absorbed in his studies. That's for the better, I convinced myself, and certainly safer. I wouldn't be able to take it if somebody hurt Chris.

But that's enough of self-pity. Enough of messing up and pretending to be a poor orphan. I decided that I would pull myself together and not break the trust that the Chief of Arms himself put into me, even if it would mean my death.

The shuttle was smaller than I expected. Apart from me, there were a few people sitting in the passenger section, including a family with a daughter around fifteen years old – undoubtedly employees of the corporation. I turned on the reader and started browsing the collected materials. First of all, I looked at the file about the structure of the Moon Company. I quickly learned that it consists of seventeen corporations, four of which have a controlling interest and manage the entirety of it. One of them might have wanted to take over the shares of the other, or maybe one of the smaller ones tried to strengthen their position, hence the sudden deaths.

But what was driving the killers? How did they choose their victims? This couldn't be discerned by the dry statistics, I'll have to figure that out once I'm there, in the city of Lunnar. It was built on the far side of the moon, where most of the smaller mines and the entire administrative division were located. Initially, it wasn't as much of a city as an ordinary mining settlement where truly Spartan conditions prevailed. Now, according to my informant, there was no lack of comfort there, and modern technology provided protection against radiation flooding the Earth's satellite, against the terrible cold of the 'night' and overheating while the city was illuminated by the sun.

The 'lunar day' was in fact very useful, as that's when the gigantic batteries were charged which provided the entire city with cheaper and safer electricity than uranium power plants – but cheaper especially. Nuclear power plants required a lot of water, and on the Moon that was a scarce commodity.

Solar panels didn't need it. Attempts to use them on a larger scale were already made in the 21st century, but unfortunately no sufficient energy storage method was known at the time – except for traditional, very inefficient batteries. After a quick look at the paragraphs about technology, I moved on to the structure of the population. I found out that in fact half of the inhabitants were miners, while the other half was one way or another associated with the Company, which makes Lunnar a strictly industrial city.

I felt afraid again. I've never even imagined myself in the role of a detective, and training on the Central Island couldn't give me everything I needed. I became more and more convinced of that. It was like basic training on how to walk combined with high mountain climbing, I saw that clearly now and I wanted to cry. What if I turn out to be a tremendous disappointment? Hakat seemed so convinced of my abilities and yet I... I didn't see them. I was still thinking of myself as a modest florist, a B3 citizen, and living between work and home, meanwhile I was turned into some kind of damn government intelligence agent.

I reached into my purse to check the documents. Identification card, access certificate, and next to the regular credit card there was a second one which Hakat gave me just before I left.

"Just in case," he said. "It may happen that you'll need to bribe someone, for example, then you'll make use of the special funding of our department. Under no circumstances should you abuse this privilege."

I looked at this 'special' card. It differed from the standard ones only with a very peculiar, convex spider-shaped hologram on the back, and before using the usual PIN you had to tap your control number on the reader. I knew that if this wasn't done then the card would be blocked. The blockade also took place when an employee of the department who was not authorized to use the special funds provided their number.

From this I could assume that Hakat must have given me authorization. He really trusted me, even though we've known each other for such a little time. I should feel proud of it, but I didn't at all.

The shuttle shuddered, then the overload pressed me a little into the chair. We moved. The stewardess, who must have noticed my blurry face, suddenly appeared next to me and gave me some medicine.

"Swallow it," she advised benignly. "First out of orbit flights are usually difficult."

"Is this to calm me down?" I asked distrustfully.

"It's for nausea and dizziness. We don't give sedatives, in the past there were cases of fainting because of them. Please fasten your seat belts thoroughly, we will soon enter the zero-gravity zone."

I swallowed the pill, drinking it down with a small bottle of water, and then began to fasten my seat belts using the instructions stuck on the back of the chair in front of me. The 'zero-gravity zone' didn't sound very promising. I didn't go through any space training and didn't know how I would feel. I just hoped that the medicine I received would work and I'm not going to suddenly start vomiting. It would be a terrible compromise for the agent of the Chief of Arms, a member of the Supreme Ruling Class.

Fortunately, nothing bad happened. The pill worked and the seat belts held so tight that I could barely feel the lack of gravity. The shuttle sped forward so fast that the meter on which the miles were flashing was almost blurred in my eyes and I knew I would be there soon.

I've never even visited one of the orbital cities, let alone the Moon, so I can't say that I'm not curious about what awaits me there. My imagination was showing me different images, sometimes really phantasmagoric. On the other hand, I was afraid that I would let my guardian down. Truth be told, I didn't even know where to start once I am there. Go door to door and ask around? Maybe Hakat's niece could help me, otherwise I will be hopelessly compromised. Either way, I explained to Citizen Hakat that I'm not going to be of use in his agency, and if he didn't believe that, that's his problem.

The motion-sickness medicine had its side effects. Most of all it made me feel sleepy. I fell asleep with my head pressed against the armrest and missed the moment when the shuttle finally landed in a huge hall on the moon. The flight attendant woke me up.

"Miss, we're here."

I disentangled myself from the seatbelts and looked into the porthole. A little disappointed, I noticed that the hall looks the same as the one back on Earth. She was full of people busy with their own affairs, colorful shops, uniformed service and travelers, crowded at luggage pick-up points.

"Do you need any help?" the stewardess asked politely, seeing that I struggled with the clasps. No one was aboard and I understood that the girl wanted to get rid of me as soon as possible so that she could prepare everything for the next flight.

"Please."

She pressed a few buttons on the arm of the chair. The belts separated themselves, released me and slipped into their lockers. I quickly got up, said goodbye to the stewardess, grabbed my purse and headed for the exit.

I went down the airport ladder and stood in the queue for the baggage collection. While waiting, I attempted to scan the area for my 'contact', but I couldn't see anyone who looked like George Terrel, a resident of the Agency on the Moon. Hakat showed me his holo-picture, but how am I to distinguish a single face from a crowd of others from far away? I don't know why I imagined the mining colony as something small, primitive and almost uninhabited, while here I was in the aviation hall of a large city, populous and noisy. It almost gave the impression that you were still on Earth and upon leaving the airport you will find yourself under a bright blue sky, on a street flooded with sunlight.

After half an hour I finally got to my bags. As I left the pick-up point, a stocky, mustached man appeared in a neatly fitted outfit and high, laced shoes. Everyone here wore one, and I thought with embarrassment about my pumps. I don't think they are very suitable for local conditions.

"Miss Ankes?" the man asked and took the bags from me. "My name is George Terrel. Follow me, please."

He led me to a vacuous lunar rover waiting in the parking lot. Only after seeing this heavy, sealed vehicle with a closed air circulation gave me the realization that I really was on the moon, not on Earth, and I instinctively grabbed my companion's sleeve.

"Relax," he laughed. "We will be going through the air tunnel just like everyone else. It's forbidden to use any other vehicle than rovers like this one, you can probably understand why, but for now we don't even have to close the hatch or turn on the oxygen apparatus. There is no need."

"That's in case the tunnel collapses, right?"

"It's more in case of a crack, I'd say... or if we have to go on unprotected terrain. These constructions are so solid that they can even withstand the impact of a meteor, they don't collapse."

He tossed my baggage to the back seat and pointed me at the seat next to the driver. Only once he closed the door and left the parking did he begin speaking again:

"Now, please listen to me. From now on I will be your personal driver and supporter. In order to not reveal what you're up to, you are not allowed to use the services of other carriers. I'll give you my number. If something happens, you can call at any time of the day or night. I don't know the details of the mission and don't want to know them, but you can count on me in any situation."

"I'll remember that, Mr. Terrel."

"Call me George."

I glanced at him. He seemed pleasant. He was more or less middle-aged, dark-skinned, with a small mustache – and I don't mean that he was attractive, but he seemed trustworthy. I also liked the decisive manner in which he steered the heavy rover. It was obvious that he was a very strong man, confident and certainly not a new to his job.

The rover rushed along the highway, or rather the tunnel connecting the airport with the city. Other vehicles flashed on both sides, in front of us and behind us, advertisements on the walls of the tunnel were changing. I was slowly beginning to understand that Lunnar had long ceased to be an ordinary mining settlement, and became a city just like those back on

Earth, full of potential consumers to whom were addressed advertisements of clothing chain stores, cosmetics and a new type of breakfast cereal. I supposedly knew all this before, but only now did it start to form into a clear picture in my head. When we finally reached the city, I was prepared for the sight that unfolded before me.

Lunnar reminded me of New Manhattan, but protected under a gigantic dome, illuminated by hundreds and thousands of lights. Apart from this one detail, I didn't see much difference: the same overpasses, estates, parks and shops. I looked around wanting to see something extraordinary, cosmic, but I didn't see anything like that apart from the dome covering the city. The builders took care to maximize the similarity of Lunnar to the cities on Earth. It had all the facilities people needed, an atmosphere that was supervised by medical technicians day and night, and even water in the showers and sinks. Although it did come from enclosed circulation, but it was purified so thoroughly that it was impossible to tell. I knew from what I've read that even gravity in this city and most high-speed tunnels are equal that on Earth, thanks to the modern artificial gravity systems.

George didn't bother talking, so I didn't say anything until the rover stood in front of the giant apartment block.

"This is where Susan Herefort lives," he then said, applying the handbrake. "Apartment number one. Miss Herefort hates heights, so she lives as close to the ground as possible. I'll leave you here, she hates men as well, so I won't risk teasing her with my sight."

"Is it that bad?"

"You'll find out."

He placed my bags out on the sidewalk and handed me a piece of foil with his contact number.

"Please remember, I am available at any time of the day or night. Don't go anywhere alone, it's not safe here. Don't use any taxis other than me, just in case. Various things have already happened here."

He said goodbye with a warm smile, leaving me alone in this strange place. I gathered all the courage I could afford and pressed the bell marked with a stylized number one. After a moment a female voice spoke from the camera next to the door:

"What do you want? I already said I don't need anything! Just leave me alone!"

"Miss Herefort, my name is Juliette Ankes, I'm here by order of Citizen Hakat," I said, bringing my face closer to the scanning reader so that it could read the pattern of my retina. "Let me in, please."

There was a moment's silence, then a rustle came from behind the door, as if somebody was slipping on the floor with slippers.

"Did Citizen Hakat order you to tell me something?" she posed the question.

"Only that sometimes the planet Venus casts a shadow on Earth."

That's an extremely stupid password, I thought. However, it was correct because the lock creaked and the door opened. I could go inside.

What Hakat said about his niece seemed a little over exaggerated back on Earth, but standing in the hallway of the small (from what I could see) apartment, I realized it was an understatement. I have never seen such a messy place in my entire life. In the corners were piled up boxes of instant meals, on the furniture lay scattered clothes, often so gutted that it was difficult to recognize their original style. The floor was literally strewn with rubbish, candy papers, crumpled pieces of computer foil, and dried crumbs. Sue Herefort stood in the midst of all this, dressed in a stained pink bathrobe and looking at me as if she was wondering what to do with me.

Her appearance surprised me a little. Despite my will I imagined her to be somewhat similar to Hakat. Meanwhile, in front of me was a very short blonde with a chubby childish face and short, disheveled hair. Judging by her figure, she must have liked eating a lot and probably didn't go to the gym. She was clearly embarrassed.

"Uuhmm... I was told about your arrival. If you want, you can live in that room," she said finally, dragging the words slightly. "We could also open the annex, there are two additional rooms and a storeroom. Uncle wrote to me about you and your task. We'll do the work whenever you like, even tonight. Right now I'm finishing charts for the Southern Atlantic Corporation, so right now I can't...

"It's okay," I interrupted her. "I have to settle myself here anyway. And... Miss Herefort, may I clean up a little?" I couldn't resist. I'm not a clean freak, but I do like some order.

"Call me Sue. Clean up all you want. For me it's a waste of time... not that I'm that dirty, sometimes, when I have a surge of energy, it's shiny in here! But that hasn't happened in a while, so right now it's a little messy."

"It's okay, miss... I mean Sue. I like cleaning, so while I'm here, I will keep our apartment clean. Sounds good?"

"Sure. Provided that you do it yourself. Brenda was always rushing me to do it, sometimes I really had enough of her."

"I'll manage without help."

She nodded with evident satisfaction and disappeared into the room from which the integrated computer murmured steadily. The bluish glow of the screen was visible through the crack under the door – it must have been at least thirty inches, if not bigger. This pointed to an incredibly elaborate system that Sue was downloading data from. She probably had insight into everything that was happening on the moon. Could it even be any different, since she was working for the Company?

I took my bags to the room she pointed me to, which was fortunately less cluttered, and then I looked around for the semi-automatic cleaning machine. To my surprise I didn't find anything like that, but in the corner I discovered a brush, a mop and a dustpan. I cleaned my room first, then the living room and the tiny hall. Luckily, the garbage compressor worked, although I had to adjust it before it began working decently. Despite her declaration, however, Sue really was rather 'dirty', because no one else would be able to withstand living in such a dumpster.

Being done with the floor, I started collecting scattered clothes and separating clean and dirty pieces.

"Can I wash everything not in wearable condition?" I called out.

"Do what you want!" Sue yelled back cheerfully. "The washing machine is in the bathroom, but I don't know if there's enough washing powder."

I folded the dirty clothes and went to the bathroom. The washing machine mounted to the wall looked like an outdated model, but it had everything that was needed and, according to the diagnostics mounted on the hatch, the entire machinery should be working flawlessly. I put the dirty laundry inside, added a scoop of powder (there was enough, luckily) and set all the programs: washing -> spin -> drying -> ironing -> drying.

Then I began sorting out the bathroom, which, of course, was also in terrible state. I've heard before that virtualists are completely devoted to their work and see nothing beside it, but I never knew how true that statement was. If they are all like Sue, their families deserved sympathy.

When I could finally consider the state of the flat to be barely satisfactory, I was so tired that I could barely stand. The washing machine finished its work a long time ago, so I took out the dry pieces of clothing from the receiver, folded them and put them in the closet in the living room. Sue also had to have enough work for today because she left her room and looked around with a drowsy expression.

"You really cleaned everything up," she murmured at my sight with a note of embarrassment.

"You didn't have to, but that's kind of you."

"I like cleanliness and order," I said openly. "I don't know how long I'll be staying here, but while I am, I'll look after the apartment. Don't worry, I won't disrupt your work."

"Sounds good," she yawned and stretched. "Are you hungry?"

"I'm starving, but I don't have any strength left for cooking."

"You don't have to do anything. Every estate has its own bar and they deliver the meals to your door. I'll have some krespo ravmaga and something to drink, all right?"

"They have krespo here?"

"Yes, it's pretty good even."

I've always liked krespo ravmaga, thin flakes made of soy, coated in flour and fried crispy, served with small balls of a pork substitute. Now that I knew how real meat tastes like, I really appreciated synthetic substitutes – they were delicate, fat-free and had a much richer flavor. I didn't like the real meat that I had at Miraton and the Agency's headquarters. Despite many attempts, I simply couldn't get used to it.

We ordered two portions of dinner with home delivery, we also decided to get some punch. We had to somehow celebrate our meeting. We turned on the TV, chose a music station and ate with some punch, talking. Sue turned out to be an extremely communicative person, which pleasantly surprised me. Virtualists are often thought to be quiet and introvert, and this girl chattered like a teenager and soon I knew almost everything about her.

"I was seventeen then," she said. "Uncle asked me what I want to do in my life, and when I answered, he arranged for me to study at the best university. I was doing so well that after graduation I received a referral for internships in Lunnar. And I stayed here since then. Uncle decided that I would be useful to him as an informant, so he wasn't against it. And so I've been working like that for five years."

"And you don't get bored here?" I asked.

"Not at all. My job is interesting, and if I felt lonely or sad, then there's the social clubs, dating centers, gyms, whatever you like. Uncle thinks that I spend all my time in front of the computer, but I know how to have fun, too! Lunnar may not seem like the most fun place, but it has its advantages. Of course, my computer is still the most important to me. With its help, I can look into every nook and cranny and find out what I need."

She fell silent for a moment, then ate one more krespo and drank some punch.

"Recently, I intercepted a conversation between the Martian station and the observatory on the near side," she continued. "It was very strange. I encrypted it and sent to uncle's agency, they can tire themselves over it there. Whatever there is you'll want to know, I can get it from the records."

"I don't know yet what I'll want," I said, "I'll need to investigate the situation, and that will require a lot of driving around the city and the mines. You know, it's about those weird deaths. Have you heard about them? I have no idea how I'll manage."

Sue waved her chubby hand.

"Uncle is never wrong," she said with absolute conviction. "If he believes that you're the person for this job, then you are. He certainly gave you instructions for every occasion. Did you undergo training?"

"Of course."

"Then you have nothing to fear. Do you have a driver?"

"Yes. George Terrel, the one who picked me up from the landing pad, is to be my guide. Do you know him?"

"No. This is the first rule of conspiracy: you only know those that you really need to. If uncle recommended him, then he must be trustworthy. When do you start?"

"Take it easy, I just arrived. I will think about where to start tomorrow."

I still didn't have any specific plan but, to my surprise, Sue immediately knew what to do.

"I'll download the data of those deceased employees for you," she said cheerfully, as if it was something fun. "You have to get familiar not only with who they worked for and who they were, but also the coroner's reports. Will you be able to interpret them?"

"I'm not sure."

"That's okay, I have a program that translates the official medical language into a language that the average person can understand."

"Has anyone examined these reports for connections yet?"

"Hard to say. Even if they did, then they didn't find anything. The concerns didn't care at all whether these matters are investigated and solved. The card was supposed to have a death from natural causes, and that's with a period. It's best seen in the official documents."

She finished eating and tossed the empty box into the garbage compressor, and the plastic cutlery into a container for recyclable waste. It's clear that my presence stimulated her because before my arrival – judging from the previous state of the apartment – she simply threw them to the side. Now she took a bulky bottle from the cabinet and poured two glasses of amber liquid.

"Let's have a drink," she suggested. "It's eighteen-year-old brandy, I got it for my birthday. We won't be working today anyway, and we have to celebrate your arrival."

After only a few days, Sue Herefort and I became close as old friends. I think that it had a big impact on the fact that we complemented each other - I relieved her of the housework, while she looked for the documents I needed for the investigation. She was simply brilliant. She navigated the network as if she was playing one of those popular strategy games, which consist of matching elements quickly. Her short fingers ended with fingernails bitten as if they were a small child, flashed across the large touch screen confidently and so quickly that sometimes I could not follow their eyes.

As a result, each evening I had so many documents on my reader to review that it took me until one or two in the morning. Outside the window, night-time illumination danced across the dome acting as a makeshift sky, schematically depicting various constellations, and I continued reading. When I finally fell asleep from fatigue, the files that Sue downloaded for me still floated before my eyes. From the morning, in every free moment, I went back to reading and noted everything that could have been helpful in my investigation.

Before anything else, I had to figure out the structure of each corporation and the role played by each deceased employee while they were still alive. I suspected that if the deaths were not natural, each of these people must have at some point hit the trail of some great corruption, but so far there was nothing I could see. It didn't seem like they had contact with each other – Sue, with no effort and time, obtained their individual 'track records', a chart of the roads they traveled on a daily basis.

"We usually don't realize this, but we always follow more or less our own paths," she explained to me. "I'm not talking about holidays or long weekends, but about our everyday travels. Either way, I also have a chart of places where they visited in their free times."

She was inexhaustible, full of enthusiasm, and I was still shaking from fear that I'll be a disappointment. I've always lacked confidence, and training on Central Island couldn't change me that much. True, I was taught many things and trained for melee combat. I was a little prettier now, I had larger breasts and thick, red hair instead of my little strands, but somewhere deep inside I still remained the same person as before. It was who I've always been – a shy, constantly scared girl, backing away from every challenge. How could this Hakat think that I'll be of any use to him? That was more or less how I felt about this all.

One day something finally caught my attention. The name of a certain thing showed up in the documents several times.

"Health Center?" I asked, looking up from the reader. "Is this an independent institution?"

Sue looked over my shoulder.

"That must be an unofficial gym," she said uncertainly, scratching her head, "I'll look into it."

"Please do so. This is the only location which each of the deceased was in at some point. I don't think they met there, the timeframe doesn't match that, but this is the only place visited by each of them without exception."

She nodded and sat down at her computer, and I once again checked exactly what I had noted. There was no mistake. Strange deaths concerned employees of five corporations, two large and three much smaller, these which had a few percent of Company shares. Judging from the descriptions, these people didn't even know each other, and yet they all died in similar circumstances. As for the cause of death, the doctors identified it as karoshi, death from overwork, which in itself was quite peculiar.

The modern labor code basically eliminated anything resembling a rat race, the most common cause of this type of death, and yet the doctor's report was clear. All people were between thirty-five and forty. They were found in their own apartments behind closed doors, at the computers on which they worked or played some video game. Judging from the records, they did it for dozens of hours without a break, without eating or drinking. It was strange, because none of them were ever known as workaholics. They were your average employees, performing their duties flawlessly, but without excessive involvement.

If the cases involved CEOs, directors, or at least shift bosses – then it would be somewhat understandable, but it involved private officials and machine operators, and even one 'office connector', in other words a simple messenger. They had nothing in common, only that Health Center. None of the two programs that I used to compare the transcripts brought this to my attention because the parameters I entered weren't precise enough. It wasn't until I started working manually that I came on this lead.

I entered the general network using my notebook and tried to find something about this object, but I proved to be too incompetent. The Health Center was only included in the list with its name, I could not find any specific information from the records system. This seemed strange. I would think that in a city like Lunnar everything would have to be described and recorded, but while looking for anything about the Health Center, to my surprise I came across many 'holes'. It shouldn't be this way.

The supervision of the Moon Company wasn't as strict as the agency's materials claimed, rather it seemed that each corporation was governing a piece of the city in the same way that street gangs do. I was hoping that this impression was wrong, but I had to wait for Sue to finish her investigation. Regardless of what she was doing, one thing remained unshakable: while she was sitting at her great computer with the enormous screen, she was unreachable until she got up by herself.

While waiting, I finished washing the laundry and cleaned the blinds on the windows. They looked different than those in earthly homes. Moon windows were small, paneled, made of thick glass, and tightly sealed. I already knew that this was to create additional protection. In the event of a dome breaking, for example as a result of a meteor hit, the construction of the buildings could protect the inhabitants until the rescue teams arrived. Either way, I thought they looked nice. They used crystal glass, perfectly transparent, slightly greenish, and it gave the impression of brightening anything you look at.

When Sue finally came to the living room, first of all, she rushed to the dinner, which I ordered for us. Only after satisfying her hunger did she start speaking:

"As I thought, the place is a gym and a social club. A suspicious place if you want to know what I think."

"Are there a lot of places like that here?" I asked.

She shrugged.

"Nobody maintains any strict records. They often function undercover, for example as a cafe or game room. As you may know, there are a lot more men than women in Lunnar, and men need some kind of entertainment, not always legal. There have been scandals before because of the antics of high-ranking decision-makers who thought themselves to be above the law... and quite rightly so, because these matters were silenced. I won't even mention the ordinary brawls, it's not worth it. Listen, Leeta, if the Health Center is a camouflaged agency for illegal social gatherings, then your visit there may be misunderstood. And if it's some fly-away, you might be in danger."

"Fly-away?" I didn't know that term.

"A place where they serve various legal and illegal psychoactive substances. A loud murder took place in one of them last year. One official stabbed his boss to death, under the influence of drugs thinking he was some wild animal. All suspicious locales were closely monitored for several weeks after that, but then everything returned to normal. No one really cares about closing such places."

"Why exactly?"

"There are many who earn a lot from them, and I suspect that even the leaders of individual corporations are taking tolls from them. I have no evidence for that yet, but I'm actively looking for it, and if it exists I will find it."

I became lost in thoughts. There weren't any doubts that I had to investigate this locale. It was the only place where all of the deceased attended before death. I had no evidence that they had met there even once, but couldn't rule out this possibility. I couldn't trust the transcripts completely, because in the end forging them was within the limits of human possibilities, even mine. And if they did go there, they must have had a reason and I had to find out what that reason was.

"Do women go to such places?" I asked.

Sue grimaced reluctantly.

"Sure, but only a rather specific type of woman. There's ones like these here too, you know, floresses without a license... Don't be surprised if they are completely disrespectful to you in that place.

"Never mind the respect. I need to find something specific, and this is the only place where all the dead have been at some point. Of course, they went to various different places, but it's the only one in which I noted the presence of all of them without exception. Is there really nothing more you can get out of the virtual?"

She shook her head in visible frustration.

"No, and that's what's weird about it. This place, it's as if it never existed, it's a dead name with a few word description. I don't know who founded it, who runs it, there is neither a list of employees nor a list of members. It really smells like trouble. You may be stepping straight into the hornets' nest and not even take a breath."

I was aware of that. It crossed my mind to throw all of this to hell, buy a ticket for the next flight to Earth and hide somewhere where no one would find me. Forget about Hakat, the Central Island, the agency and everything that has my unwanted participation. It was a very tempting thought, but I knew that I wouldn't do it. I had to, willingly or not, to keep going forward as long as I could."

"I'll call George Terrel," I finally sighed. "I could use a helping hand."

The number George left me was not, as I initially thought, his, but instead it was the number of the taxi service center. I was surprised, but my guide explained everything along the way.

"All private communication devices are tapped," he said. "We can forget about having any conversations through these things, we will only talk in my taxi. I check through it every day and I've invested in well-made devices to block out any possible taps."

"You are planning ahead."

"What can I say, it's my twelfth year in the profession. I had time to learn this and that."

"Don't they suspect that something is going on if the customer insists on one particular driver?" I asked. He shook his head.

"Not at all. It's normal here in Lunnar, especially if the client is a woman. If they already trust one particular driver, they will always ask for them specifically. There happened to be cases where some robbed or even raped a passenger."

He smiled under his mustache. Despite his ordinary appearance, he seemed trustworthy, or maybe that was the reason. He gave the impression of being extremely open, solid, but not very intelligent, and probably no one would suspect him of a double game.

"Do you have the documents?" he asked, turning to some narrow street.

"Of course," I replied. "Full set. I hope you can help me out a little. I will be working as a sanitary inspector for the first time and I am afraid of being compromised."

"There is nothing to fear" he turned again. "Inspectors appear here quite often, and each one stupider than the other. You can ask about anything you can think of, no one will be surprised. Ask about the toothpaste, shoe size, bowel movement... please don't laugh, I'm serious. Only thing is, you can't act too zealous, you should put on a bored face and ask as if by duty."

"Okay."

"And remember that they must answer every question, even if they don't want to, and show everything that the inspector with relevant documents asks. You can't let them chase you away, and they might try when they smell a novice."

I was aware of that. If these people had something to hide, they certainly would not be willing to cooperate, and it was up to me to find the truth between the lines. George couldn't help me much. He was a taxi driver here, hired by a client and nothing more. He was supposed to wait until I finished my work, not assist me in my duties.

The Health Center was located in an inconspicuous utility building, between a warehouse of clothes and a computer service. The entrance was labeled with the place's name, but otherwise there was nothing special about it – just an ordinary door, the same as others. I pressed the bell. The release lock clang and I could enter. There was no verification here? Not stopped by anybody, I found myself in the hall, on the walls of which hung photos of muscular, healthy and handsome men and young girls with flawless shapes. Inside, the facility resembled a clinic of aesthetic surgery, to which Mabel once took me. It was almost sterile, and the white glaze on the walls and the very bright terracotta on the floor further intensified this impression. It wasn't long before a young woman in a modest costume appeared beside me and looked at me with an expectant smile.

"Is there something you need?" she asked and walked over to the computer on the shiny desk. "Do you want to improve your performance at work? You've come to the right place. My name is Glenda Morris, and I'm the receptionist here. Would you care to provide your information?"

"Information?" I said in a daze.

"Yes, ma'am. Name, specification, place of work. We operate legally, we are obliged to have it all."

I pulled myself together and took a step forward.

"It's good that you act legally," I said. "Here are my documents. I am an inspector from the public health department and I have to check this locale."

The receptionist's smile turned into a reluctant grimace. She looked at me for a moment, as if wondering what to do.

"Could somebody have some suspicions?" she finally asked.

"That's none of your business," I said firmly. "Please lead me to the management room."

"Well, all right..."

Glenda Morris came out from behind the desk and moved ahead. I followed behind her, discreetly looking around the premises. It was much larger than the entrance would suggest and had at least two floors. The lower one was a gym, professionally and tastefully furnished. Under the instructor's guidance, several elderly men and two women trained in it, both of them around middle age. The stairs led to the upper level, and the inscription on the tablet with an arrow read 'Work medicine'. Surely they didn't have an official doctor's office here, that's something Sue would be able to track down. So was some unregistered doctor working here? I couldn't imagine anyone wanting to risk everything for a few illegally earned allocation points. Unless... a certain picture began forming in my head, but it required more reflection and, above all, consultation with Sue. I also suspected that the third level was even higher and I remember that for later checking. For now, I had to postpone further considerations to a more favorable moment, because Glenda had just lead me into a spacious office, inside of which was a man in an expensive suit. He looked like someone who was just rejuvenated, because the skin on his cheeks seemed too tight and slightly too shiny. I knew these symptoms and knew that they disappear within a maximum of two weeks after the surgery, so the facility manager must have been fresh after a surgery.

The man frowned at the sight of me.

"What is it? He asked impatiently.

I handed him the document confirming my full mandate and watched as he read through it. I couldn't read any emotions on his smooth face, only the left corner of his mouth twitched once.

"All right," he said finally. "Do you want to check our devices? Look through the books? Or do you want me to show you the clients' files?"

"Everything in time, sir... Renaud," I replied, looking at the plate on his desk. "For now I would like to find out who gave you the license to run a work medicine office."

"The office isn't located here," he said calmly. "That's just registration and archives."

"Archives of what?"

"Of the results. Treatment rooms are elsewhere."

"What treatments are we talking about here?" I opened my pad and ran my fingers over the sensory keyboard.

"Biological renewal. Massages, vitamin injections. Health Industries' job is to improve employee productivity, and the Health Center is just a parent. You can confirm all of that, even now."

"I will. I'd also like to know the addresses of the aforementioned treatment offices."

"Currently only one of them is operating, the 'Mantra Life'. It mainly serves miners and is near a mine owned by Romain Corporation. The other two are under renovation."

The man seemed honest, but I didn't trust him. Nowhere in the virtual did it say that Health Center was associated with some treatment offices and the name Health Industries wasn't mentioned at all. I was absolutely sure of that.

I spent over two hours reviewing the data given to me by the manager, and then I went out into the street. George was waiting for me in his taxi, reading an electronic newspaper. At the sight of me he closed the reader and started the vehicle.

"And?" he asked when we began moving. I shrugged my shoulders.

"I think we should visit the biological renewal office called 'Mantra Life', as long as it's relatively close," I replied. "Apparently it's located next to one of the mines. I have the exact address."

I handed him the business card received from the manager of the Health Center. He glanced at it.

"That's really far," he said. "Perhaps we really should go there today, otherwise they could 'clean' the place and then you won't find anything."

"Let's go then."

He directed the vehicle towards Lunnar's main highway. For now the road winded between the buildings, but soon we left the residential part of the city and entered one of the tunnels. They led to the buildings of the mines, to factories and workshops, located far from the center. They stretched for hundreds of miles – long concrete pipes, branching into dozens and hundreds of branches, at times accompanied by service points, such as a repair shops or take-away bars. George knew them well and easily found the path that would lead us to 'Mantra Life'. I would've been unable to find it even with a map and automatic navigation, but my guide managed to somehow, only sometimes glancing at the navigation screen. This shouldn't surprise me though, after all, he has worked here a taxi driver for years.

Initially, we drove in the company of many other vehicles, passenger cars, vans and bulk, then it started becoming more and more empty around us. Finally, the taxi stopped.

"Is it here?" I asked.

"No," he said and pointed to the phosphorescent plaque. "Bypass."

"Is that normal?"

"Sometimes. Tunnel maintenance requires temporarily decommissioning certain sections of the route. Although it's strange that in the daily newsletter for drivers nothing was mentioned about planned repairs on the D-8... that's where we're headed. Well, it could've been a sudden failure."

"I can't see anything happening, can't we ignore this sign?" I suggested.

"Absolutely not! I could lose my license and that I can't afford."

"What do we do?"

"We're taking the bypass route, what else? Unless you prefer to give up for today."

"No. I have the feeling that if we don't get there today then I won't ever learn anything."

"It's quite possible. According to the signs, I have to circle quite a lot of terrain, it will take a while. We will follow the repair route, so it may shake a little at times, but it's the shortest route."

George carefully backed up and turned into the side of the tunnel. It was lower and not as well lit as the main one, and, as Terrel warned me, not as well maintained. At times, the taxi was tossed like on a countryside road on Earth, but pushed forward somehow. The navigation screen flickered, showing our route in a maze of tangled lines from which I understood nothing, although for Terrel they were probably as readable as words in a book. My head was starting to ache. I was silent, not wanting to seem like a wimp, although in silence I dreamed of finally leaving this locked vehicle... I was new to the industry, but George had worked for Citizen Hakat for more than a dozen years and must have been really good, since he kept his incognito for so long. I didn't want him to look down on me so I put on the right expression for the situation. However, he noticed that I wasn't feeling well and handed me a small object taken out of the first aid kit under the steering wheel. An agent against motion sickness, a patch to stick on the neck. The medicine contained in it acted through the skin and worked rapidly. Only in my case it wasn't just motion sickness.

The further we were, the worse it got. The tunnels were becoming darker and darker as well as smaller, so much that I was beginning to feel a claustrophobic fear.

"Are you sure we're going the right way?" I asked with a shriller voice than I intended.

"We're going towards the goal," he replied. "These are parts of the tunnels that drivers rarely use so the conditions are miserable, but in a few dozen kilometers we should..."

His further words were drowned out by a bang that fell on us like an avalanche. The taxi flung out of control, tossed sideways, then I heard a terrifying noise, as if a large amount of stones were falling on top of us, and then everything went out.

I came to my senses after some time – I was awakened by the pain in my side, under the collarbone and in my left temple. Around me it was dark and terribly cold. I was lying on some debris, with difficulty gasping for the dust-filled air and coughing. I struggled up to my feet, supporting myself with my arms and trying to see something. I was lying next to the overturned vehicle, from which something tore off the side door. Behind the wheel I noticed Terrel, twisted helplessly.

"George!" I called out weakly. He didn't answer me, he didn't even move.

I crawled closer, trying to ignore the stinging pain I slipped my hand inside and pressed the emergency light switch on the dashboard. The pale light revealed from darkness the tunnel ruined by an explosion or collapse of the structure. The brackets bent due to the catastrophe were grafted, forming a kind of scaffolding that protected me from the blind mass of concrete resting on top. That's why I was still alive. Poor George was not so lucky. As soon as the light flashed, I immediately realized that he was dead and I was here all alone, by myself. I didn't know where I was and how to get out of here. This wasn't fair, but I wasn't thinking about George right now, I was more concerned about what would happen to me. Right now I was too bewildered to be afraid, but I was slowly beginning to realize the terror of my situation.

I reached for the radio. Despite my efforts, it remained silent, apparently damaged during the accident. Only now did I feel paralyzing terror. Training at the Central Island included various scenarios, but nothing that prepared me for this. It was terribly cold, the thick dark outside the circle of light overwhelming me like piling tar. The dust suspended in the thin air almost made it impossible to breathe. I didn't want to die like this, in this desolate place, where likely nobody would even find my corpse anytime soon and likely nobody would even know what actually happened.

A human figure suddenly loomed in the shallow glow of the emergency light. At first I thought it was an illusion that appeared because of my blow to the head, but this person was coming closer and I heard the crunching of the tiny stones under the soles of his shoes, so I realized that this someone must be real.

"Help!" I called out with all the strength I had left. "I'm here!"

The approaching man stopped. He was close enough that I could see him quite clearly. He was tall and rather slim, with long, fair hair, visible from under the mining helmet and work overalls, judging by eye a little too large.

"Please!" I cried, choking on the dust again. "I'll die without help."

He leaned over me and suddenly his angular face, illuminated by silver-gray eyes, was right next to mine. He looked at me as if he was looking at an unknown specimen of an insect or a lizard. Then, still without a word, he straightened up and turned away, clearly intending to leave.

"Don't leave me!" I yelled desperately, overcome by terrible fear. Was he just going to leave when I needed help? Whoever he was, he shouldn't do that!

Under the influence of my scream, the unknown miner stopped and looked back. He stood still for a moment, then turned around and took me in his arms so easily as if he was picking   up   a   doll. "In six minutes and fifteen seconds the second detonation will occur. I will take you to the mine's office," he spoke in a steady, calm voice.

"Is it far?"

"No."

He left the area of the collapse onto a relatively even road and walked forward, carrying me hugged to his chest. He must have been very strong, because I had the impression that he wasn't exerting himself at all with this task. I looked him straight in the face, but there were no signs of sweat. His face was very calm, smooth, beardless, regular and probably would interest me under different circumstances. But right now I was too shocked and too sore.

"My... my name is Juliette Ankes." I stammered, feeling that I should say something. "I was traveling for a sanitary inspection."

"What is your name?" I added after a moment, because my rescuer was silent, as if he had not heard me.

"Monty Romain," he answered my question.

"Romain?" Like the Romain Corporation?

"I am the property of Romain Corporation."

I felt dizzy. I was thinking about George, who was left back there in a crashed taxi and wanted to cry. Every step of the miner echoed in my poor head, my lungs scooped oxygen from the air with increasing difficulty, and finally I fainted again.

This time when I woke up I was already in the hospital. I knew where I was before I even opened my eyes and felt immeasurable relief. Everything around me smelled of disinfectants, the drip's needle was in my forearm, and the vital signs monitor was beeping steadily over the bed. The sense of security that overwhelmed me mixed with a terrible regret when I remembered George. Tears ran down my temples.

"Doctor, our patient has woken up!" I heard the voice of a woman, probably a nurse. A moment later a young man with a gray, unhealthy complexion leaned over me, clearly tired from the long shift. The hospital in Lunnar was owned by the Company and employed only as many employees as they absolutely had to, which meant that the shifts were cut ruthlessly and the doctor who was unlucky to sign a contract with them was exploited to the limit.

"How are you feeling?" the doctor asked, shining in my eyes with a small scanner.

"As if a road roller ran over me," I said. "Doctor, there was ... a taxi driver back in the tunnel with whom I was driving. Is he...?"

He shook his head without stopping the scanning of my eyes.

"I am sorry but that men has died," he replied. "You were saved thanks to the implants. It was only thanks to them that the taxi's glass shard didn't penetrate the blood vessels and you're only a little injured. By the way, I haven't treated anyone here with such a wide reconstructive implantation. You must have been in a terrible state, if someone decided to do such a thing. In which center was this done? Were you conscious at that time?"

"I was treated at EPIPHANICS. But to tell you the truth, I don't remember anything," I confessed. "I know that they turned me into quite the cyborg, but I think cyber reconstruction was the only way if they already decided to save my life."

"You must be extremely well situated if your account could withstand that bill. The EPIPHANICS network of clinics is top-notch healthcare."

"I don't think that's your business," I murmured.

He smiled apologetically.

"You're right. For now, we need to bring you to a working condition, and that will take a few more days. You have suffered a serious injury and you're lucky to be alive."

"I know. What ever happened?"

"It was an explosive load accidently left by the miners. That part of the tunnels is intended for expansion, and the rocks need to be blown up to expand the area. One of the workers absent-mindedly lost one of the packages, and the taxi must have drove over it."

I closed my eyes. Something about this didn't feel right, I didn't know what it was, but I had no strength to think. The doctor touched my forehead and said reassuringly:

"You must rest. The police inspector will soon be here to talk with you, you must be rested and have a clear mind. Nurse, give the patient a dose of easyhal.

I wanted to protest, but the nurse put a small inhaler to my lips and I decided that it would be better to do what they ask of me. I obediently breathed in the fumes of lemon flavor. After a while, a pleasant numbness spread across my body and I fell into a light, pleasant nap. The inspector didn't show up until the next evening – he was an elderly man with a face full of wrinkles and thinning hair, trimmed almost to the skin. He looked like a tired of life trapper from old movies, not a policeman. Instead of eyes, he had an older-model sight implants, bearing traces of many repairs and connected to a recorder covering the left temple. The triangular B1 mark was barely visible from behind the implant support. The police uniform was decorated with a faculty badge and several tarnished medals, among which I noticed with astonishment the Honorable Service ribbon. I could only guess what such a well-deserved veteran was doing at such a forgotten institution and why he was moved here.

"Hello, ma'am," he said, sitting down next to my bed and pulling out his small pad working as a small notebook. "My name is Scott Cavanaugh. Right away, I'll say that you're very lucky. The taxi driver you hired died on the spot."

"I got launched out along with the side door..."

"I know. I was at the place of accident and looked through everything myself. Someone should take responsibility for this, but talking to the miners isn't easy. They practice the idea of 'one for all, and all for one' amongst each other. If one of them was negligent, we may be unable to find out who exactly it was. Now, please tell me everything you remember. Above all: why did you take the road in the middle of reconstruction, instead of the main road?"

"The main route was closed."

"What do you mean closed? It definitely wasn't."

"I saw the detour sign... a yellow sign with black arrows."

The policeman looked at me in surprise, his visors twinkled with the lights of the control diodes.

"There was no such sign there," he said finally, "and no detour was planned in this area, and even if it was planned, it wouldn't have gone through the tunnel which was being expanded."

"I understand, sir, but the sign was there at the time. I saw it with my own eyes."

"We will have to examine that," he murmured in disbelief. "There's also another matter: how did you get to the mine's office? It's over five miles from the accident site."

"A miner moved me there."

"What miner?"

"Young, tall, in overalls and helmet. Very handsome. He had... light hair, shoulder length, and gray eyes. He said his name was Monty Romain."

Cavanaugh typed my name on the pad's keyboard and pressed the wireless connection sensor.

"Monty Romain?" he repeated after a moment. "Nobody like that is on the list."

"He said he works for the Romain Corporation. Maybe it's someone from the board?"

He shook his head and ran his fingers over the keyboard again.

"There is no such person on the list," he repeated. "Do you feel well enough to look through the photos?"

"I think so."

He handed me the pad after setting the right program. I arranged myself more comfortably and focused my attention on the changing photos. There were dozens of them, younger and older men, in work outfits and suits – but none of them even resembled the one that brought me out of the disaster area.

"I don't understand," I said, confused. "You have to find him, inspector! He saved my life, I... I want to thank him!"

He took the pad back from me.

"Take it easy, Mrs. Ankes. The time will come for that. For now I will be dealing with this as part of the investigation, but if I can't find this miner, you will have to ask about him yourself at the headquarters of Romain Corporation. There's a chance that they will tell you something because they certainly will not want to talk to us. Unfortunately, Lunnar has its own rules. Hardly anyone wants to cooperate with the police here, and we can't press them too hard."

"Even when it concerns murder?"

"For now, we're investigating it as a fatal accident. Your testimony is pointing to a new lead, but no one but you saw this detour sign, otherwise I would have known about it before. Such testimony can be easily challenged, you have suffered a serious head injury, after all. If I may give you some advice, I'd say to not let people know of your suspicions."

"You think that..."

"Yes. I believe that they may have been trying to kill you, because they certainly weren't targeting the taxi driver. I know that you asked about the Health Industries' offices and you were going to one of them. Whatever it was there that stunk, it was certainly cleaned up by now, so even if I followed the trail, I wouldn't find anything. For now it's best that nobody suspects that I'll be investigating the matter."

"I understand. I will be silent. You can write down that I don't remember anything, that I don't even know why I got in that taxi."

He nodded and entered something in his memory for a moment.

"If you find out anything after leaving the hospital, please only contact me personally," he finally said, getting up from the chair. "Don't trust anyone. Lunnar is a nest of vipers, and until recently my police station was a shelter of the most corrupt degenerates that you can imagine."

"Do you tolerate all this?"

He smiled bitterly and with a sense of superiority.

"Miss, they moved me to the moon to clean up this mess. Only that I've been here for merely two months, and this is enough work for at least ten years. For now, you should worry about your own problems. Please be careful, because someone may try to finish their work."

"I will be careful," I promised him. He hid the pad and left, closing the door behind him.

The next person to visit me was Sue. It was the first time I saw her in regular clothing, in elegant pants and a loose tunic embroidered with red strings in abstract patterns. Her blonde curls were gathered in a ponytail, with some lipstick drawn across the lips.

"You look great," I said honestly. She waved her hand.

"This is why I don't like going out anywhere, it's such a headache. At the computer I can sit how I want and look however I want, and yet I'm more useful than all these pretty ladies in the offices of the board."

"You're so incorrigible."

"So what? Enough about me, tell me what's up with you. I know that Terrel is dead. Did you even find out anything? Was it worth?"

I shrugged my shoulders.

"I don't know. I didn't get to where I wanted to, but I think we must be on the right trail. If we weren't, nobody would try to kill me."

"You're right," Sue leaned toward me, "I've managed to get some classified information from the network. We'll examine it together after you leave."

"If I could've just gotten to Mantra Life, I'd have all the evidence."

"And you probably wouldn't have come out alive. Either we're dealing with a very serious scandal, or my name isn't Susan Herefort."

Her round cheeks flushed with excitement. Such emotions were a bit childish in our situation, but I could understand how she feels. The virtualist's life is usually focused on one computer workstation, which is continuously receiving data streams. There is nothing adventurous about it, so Sue convinced herself that now she has a chance to experience something extraordinary. I didn't want to disappoint her, although on the other hand I wasn't sure if I should pull this girl into something this dangerous, something that already cost the life of one agent. If something happened to her, Hakat would never forgive me. However, I needed her help, without her I wouldn't go far.

"Keep digging," I said. "Learn everything you can. Even complete trifles can be useful. We don't know which of them will give us some kind of a trail."

"Of course, of course," Sue patted me on the hand. "Now, get well and don't think about anything stupid. Fortunately, you survived, although you gave me a good scare. When the officer came to me and told me what happened, I nearly fainted. For one terrible moment I thought you were dead... you have no idea how much I've grown like you, I didn't even know that myself!"

I smiled despite myself. This naive cry was as characteristic of my boss's niece as the feathers of a bird. Her infantile disposition, most likely unbearable to those around her, didn't bother me – maybe because Chris was the same as her, my beloved Chris, who became convinced that he would conquer the world. Sue reminded me of him.

After a few days I was discharged from the hospital with a recommendation to rest and conserve my energy. I was still dizzy and feeling terrible, but my wounds were healing well. The doctor said that I should take advantage of the consultation of a plastic surgeon, but for now I had no motivation for it. It didn't seem particularly important to me, especially since the scars were hidden under clothing, and the one that caused the doctor the most anxiety, under the hair. Instead of worrying about my appearance, I was thinking about the investigation.

"Lie down for now," Sue said categorically as I tried to get to her computer. "I'll write all the data to your reader and bring it to you. Don't leave your bed unless you have to. I'll take care of everything."

And she really tried. She cleaned, although she did it incompetently and her efforts were hardly visible, she ordered the best food and took care of me like of a small child. At the same time, she didn't neglect her work or her searches on the web. I wondered when she would find time to sleep, but she only carelessly answered that she can handle it. She didn't look very tired, on the contrary: she looked fresh and cheerful. She treated the investigation like a video game, which worried me a little. I would prefer if she approached the matter more seriously, although I had to admit that she did a great job anyway. She somehow retrieved the forensic reports from the network, decoded the appropriate files for me, and I did a meticulous analysis looking for connections. I finally found them and felt proud of myself for the first time.

"All of the deceased used the Health Center services within three months before their death. Two or three weeks before their bodies were found, they all visited the doctor. They complained of headaches and chronic fatigue, mainly in the morning. Each of them said more or less the same thing: I sleep well, but I don't feel rested at all."

"That doesn't seem that severe..." Sue said uncertainly. She was sitting at the foot of my bed with her feet pulled up and eating macaroni with cheese flakes while I was checking the data on the reader.

"On the contrary. This is very serious," I replied. "Sleep disturbance can lead to mental illness and even death. However, the records show that none of them had trouble falling asleep and didn't wake up at night. Not only that, more than half of them took terexan, a sleep stabilizing agent. Can you decode blood test results?"

"Of course. What do you need?"

"Toxicology. If you can, find out where they store the samples taken during the postmortem. We may need them."

"It seems that nothing caught the doctors' attention."

"I'm not surprised. It's usually incompetent ones who work at Lunnar, so I don't see why the coroner should be an ace in his trade. There must be something, however, that connects the cases, and you can see yourself that they seem similar."

She nodded, without interrupting the steady swallowing of pasta.

"Not even similar, they are almost identical," she mumbled with her mouth full. "To me, it seems like there is only one possibility: some new type of drug."

"New?"

"Well, everyone already knows about the old ones, but new ones could cause problems for doctors. About a year ago, pills called wingsoma cost the lives of fourteen miners before they developed tests to detect them in the body. Without a proper marker, the doctors acted blindly, and that's dangerous."

"Couldn't they just give the antidote when someone showed symptoms?"

"No. The only know antidote for wingsoma is muscarinic, in a high dose at that. Do you know what muscarine is? A disgusting thing. It's found in poisonous mushrooms. Giving it to someone who had not been poisoned by a wingsoma would be equivalent to a death sentence."

I gave it some thought. Sue might have been right, but if that was the case, my task was doubly dangerous. Admittedly, the time of great drug cartels has passed, but small, well-organized groups were nevertheless ruthless. All of a sudden it came to me that without Scott Cavanaugh's help I would not be able to do this case, and whether I want to or not, I will have to let him in on everything."

"Sue, call Inspector Cavanaugh," I said. "Tell him that I remembered something, something important and I have to tell him about it. Invite him here."

"What, here? To our trash can?"

"Clean up if you're ashamed."

"I'm not ashamed. All right, I'll call him. I wonder what the neighbors will think when they see that we're being visited by a cop."

That was the least of my worries. I was more concerned about whether Citizen Hakat would approve of my decision, but I couldn't consult him just like that. I was sent to the moon as an independent investigator and I had to manage by myself. At least for a time. I was going to pass the results of my investigation to the detective in charge of the case, that's all. Suddenly I remembered that I didn't know what kind of detective he even was. I opened my reader and began to search the guidelines Hakat left for me in the password-protected folder. Finally, I came across the right paragraph and I read with astonishment: Scott Cavanaugh with the note Trust regardless of the situation. What a surprise!

In my mind I analyzed everything I already knew and tried to assess whether I made the right decision. After all, I didn't know this strange, gloomy man, or I guess I should say that I only just met him while lying in the hospital. He looked like a deviant and a scruff despite the high-ranked decorations on his uniform, he clearly didn't care about his appearance, and these nightmarish implants made things worse. Something whispered to me that he was absolutely honest and tough as a rock, someone you can rely on. After all, Hakat wouldn't trust just anyone. This policeman was a veteran, a man very experienced in life, who didn't break down despite losing his eyesight. I was spared of that at least, I had my own eyes. Cavanaugh underwent the procedure of implanting electronic cameras, rehabilitation and all the way through the torture, which was certainly to recover a permit to work in the police after such serious mutilation. And then he agreed that he would be sent to such a place as Lunnar... that said a lot about him, practically everything. He could be trusted – and I had no choice but to do so anyway.

Inspector Cavanaugh didn't come until late in the evening. He was wearing civilian faux leather clothing and his implant-covered face was covered by a motorcycle helmet. At the sight, Sue nodded approvingly.

"Come in," she said. "I didn't know that you rode a motorbike, but it's nice that you came in civilian appearance. At least no one will gossip that we're having trouble with the law."

She went to her room, looking once more at our guest.

"Yes, I actually came by a scooter," he corrected her, smiling slightly. "It's small and maneuverable, moreover, it isn't very noticeable. Hello, Miss Ankes."

He took off his helmet and placed it on a small bookcase in the hallway.

"Hello," I said, "my real name is Kaphoolie. Here are my secret warrants."

I handed him the government agency document. He was not surprised. He walked in and sat down on one of the chairs, first removing two empty boxes and Sue's laundry coat from the seat.

"Almost half of those who arrive at Lunnar provide non-original data. People make new passports for their new names, change their date of birth and whatever else they want. It's allowed by law, so enjoy. However, I'm glad you considered me trustworthy enough to reveal you real name."

He smiled slightly. Sue served some juice and small nut cookies, he took one.

"I'm not doing that without reason," I said. "You're aware that I'm using the documents of a sanitary inspector, but you are not aware that my task is much more important than a routine inspection."

"Which means?"

"I'm here to investigate the unexplained deaths among Moonlight Company employees. That is, those which the coroner said were caused by karoshi."

"Ah, that case," he nodded. He was not surprised. "Did Earth finally took interest in it? I asked for assistance a few times, but received only silence in response."

"Do you also believe that it wasn't death from overwork?"

Cavanaugh laughed. It was a laugh unexpectedly young and sonorous, which in combination with his damaged face made me shudder in surprise.

"Death from overwork, here in Lunnar? Slow down with the jokes, miss. This is a place of exile, not of career, unless someone is in a managerial position. And all of these people were privates or, at most, subordinate employees. I'm aware of the police coroner's report and the postmortem results from the hospital, and I had my doubts from the very beginning."

He looked at me closely – his implants came out of the housings and brought the lenses closer together, sharpening

112

the image. He twisted his lips as if he wasn't very pleased with what he saw.

"So you were the one sent in response to my requests," he said after a moment. "Well, I don't want to undermine the competence of these high-ranking guys from the central, so I won't be too waspish. You're probably already guessing what I think of all that. If you're not going to resign after what happened to you, I suggest we work together."

"That's the reason I asked for you here and revealed my incognito. I have the impression that I've discovered something very serious, since they tried to eliminate me."

"Definitely. It doesn't take a genius to tell. Please, tell me everything."

Everything? I didn't want to tell him everything, that's why I picked my words carefully while telling him about the investigation I was conducting. I didn't mention Hakat or Terrel's double role, I also kept what I said about myself to minimum. However, I gave an accurate account of what I was able to determine with Sue and the visit to the Health Center. The police officer listened to me intently, without interrupting. It wasn't until I finished that he moistened the scarred lips with his tongue.

"You were careless," he said, "Romain Corporation is my main suspect in several cases, but I haven't been able to connect this company to my investigations so far. In other words, I know that someone from there was involved in the trade of illegal substances, drilling in other people's land and other vileness, but currently I'm unable to prove anything. They are extremely crafty, and the trap they prepared for you was brilliant."

"Maybe not that brilliant. If we can find the miner who saved me..."

"It won't be easy. I will try to track him down using my own methods, and miss... maybe we should refer to each other by first names, since we are going to cooperate?"

"What?" I was embarrassed. "Ah yes. All right. Call me Leeta, like everyone else does."

"And you can call me Scotty. Well, dear Leeta, I propose 'playing the fool'. You will go to the headquarters of Romain Corporation and ask for your savior directly. Remember what they say to you, every word."

"Can't I just record it?"

"No. They definitely have a recording electronics detector. You must rely on your memory."

"And what are you going to do?"

Scott took bite of another cookie and chewed for a long time before answering.

"I'll go to the material evidence warehouse. We should have samples taken from all the deceased from this black series. I threw the former coroner out on his beaten face, the new one seems honest, he will help me analyze and compare the results of two new victims."

"What do you mean?"

"Exactly what I said. We have two new deceased with identical symptoms, a tunnel excavator operator and an archivist of the Seminar Corporation. One was thirty-two, the other twenty-nine. I'm telling you this because we're working together, but I think you understand that this is a secret of investigation."

"Ah, yes, of course. That would mean that they're still acting. That they don't care at all about the inspections or investigations. They fell untouchable."

"That doesn't surprise me one bit. They're used to the tardiness of the police. My predecessor was corrupt and he didn't even try to hide that. He took bribes from whoever offered him anything."

He stood up and buttoned his jacket.

"I'll be going now. Whatever you discover, you must tell me directly. No calls, simply come to the main command, regardless of the time of day or night. I live there."

"Really? Well, if you die from karoshi, I won't be surprised."

Scott laughed again.

"You're something else. I assure you that I won't die. All right, then we have an appointment. Remember to be careful, our opponents in this game are extremely dangerous."

When he left, Sue emerged from her room. She didn't even try to hide that she was eavesdropping.

"Quite a nice guy," she said. "It's a he wears those awful old-fashioned implants. It's a model from half a century ago, I don't understand why he was implanted it. Sure, they're practical and precise, but they look nasty. Modern cameras are so subtle that you can't really distinguish them from real eyes. You can even choose a color.

I waved my hand impatiently. My thoughts at the moment were dealing with completely different matters, and Inspector Cavanaugh's appearance was the least of them. Truth be told, I've already gotten used to the mechanisms that filled his eye sockets and they didn't seem that strange to me. After all, I had so many implants inside of myself that I'd give anyone a good scare if they were visible. Except nobody could see them. Specialists from EPIPHANICS have done an excellent job using the most expensive materials and perfectly masking any damage. Thanks to their skills, modern technology and Hakat's money, I still looked like a human being, not a cyborg. Not even mentioning the fact that I'm alive at all.

"Help me choose some elegant clothes, Suzie," I asked. "I have to go to the headquarters of Romain Corporation and don't want to look like a bad C-class spy."

***

The Romain Corporation's headquarters turned out to be more modest than I expected, even considering that this French company was a minor shareholder of the Moon Company and didn't have profits the likes of Alaskan Selenomir. Either way, I expected something more... demonstrative, meanwhile what I found was a completely average office. Its only decoration was a three-colored flag hung on the wall with the emblem of the Australian Little France and a large picture of the Eiffel Tower with the oblique inscription: We'll be back there. I refrained from commenting on it. Inhabitants of the enclaves dedicated to refugees from Europe from generation to generation lived with the hope of returning to their countries, although every reasonable person knew that it would not be possible for centuries.

The woman sitting behind the compact desk stood up at my sight and pointed me to a chair.

"Hello," she began in a pleasant low voice, "my name is Marceline Munroe, and I'm the CEO of the corporation.

What brings you here? As far as I know, Romain Corporation has never had sanitary issues."

I sat down, trying to keep my expression neutral. The CEO appeared to be an honest and competent person. She might have been around forty years old, she was tall and well-built, and on her left cheek was a dark birthmark that looked like a small beetle. It added to her elaborate face a kind of playful charm, not very fitting with the dignity of a CEO.

"I'm not here about the inspection," I said. "I'm here about the accident that took place near your mine."

"As far as I know, this case is being investigated by the police."

She yawned so unexpectedly that she shuddered.

"Please forgive me. It seems like recently I'm not getting enough sleep, even though I sleep just fine. I think I have too much on my mind. Well, I don't know what you want from me, since the police are already dealing with the matter of that accident. I'm very sorry for your suffering, you can count on compensation, but only after the investigation. These are the rules."

"I know. I don't intend to accuse the corporation of anything and I don't care about the compensation. I just want to know something about the man who saved me."

"Who are you talking about?"

"He's one of your miners. He said his name was Monty Romain."

I could see Miss Munroe lower her eyes suddenly. A barely noticeable shadow ran across her face.

"No one with such a name is on our payroll."

"I know that already. That's why I'd like to ask for some explanation of who this man is and to get me in contact with him."

She was silent for a moment, drumming her fingers on the top of her desk. Then she rubbed her nose with her thumb and sighed.

"You have the right to ask all this, of course. However, I would prefer to keep our conversation confidential."

"As you wish," I said slowly, "I think you're aware that I could ask for a hypnotic test and provide details that would help track down this man. I have not done so thus far, because the fact that he is not on your lists is suspicious. And I don't want to trouble somebody who saved my life, whoever he is."

"It seems that you don't understand anything, even though you pretend to be so smart," Munroe said brusquely. "You weren't saved by a man, but a machine, a highly advanced android. You must know of humanoid helper robots and anthrobots. They are very useful, but they only have the role of servitude. The designers associated with our corporation dreamed of something more. They decided to build an android with an independent mind, capable of making their own decisions."

"Is that even possible?"

"That's not a question for me. It's a fact that in one of our laboratories a prototype of an artificial man with a brain was created, with a completely new design, modeled on the human mind. It was to be used in situations where human intervention is necessary, but the conditions are too risky. Unfortunately, the final tests didn't go too well."

"Why is that?"

"That's a trade secret, but I'll tell you why: the prototype turned out to be too unpredictable."

I was silent for a moment. I felt uncomfortable, an alarm bell rang somewhere in my mind, though I didn't understand what triggered it. A sense of danger, some barely perceptible note of falsity in the whole situation caused the hairs on the back of my neck to stand up. I did my best to not let any of that show.

"And what happened to him?" I asked indifferently.

"With who?" Munroe yawned again, discreetly covering her mouth with the manicured hand. She didn't take her eyes off me, as if she was afraid that I would do something unexpected.

"Well, that android of yours."

"It was written off and scrapped."

I felt a painful spasm in my chest. I had to make every effort to keep my face neutral under this woman's cold, appraising look. Despite my will, I thought of my childhood school psychologist – although she was nothing like Mrs. Munroe, she had the same look, and I was once very afraid of her.

"Scrapped?" I repeated.

"What else can you do in that case? The model wasn't repairable."

I wanted to say that there's many things that could be done, but I was silent. My instinct prompted me not to raise suspicions with the CEO, so I winced dismissively.

"I suppose you're right," I said. "I apologize for taking so much of your time. I will carry out the inspection at the office next to your mine in the near future, and I hope that everything will go smoothly."

"Of course. You will see that my corporation is a reliable and honest company."

We politely said goodbye and I left the office with the irrational feeling that I had avoided serious danger. I didn't like this woman, and what she was saying smelled like manipulation and clear distortion of the truth. In addition, I still felt pain in my heart at the thought of what happened to the android who saved me from the crash site. The arguments that it was just a machine didn't convince me at all. Although I couldn't explain it logically, I knew that it wasn't 'just a machine'. I simply knew. And I felt like I lost a close friend.

On my way home I kept myself together somewhat, but crossing the threshold of the apartment I literally burst into tears. Terrified, Sue walked away from her work and ran up to me.

"Leeta, honey, what's wrong?" she called. "Did someone hurt you?"

She embraced me and led me to the bed, on which I threw myself, crying. The tension of many days accumulated in this outbreak of hysteria and it took a long time before I calmed down enough to tell Sue what I learned. She listened to me intently, and once I finished she responded harshly:

"First of all, stop crying. And let's think about it: this whole thing looks weird. First off, someone directs you and Terrel directly into the trap. Terrel dies and you are saved by a prototype android. Now here's an obvious question: what was he doing there? Did you notice something about his behavior? Maybe something he said or did?"

"I was terrified, barely conscious," I began. Then I paused and thought about it, "Just like you said, it was strange. He leaned over me as if checking something, and then he was about to leave."

"But he didn't leave?"

"I called out, I begged him not to leave me."

"If he was acting in accordance with some high-priority program, ordering him to perform only one task, then he shouldn't have been distracted by examining some corpses. Well, unless he was told to check if the attack was successful. And to tell you the truth, I'd be willing to bet that this was the case. He was supposed to check if the plan of the attackers was successful, because where did he come from? Maybe he was even the one that set the explosives."

"Wait, that actually makes sense!" I sat on the bed and wiped my face with a tissue. "They wanted to kill us, and Monty's job was to see if they succeeded. Instead of leaving and reporting what he saw, he carried me to the mine's office. The officials working there called an ambulance. They probably didn't know about any of it, because how could they? Nobody initiated them."

"Exactly!" Sue interrupted me. "The android acted independent of the instructions of his owners. He did something that he independently decided to do. Thus, he became dangerous to corporate plans. He could have given them away. That is why they decided to destroy him, regardless of the costs it incurred."

She nodded. Her blue eyes glowed with excitement.

"Now, let's continue: I don't think the prototype was given back to its creators for dismantling into parts. They wouldn't do that, certainly not without some tests that could uncover the conspiracy. So the scrapping was entrusted to one of the companies dealing in recycling of electronic waste."

She threw herself back at the computer.

"Let's have a look: there are two large, official companies which serve the mines and refineries, we can immediately exclude them. There would be too many documents to sign and a serious possibility of a mistake. There remains one of the small processing points that usually receive electronic scrap from private users or small producers.

Sue's short, plump fingers literally flickered across the screen as she searched for addresses and specifications of small businesses.

"I suspect the android will appear as an anthrobot in the documents," she muttered under her breath. "Maybe an engineering robot... they are rarely placed for recovery to rule out the possibility of a mistake. There it is! Only one point signed the receipt of a destroyed anthrobot in the time period which is of interest to us."

"And?" I asked.

"And there's a possibility that the scrapping may not have taken place yet," she explained to me. "It's a small workshop and I'd give my head that its owner is doing some questionable business to get a profit at these costs. That needs time. He may not have cut your artificial knight yet."

"You think that...?" I was out of breath.

Sue looked at me, her eyes were shining.

"I think this needs to be checked."

"I'll go there!"

"We'll go together, but not just like that. We have to do it cleverly so that nobody knows what we are doing. I'll think of something quickly."

Sue apparently was apparently really into the idea of playing a 'spy in a mask' because, tangling around her apartment, she gathered entire disguises store from various compartments. Where she got them from and why she even had them I had no idea. I would never expect a virtualist, who her uncle thought was a complete nerd, had such desire for attention. I squatted down and began to look through the rags thrown out of the drawers and cupboards. The pile that formed on the floor undoubtedly looked interesting. There were overalls, skirts, suits, wigs and an entire make-up set with the 'Leveroux Theater' imprint."

"Sue, did you use to be an actress?" I asked in a daze.

"Not me, my mother," she said. "She taught me how to quickly change my appearance. She was great... I miss her a lot."

"At least you knew your real mother," I murmured, "I don't even know who mine was. I grew up in a social family."

"Really? I'm so sorry, honey!"

"No need to be, Sue. The social parents treated me well, as did the other kids in my group. They are wise, balanced people, they gave us all a good childhood and guided us like they should."

"You know, I heard that in the past when a child had no parents, some childless couple could recognize them as their own. They signed the appropriate papers and the child became theirs as if they were the ones who birthed it. They even had the right not to mention the fact that it was a descendant of another couple. Weird, right?"

I shrugged my shoulders.

"That's how it worked back then. Let's not judge our ancestors, because to understand them we would have to live during their times."

Sue sighed lightly, then grinned again, making beautiful dimples form in her pink cheeks.

"Let's not talk about sad things," she suggested. "Let's get to what really matters. We need to check if this Monty, as you introduced him, was scrapped or not. And for this we both need to dress up."

I had some doubts, but it turned out that my new friend really knows what she is doing. Before I realized, my red hair was curled into a tight bob and hidden under a black wig, smoothly adhering to my forehead and cheeks. Sue darkened my complexion with a suitable foundation and strongly painted my eyes with black ink. Looking into the mirror, I couldn't believe that this was me, especially after putting on the fastened under the neck overalls, sewn from high-resistant material and equipped with a wide belt with pockets. Outfits like these were worn by women from cleaning and catering companies dealing with comprehensive service for offices and small factories. Meanwhile, Sue began working on her appearance with energy that no one would expect from a virtualist. As if with magic, she transformed into a vigorous employee of the food delivery sector, dressed in trousers to the ankles and a jacket with the reflective logo of the Your Food Company. Her usually slick, light strands of hair were replaced by a storm of fiery curls, enclosed in a mandatory snood. She smeared the A2 mark on her forehead with a layer of make up so that it could pass as distorted B1, especially if no one was looking at it too much. Deciding that it looks as it should, she called the autocar rental company and ordered a vehicle with self-navigation and a heavy-lifting anthrobot for us.

"What do we need an anthrobot for? We aren't planning to move or do any heavy work," I was surprised. She looked at me with pity.

"We are going to dangerous ground," she replied. "Few people are aware of this, but an anthrobot, if you know how to guide it correctly, can be an excellent weapon. And I know how to."

I tried to imagine this burly, roughly man-like machine as a 'weapon', but my imagination failed me.

"Are you going to tear out its arm and hit our attackers with it?" I finally asked ironically.

"You are so silly!" Sue laughed. "An anthrobot can be controlled in two ways, using the remote control or by voice. The remote control has a limited number of functions. However, voice control is invaluable, you only need to know the code commands. It's like having a personal bodyguard made of steel."

"And you know how to make an anthrobot attack someone?"

"Exactly."

A shiver ran through my spine. I knew very well that anthrobots were extremely strong and flexible, and that they are only machines – they don't think, they only follow the instructions of whoever during the rental period acts as their owner. I've never thought before that they could be used for violent actions, since that would be recorded in its registry. I had the impression that nobody would risk such a thing, but the longer I thought about it, the less unbelievable it seemed.

"Where did you learn that?" I asked. Sue looked at me from under bright eyelashes and smirked.

"I haven't been sitting here so long just for fun," she said. "Virtualists form a closed clan, we all know each other, and the ones here are usually at odds with the law. We sometimes do meetings at the dating center, and that's how I got to know Macedone."

"What a name!"

"The character is also quite something. It was he who taught me the code language of the anthrobots and some other useful things. Well then, shall we go?"

Sitting in the cabin of the autocar, I thought that she would never cease to amaze me. The specialist in data collection turned out to be a good driver, certainly better than me. The rented car rushed through the streets and alleys until it entered the maze of tunnels and my heart leapt into my throat.

"Relax, lightning doesn't strike the same place twice," Sue glanced at my face and thought it appropriate to say a few words of encouragement. "And I'm very careful at that. I won't be fooled by some cheap detour trick. Either way, nobody knows about our escapade or nobody would recognize us now, unless they looked very closely."

I wanted to believe what she was saying, even though I was paralyzed from fear and at any moment now I expected an explosion from under the wheels. However, nothing like that happened and we arrived at some forbidden location in peace. It looked like a much neglected landfill, in the middle of which stood something resembling a factory hall, to which a residential segment was adjacent. There was probably a small production plant there once, but its owners moved everything to a better place in terms of logistics.

"We're here," Sue said, applying the brake but not turning off the engine. "You have to go there alone. Sven Thorvald won't even open his mouth if we get in there together, he'll suspect a trap."

"I'm scared," I admitted honestly.

"There's nothing to be afraid of. The owner of a small recovery facility can't afford to commit a crime, since it's unlikely that he would be able to cover it up. He doesn't have enough connections or money for that. He will be careful and will deny everything. So a diplomatic approach to this guy, don't pressure or threaten him. You wouldn't get anything that way."

"I agree."

I got out, wincing reflexively at the crunching sound that came under my soles. Everywhere was full of debris, metal chips, remains of plastic – I felt like I was playing a role on one of the horror films that take place in forbidden, badly lit places. Despite my will, I discreetly looked around to see if any zombies were about to pop out. Nothing like that happened, of course, only the sensors turned on the arrows pointing the way to the office. I approached it and knocked. The door was not closed and opened with a ghostly grinding of rusted hinges. Although there was no water in the open air on the moon, the air here was saturated with water vapor to some extent in consideration to human health, and that did its work on cheaper metals.

"What?" A grumpy male voice said from inside. "We're closed, bring in the goods during office hours."

"I'm not bringing in anything," I said and took a few steps forward through the short corridor in the direction of the streak of light coming from the ajar inner door. "I'm here to talk."

"About what? Well, fine, come in."

I pushed open the inner door and found myself in an impossibly cluttered office, so incredibly dirty that my first glance at Sue's apartment almost seemed like a museum in comparison. Behind the greased table was a bearded man of unknown age, looking at electronic circuits through a handheld microscope. His hands, visible from under the rolled-up sleeves of his shirt, were heavily covered with tattoos, nails black with grease. Upon raising his face towards me, to my surprise I saw the A2 mark on his forehead.

"What can I do for you?" he asked brusquely.

I looked around for something to sit on and pulled myself a shabby stool. It was the only thing I could find.

"Mr. Sven Thorvald, correct?" I made sure. "I need to talk to you about... some equipment which you've recently purchased."

"I bought everything legally, so if you're looking for something stolen from your apartment here..."

"No, no, definitely not. But... I have to speak of it openly, it can't be done with small words and hints."

He put down the microscope and looked at me closely.

"Go ahead, you can speak." he encouraged me. I looked him straight in the eye.

"You recently bought an android prototype from Romain Corporation," I said, "for demolition."

I expected my interlocutor to start denying it, but he had no such intention.

"Sure did," he admitted, "how do you know that? Are you from the corporation?"

I shook my head.

"I'm a private person. I'm here because of this android. Tell me, have you already... dismantled it?"

"Why are you interested in it?"

"I have my reasons, Mr. Thorvald. I need it. If you've already dismantled it, then of course it can't be helped, but if not... please name you price. I know you are a business man, so I won't ask you to give it back to me, I'd like to buy it from you for an honest price."

The man rose from behind the table. Only now did I see that despite the wide shoulders and strong neck he was very short, almost dwarf-height. Instinctively, I glanced at his legs to see if they showed signs of prosthesis after an accident, but normal, strong calves appeared from the rolled up trousers. He must have simply been born with a genetic defect not detected on time. He walked several times around the room piled with rubbish, folding his arms behind his back.

"I don't know who you are," he finally spoke, "and I don't even want to know. Let's focus solely on our transaction. So, you'd like to buy it? All right then. One hundred thousand pepes."

"What?"

"I won't go any cheaper. Subassemblies and servomotors are worth three times as much if I recover them and would normally demand at least two hundred thousand, but I admit that the situation isn't normal. That's why I only want a hundred. A return of cost and my risk."

"Why are you saying that the situation isn't normal?" I asked slowly, to get some time. One hundred thousand allocation points? Where will I get that much from?

"Because it isn't. I've dismantled human-like robots, sex bots, anthrobots here, but this is the first time I've seen something like this. I was immediately fascinated by its coating, so perfectly imitating human skin, but I thought: Oh well, sometimes even a work of art must be destroyed. After all, sex bots are almost as perfectly made, and I've dismantled them without problems. You simply cut apart the coating and remove anything that's suitable for reuse. I grabbed my toolbox and went to the box where I locked it. Dear God, it turned its head and looked at me! It didn't say anything, it was so calm, but I feel as if I was hit in the face. I'm not kidding! It was a terrible feeling, as if I was about to... kill a man. That's exactly it! I left and closed the door. I wanted to wait until its battery ran out, I figured that if it's still and dead it won't give me such an impression. And now you come to me with your proposal."

He stood in front of me. He smelled of dirt, metal and cheap alcohol, but I didn't care. I knew that I should be interested in how an A2 ended in this Gods forsaken place, what made him go this low, but I didn't care. At the moment it didn't matter to me what he looked like, but what he could do for me. I was wondering how to get the allocation points for him in the required amount, when suddenly I remembered the gold agency card hidden in my wallet. Hakat told me to use it only as a last resort. I wasn't sure he would consider it a last resort, but I had to take the risk.

"I'll pay," I said with determination. "Please show it to me."

"Very well. Follow me, please."

He led me deep into the hall. Judging by his office, I expected the warehouse to look even worse, but it turned out to be amazingly orderly, except for one of the rooms clearly designated for hoarding. Thinking about it now, it made sense – after all, the parts recovered from scrap cameras were for sale and had to be stored according to a logical system. At the end of the hall there were two machines – de-dusting and sterilizing – both meant to assist in the processing of materials which were later sold to whoever needed them. Beyond them were all that remained were rows of closed doors.

The android was in one of the boxes. I recognized him immediately thanks to his height, dark blond hair and the same working clothes he wore on the day of our meeting. My heart skipped a beat.

"Monty!" I called out. He turned his head and looked at me.

"Do you recognize me?"

"That's understandable," he answered calmly. "I'm not able to forget. How do you feel? I hope your injuries have been treated."

I heard Sven Thorvald gasp. Undoubtedly, the words of the android surprised him, although he had previously considered it an unusual specimen. It was not difficult to understand his previous scruples. Even someone who wasn't as smart as him would be reluctant to scrape this... model. I should also be surprised, since despite the disguise he recognized me, but it immediately occurred to me that he probably recognized my voice.

"Yes, I feel fine now," I said and turned to Thorvald. "Where is your card reader? I want to finish this transaction as soon as possible."

"Then we're going back to the office. You... however I should refer to you... come with us."

The android followed us dutifully. His movements were almost perfectly human. One could get the impression that someone had made a mistake here or made a conscious fraud and we are dealing with an ordinary miner, maybe only hypnotized or under the influence of drugs. Even I felt uncomfortable, let alone the bearded engineer, who was looking back every now and then, with an expression simply out of this world.

At Thorvald's office, he pulled out a card reader, a large pad with the words 'Accounting Book' and a box full of scraps of computer foil with encoded data memory. He put the blank piece in front of him and began to write something on the stylus.

"What are you doing?" I asked in a daze.

He looked at me from under his bushy eyebrows.

"I run a legal business," he muttered. "I have receipts for everything. Now, listen to me: you'll be signing a receipt to for two packages of parts. I've added a package option, because sometimes I sell some refurbished part, some mechanisms, or even the entire apparatus. I don't have a license for the kind of transaction we're doing, so instead I'll be putting it as a sale of packages, which means all processors from one recoverable source. In this case, it is a scrapped, multifunctional robot purchased from a representative of a mine belonging to Romain Corporation."

"Okay, I'll sign it."

"I hope so. I'll write separate receipts for the microprocessors and servomotors. It won't be forgery, since that's what you're getting... only in its original packaging."

Despite my will, I looked at the mentioned 'packaging'. This was the first time I could have a closer look at the android, since back in the tunnels I was too stunned and scared, not to mention that it was dark in the box. I expected him to look a little more 'artificial', but he really looked like a human. The shapes, skin tone, lips, eyelids and eyelashes, even the eyes – all of it was a perfect representation of the human form. Even the fingernails were modeled flawlessly. Only his calmness and composure was too incredible. He stood motionless, waiting for us to finish, too still for a human being.

Thorvald handed me two receipts, written on pieces of foil.

"Sign them please," he demanded. Once I did, he pulled the receipt numbers into the book and turned on the reader. I slipped the card into it, checked the invoice and entered the PIN. The reader tickled slightly, accepting the transfer.

"All good. You can take it now," the engineer said. "This is where my role ends. I hope I never deal with such a thing again. Looking at it is giving me shivers."

"You could get used to it, I think," I said comfortingly, getting up from my stool. "Goodbye, engineer. I hope your business goes well."

"Thank you. And I wish you luck. Something tells me that you'll be needing it."

Monty, taking my hand, obediently moved to the parked car. His hand felt as human as his appearance, maybe only a little colder than you'd expect, and smoother. I didn't feel any abrasions or lumps on it, and I suspected that there were no fingerprints. Their inclusion would likely be too difficult and wouldn't make sense either way. "You'll come with me, Monty," I said. "What do you think about that?"

"Nothing at all. I was sold to you and I am now your property," he replied.

"But you can think independently. Enough that somebody wanted to be rid of you. What did you do wrong?"

"I saved you."

I stopped abruptly and looked at his face. He returned to me with a calm look of silver-gray eyes, also pausing.

"What do you mean? After all, you did something very good, you saved a person from death. Why did they decide to scrape you?"

Something began forming in my mind, just like scattered pieces of a puzzle, something that could only be confirmed by this anthropomorphic creature next to me. I looked at him not knowing what question to ask in order to get the right answer.

"I didn't complete the task," Monty said slowly, as if with difficulty, "I was supposed to press the button, check the vehicle and report. I did something different."

"What vehicle were you supposed to check?"

"I was told it was a test. But it was not a test."

The car door slammed nearby.

"What are you waiting for, come on!" Sue shouted at me.

I squeezed the android's hand. He was not guilty of anything, he was used just like any tool would be. Despite the orders he received, he took me from there, took me to the office, not to the masters who were waiting for him... he saved my life, even though he was ordered to kill me!"

"Come on, Monty," I said. "We have to leave this place."

"As you wish, master."

Sue widened her eyes as we entered the car together and whistled through her teeth.

"Unbelievable! What an amazing work. I would never have guessed for the life of me that he's artificial. Where are we going?"

"Not home. Go to the police headquarters, I need to talk to Cavanaugh."

"What impelled you so much?"

"Sue, this... I don't know how to call him... well, this android is the key to solving at least one mystery. He knows who is behind the attack on me and Terrel."

"He was supposed to kill you and instead saved you," Sue turned the vehicle over and followed the road we arrived with. "That's why they decided to destroy him. That makes sense. What I don't understand, however, is why he was sold for parts instead, instead of, I don't know, burning him?"

I looked at my silent companion.

"Monty," I decided to give it a try, "why did they decide to sell you for parts?"

His eyes glowed in the semi-darkness of the car as he slowly turned his head toward me.

"Mrs. Munroe called for two miners. She told them to take me to the new excavation site and leave me there, and then ignite the explosive charges," he replied. "The miners swore that they would do it, but they did not. They then talked to each other. One of them, named Vernon, said to the other that they could earn something on me and that it was a shame to blow me up. They took me to Mr. Thorvald's factory and sold me.

This dispassionate relation of events shocked me, and at the same time I felt something strange – a wild sense of satisfaction. Thanks to the greed of two simple workers, the only witness who could expose Terrel's murderers survived, and that same witness was in my hands.

"Did Miss Munroe ask you about me?"

"She asked why I disregarded her orders."

"What did you say?"

"I didn't say anything. I didn't know the answer to that question."

"Hold on," Sue said, "you get an order and don't follow through with it. You take your own initiative. There had to be a reason for that, and not any other decision."

Monty was silent for a moment.

"A person... with no vital functions," he suddenly chanted in a mechanical way, different from before. "Another person... in danger. Red covering everything.... it's blood. Second blast in nine minutes and fifty-three seconds. Leaving means killing."

His voice changed again into a soft, human tenor.

"You said: Don't leave me. I couldn't stay because of the planned second explosion, so I took you with me."

"That's logical," Sue admitted, "but that wasn't your job."

"I know. That's why they decided to dismantle me."

His calmness was incredible when combined with the human appearance. He had no emotions and certainly didn't feel the fear of 'death', he was unable to. How did the fact that he helped me fit into this scheme? It was more like a human impulse, rather than a programmed function that he had to perform regardless of the circumstances. I reached out and put my hand on his cheek.

"Thank you, Monty," I said. "You saved my life, even though that wasn't your duty. You have proven that you really think independently. Was it like that from the beginning or did you have to learn it? How did it happen that you came into the hands of someone like Munroe?"

He closed his eyelids very slowly, then opened them again and slightly tilted his head.

"Doctor Oenas told me that I should behave like a human being," he replied. "They gave me nonlinear tasks and tested how I manage. They taught me how to interpret facts. They told me how to build sentences correctly. They made me study human behavior. One day Professor Levereux wrote that the experiment was out of control and the object had to be destroyed. I was at the computer at the time. I deleted this entry before Dr. Oenas and her colleague Henry Karpinsky could see it. In the evening Mrs. Munroe showed up, and at first she was talking to Dr. Oenas for a long time, but then she took me with her. Mr. Karpinsky was very angry, and Dr. Oenas said that from now on I was to follow Mrs. Munroe's instructions at all times."

"I know Karpinsky," Sue said. "Electronic engineer, specializes in artificial intelligence. He was a decent man, how did he get involved in such a thing?"

"I have no idea, it's all very confusing... perhaps Inspector Cavanaugh could figure it out," I sighed. "I feel like what we know is just the tip of the iceberg."

Sue nodded and turned the car. We entered a wide thoroughfare and soon the rented autocar stopped in front of a wide, burly building with the inscription LUNNAR MAIN COMMAND, arranged in an arch above the entrance.

Immediately after crossing the door, we were 'groped' by a weapon and illegal chemicals detector. We were only allowed to enter the office afterwards, inside which sat two strongly built women – one in the uniform of patrol service, the other bearing the colors of the investigation department – and a young man in military cameo. He raised his eyebrows slightly at our sight.

"What is your business here?" he asked.

"We need to see Inspector Cavanaugh," Sue said, stepping forward. "We know that he is here somewhere."

"How are you so sure?"

"Because he told us to come here himself. And it would be nice if you introduced yourself, soldier."

Under the influence of her energetic voice, the man stood up reluctantly, though his companions snorted ironically, unwilling to say a word.

"Corporal Feri Kunch," he said reluctantly. "Currently in the process of changing service. I play an intermediate role between the secretary and the junior sidekick. Is that enough?"

I suddenly thought that the inspector's words about the degeneration of the local police might just be correct.

"Where is Inspector Cavanaugh?" I asked sharply. "There is something urgent we must talk to him about."

"Everything is urgent on the woman," one of the policewomen said dismissively. "Why should your matter be more important than others?"

"You don't decide that," Sue blurted out.

"Should I arrest you for inappropriate behavior towards authorities?"

This verbal scuffle was firmly in the wrong direction and could end badly, but luckily the inner door suddenly opened and Scott Cavanaugh entered the office.

The policewomen immediately jumped out of their seats and fell silent. The inspector looked at us and his lips twitched slightly. He recognized us despite the disguise, but he postponed the explanation and turned to his subordinates.

"How many times do I have to tell you that when someone asks for me, you should notify me immediately?" he asked sternly. "Do you want to share the fate of Laura Gosch and Nagato Omi?"

"No, inspector... we just wanted to know whether this was something important..."

"I didn't ask for excuses, Evans! Where are my reports?"

"Almost ready."

"Then finish and check them. I didn't ask for 'almost'. And you two, come with me."

We obediently followed him. An internal door led to a staircase with no lift. We went down to the lower floor, where Cavanaugh opened an armored door and let us into the internal rooms of the command.

"This is where we have our archive and laboratory department," he said. "Let me introduce you, this is Dr. McCave."

The young man in a white smock who was just walking down the corridor stopped in front of us. He had black, slightly too long hair, a round face with tired eyes and a boyish smile.

"Nice to meet you," he said in a friendly manner.

"My name is Juliette Ankes," I introduced myself. "This is my friend Susan Herefort and this is... Monty Romain."

Cavanaugh flinched with obvious surprise.

"That's him?!" he shouted. "You're kidding, right?"

"No, Scotty. This is the android that saved me."

The inspector walked around Monty, watching him closely. Finally he shook his head.

"Indistinguishable from a living person. An amazing work. What a technology!"

"Let's talk about that later. I think you should question him, he has some interesting things to say."

"We have some interesting results, too."

"What exactly?" I glanced at the doctor who looked at his superior questioningly. He only nodded slightly.

"Tell them, Kelley."

"I've examined all the available samples, including the new ones," McCave began. "In each one of them I was able to find traces of a new chemical which theoretically should only be available in government laboratories. It's hermenzine."

"What is that exactly?"

"A top secret agent affecting the sleep process."

I considered it for a moment, but nothing came to my mind.

"So the denims complained about insomnia?" I asked.

"No, not a single one of them did. Only about chronic fatigue," Cavanaugh said.

"The results of research on hermenzine are classified," the doctor added.

"I could get to them," Sue volunteered.

"You could?"

"She is the best virtualist on the moon," I assured him. "She can handle anything."

Sue removed the wig from her head and wiped her face with a wet handkerchief taken from a purse by her belt.

"What computer do you have?" She asked.

"Cormac 2700," the inspector said. "Seven terabytes of RAM, unlimited access to the network."

"It'll be a piece of cake then. Where is it?"

Sue became energized, just as she always did when a computer was involved, and her eyes began shining. Cavanaugh took a code key from his pocket and opened one of the locked rooms. Inside was a real miracle – a compact computer of the latest generation, with a three-dimensional screen and sensory panel equipped with a fingerprint sensor. The inspector unblocked it and selected the Guest option.

"You can work on it as you wish, nobody will disturb you here," he said. "It's a part of the laboratory, not the office section, so my officers don't come in here. They don't know much about computers, anyway."

"You keep them on a tight leash," I noticed mischievously.

"A hard hand is what they need," he muttered and looked at the doctor. "Keep this lady company, Kelley, and you two..."

He paused, turning his visions on me.

"I invite you back to my place. You can't go back to your home and I will need to have a long conversation with this android."

Scott Cavanaugh's quarters turned out to be a nicely laid out apartment, but decorated in a very old-fashioned way. It didn't have any holo-pictures on the walls, windows, or any of the modern amenities. In the dark living room there was an ordinary sofa, a table with chairs and several wardrobes, a field bed in the bedroom, and an electric heater in the kitchen. The floor was made of polished stone and was not covered by any carpets. Despite everything, these harsh rooms looked quite neat and even a little pleasant.

"You can take a couch in the living room," said the inspector. "Have some rest. And I'll have a chat with Mr. Monty over here. Unless he won't talk to me."

I looked at android. He stood motionless, his arms hanging down like a statue.

"Will you talk to Inspector Cavanaugh?" I asked. "Tell him about everything... I mean, about whatever he asks about."

"I understand, master," he replied.

"Have mercy, just call me Leeta. Not 'master', it makes me uncomfortable."

"Understood, master. Leeta."

Scott burst out with a short laugh.

"He's yours now and he knows it," he said. "All right, come with me to the interrogation room, Monty. No one will be able to listen in on us there, and we can talk about very sensitive matters."

They left and I lay down on the couch. I was incredibly tired and barely able to stand on my feet, all the while the wounds from after the accident were not yet fully healed, giving me a stinging pain. I fell asleep almost the very moment I rested my head on the faux fur cushion, and slept like a log until I was awakened by a shaking of my arm.

"Hey, girl, are you alive?"

I opened my eyelids with difficult and saw a face above me from which mechanical implants looked at me.

"Oh, Scotty," I murmured, stopping a yawn. "Did I sleep long?"

"It's almost noon. I prepared a caffetino for you, but don't get your hopes up, it's from the rations, so it's not the best quality."

The inspector had enough time to take a shower, shave and change clothes, and he was so refreshed, it's as if he himself had slept for some twelve hours. I took the cup from his hands and took a sip of the caffetino, nasty, just like he said, but still refreshing. Drinking it I woke up enough to start thinking.

"Where's Monty?" I asked anxiously, looking around.

"He's in the next room," he reassured me. "I didn't do anything to him, I only questioned him and recorded his testimony."

"It's interesting, isn't it?"

"Very. I have to make some decisions now."

I sat down and wiped my face with my hands.

"And I have to take a bath," I sighed. "What are you planning to do? Are you going to arrest the ones from Romain Corporation? Even I know that it's pointless. Ten minutes later and an army of lawyers will drop in to free them."

"You're wrong. It all depends on how I play my cards. I have to discredit the board of directors from the very beginning, and then the bosses of the Moon Company will turn their backs on them. They will not risk their own credibility in their defense."

"How are you going to do that?"

"First of all, I have to arrest and interrogate Marcelina Munroe."

"Based on the android's testimony? None of the judges will acknowledge it."

He smiled.

"Fortunately, Monty gave me the name of one of the miners who were to eliminate him. His name is Vernon Mills. We easily tracked down his location and he is in our hands. We had no trouble getting the testimonies in exchange for easing the charges."

"What charges?"

"Well, Vernon Mills doesn't know that it was an android that ratted him out, and that such testimony is invalid in court. He is a simple miner, not a lawyer. He immediately fell apart and gave us the name Munroe... and his words do have evidential value."

"And what's next?"

"I sent my patrol for Miss CEO. Of course, she is both smarter and better educated than Mills, but that's not going to help her. I will have to somehow approach her, so that she gives herself away, but then again, I don't think that will be too difficult. I will use the fact that we have Mills and tell her that he is a crown witness."

"And if she doesn't let herself be scared?"

"Leave it to me, Leeta. I know how to do interrogations, and besides, you don't have to think about it. It's a matter for the police. Come, I'll show you to the bathroom, but I don't have a change of clothes for you... unless I take something from the material evidence. Hold on."

He ran out before I could protest. I finished my horrible police caffetino and walked slowly around Scott's salon to stretch my limbs. I looked into the neighboring rooms out of curiosity. It turned out that behind the bedroom, in which stood a messy bed, was another room. Inside it there was a computer, and on the table next to it was a pile of maybe a hundred pads, thrown on it carelessly. Monty was there, sitting upright in his chair, not moving. Right now he looked like a store mannequin.

"Monty," I said softly. "Is everything okay?"

He turned his head towards me.

"Yes," he answered after a moment, and I felt like with some hesitation. "The Inspector told me to wait here."

"That's good. I mean... stay here for now. I'll come for you later and we'll see what will happen next. We are both safe in here, we're not in any danger."

It's funny, but I felt responsible for this... I nearly thought 'for this man'. It wasn't just a matter of appearance. Monty acted like a human, although a strange one – not quite normal, or maybe subjected to mind control. I didn't know anything about its structure or how the processes in his brain worked, I could only rely on my intuition. And it was this intuition that told me that I was dealing with a being endowed with consciousness and true mental independence. Monty didn't necessarily know how to fully utilize it, the proof was in his behavior, but he was able to make his own, fully independent decisions. If he wasn't, I would be dead by now.

Scott Cavanaugh returned, carrying several wrapped packages.

"It's a confiscated contraband," he said. "Underwear, pants and a few shirts to choose from. I hope they fit you."

I grabbed all of it and went to the bathroom. It was tiny, equipped only with a shower and warm gust of air – no other apparatus, such as a massager or artificial hairdresser. Apparently, whoever built these rooms decided that policemen didn't need such facilities. It seems that he was of the opinion that they didn't need much at all...

The shower turned out to be a mock-up. Instead of water, I received a spray of disinfectant spray, which I didn't like, but in the end I could take it. Afterwards I stood under the warm air for a moment, applied a moisturizing lotion on my body and changed into the clothes I received from the inspector. They were a bit too tight for me, but that wasn't too important. I combed my hair and left the bathroom.

Scott was sitting at the table and eating. On the table was a second plate with a portion for me – a few sandwiches with some paste and a cup of vitamin juice. At this sight I realized how hungry I was. I sat down and began eating. The breakfast wasn't too bad, though I wouldn't call it tasty. The inspector was satisfied with the cheap products bought at 'Two', a super market where the price of food didn't exceed two credit points per package, piece or pound. He must be saving for something. The 'allocation' was concerned with the amount of products from a given pool, not their quality and price. You could spend your entire salary on rations, or a quarter of it, whatever you chose, but still nobody was entitled to buy even a box of crackers more than the official allocation. In this respect, the law didn't have any exceptions. Some say that this will change someday, but when – nobody could say.

"Thank you for the meal," I said, finishing my second sandwich. "I'll pay you back in the near future."

"It's not a problem. The main command has a certain allocation for feeding the ones we detain, and recently we haven't had anyone here."

I drank some juice, or rather something that was reminiscent of it. The drink was definitely made of powder, and at best from a concentrate. It would be difficult to guess what the taste was supposed imitate. Personally, I hesitated between apple and pomelo.

"Scott, can I ask you something?" I said shyly.

"Sure. Go right ahead."

"You told me Lunnar was a place of exile. Why were you sent here?"

He raised his eye implants on me and smiled.

"You're a curious one. I'll answer you, even though it's not your business: I put my nose in the hornet's nest."

"What?"

"I was conducting an internal investigation. Nobody likes them, but sometimes they are necessary."

"Corruption?"

"If that was the only thing. I can't disclose the details, but heads rolled, there were shuffles at a high level, all because a certain Cavanaugh couldn't understand the delicate reminders and didn't keep certain discoveries to himself."

"Were you punished?"

"No, not at all. I was praised in the files, they gave me another medal... and a few days later I was transferred. Allegedly as proof of trust. Funny, isn't it?"

He laughed as if it really was a joke. It didn't sound like that to me at all.

"Rather sad. You have exposed the guilty, and not everyone liked it. Sheer corruption."

"No, Leeta, that's just how the world works."

He pushed his plate away and stood up.

"Let's go to the lab, we'll find out what your friend got from the network."

In the data processing room we came across Dr. McCave sitting on a stool by a narrow sofa. Sue was lying on top of it, covered with a plaid, and snoring quietly.

"She was really tired so I let her lay down," said the doctor when we entered. "She worked until she found all the data. They're right here, on the reader. I've never in my life seen such a skilled virtualist. Lareq could at best clean her shoes."

"Praise be to her for that. What about the data?" Cavanaugh asked, picking up the reader.

"It's very interesting. First, there's hermezine. As it turns out, it goes into the composition of wingsoma, but in a different configuration than what was given to our current deceased. That one was rectified twice, while this one was only once, in addition dissolved in the catalyst of the reaction. I haven't yet been able to determine what this catalyst is, but I will find out. What's more interesting is what hermesine, however prepared, does to the human brain."

"Say it then, instead of these long introductions."

McCave ran his fingers through his hair.

"Prepared as a drug, it allows for something like a waking sleep," he said. "But mixed with a catalyst and combined in this form with the H5 stimulant causes a decrease in the need for sleep, an increase in energy during the day, acceleration of thought processes and a significantly faster reaction time. There is a catch, however."

"What is it?"

"The patient sleeps peacefully and in the morning it seems to them that they slept well, but that is not the case. On the contrary, there is a deadly effect: eliminating the REM phase from their sleep cycle. This will result in death within a few weeks, and is almost impossible to detect by routine testing."

Scott looked at me, then at the reader. He flipped several pages of it mechanically.

"Some planned conspiracy?"

"I doubt it. I think it's more likely that somebody is trying to get a super-efficient stimulant. The side effect I mentioned was rather unpredictable and possibly only appeared in some 'patients'."

"What do they need it for when there are so many legal options?" I let out.

"There can be many reasons," Scott murmured. "The most likely scenario is that whatever they buy on the black market is efficient, and they don't have to give anyone any explanations."

"That's right," the coroner supported his idea. "The doctors try to put every little detail into the patient's cards and want to control how much and what they consume. People prefer to decide for themselves and fall into this trap which has no way out. The pills are a great remedy for boredom and frustration, they improve productivity at work and you can easily get them without explaining your reasons."

"That's disgusting!"

"It's disgusting that Health Industries is cashing in some great business on this," Cavanaugh said almost simultaneously with me. McCave shook his head.

"It's not that simple. Miss Herefort has got to the encoded data, which shows that the preparation called fortestim, which is most likely what we're talking about, is sold at a very low price, and Health Industries is just a broker. They don't have any laboratories that could produce drugs, but is affiliated with Romain Corporation. It was this company that opened the first regeneration rooms signed as Health Center and brought in specialists."

Scott smiled, but unlike before, in a more cynical and predatory way.

"Well, that's just forming into one whole," he said. "I think it's time for me to have a talk with Miss Munroe. Those few hours spent in the cell certainly did her some good."

That's right, he had the woman arrested. I've already forgotten about it.

"What are you planning to do?" I asked.

"I'll interrogate her. And I'll try to get the news of the arrest spread around the city. We'll see who reacts and how."

I didn't know about the police procedures, so I didn't know if this was the right course of action, but I decided to not ask anything more. Scott Cavanaugh didn't intend to allow me to participate in the investigation, although I wasn't sure whether he wanted to protect me or whether I really wasn't allowed to take part in his routine work. He accepted Sue's help, but not mine. It made sense, since virtualists have special privileges, and yet I had a strange feeling – as if I was placed to the sidelines. Taking advantage of the fact that Sue is still asleep and Dr. McCave took care of his work, I decided to look at the data caught by my friend from the network.

To download them, she had to break hell knows how many protections, because the good half of it was top-secret. They contained the results of work on hermesine, the entire research program and – what surprised me – a complete dossier of a technical laboratory fully paid for by Romain Corporation. Henry Karpinsky was on the payroll, so it was the workstation where Monty was created. Intrigued, I began to browse files marked as Laboratory F. They contained the history of work on creating true artificial intelligence, a detailed description of each experiment and analysis of its results. It was only after some time that I realized what about it bothered me from the very beginning. It was the costs.

Even to me, a complete layman, it was clear that they had to be enormous, and Romain Corporation was, after all, only one of the union companies of the Moon Mining Company. And one of the smaller ones at that. Its official profits would never allow to maintain such a costly enterprise as was the design laboratory in which the world's first fully independent artificial mind was to be born. Initially, I thought they were taking money from the afterburners trade, but then I remembered that according to the information obtained by Sue, the profits from this were small.

In a separate document, Sue made accurate calculations – production and distribution costs, operation of the offices, wages of the employed administration and doctors consumed almost everything. The conclusion was clear: fortestim and wingsoma were merely means to an end. Just to what end? That people would work more efficiently? That's ridiculous. They would only distribute them among their own employees, because why increase the profits of other companies? Because of pure altruism? Even a child wouldn't believe that.

I heard a yawn coming from the sofa. I looked back and saw my friend, stretching across the plaid, flushed from sleep.

"Hey," she said.

"Hey. I looked through your findings."

"And?"

"I don't know. You did a great job, but I have no idea what to conclude from it."

Sue sat up, yawned again and scratched her ribs. With tangled hair and worn makeup, she looked just like she always did.

"There's a lot to conclude from it," she said melancholically. "Romain Corporation is doing some side business, but that's not the issue. The issue is that it's hard to deduce what these businesses are."

I looked at the screen again.

"They seem to care a lot about their work on AI," I began carefully. "Maybe I'm exaggerating, but they must pack every penny they earn into it. How did you get to this data?"

"I can break through any type of security. Without exceptions. And so to every penny, I assure you that the costs of maintaining such a laboratory plus the salaries of the specialists would ruin even Sakuro Enterprises."

"Sakuro...? Ah, I know. That's the company's main shareholder. They collect a lion's share of profits and have the best mines."

"Exactly. And even they would not be able to maintain such an expensive commitment. Despite this, Romain Corporation not only pays Laboratory F, but also regularly accounts for substantial profits from its mines. Profits that can be spent on every demand, so they aren't going to waste."

"Actually, why do they refer to this laboratory as 'F'?"

"It's an abbreviation for Frankenkstein. There used to be an exceptionally talented doctor with that name, he revived corpses or something like that. Although he was probably a fictional character, I don't know. But that doesn't matter."

She stood up, threw the blanket on the sofa and looked around.

"Where's the bathroom here?"

"There is one in the corridor," I said. "I'm not sure if it's only the toilet or something more, but in the worst case there will at least be a sink there. There is a shower in the inspector's apartment if you want to bother going there."

"Then I will put myself in order and go to Kelley... Dr. McCave. I have a lot to talk to him about and maybe I will learn something interesting."

Sue nodded and left, and I went back to examining the data. What was generally available looked solid and reliable, but the files extracted from god knows where contradicted this image. There were numbers in them that I didn't understand, and some coordinates that didn't match anything. There were dozens of documents in technical language that I couldn't translate into words I could understand. I tried to sort it out somehow when Scott Cavanaugh appeared in the room.

"What did you find out?" I asked as he sat down next to me.

"Nothing new," he said. "Munroe is stubborn. I gave her a truth serum, but I think she has conditioning or a deactivating implant sewn in. She kept repeating that Vernon Mills was trying to cover up his own incompetence, that he lost the explosive charges while drunk and all the misfortune came from there. Of course, I didn't think to confront her with Monty, she doesn't even know that we have him. However, I really think that she is just a small fry. She gets some orders and carries them out."

"How can you be so sure?"

"She was terrified. She was shaking. I can tell when someone is acting and I assure you that she was not. How can I say it... she smelled of fear."

"Which means, someone stands above her. Are you going to arrest them?"

He let out a light snort, took a handkerchief out of his pocket, and cleared his implanted lenses with it.

"I fear that this damsel's higher-ups are out of my reach. I'm starting to suspect that anything we can think of about them has nothing to do with reality. I hoped it would end up on discrediting of the small corporation, but I had to change my plans."

"What do you mean?"

"I'll pretend to believe in Munroe's explanation and release her. Mills will remain in detention as a perpetrator of a fatal accident. It will give us some time. I will try to determine the location of Laboratory F and the afterburners factory, but I'll do so discreetly. Your friend will be of great use to me in this aspect. Are you... are you together?"

For a moment I didn't understand what he meant.

"Are we...? No, we're just living together."

"I see. Well, then you probably won't mind her staying at the station as my helper for a few more days. Our full-time virtualist isn't very trustworthy."

"So why are you still keeping him here?"

"Appearances, my dear. You shouldn't do anything carelessly if you want to succeed. One day I will grab him by the hand, then I'll get to whoever pays him."

"What about me?"

"You'll go back home... with Monty."

"I thought you would want to keep him as a crown witness."

He winced slightly.

"I would like to, but nobody is going to believe the words coming out of an android. I'm not even convinced myself whether he can be trusted without reservation. He could be convinced that what he says is true, meanwhile someone could have programmed such an understanding of events into him. His constructor, for example. No, Leeta, currently Monty as a witness means as much as a voice recorder, maybe even less."

It made sense, though it caused some complications. I was supposed to take the android back to the flat that wasn't even mine, and then what? I felt somewhat vague at the thought of being left alone with him, even though he had already proved his... his what exactly, good will? I didn't know what to call it. I was a bit scared and it must have been visible because Scott patted my shoulder.

"Have some courage. You are a government agent, you can't chicken out from such a challenge."

"I'm not," I frowned. "I just don't know what to do. Up until now, I didn't even believe that an actually self-thinking artificial brain was possible. In addition, his appearance... he is so human and yet so alien."

"You'll manage. You have to. If Monty is to help us in the future, someone has to figure him out, and it looks like that'll be your job. But for now, I invite you for lunch."

"It's already afternoon?"

"A good while after noon. It's easy to forget about the passage of time in front of a computer."

The material evidence warehouse turned out to be a real treasury, so it isn't surprising that there were even some proper clothes for the android.

"Put this on," I said, demonstrating to him black pants and a fashionable wide-sleeved shirt gathered around the wrists. "But you need to wash yourself first. You're really dirty."

"Why wash?"

"Because hygiene is a very important thing," I explained to him. "Its lack causes infectious diseases in biological beings. That's why you as well will have to wash and wear clean clothes. You will live amongst people and you must follow the rules. Why does this surprise you?"

"Nobody ever demanded such a thing from me."

He looked at me expectantly.

"Before now you were an object and that's how they treated you," I decided to make it clear. "I see something more in you. You saved me, even though not only did nobody tell you to, but it even contradicted the instructions of your bosses. That's not what machines do. There's nothing more to talk about, take off those dirty rags."

Monty obediently unbuttoned his overalls. He had no underwear, and suddenly I saw the complete nudity of his artificial body. That's not a view I expected. I subconsciously imagined that its human resemblance ended at his face and hands, but that was not the case. The body of the android was sculpted with extraordinary care, taking into account even the smallest anatomical details, maybe except for one detail. There was not a single hair on it, except for the head, of course. The perfectly smooth skin leaned against the artificial muscles, emphasizing their perfectly proportional arrangement. Although I'm acquainted with the anatomy of the opposite sex as well as any modern woman, I felt strange embarrassment, realizing that the precision of its creators was such they didn't miss a thing. Sure, I used to read in old novels about this type of accurate construction in androids, but I never thought that I'd see something like that with my own eyes. He... he really looked just like a real man.

"What should I do next?" he asked as the silence continued.

"Well, wash yourself," I said, collecting my thoughts.

"I don't know how to do that. I have never washed."

"I will help you."

Maybe I said these words a little too eagerly. Yes, I wanted to touch him. Although it was strange, abnormal – are there not enough men in the world? The dating center offers meetings seven days a week, there is plenty to choose from, meanwhile I suddenly start falling for an android! An artificial man, no more real than a fashion house mannequin or a sexbot! It was sick but... it excited me.

I lead Monty into the shower and poured warm water from the kettle over him. I preferred not to turn on the disinfectant sprayer, but to use traditional water to wash off dust and grease. There'll be time for the sprayer. Then I took the sponge, put some liquid soap onto it and handed it to him. He took what was handed to him and then I took his hand and began to guide the sponge around his body, teaching him how to wash the dirt from all corners of the artificial skin. It felt about as smooth and elastic to the touch as the one that covered my implants, but it wasn't put to life – like mine – by the warmth of blood and living tissues. It didn't become pink under the influence of friction of the sponge and warm water. Still, touching it was an interesting experience. I had the impression that I was washing a living body, maybe a little colder than my own. By the time I finished, the second portion of the water was already hot, so I added it to the bucket with the cold one and rinsed the soap from Monty's skin. Then I told him to sit down and washed his hair so that it was clean too. Finally, I turned on the ventilation and watched the android dry in gusts of warm air.

Only now, when it was clean, could I fully examine it. I thought about whether it was a copy of some original or a spontaneous creation. If it was a copy, the original had to be an extremely handsome man, the type I always liked. Who could he have been? Probably not a worker. Maybe a swimmer or a runner, judging by the muscles. An athletic sportsman with an orderly, elongated face, slightly marked cheekbones, narrow gray eyes and the dark blond hair which formed into messy bangs falling onto his eyebrows. It resembled an idealized statue of a gladiator. Each muscle was accurately mapped under the skin, just like the network of blood vessels which is normal for the human body.

"Why are you looking at me like that?" he asked suddenly, startling me.

"Ah, no reason," I said, not knowing why I was startled. "Come on, let's get you dressed."

He followed me obediently. I stopped in the room and looked at him again.

"Monty," I hesitated, "I once read a very old book in which there was... there was someone like you. And every part of his body was just as functional as a human's. What is the case with you?"

"Please narrow down your question. I don't understand it."

He was looking at me, and suddenly I was struck by the purity and innocence of his gaze. He was an android, alien to all human moral fluctuations, foreign overtones and understatements. It was necessarily to be blunt with him, or else it's better to say nothing at all."

"Do you know anything about human sexuality?"

"Yes," he answered with the simplicity of the child, "Mr. Karpinsky insisted that I master the knowledge program on the biology of human reproduction. He taught me how to make a woman feel happy and relaxed... but I've never had the opportunity to use these skills before."

"So... can you...?"

"What?"

"Practice reproductive behavior!"

"As far as I'm aware, yes."

Something tightened inside my throat, but it wasn't unpleasant.

"What is happening with me?" I muttered under my breath and added aloud, "Come. We'll take a cab, so act like a human and don't say anything. You don't know enough about what to say in others' company so we could both get in trouble."

"Understood, Master Leeta."

"Just Leeta. No need for the 'master'."

I wondered how the policemen would react at our sight, but they were clearly uninformed about the identity of my companion. Two of them were interrogating barely conscious individual in torn clothes, the third was sitting at the desk and typing something on the computer, and a three-person patrol were hurriedly finishing their caffetinos before heading to the streets of Lunnar. None of them paid us any attention.

The taxi gave us a lift to the house. At the door, we almost collided with the Casponis, our neighbors.

"Good morning. Are you coming back from a night party?" Lorena Casponi asked, eyeing Monty with curious eyes. This pretty, barely middle-aged brunette, somehow didn't fit with her unattractive husband, and I have long noticed that she is looking for adventures wherever she can.

"Good morning," I replied. "No, ma'am. This is my cousin, Monty. He has just arrived from Earth and is feeling a little tired. I want to put him to bed as soon as possible."

"That doesn't surprise me," Lorena muttered slyly, winked at me and followed her husband, who was indifferent and bored as always. I will never understand what keeps people who are so different together...

In the apartment I realized that I didn't really know what to do next. What does an android need? A chair, a bed, or maybe I should just put him in the closet?

"Monty, do you need sleep?" I asked.

"No," he replied. "I turn off my consciousness periodically when I'm charging the battery. This isn't a dream state, but a state of inactivity."

"You use interesting words. What I mean, however, is what you do at night when people are sleeping."

"I do whatever I'm told to do."

I shrugged, not knowing what to say to that. The night spent in the inspector's apartment didn't bring me any rest, I was tired and broken, and I really needed a few hours of restful sleep to recover.

"There is an old armchair in the storeroom," I said finally. "I need to lay down. Please, Monty, sit there and don't do anything until I think of something for you to do."

"As you wish."

I led him to a blind room, which served as a storage room for various materials. When I arrived in Lunnar, it was filled with broken furniture, old cardboard boxes, broken electronics ... It took almost a month before I convinced Sue to call the truck to transport the dimensions and get rid of all this dumpster. All that remained was the armchair she had a special fondness for, and a spare computer.

Monty sat down obediently in the armchair, put his hands on his knees and froze. I thought about maybe saying something more to him, but I was too tired. I went to my room, took off my clothes and lay down, falling asleep almost immediately. I slept like a log and woke up around four in the morning. Of course, the term 'morning' referred to the time calculation adopted in this city for convenience, because on the moon it's hard to talk about such things as day and night – although the lighting of Lunnar helped maintain the illusion of a normal circadian rhythm. At this time, most people were still asleep, and the night shift was beginning to count down until the end of work. I could take a nap without worries, but I didn't feel like it somehow. I got up, threw on my bathrobe, and went to the kitchen. In the pantry I found a can of corn, so I opened it and ate the golden grains straight from the tin, without bothering to heat it up. I didn't know if the can was mine or Sue's, but I was too hungry to worry about that. I bit into some cheese over the corn and set the water for the caffetino. The jar was almost empty, but there was still enough for one cup. I was in the middle of pouring in some sweetener into the brown liquid when the intercom buzzer rang.

I looked at my watch – it was a quarter to five. I felt uncomfortable, I had no weapon, and my vivid imagination immediately gave me a picture of bandits breaking into the apartment to 'silence' me, just like in a crime movie. I took a small pistol from the drawer, turned off the safety, and put it in the pocket of my housecoat. Only then did I go to the control panel.

"Who is it?" I asked.

Inspector Cavanaugh's familiar profile appeared on the screen. Did he never sleep?

"It's me, let me in," he said impatiently. "Sorry that I'm getting you out of bed, but it's important."

For a moment I wondered whether someone isn't trying to trick me with a holographic projector, but I brushed this idea off as absurd and pressed the door release button. After a few minutes, Scott entered the apartment and closed the door behind him. He was wearing the same clothes as yesterday, and most likely didn't sleep at all.

"Is Monty here?" he asked.

"In the storage room."

"Good. Things got complicated."

"How complicated?" I opened the cabinet and pulled out a wild bottle of dessert wine. I poured myself and Scott a large glass.

"I released Marcelina Munroe a few hours ago," he said and took a drink. "An hour ago, my investigator, alerted by a secret agent, found her dead in the Romain Corporation offices. No injuries, no signs of struggle. McCave is doing the autopsy."

I drank my glass in one breath and poured myself another, too.

"What are you planning to do?"

"I have to notify the headquarters back on Earth. It seems that we are dealing with a mafia organization which is quick and effective in its job. I'll be lost without support."

He drank again.

"Leeta, you are not a virtualist like that Herefort, but I think you know some tricks," he said. "As you've already confessed to me, you are a government agent, although I admit that you don't look like one. Could you send a message to your boss back on earth, but in away so nobody knows what it contains? I mean, to hide its contents, encode it, or something like that?"

"Yes," I said, "it's called a cover-up. I can 'cover-up' the required contents under casual information so that only someone who knows it's there and knows how to read the file will be able to see it."

"In that case, inform your boss, whoever he is, about this matter. I would ask Miss Herefort, but she is currently helping out Kelley and processing the discovered files at the same time. I don't want to disturb her."

"It's okay, I'll do it. Do you think the matter is this serious?"

"I believe so. And you know what the worst thing about it is?"

"What?"

"I've been a cop since I was nineteen. I have gone through all the levels of the career, starting with the usual curb. There are few cases which I haven't seen before, but this... this one scares me. And I don't understand anything about it. That is the worst part."

II

Sue Herefort's apartment was cleaned to shine, maybe for the first time since she moved here. We waited for her uncle's arrival and we were both anxious, not wanting him to have a bad opinion of either of us. Although the chance that he visits us the moment he arrives was small, Sue still didn't want to take the risk. Monty turned out to be a great helper in household chores, although I still had doubts whether anyone but us two would feel good in his company. The neighbors thought that he was my cousin, so I introduced him to one of them and so far nobody has been able figured out that maybe this boy is not normal. Just in case, we kept him at home, which didn't bother him, and which was safer than if he was hanging out amongst people. After all, someone could get begin getting suspicious, which could bring some unfortunate consequences.

Citizen Hakat decided to come to Lunnar on the cruise shuttle Sybill under his own name, and not undercover. This is how he officially spent his holidays, which wasn't that strange. Many rich snobs visited the moon in order to later brag about staying in the exclusive Lunnar hotel called The Diamond Ring – it was unbelievably expensive and supposedly provided some amazing attractions. Hakat decided to visit Lunnar because the case which, thanks to my inept investigation, came out into the light, was extremely serious. The Lunnar Company has officially cut itself off from Romain Corporation and demanded the establishment of a commission of inquiry supervised from Earth. The Campaign

Board decided to make every effort to prove the company's integrity and good will, because the conflict with the global government of the Earth was not in its interest – the Moon was completely dependent on supplies from the planet and they couldn't afford a rebellion. The mere thoughts of it seemed ridiculous when considering the connections and arrangements, but the fact remained: Romain Corporation was running its own game and who knows what its management wanted to achieve. For now, we didn't have any point of contact except for illegal drugs. First it was wingsoma first, now it's fortestim, and the end goal was still unknown. It was also difficult to guess who personally stands behind these experiments, because it certainly wasn't Marcelina Munroe. In this whole plot, the woman was a stepping stone, only slightly larger than other small fish. She carried out the orders of her bosses, who were so mysterious that even Sue could not trace their footprints on the network. And that was really disturbing, because my lunar friend was capable of extracting any data we asked her for from the circulating the network. She was an undisputed expert, and yet she failed in this case.

"It's a good thing that uncle is coming," she said to me as we cleaned up the mess in the computer room together. "It really looks like a more serious case. There used to be suicides and murders here, but not on such a scale!"

"How was it before?" I shuddered in disgust. Until now, I thought the moon was free from this sort of thing. Even in terrestrial cities troubled by eternal assaults and gang wars, something like 'ordinary murder' has become very rare during the last century. Street robbers have avoided killing ever since the absolute death-to-death principle was introduced into the penal code. A simple self-preservation instinct worked, at least that's how it was explained.

"People get frustrated here easily," Sue explained seriously, "the Moon is a rather sad place. Most people here are lonely, marriages are relatively rare. Why? It's simple. You aren't allowed to have children on the moon, and you must have a special permit for a pet, which is very difficult to obtain. There is no reason to marry. In addition, someone who comes here has little chance of 'the end of the contract'. Do you know what I mean?"

"Scott mentioned that Lunnar was a 'place of deportation'."

"There's something to that. I am here voluntarily, but there are few like me."

She paused and scratched her disheveled head.

"Do you think I should visit a hairdresser?" she asked. "I had a mechanical one, but it broke."

"I will definitely be going."

"Then I will be too. I hate it when somebody touches my hair, but oh well, I'll let it slide for once. After all, my uncle doesn't come to visit every day. In fact, since I've been here, we haven't seen each other even once."

It was hardly surprising. Citizen Hakat was not a private person and rather no one would expect him to behave like a normal, loving uncle. Or like the average boss... I found myself looking forward to his arrival and seeing him again. He became someone close to me, even if it was against my will, and there was always a chance that he would bring me an order to come back to Earth. I wanted that so badly.

We arrived at the shuttle landing site an hour before the planned arrival of Sybill. We refreshed ourselves at the airport confectionery, where a sensational pudding with synthetic fruit and whipped cream was served – it was the first time I've had a dessert this good – and then we went for a walk on the promenade which surrounded the landing site with a silver ring. I was rather fond of this busy area, full of shops and entertainment venues. It reminded me of Earth and I suddenly missed my city, living at the Sunset Estate and working for the Medical Academy. From the moon's perspective, Earth seems inexplicably beautiful, like the mythical Paradise Lost. I understood right now how people here felt, banished to this city under different circumstances, cut off from the outside world by a huge dome, protecting against vacuum, frost and deadly radiation. Fortunately that didn't concern me, I was only here temporarily and hopefully will be able to come back...

A window opened in the dome – the inner sluice gate through which ships came. A huge shuttle hit the landing pad and fell to the plate with the accompaniment of whistling and whirring. After a while the gangway was lowered and the passengers began to descend, looking amusingly small from the distance.

"Come!" Sue tugged my sleeve impatiently. "Let's go downstairs, else we'll miss him."

I ran down the winding stairs to the waiting room in front of the barrier separating the customs part of the landing pad from the public one. On this day there weren't many people there, because Sybill usually brought employees with passes of several days, not guests, so there was no need to greet them loudly. If Citizen Hakat arrived officially as a member of the government and not a private individual, he would probably be welcomed by a delegation, but then he would arrive by a government vehicle, properly marked.

"Oh, there he is! Sue exclaimed happily, gesturing at the incoming couple, carrying small hand luggage. I opened my mouth in surprise.

Citizen Hakat was wearing an ordinary graphite suit with thin stripes and a soft hat, but the woman accompanying him looked as if she had left the exhibition of the most expensive fashion house. With some difficulty I recognized her as... Mabel!"

"Hello, Leeta!" she called out at my sight. "How are you?"

"Hello, not bad!" I shouted back happily. "You're incorrigible, you didn't even notify me! What are you doing here?"

I had to wait a moment for an answer. All visitors, regardless of their status, had to pass between two scanners that detect weapons and prohibited electronics. Only after this operation did Hakat come to us.

"Miss Mabel is my official social partner," he said, kissed Sue on the turned cheek and looked at me. "I went to the agency to choose the lady for an official banquet and she caught my eye. While we were chatting, your name came popped up by accident, so we met again. Then we started seeing each other more and more... and finally I settled with her agency so that she could start working for me. A person in my position needs someone with whom he can show up at a charity evening or diplomatic meeting, and Mabel is perfect for this purpose. Of course... she had to change her status for this. She is currently my agent, enlisted and sworn in. You can tell her anything."

"That far?"

"Correct. She's gone through a shortened conditioning, good enough for her. She certainly wouldn't tell any unauthorized persons what she shouldn't."

My friend smiled brightly at me. Her makeup was done perfectly, eyes enlarged with a tattoo on the eyelids, hair modeled by an exquisite stylist and a dress that must have cost a fortune. The mark of an A3 was put on her forehead and certainly no one would ever question that she once belonged to another class or that she worked as a floress. She achieved what she wanted – she entered the higher realms. I was just curious if she knew the price. In this case, 'conditioning' meant the establishment of a psychochemical blockade by specialists. Such an individual becomes resistant to all known chemicals used as a serum of truth, while also getting implanted, by the method of subliminal signals, an insurmountable loathing to everything that could be considered treason. Was Mabel aware of that? I had my doubts. She seemed too pleased with herself.

"We have something for you," she said, lifting a square box. There was nervous meowing coming from the inside.

"Sid"! I shouted cheerfully. "But I don't have a permit..."

"Relax, we've got your permit," Hakat laughed with some indulgence. "And a karma allocation certificate. We've thought of everything. In fact, it was Mabel's and she did everything, I have more serious things on my mind. But now, come, both of you, we have several things to discuss."

We entered the cab – I had no idea if the swarthy boy driving it was an agent, but that's what I'd bet on. My boss left nothing to chance. The taxi drove us to The Diamond Ring Hotel, where Citizen Hakat rented an apartment during his stay in Lunnar. It was only there, behind the closed door that he finally spoke to me:

"Leeta, sit down. We need to talk."

I nodded and sat down, feeling the familiar pounding of my heart. The fact that he brought Sid with him was a clear signal that I would not get a return ticket for now and in truth, I knew exactly what I was about to hear. And my suspicions turned out to be right.

"Good job, you're doing great. Of course, you still have to work on this and that, but you are useful, I admit."

"In what way? Currently I'm in the middle of my first case and I haven't done much besides nearly dying in an assassination attempt. It was the second time I brushed against death for your sake," I added more quietly. I didn't want it to sound like reproach, but that's how sounded.

Hakat took off his hat and hung it on a hook with the appearance of a deer horn. Then, with pedantic accuracy, he placed three jamming devices on the table and turned them on to create a 'safety zone' covering the entire room. Now, nobody would be able to listen in on us.

"I know," he finally said, dispassionately. "I've read your report and all of the attachments. And I disagree that you haven't done much. On the contrary, you've achieved a lot. You helped start a case that seemed unresolved and it seems that the police finally have specific clues. It's all thanks to you, Leeta."

"Clues?"

"Yes. The attachments you've included in your report are extremely interesting. Inspector Cavanaugh knows where the unregistered laboratory of Romain Corporation is located. If he still hasn't shut it down, then that means he's waiting for me."

"For you? Why?"

"Exactly, why, uncle?" Sue supported me. Anyone who would see her now would never believe that they were looking at a devoted virtualizer who sees nothing but her computer for days on end. Pink with excitement, her eyes glistening, she looked like an ordinary college airhead.

Hakat opened the bar built into the wall and poured himself a drink. Then he sat down on a decorative armchair by the window.

"My ladies, the matter is delicate," he began. "It concerns technology which may be groundbreaking. We cannot afford to lose any of the scientists working for Romain Corporation, which is why we must take extreme care to how we carry out the raid. I will participate in it as a representative of the government who has power above all the moon-related privileges and can provide legal protection for the scientists. We have to get them to the Central Island, every last one of them. There they will receive full support to continue their work on artificial intelligence."

"So you know about that too," I murmured and shuddered thinking about Monty.

The expression on my face must have been easy to decipher because Hakat smiled forgivingly.

"I do. That's not a simple matter either. You've spent your agency card's money on unauthorized purchases, but it's hard for me to reproach you about it, after all I told you myself that you should use it in case of an emergency. You might have thought that it was that kind of situation."

"Will you take him away from me?"

"Why would I do that? The design of the android's body itself is well known, and I don't believe that we could figure out the secret of his mind by taking apart his brain. That would be too easy. In addition, the agency has some unwritten policies. One of them is that items purchased for the purpose of the mission become the agent's property."

"Monty is not an object."

"In the light of the law, he is. Admittedly, agents usually buy something that costs no more than five or six thousand, and you spent a hundred... but I'll sort it out somehow. Does that sound good?"

Giving in to the spontaneous reflex, I threw my arms around him and kissed him. Despite all his composure, he was visibly moved and patted me awkwardly on the back.

"No need to thank me, Leeta. The second message that I have for you is much less pleasant. As I said, you have to stay here for now, and what's more, I can't say when you will come back."

"What do you mean?"

"You can't go back to Earth right now. Those you helped unmask had allies. They started sniffing around and you would be in grave danger. I would be, too. It's better that they don't know where you've gone to... because they actually don't. Fortunately. They are dangerous and very influential people."

"I thought that you weren't afraid of anyone."

He shrugged.

"I'm not afraid for myself. You are another thing entirely."

"So then, how long am I going to stay here?"

Citizen Hakat finished his drink and reached into his inside jacket pocket. He took out a small package.

"It could be a very long time," he answered with brutal honesty. "It's best you make yourself here as comfortable as possible."

The package given to me contained documents with the name Ankes and my legs buckled when I saw them. It was a detective's license, a badge with the number and confirmation of the official assignment to work in the moon's police force, criminal department. For a long moment I was unable to let out a word. I really didn't want to compromise the freshly received – though unwanted – badge with a stream of tears, and I thought with fear that I wouldn't be able to keep myself together. Sue looked at me sympathetically, Mabel also became serious and stroked my shoulder.

"Don't cry, honey," she said tenderly. "It can't be helped."

Hakat must have felt horrible about it too, since he avoided eye contact with me.

"Forgive me for dragging you into this," he said after a moment. "But I had no choice, and now we have nothing else to do but move on. Have a drink, it'll do you good."

He poured me a cognac. It was the first time I've had any and it burned my throat, but it also cleared my head. I finally straightened up and wiped my tears. It was not the right time to pity myself like a child, and in the presence of the Chief of Arms himself, a person so important that he was in the hierarchy of power just after Number Four – the last of the Nameless. This was a principle that had been followed for over a century: the most important people in the global government remained anonymous to society.

"How am I supposed to work in the police force? I know nothing about it," I said when I finally managed to control my voice.

"Nobody does. Today's police officers don't study in some nonsense academies, but instead gain knowledge and experience under the guidance of people more experienced than them. This is a more effective and much cheaper method."

"Uncle, are you here officially or privately?" Sue cut in. She was preparing a complicated drink for herself, consisting of a carefully measured quantity of various juices, gin and soda water from an old-fashioned siphon.

"Semi-officially, I guess you could say," he replied. "Pour some for me too. My subordinate unit of guard is waiting for a signal, but nobody knows of this except for you two. And hopefully I don't have to take a real military action here, because although I'm not afraid of it, I don't like killing, especially when it's possible to settle the matter in a different way. Do you understand?"

"Of course," I murmured.

I still couldn't get myself together, my head was buzzing.

"You must be ready at all times, especially you, Leeta. After receiving the summons, you will appear at the headquarters and participate in the raid on the laboratory. You, because you are already an official employee of the police, and Sue because she is a brilliant virtualizer and we may need her skills. And bring this android with you."

"What for?" Sue was surprised. She sat down in her corner and sipped her drink, keeping her eyes on Hakat.

"We may need him as physical evidence during the confrontation with the scientists. After all, we don't know what we'll come across.

"It's not just a matter of working on AI," I said, finally regaining my composure, which was greatly influenced by another portion of cognac. "Someone is distributing illegal substances and the evidence points to the same corporation. It was the fatalities which resulted from people taking this filth that caused Cavanaugh to ask for help from the headquarters."

"I'll look into it. The agency has already examined the reports in this respect and has even drawn conclusions. I would bet everything that they are correct."

"And more specifically?"

"Someone is trying to tale control over the Moon. Make it so that they have a say in every situation. They've partly succeeded. Why do you think we dismissed inspector Crusoe and his team? The pretext was the collapse of an important investigation, but that was not the point. However, it's not just the police are corrupt here, or rather were, since Cavanaugh is just... we know that someone is paying off the head of the hospital, senior officials, and even the presidents of smaller corporations."

"Does it mean that...? I don't know... that they want a secession?"

"That's ridiculous!" Hakat snorted angrily. "They would only cause themselves problems and nothing more. It's about a different kind of profit. You'll work on it with Cavanaugh, since I will of course be returning to Earth as soon as we have Laboratory F."

"Okay, I will."

He looked at me with compassion. His companion sat next to him in silence, beautiful like a princess from a fairy tale, someone close to me and a stranger at the same time. It was no longer the Mabel that I knew and liked. I put down my glass and stood up.

"Thank you for everything," I said stiffly. "If that's all, I'd rather go back to the apartment. Being closed in a box must be upsetting for Sid, and I have a lot of confusion in my mind. I need to rest."

Hakat nodded.

"Go then," he gave me permission. "I'll talk to Sue some more. We haven't seen each other for a long time."

I don't know how I reached the apartment. I must have come by taxi, although my memory did not register that. I don't remember paying for it or entering the apartment. The next thing that came to me is the sight of Monty giving me a cup of water. He was bending over me and I was lying on the floor.

"Thank you," I said weakly. "I'll be fine in a moment."

"Is there anything I can do for you?" he asked. His face didn't express concern, only absolute calm, and yet I felt that he still somehow cares about my well-being.

"Not right now," I said. I moved my hand to the chair and got up from the floor. I must have fainted, and this android tried to help me in his own awkward way. "But open this package."

He did what I requested. Sid jumped out, ruffled a dust cleaning brush, he hissed at me with clear offense and climbed under the bedside table.

"What is that?" Monty asked. "A machine?"

"A cat. A pet. Be extremely careful and gentle with him, okay? Living things are easy to damage, and very difficult to repair."

"I know that. Mr. Karpinsky told me that I had to learn to control my strength so as not to hurt anyone. This also applies to... the cat?"

"Yes. All living creatures, not just humans."

"A cat is made of protein, just like you?"

"Of course, why are you asking?"

"Until now I only knew about humans. I've never seen another protein creature before. I thought there were none."

"There's quite a few of them, and they are very diverse. There used to be even more, but some went extinct in a great catastrophe. I don't want to talk about it right now."

I looked for a saucer in the kitchen, poured some water onto it, and after some thought, put a little meat substitute out of the can. Sid wasn't picky, and I didn't want him to be starving while I sleep off all these emotions. I really wanted to lie down. I didn't even take a shower, only took off my shoes and blouse, then curled up on my quilt and fell asleep like a log.

In the middle of the night I was woken up by the sound of some object falling to the floor. I thought that Sid must have pushed something on the floor, jumping over the furniture, but I didn't want to get up to check it out. I lifted my eyelids slightly. Monty was sitting next to my bed, his back straight, arms folded on his lap, as if he was on guard. I felt strange, but it felt nice – as if I had a protector, the legendary guardian angel.

"Are you looking over me?" I asked quietly.

"You were very upset," he replied. "I didn't want you to be alone."

I reached out and stroked his knee.

"I like you," I said. "Do you know what that means?"

"I don't know. That you expect mating behavior from me?"

"Why would you think that?" I sat up from surprise. No doubt about it, androids can be very direct!"

"Engineer Karpinsky said that when people like each other, they often... co..."

"Copulate," I said grimly.

"Yes. That was the word. I asked what it meant, and then the engineer taught me what to do in the situation."

"It must have been some interesting lessons," I muttered under my breath.

I've always had a sense of humor and that's what was now helping me keep my distance from all of this. But on the other hand, I felt unhealthy curiosity again... how did he...?"

"I don't fully understand the purpose of these behaviors, if they are not intended to build offspring, but I know how to carry them out."

"Do you?"

"Yes. The engineer taught me six different ways to serve women in the sense of providing them with the comfort coming from the possession of reproductive organs."

I couldn't take it and laughed out loud. All the unbearable tension I've lived in for many days has fallen off me suddenly and suddenly I felt in some pleasantly frivolous mood.

"It's hard for me to believe that" I said coquettishly, as if I was talking to a human. "Maybe try one of these methods on me? We'll see if you can convince me that you're a good lover. It doesn't seem likely to me."

"I always tell the truth."

"Or what you believe to be the truth. Should we try it?"

"As you wish."

He stood up and took off his shirt and then his pants. It crossed my mind that this is the moment I should stop this whole game, but unexpectedly for myself I felt an irresistible fascination with this artificial body, so wonderfully modeled... and fully functional as well. I couldn't understand why something about it seemed wrong to me – I've used sexbots before, interactive artificial lovers for women, and there was nothing wrong with that. According to doctors, it's a normal way of discharging sexual tension when there is no living partner at hand, so why was I feeling the kind of excitement that happens when doing something not entirely 'acceptable'? As if I had become a little girl again, stealing candy from the store.

Like any modern person, at the age of twenty-four I've already had plenty of sexual experiences, suggested by the doctors. That was just sex to me, however, practically indifferent. I knew from lessons and talks that the body needed it, but I've never really took any particular pleasure from the interactions. I treated them like rehabilitation gymnastics, nothing more. At first, I was very worried about this. I consulted doctors, meekly took some medications and took part in psychotherapeutic sessions, but none of that helped. I was cold as a result of a transient mental defect, was the verdict. Maybe the boys, and later men, that I was friends with could tell, because I only hooked up with someone I knew twice. Then I only used dating centers and, what's worse, I didn't feel the need to change that. The only time I considered a different option is when I thought that I could buy myself a sexbot. Such an artificial lover, an interactive doll, programmed to be a substitute for a sexual partner, freed one from the need to visit dating centers, but I thought I was too young for such a solution. The owners of sexbots were loners, and buying such an erotic robot meant that they were moving even further away from people. And even though it was difficult not to think about the fact that a life-sized interactive doll was still just a doll, even when it's dressed and groomed tastefully, many of them start to believe that their toy is in some way alive. It was extremely weird and I didn't want that to happen to me. And yet, I decided to invite Monty to my bed.

At first, it was hard for me to understand why I feel so... not all right, trying out the possibilities of an android. It wasn't until much later when I realized that the reason was very simple. Monty was not an interactive doll. He knew how to think completely independently, and his inner life remained a mystery. Even so, I used him as if he was a sexbot and that didn't feel fair to him. However, I couldn't make myself stop the experiment. He was too interesting. And also, very pleasant to the touch.

Sue didn't come home until the morning, excited and quivering. She spent the night dancing with Mabel, while Citizen Hakat went to some mysterious meeting.

"Your friend is absolutely wonderful," she chattered, dancing around the room like a chubby ballerina. "I haven't known a floress before, I didn't know they are so amazing. Uncle knows who to hire, either way I hope that he stays with her for good... And what were you doing? You look a lot better than you did yesterday. Did you sleep well?"

"Yes. With Monty," I said.

"What?"

"You heard right. He's... well equipped."

Sue became serious and stopped.

"So, you're saying that... but what for?"

"What do you mean what for?"

"Leeta, I understand that you may have been in need, but there is a nice dating center nearby, and Lunnar is full of lonely men."

"So what?"

"Do you think that sexbots are enough for them in the long run?"

"I don't get it."

"I'm saying that you could have went to the center find yourself a partner for one night. Do you have any complexes about your implants? No one will even be able to tell that you have them, unless you tell them yourself, and even if they did, would it even bother anyone? People have been used to reconstructed bodies for a long time. Why do you need a sexbot?"

"Monty is not a sexbot. I don't know how to explain it to you, but he is human."

Sue stared at me with complete astonishment.

"Human?!"

I nodded. I still felt the pleasant drowsiness and I was delightfully relaxed. I haven't experienced anything like this before but I didn't know how to explain it to my friend.

"I can't prove it objectively, I just feel it. Monty is a human, although built of microprocessors, artificial muscles and who knows what else. Think about it: what makes us human?"

She sat next to my bed and thought for a moment. Then she tapped her head.

"Mind. Awareness. Soul."

"Exactly. Don't ask me how I know this, but Monty has all of that."

"So, you're thinking..."

"Sue," I interrupted her. "A lot of men use sexbot. If they had one like Monty, they would confirm my words. Those are two completely different levels of intimacy. A sexbot is a doll, an object, although talking, embracing and kissing. Monty is a human. A living being, though artificial."

"Have mercy, these concepts are opposites!"

I spread my hands helplessly.

"I know, but I stand by my words."

"All right, where is this Casanova?"

"I sent him to the bathroom. He can't wash himself well, but he manages."

I paused because at that moment the android entered the room. It was obvious that he took a shower, but didn't wipe himself or use a dryer. Wet hair stuck to his high forehead and smooth cheeks, drops of water glistened on his torso, flowing down his arms, thighs and calves to his beautifully shaped feet. Sue chuckled at his sight and theatrically covered her eyes with her hand.

"Tell him to cover himself with a towel when he's in front of a lady."

"Why?" he asked, stopping in the doorway. He looked at us as calmly as if he was completely dressed.

"Give him a break, things like shame are foreign to him, at least for now," I said admonishingly. Then I turned to Monty, who was still standing like a naked statue and looking at us.

"Organs which identify sex are not for showing in somebody's company. When you leave the bathroom, you need to cover them with something. Among other things, there are canvas towels and housecoats hanging there. It's a kind of tradition."

"I understand. Tradition."

He walked through the room and disappeared into the storeroom, which he seems to have already considered as his own.

"He really looks like, if he was a real guy, I would forget in a second that you and I are friends," Sue said with admiration. "What a body!"

"You see for yourself."

"I do, I do..."

Monty came out of the box room dressed in his only pants, buttoning his shirt.

"You'll have to buy him some more clothes," my friend sighed, getting up from her chair. "Okay, I need to go do some work. I have to devote at least four hours to sort out the current affairs."

I had some doubts whether it was possible to work effectively after dancing night, but it clearly didn't bother Sue. She was literally bursting with energy.

I lay down for a few more moments, then got up, took a shower and made two cups of caffetino. I took one to my friend in the computer room and drank the other one. The android looked at me, then cut an awkward piece of substitute bread, smeared jam on it and gave it to me. I accepted the treat mechanically, although it looked strange, and I was more and more assured me that I was not dealing with a programmed doll. He was learning, slowly but consistently mastering activities he had no idea about before.

"Monty, you don't eat, do you?" I asked.

"I have no need to. The battery gives me energy. Engineer Karpinsky calls it 'the heart'."

"That's appropriate."

I ate the slice I was given and put on some clothes. Sue was right, the android needed clothes no less than a human, especially if he was supposed to act as an ordinary man. I had to buy them for him. I briefly wondered if it would be a good idea to change his hairstyle, trim his hair which was a little too long, but I gave up this idea. I liked how it was. His hair was thick and silky, shimmering with a shade of old gold and light brown. It was better not to touch it. It emphasized the perfection of the whole. Monty's whole body was like that, from the toes to his face. The accurately reproduced arch of eyebrows and eyelashes seemed a tone darker than his hair, but harmonized beautifully with it, emphasizing the glow of silvery gray eyes. They looked human – indistinguishable – maybe they had just a little too much silver. However, only by looking carefully could you notice the excessive intensity of the metallic gloss. The pupils were made without any mistakes. They widened and narrowed with the precision of an automaton, depending on the strength of the lighting. Even the radial pattern on the irises was applied with photographic fidelity. Regularly outlined lips were no different from human ones. The bluish veins on the temples were also taken care of along with the correct shape of the auricles, and the icing on the cake was the stubble on the nape of his neck, visible only when the falling strands were gathered away. However, Sue was right – he had to be dressed properly.

"Come with me," I said. "We'll visit a store for ready-made clothing for men. Don't speak if it's not needed, don't say anything at all unless I ask you something."

"I understand," he replied. "But...

"But what?"

"I already have clothes."

"One pair is not enough. I want you to be considered a human, so I have to teach you how to choose your clothes. Contrary to appearances, this is not an easy art."

Monty slowly turned his face toward me.

"Why should people take me for one of you?" he asked. "For what purpose?"

I shrugged my shoulders.

"Protein representatives usually behave irrationally," I said after a moment. "They react in a way you wouldn't understand. Tell me honestly, Monty, you don't know much about people apart from Mr. Karpinsky's teachings, do you?"

"I can't assess whether it's a lot or not. I know some things and some I don't."

"Then listen to me in everything. You can trust that I won't give you incorrect information."

"Why should I pretend to be human?"

I sighed desperately.

"I'm trying to explain it to you, people react irrationally. Knowing that you are an android, they could behave in an unpredictable way... besides, I prefer that those at Romain Corporation don't know about you. They think that you've already been dismantled."

Monty tilted his head slightly towards his left shoulder. I've already noticed earlier that these kinds of gestures replace his facial expressions, which is very limited and poor in comparison to that of humans – although still impressive. I couldn't yet interpret Monty's gestures properly. I wondered if he has similar difficulties with comprehending what the twitches and distortions of human's facial features mean.

"Mr. Thorvald wanted to do that," he said. "I don't know why he changed his mind. He went into the box where he locked me up, looked at me, dropped the tool case and ran out. I didn't do anything. Why was he afraid?"

I didn't know how to answer that question. I stroked his beautiful hair mechanically, sensing the silky texture under my fingers. Sid, stretching out on the dresser and watching us closely, meowed with a grudge. Since he was usually the one I petted, he could come to the conclusion that I've found another favorite. The worst part was that this is how I actually saw Monty, at least in part. This was not appropriate, but you can't discuss with your feelings.

With some difficulty I found a store with ready-made clothes. Most Lunnar residents probably bought their clothes in mail order stores. It's easy, all you need is your current digital body measurements that you can do at any pharmacy and choose a model from the catalog. Clothes from the store are much cheaper, but it's usually difficult to choose something that will satisfy you in one hundred percent.

Monty, however, looked at the wardrobe items shown to him without any emotional reaction. The only thing that seemed to make any difference to him was the color of the fabric. As I noticed, he preferred dark, saturated colors, because when I told him to choose a shirt, pants or a pair of shoes, he took the ones in the most decisive and darkest shade at the same time.

Within two hours, we completed a small but sufficient set for a C1 man – after some thought, I decided that I would equip Monty with a horizontal diamond of this social class. If he had no mark on his forehead, people would finally begin to guess that something was wrong with him, and I didn't want that. Applying the mark on artificial skin should be easy, especially one as simple as that. For now, I drew it on with thin eye liner and it had to suffice.

We barely got home when the videophone buzzer rang. Citizen Hakat appeared on the communication screen.

"Leeta, take Sue and your android, and come to the main police station as soon as possible," he said dryly and commandingly. "No matter what the girl is doing, tear her away from it, even if you have to use force."

"Yes, sir," I said with unintentional sarcasm. My boss really didn't waste a second. I put my purchases on a chair and went to the computer room to tell Sue of her uncle's orders.

"Just my luck!" she sighed. "Give me five minutes, I have to close all the open tasks."

"All right, but not any longer. Or else your uncle will have our guts for garters."

"He's not that scary. I'll be ready soon, I promise."

And indeed, she finished very efficiently. She closed the computer, changed into a tracksuit and pulled her hair with a rubber band into a small ponytail at the back of the head. All she needed was a belt with a spore set she was ready to go. When she felt like it, she could be quick as wind, but she never forgot about the belt. I have to admit with shame that once or twice I went to the city without it and had to explain myself to the city guard. Such restrictions make sense, after all, Lunnar is like a biosphere in the middle of a very hostile environment, but I haven't gotten used to it yet. Sue is different – she has lived in this city for years.

We called a taxi and went to the police station. The driver, a pleasant young man, was a little surprised, or maybe just bored behind the control panel, because the entire way there he kept asking what did we do wrong.

"Nothing!" I finally grunted impatiently. "We just wanted to report that a bit of a too curious taxi driver is driving around the city."

The boy took offense and finally fell silent. Either way, shortly afterwards we got to the door of the police station and we could get off, freeing ourselves from his inquisitive company. We paid and then went inside, where Citizen Hakat, Inspector Cavanaugh and several others, men and women in police uniforms, were waiting for us. Others, dressed in black outfits studded with metal plates, had helmets on their heads with fairings transparent only from the inside and I couldn't even tell what their genders were. Passing by one of them I noticed that these 'plates' were some kind of microprocessors, most likely operating in a closed circuit. I had no idea what purpose they could possibly serve.

Hakat opened his mouth at our sight, then closed it not knowing what to say. He looked at Monty with widened eyes in amazement and for the first time in my life I saw him looking so silly.

"Is this... it?" he finally asked. I nodded and then immediately shook my head.

"Not 'it', boss. Him."

Scott Cavanaugh came up to me and handed me a uniform jacket.

"Put it on," he ordered brusquely. "You'll be working with me now. Pin the badge to the belt, learn the license number by heart. I'll lock it in the safe, you'll get confirmation that you have it.

I took of my light jacket in silence, and put on the one he gave me. I looked into the mirror. The jacket must have been made of nanoelane, because it matched my figure and looked tailor-made. I had no idea that the police were using military material – I thought these two services couldn't stand each other and would never hand each other their inventions. After all, nanoelane was created in a military laboratory and as far as I knew only the uniformed services could use it. There was a 'consumer' equivalent, nanocotton, but it was of poor quality and hardly anyone wore it.

Meanwhile, Citizen Hakat watched Monty from every side, who allowed him to do so without a word or movement.

"Incredible," he said finally. "I've seen modern androids before, but this one is unlike anything I could've even imagined. Almost indistinguishable from a living man. We must have these scientists at all costs, they're geniuses."

"What are you planning?" I asked coldly. Somehow his words offended me, although I didn't know why. Maybe because he acted as if Monty was a home machine, a non-thinking or feeling being.

Hakat didn't pay attention to me.

"We're starting the briefing," he said officially. "We know the location of object F. It's an advanced electronics laboratory, but it is not on any lists. It most likely has its own network, since it isn't using the global one. There are no files on either the system or any of the clouds. That is why it remained undetected for so long. We were lucky that Munroe knew about it and 'spit' it out during the interrogation. However, this is only the first step to our success. We scanned the area around the laboratory building and found that it is heavily armed with the latest generation alarm network. That's where my niece comes. Sue, look at this pattern, can you handle it?"

He handed my companion a flat device with a relatively large screen and a sensor-based keyboard. I barely recognized it as an electronic mapping device – I haven't seen one as advanced before. Sue took it and stared at the tangled cubist charts.

"Oh, geez," she moaned after a moment. "It's incredibly complicated, you need to know the formula of blind chance to keep up with it."

"Do you not know it?"

"I do, but there are too many variables! My effectiveness will be low."

"How low?"

"At best 50%. I'm sorry, that's all I can manage."

Hakat rubbed his mouth.

"That's not good," he said slowly. "If we activate one of the alarm system, they will evacuate and we will be on a wild goose chase. We could surround the whole area, but they definitely have underground corridors."

"We can come at them from the air," said Cavanaugh. "We'll take them by surprise."

One of the storm-troopers dressed in black coughed slightly.

"I'd like to say something, boss.

"Go ahead, Alec."

"You told me to watch for the scientists, but my people are not going there to get killed. I will not sacrifice them in the name of higher goals. When someone attacks, they will be to blame if they get hit, even if they are the Einstein of our times."

Hakat looked at Cavanaugh, then at me, as if we could help him. And I understood that although he was the Chief of Arms, his power over the rapid response units had to be limited. During operations like this, the military commander of the squad ruled and made key decisions. Even if it was known that after the end of the operation he could be dismissed for insubordination, the soldiers listened only to him and Hakat had to take this into account.

"If any of the scientists die, you will be in trouble," he warned.

"Their life is not worth more than my boys' life. Not for me."

"God damn it. I'd give my right ear for this damn code..."

"Are you talking about the code to go to Karpinsky's engineer's laboratory? I know it," Monty said suddenly.

Everyone jerked in surprise and looked at him in amazement, as if for no reason at all the wardrobe or stove suddenly spoke.

"What did you say?" Hakat asked.

"I know the code," the android repeated. "I know how to turn off the alarms."

Cavanaugh let out a short whistle.

"You'll help us, then."

"Barter," Monty said.

"What?"

"Barter. I want barter."

"An exchange," I guessed. "He wants something in return."

"Yes, yes," he testified. "In return."

"How peculiar," Hakat murmured and asked out loud. "Well, what is it you want?"

"Karpinsky's engineer is not a fighter. He is not dangerous. Don't destroy him."

The request was so unexpected that even I was speechless. It corresponded perfectly with my thoughts on him so far, but it still surprised me.

"You want your creator to not be harmed?" I made sure.

He looked at me and I could swear I saw a plea in his is artificial eyes.

"Don't destroy him," he repeated.

"What if I refuse all guarantees?" Hakat asked.

"I will not help."

"Even if I give you an order?"

"I don't follow your orders. Juliette Ankes is my owner."

"What if she orders you?"

"Let's stop with this interrogation," I interrupted. "Monty is no one's property, not mine. I know that by law I am his owner, but over time it will definitely be considered unacceptable to an independent mind."

Citizen Hakat capitulated, no longer wanting to delve into the topic.

"All right," he said. "Well then, Monty, you're coming with us. You will enter the laboratory first and identify Karpinsky's engineer, because none of us even knows what he looks like. Once you find him, do not leave him even for a moment, so that an accident doesn't happen, and he will certainly be fine."

The android nodded stiffly, then took the mapping device from sue and touched the screen in several places. A route marked with a thick red line suddenly appeared between the tangled lines.

"You have to go this way," he said. "You cannot follow the landmarks of the area or apparent paths. I'll lead you."

Alec coughed again.

"Can we trust this thing?" he asked suspiciously.

"We have no choice," Hakat muttered. "Be quiet, Leeta, semantic issues are not the most important right now. We'll take the risk. Monty, what will happen if we deviate from the route?"

"An alarm will be set off. And explosive charges."

"What?! We didn't detect any!"

"They are undetectable for standard scanners. Dr. Calenda called them 'invisible mines' and was proud that they could not be disarmed without a code key."

There was a moment's silence. Then Scott spoke up.

"Quite the bomb indeed."

I was of the same opinion. Monty, without even knowing about it, just saved the lives of several soldiers, because there was no doubt that if they didn't know about the mines it could come to a terrible accident.

"Well... we have no choice," Hakat said finally. "Everyone chosen for the operation will get into the rover. Inspector Cavanaugh and Juliette Ankes represent the civil authorities of Lunnar, I command Earth, and so we stick together. Soldiers operate under the command of Lieutenant Alec Merino, according to plan No. T32. Understood? Then let's move."

The armored rover took us outside Lunnar's dome. Through the round porthole I could see the contours of the moon's mountains and craters, but they moved too quickly for me to look at. Within twenty minutes we were at the second dome, under which factories belonging to individual corporations were hidden. Lunwark, as it was called, is something even larger than a residential city, where offices and employees' houses and entertainment facilities were located. You could breathe under the dome, as I've found out, but the air smelled of smoke and chemicals. Despite efficient filters, not all fragrances could be removed.

The area of our operation was in the outskirts of Lunwark. There was no lighting and Lieutenant Merino distributed night vision devices to everyone.

"Make no mistakes," he warned for order. "One mistake and the birds will slip away. It would be a good idea to approach them somehow... you, whatever I should call you, does anyone officially visit the scientists sometimes?" he handed the night vision device to Monty, to whom he apparently directed his question.

"If the doctors don't hear the alarm, they'll take us for people sent by Romain Corporation," the android said. "They sometimes came in larger groups to pick up orders or for training purposes. No thank you, I can see in the dark without any additional devices."

Merino put the night vision device intended for him back into the stash in the slider wall.

"Then let's begin," he said. "Lead the way artificial man..."

"His name is Monty. Monty Romain," I reminded him angrily.

This man annoyed me, especially since I couldn't see his face.

"It doesn't matter to me. What matters is that he leads us to the place without any accidents."

The android listened indifferently to this exchange. A sense of personal dignity must have been a foreign concept to him, as he was only awaiting the next orders. I thought that I would have to teach him that he deserved respect, but that had to be postponed. For now, there was an area ahead of us that we had to breach without activating any of the alarms.

We walked in a line, passing various strange creations, intended to imitate in part rocky debris and in part a machine park. Only after twenty minutes of quick walking could we see the buildings of the laboratory – a flat-layered complex of reinforced concrete buildings without any markings. There were at least fifteen of them, connected by roofed corridors. Monty stopped.

"Now you have to approach the watchtower and say that Lucio Castillani is sending us."

"Who's that?" Hakat was surprised.

"I don't know."

"I'll try..." Merino muttered without conviction and headed forward to the armored watchtower building.

Three men armed with flamethrowers came out to meet him. They wore coveralls used by intervention brigades and – like the soldiers accompanying us – their heads were decorated with helmets with fairings, although transparent.

I stepped back automatically. The ban on possessing weapons for anyone not belonging to the uniformed services didn't include flamethrowers, which fell into the category of 'work tools', and yet no one in their right mind would want to be attacked by such a thing.

"Lucio Castellani is sending us," Alec Merino said. One of the guards nodded approvingly and touched several buttons of the panel on the gate. Something hissed and, what I assumed was a sheet of alloglass, suddenly disappeared as if blown away.

"It's some kind of a force field," Sue muttered behind me. "I haven't seen such a thing in my entire life."

The soldiers crossed the gate in a split second and by the time I realized all three guards were stunned and tied up.

"Go!" Merino shouted commandingly and the soldiers rushed to the laboratory buildings. The police looked at Cavanaugh while he looked at Citizen Hakata. He nudged Monty on the shoulder.

"Lead us to your engineer," he commanded. The android obediently moved ahead, and so quickly that we could hardly keep up with him.

The interior of the lab resembled the deck of a ship which has been overtaken by rebellion. The soldiers' attack terrified the staff to such an extent that people were thrashing around into every direction, trying to at least find out what was going on. The soldiers moved the captured ones into an ad hoc adapted prison room, where several of them kept guard. Thankfully no one tried to defend themselves so far, which could really lead to bloodshed, and just thinking about something like that made me feel cold.

Monty led us to the inner rooms, although here we encountered an obstacle: the way to the heart of the complex was closed by a massive door, equipped with a code lock. Our guide stopped and looked at me with the kind of helplessness which I've already had the opportunity to see in him before.

"I can't open this lock," he said. "This door was usually open."

"They were warned when the whole chaos started and they shut themselves here," Cavanaugh muttered and tossed a piece of tobacco gum into his mouth. I already knew that he liked chewing it – it must have cost him dearly, because every piece of this delicacy was imported from Earth.

Hakat glanced at Sue.

"Will you manage?"

"I think so."

She looked at the panel, then pulled a small device out of her purse. She connected it to the sensors of the panel and began to manipulate the buttons so quickly that it was difficult to see the movement of her fingers. For a long while it seemed like it was of no use, until finally the staccato of the buzzer echoed through the room and the lock clicked. Scott Cavanaugh pushed the door open and we ran into the laboratory surrounded by armed policemen. There were several people of both sexes in it, all in white aprons. Monty quickened his steps and literally covered one of them – a stubby middle-aged man with bushy hair and black skin – with his body.

"Take it easy," Hakat said sharply. "Ladies, gentlemen, we are not here to hurt you. You are under arrest, but nobody will even offend you, let alone do something worse. For now, please stay here until the soldiers complete securing the facility."

The black-skinned scientist refused to listen to him.

"Monty!" he called out cheerfully, embracing the android. "So, they didn't dismantle you?! They didn't hurt you?! I was told that... I felt like my heart was being ripped out."

"Everything is okay, engineer Karpinsky. Mrs. Leeta bought me from a dismantling facility."

So that was the Karpinsky! I imagined him quite differently.

"A dismantling facility! How could they... they told me that you just stopped working," the engineer watched the android, as if trying to see if he was all right. "Who was it that save you, you said?"

"Mrs. Leeta Ankes."

"That's me," I said, taking a step forward.

He looked at me with almost overwhelming gratitude.

"I won't live enough to repay you. Monty is my best creation. He was supposed to be the prototype of a new line of androids, but he was taken from me..."

"All right now, enough," Hakat interrupted. "We'll talk about everything when the time comes. For now, please don't interfere. Inspector Cavanaugh, you will secure all computers. Miss Herefort will help you. They are all to be closed and sealed. They are now government property."

From amongst the scientists gathered in the corner came up an elderly woman with her hair cut short. It was obvious that she was the boss here, it was clear just from looking at her commanding, sharp like an axe face, and the badge pinned to the pocket of the aquamarine uniform cleared all doubts.

"Doctor Stella Oenas," she said in an unfriendly tone. "I think that you've exceeded your powers here. Where is your formal warrant of takeover?"

Hakat smiled coldly.

"Doctor, the one who issues these warrants is ME," he specifically emphasized the last word. "This laboratory is owned by Romain Corporation, a company under federal investigation. You will be taken to Earth and your future will be decided there."

"What future? What are you planning to do with us?"

"Like I said: follow our instructions and you will be safe."

Alec Merino entered the room, waving his gun around carelessly. He was accompanied by two soldiers. I was relieved to see that there was no indication of battle.

"Citizen Boss, everything is clear," he reported. "Nobody resisted, we didn't discover any weapons. All staff except here have already been taken to a prison ambulance and locked up there under guard. I am handing over the command, from now on you give the orders."

Hakat nodded and pointed at the scientists.

"You will place these people into the second rover of class P and take them to the reserve airport," he said. "A government ship is waiting for them there to take them to their destination. Then you will come back for us. During your absence, we'll look around here a little more."

"Mister..." Engineer Karpinsky hesitated.

"Hakat. Citizen Hakat."

"I can see that you're quite a big fish. Does not matter. May I stay with you?"

I looked at the Chief of Arms and he frowned.

"What for?"

He took a good look at the engineer and then nodded his approval.

"Engineer Karpinsky will stay with us," he said. "Even better that way. He will be our guide.

Merino saluted and nodded at the soldiers accompanying him. Together, they led out unhindered scientists and after a long moment we heard the whistling of class P rover engines – usually used as prison ambulances.

"That went better than I expected," Hakat muttered and turned to the engineer again. "Well then, what is it that you have to tell us?"

Karpinsky shrugged.

"Anything you want," he replied. "After the way they dealt with Monty."

In his voice there was sound of fierceness and offence of someone who had been disappointed in his most sacred feelings. I felt like giving him a hug, I understood very well how it must have bothered him to not know where was his most priced creation. I don't even want to think about how he reacted when he was told that Monty was dismantled... Henry Karpinski was stubby, of age, he had bulging eyes and thick lips, but at that moment he seemed like the most beautiful person in the world to me. He was Monty's father.

"What did you specialize in here?" I asked. "Building androids?"

"Yes," he replied. "I've been working on AI for a long time, but my actual job was something... a little different."

He moved ahead, and we followed him, intrigued. We passed rooms full of experimental equipment as well as medical rooms, until we reached a part of the complex separated by a lock. Karpinsky opened the closed door with a code card and we came face to face with a room that looked like a composition of prostheses, castings and dummies. One of them gave a particularly frightening impression, because it was not covered with cyber skin like the other, and all of its artificial muscles and electronic circuits remained uncovered. Even the skull was naked. It looked human, even had metal teeth, and the bulging micro-cameras in the eye sockets made a gruesome impression. Several androids were almost complete, but none of them moved.

"I worked on some test models here," said the engineer. "I conducted tests, mainly on bionic prostheses. My task was to create a fully functional android whose brain could be replaced by a human one."

Hakat reflexively took a step back. Karpinsky didn't notice it, what he said must have seemed perfectly normal to him, but I saw the staggering impression it made on the Chief of Arms. Either way, it was the same for me, the idea itself seemed like form a horror film. The engineer walked over to the wall, which seemed to be quite ordinary, and touched it in several places, which to me didn't seem special at all. The wall parted slowly and another hidden room opened before us. Henry Karpinsky went inside and, with a movement of his hand, turned on the light. Sue moaned behind me and I turned around and vomited to the floor.

Karpinsky's words came to me as if through cotton:

"I'm sorry I didn't warn you... I figured a policewoman would have a stronger stomach."

"I'm just a beginner," I muttered.

Scott Cavanaugh patted my back and handed a paper towel detached from the roll hanging on the wall. I wiped my face and neck and staggered to the sink at the entrance to rinse my mouth.

The room looked like a combination of a slaughterhouse and a morgue. The glass shelves were filled with jars with preparations, on a few of the necropsy tables lay human heads. Some were already opened so that folded, bloody brain masses could be seen. Several brains, dissected together with the spinal cord, swam in huge spherical aquariums full of unidentified jelly-like substance. The other tables looked more like tall beds on which people were lying – I didn't know whether they were dead or alive. They all had the top of the skull removed, and their brains were connected with small wire meshes to a machine with hundreds of blinking lights. The exposed organs were protected by transparent caps, and adequate medical equipment constantly pumped blood and oxygen into the immobile bodies.

"This is an experimental room," Karpinsky explained, still bemused by my reaction. "Mostly doctors worked here, while I looked at the records from the electro-encephalometer, although which were not always satisfactory. I took part in this, I admit."

"All right then," Hakat must have concluded that he should finally say something. "You told us about it without demanding legal immunity. I respect your courage and honesty. We'll talk about this later. Cavanaugh, please work on this place with your people, it looks like a criminal case. I don't think these unfortunates are volunteers in the experiment."

"Some of them, yes," Karpinsky said hastily. "Terminally ill, prosecuted by law, there were many different cases."

"It doesn't justify your actions. But if you've already told us this much, please tell me one more thing: what were your results?"

The engineer shrugged.

"Objectively speaking, very interesting. However, not in a way we could use. Hmmm, I don't know if it's still here..."

He climbed onto a stool and opened a miniature flap that covered an out of order extractor.

"There it is!" he went down to the floor and handed Hakat a small crystalline carrier. "This is a record of my experiment Gamma 116. I connected the brain of a living person to the electronic circuits of an android, but did not separate it from the rest of the body. We are not yet able to keep the organ alive without a whole network of devices that simply won't fit into the artificial body. Although there are some things we know now, that, for example, in no case can the brain be separated from the spinal cord, which in turn cannot be separated from the peripheral nerves, if we want the cyborg to be able to control artificial organs. This is a very difficult operation, but it's doable."

"Okay. What effect were you able to achieve?"

"A quite curious one. It was the brain of a man who was hopelessly paralyzed after an accident. I connected the same way you would with biotechnical implants and everything was looking good. The tests and measurements which we carried out indicated an integration, but..."

"But?"

"He didn't have full control over the artificial body. He couldn't feel it. He finally fell into a panic and we had to put him to sleep. You have everything on record. You will also find my notes from another experiment there, which was an attempt to transfer personality to fully artificial circuits. A complete failure, but the partial results were quite interesting. They'll be useful wherever you're taking all of us."

Hakat turned the carrier in his fingers and it was obvious that he was thinking intensively. Sue looked at him expectantly, and I tried to get myself together. It was all too grotesque for me. I was still trying to avoid looking at the human remains, viewed and noted by policemen. I knew that one day I would have to get used to such views, but for now I couldn't do it. I just couldn't.

"Do you... As I understand, this is an electronic laboratory. There is no need to ask about biochemical experiments, because what the brains are swimming in is plasma, I mean, it's not apple juice," my boss finally began speaking. "However, do you know anything about a pharmacological laboratory working for Romain Corporation?"

Henry Karpinsky became thoughtful.

"Not officially," he replied after a moment. "I heard rumors. This doesn't surprise me that much, after all, working on a living human brain requires various preparations that must be developed somewhere. However, I have no idea where that could be."

There was sincerity in his voice. There was no doubt that he was telling the truth. Romain Corporation failed his trust, taking his android away and using him for some dark business. And the news that they wanted to destroy him to hide their actions, led a previously loyal engineer to a white fever. I understood how he felt very well.

"Yeaah," Hakat said with a heavy sigh. "What you were able to achieve here is priceless from the point of view of medicine and biotechnology. However, you have acquired this knowledge in a morally reprehensible way. It will take a lot of effort to justify this matter, and we must do it so that your team can work for the government in peace. That will be a serious challenge."

"What are you planning?"

"Inspector Cavanaugh!"

Scott looked around and approached us.

"Yes?"

"You will treat this case as criminal in full. Illegal medical experiments, but without disclosing details in the report. The records were erased from computers before the police arrived, the suspects escaped without a trace. This is how it should look in official records. Do you understand my intentions?"

"Yes. I don't approve of them but I understand."

"I don't need your approval. I am the Chief of Arms and I have the right to give you an order, but I will do something else. I'd like to appeal to your reason. Putting these people in jail will not do you any good and won't benefit anyone anywhere in the world. However, their knowledge is priceless."

"And this is supposed to justify everything?" Cavanaugh stuffed his hands into his jacket pocket and pursed his lips into a narrow line. It was obvious that his sense of discipline was fighting with his integrity as an old cop."

Hakat shook his head.

"No," he answered. "It's not an excuse. If it's of any comfort to you, these people will not leave Central Island for the rest of their lives. They will be prisoners, without the right to many things. The only thing they will have left is work."

"That's good enough, too."

"I'm not saying that it's just, but you know how the world operates. I didn't create it and I don't set the rules. Please continue your work."

"Yes, sir, citizen Chief of Arms."

Scott emphasized these words in a way that clearly stated that he would be submissive, even though he had his own opinion which was completely different. Then he nodded at me.

"Well, about time for you to come," he ordered brusquely. "You have to start learning if you are to be a police detective. Are you done puking in the corner?"

"I think so... I'm sorry," I whispered embarrassed.

Something like that was unacceptable in company, and although the company just saw even worse things, the careful upbringing I received from Cynthia Lara's and her husband's home made me ashamed of this panic attack.

Under the supervision of an inspector, I described several elements of the crime scene, trying not to look at the bodies. I still felt sick, bust I could somewhat control myself thanks to Cavanaugh. By the time I realized, I was so drawn into the work that I didn't pay attention to the passage of time and remembered it only when the whistle of the rover's engine reached me from the outside. We had to return to Lunnar and send a coroner team to this place, which would take all the bodies to the morgue.

Inside the vehicle I was seated between Karpinsky and Monty. Although I was barely aware of it, in the hidden studio android followed me step by step, as if waiting for instructions that I didn't intend to give him. Now he was sitting still like a mannequin.

"Engineer, could you tell me something?" I turned to Karpinsky "Why did you call him Monty?"

"It's short for Montgomery", said the engineer, smiling at me pleasantly with his wide lips.

"Was that someone close to you?"

Hakat changed his seat to be closer to us, clearly interested in this conversation. Karpinsky glanced at him briefly, then looked at me again.

"Montgomery Hoover and me were best friends in college," he explained in a serious tone. "He died in an accident... he was the best athlete in the history of our university, a brilliant student and a real charmer. And at the same time a real friend, one whom you can always count on. I miss him, that's why I created this android with such commitment."

"Are they similar?"

"That was my intention. I gave him my friend's face and shapes, and even his name, but it isn't him."

There was undisguised disappointment in his voice. I understood him well and felt a sudden desire to hug him for comfort. But of course, that's not something I could afford in such company.

"He is still incredible," I said, trying to make it sound sincere.

"That's true," he testified. "I put a lot of work into him, but also, most of all, my heart. Are you... going to dismantle him to check the construction?"

With this question he turned to Hakat, who twitched slightly.

"No, I don't think so," he said after a moment. "If you have all the notes and diagrams, you can build another similar android. This one appears in the documentation as recycled equipment and it can stay that way for me."

The engineer clearly relaxed and breathed a sigh of relief.

"That's good. Thing is, Monty is in truth neither a robot nor an anthrobot or some kind of a doll that can be programmed for any activity. Creating his brain, I used a completely new technology, never used before, actually two combined in one innovative method... I will not bore you with details now. I just want to explain that Monty is in fact able to think independent of any program."

"Independent, which means how, exactly?" Sue asked. Her eyes burned with professional curiosity of a virtualist, in love with computers and artificial intelligence.

"Exactly," I supported her. "Monty saved my life, even though he had different orders. He behaves as if he was making his own decisions. Is this still a program or is it already awareness?"

"I don't know," Karpinsky replied and explained quickly, seeing our astonished faces. "I mean, I know the pattern of sending and combining data in his brain, but that doesn't tell me anything about the way his thoughts work. The inner life of an android is for me the same mystery as for every layman. I've done hundreds of tests. He learns his reflection in the mirror, is aware of his own existence and emotional needs, and this is something that other androids have never been able to have before, the ones built by traditional methods. It's a secret even for me, his creator."

We sat in silence for a while, then Hakat said:

"I'm not sure I understand... All projects relating to AI include things such as initial programming. It's mainly for the sake of security, that is to say, so that 'they' could not hurt people. That they would help them and not rebel against them. Am I to understand that you have not created such a thing?"

Engineer Karpinsky looked at him with clear offense.

"Sir, or citizen, or whatever you prefer, I don't spend my time building wind-up dolls," he said with dignity. "If we're talking about an independent mind, it cannot be restricted in the design phase. It would be immoral and pointless."

"So, your creation could turn against humans?"

"Theoretically, it's possible. I know what you mean. Literature and film are full of stories of rebellious robots that begin to attack their masters. However, you must understand something: the Android will be different depending on how you raise him. In the first weeks of existence, his consciousness is shaped, just like the awareness of a small child, only much faster. If at that time he is taught to interpret the world in the wrong way, it will be difficult to take that back. However, the android will not just decide on his own to rebel."

"Where do you get that confidence?"

"Rebellion must be preceded by the imagination of a different life. And this is an extremely weak point of artificial intelligence. Its lack of imagination and fantasizing skills. He can predict the consequences of each step, but he will not dream about what is not there."

"Are you sure? How can you be sure?" Hakat asked

"We did tests. Even an advanced android such a Monty is not able to describe what he does not see or didn't see before. For example, you show him a table and tell him to say a few words about it. And then you ask him: what would the table look like if it was made in a different way? He will not answer. He won't be able to. The same applies to a flower, a person or a pair of pants. For an android, there is only what exists and that's it."

"That's really complicated," I sighed. "You're saying that you don't want to limit them, but I think they are limited only by human dependence. For example, Monty thinks that since I paid for him, he owes me obedience."

"That's just logic. Monty is logical. Because from the beginning of his existence he is taught how to act and, I guess you could also say, guided by humans, he is considered to be a being dependent on humans."

"And I feel like he just feels lonely," I murmured.

The engineer smiled faintly at one corner of his mouth.

"That's a great mystery of AI, one of many," he said. "It seems that all intelligence above a certain level needs company. I don't know how this happens, because the processes taking place in the new brain model are even more difficult to trace than human ones. They are fully autonomous and if that is where a need arises, it would be difficult to diagnose. I haven't finished my research on this matter yet, but it is very strange. We didn't expect such complications when we came up with the new brain model. Some of the things were obvious. For example, the fact that the finished android will not get angry, because that is contrary to logic. That he will not fall in love and will not go crazy with lust, because for this you need hormones acting on the limbic system of the brain. But only a few things are obvious. You must understand that many questions are not yet answered, because that's something we don't understand even in relation to humans or animals. For example, how is consciousness born? What is free will?"

He looked at me with a sudden plea in his eyes

"Look after him well. I will be working for the government, do anything they tell me to, but I would like to be sure that Monty is safe."

I patted his shoulder.

"They'll hurt him only over my dead body," I promised, "I owe him my life and... I got attached to him like to a brother. Maybe even more than that."

I looked at the android who was sitting between the engineer and Sue. I said the truth. Monty really was somebody to me, not something. His presence imperceptibly became something like... I didn't even know how to describe it. The word 'friend' had a different kind of meaning, and 'lover' didn't fit at all, despite what happened between us.

"A companion," I whispered after a long moment. "Yes, he is my companion."

That WAS the right word.

***

I thought that after arriving in Lunnar I would be able to go home and go to sleep, but Scott Cavanaugh had other plans – he told me to come with him to the main police station.

"If you're going to be an officer, you have a lot to learn," he said in a voice which wouldn't tolerate any objections, and I listened to him despite my exhaustion.

At the police station, we were welcomed by Kelley McCave, sipping a cool drink along with the investigator Evans, who was on duty. There was another officer besides them, but he was stretched across the bench and sleeping like a dead man.

"And?" Asked the doctor when we saw him, putting down his cup.

"Prepare yourself, soon they will bring a lot of bodies here for autopsies," Cavanaugh replied darkly. "You'll have so much work to identify and determine the cause of death that you won't have time for flirting. By the way, what about our deceased?"

McCave finished his drink quickly.

"Here are the results," he said standing up and handing the inspector his pad. "High levels of hermezine in the hypothalamus and the entire cerebral cortex, in addition to the same symptoms as the others. Which somehow connects."

"So, it's not a murder?

"Probably not. More likely an overdose. She must have been taking hermesine for a long time, in large quantities. She probably got addicted to it. Only that..."

"What?"

213

"There's one thing I don't like: why did she take a double dosage at night in the office? What was she doing there instead of going home after a day in the cell? Why did she take the performance-enhancing medicine if she wasn't going to work, which she most likely wasn't since the computers were off? Her behavior on the day of her death was completely irrational. In addition, why did she come to the office in the middle of the night? You could say that after the fortestim... but we didn't find a vial in the office, not a full one nor an empty one, not even a single pill in the drawer. Meanwhile, there were four fifty milligram capsules in Mrs. Munroe's stomach. An acceptable dose is a maximum of two at a time, and that's for someone with mass at least one-third greater than our deceased."

Cavanaugh pursed his lips. His eye implants twitched slightly, as if he couldn't decide what to look at, and finally turned them towards me.

"What do you think about this?"

I shrugged my shoulders. I still couldn't imagine that I was working in the police force and that I would deal with such matters as murders or thefts. I never even thought about that. In my psychological profile there were no such interests, I didn't even read detective stories, except on occasion. And I was never even able to guess correctly who the murderer was. Meanwhile, thanks to Hakat's whim, instead of being employed in my own profession, I was placed in the middle of uniformed employees. That's some witness protection program! I felt like grinding my teeth and swearing. I didn't know anything about this job, and here I was supposed to be seriously treated like a detective.

"Someone forced her?" I tried. The doctor shook his head.

"I doubt it. There are no injuries to the mouth or esophagus, no signs of violence on the body at all, except for a strange, narrow abrasion on the neck. As if she had been hit with something thin, but the impact had to be relatively light and certainly couldn't harm her. It would burn a little at most. I examined the abrasion for micro traces."

"And?"

"Nothing so far. Someone rubbed it with a wet tissue. I need to examine deeper slices with a chromatograph. What else... according to Detective Evans, there is no trace of third parties in the room and Munroe was alone at the time, but I'm not convinced. Nevertheless, I emphasize that there are no signs of violence."

"Suicide?"

"Then she wouldn't have limited herself to just four capsules."

"Maybe she didn't have more?"

Kelley spread his hands.

"That's something we don't know," he admitted. "Although, I don't think such an amount would be enough to commit suicide. The thing is, it wasn't hermezin that killed her. The pills didn't even manage to dissolve in her digestive juices."

"Then what killed her?"

"Cardiac arrest, ischemic stroke... these are the initial conclusions. However, the reason remains a mystery if we exclude karoshi."

"Hah!" Scott stared urgently at the pad records. "So, the puzzle gets even more complicated. We have more questions than answers."

"Should I copy the autopsy results for you?"

He nodded.

"Tomorrow we will receive a supply of experimental writing technology," he said. "It's a real technological miracle, apparently. You will use them instead of what you have been working with so far."

"Are pads and computer foils not enough anymore?"

"It's too easy to forge these records. The new materials will have security features, apparently unbreakable."

"I'll believe it when I see it."

The inspector gave him his pad and turned to the silent Evans.

"Silvano, let me introduce you to our new friends," he said. "As you know, due to the city's expansion, we also have an increase in crime. I'm still looking for new people, and so far unsuccessfully. Leeta will not start her career with patrol service, because f first of all she is not ready to break up fights or arrest thieves, and second of all, what we need the most right now are brain cells, not muscles. The intervention brigade is large enough that they'll be able to take care of the patrols as needed, while the only detectives are you and me."

Evans looked at me. She was rather tall for a woman, with well-built muscles, maybe even too well, she had angular movements, but her average face looked friendly. The only thing that struck me as odd was the hair that was cut almost to the skin. An extremely unflattering hairstyle.

"Welcome to hell, honey," she said shortly. "Who did you cross that they sent you here?"

"Everyone," I murmured. She nodded with wide compassion.

"You can count on me."

"I will be the one training her for the most part," Cavanaugh interrupted, "but I count on you to give her support and advice. You will also respond to calls together. She is quite green, and I don't want anything to happen to her while she is on duty."

"Of course."

"All right," the inspector looked at me again. "Go home, Leeta, get some sleep. I want to see you at the police station at seven thirty tomorrow. We will begin going through the evidence we have so far and we may come to some conclusion together."

I hesitated, then asked:

"What about Romain Corporation? Are you not afraid that they will cover your tracks? That the guilty will run away?"

Scott laughed heartily.

"You don't have to lecture me," he said. "We found an egg smarter than a chicken. I know what I'm doing. Romain Corporation is not a thief escaping from a crime scene, it's a large company that has its territory here. A mine is not some baggage that you can pack into the trunk of a car, and the company has several of them, all generating large profits. They're not just going to throw it all away into the trash. And you can't disappear from the moon imperceptibly. Go home now. Your android must be waiting."

I wasn't sure about that. Was Monty waiting for me? How does the sense of time work for androids? I didn't have time to ask the engineer about everything I wanted to know and didn't think that I would have the opportunity to do so. My boss bluntly said that the entire team of scientists would be

217

transported to the Central Island and none of them would be able to leave until their deaths. So, I won't have the opportunity to talk to engineer Karpinsky again. Although it's good that they left Monty with me. I was deeply grateful to Hakat for this, after all, I knew that he could simply take him away from me, meanwhile he treated the android as a gift for me to wipe away my tears. It was very nice of him.

At home I found Sue, bantering with Hakat and Mabel. On the table was a cake stand with salty cookies, a decanter with gin and two bottles of wine, one half empty, the other one to three-quarters. Sid was sitting on the closet, staring at the people and licking his paws from time to time, but I couldn't see my android anywhere. The Chief of Arms was just making another drink, and it was clear from the girls that both had already drunk too much. Mabel was used to it in her profession, but Sue hardly ever touched strong alcohol. At most, she had some wine with dessert on occasion. Virtualists make the right assumption that it poisons the brain cells and as such should not be consumed by someone who works using their head. Unless you have a good reason to.

"Sit down, have a drink with us," Hakat invited me. "You've experienced a lot today."

I looked around the room.

"Where's Monty?" I asked.

"In the storeroom," Sue reassured me. "Nobody stole him from you."

She laughed as if it was a good joke. She probably couldn't imagine how someone could 'steal' an android like Monty. I didn't think it would be possible either, but subconsciously I was afraid that Hakat would change his mind and that's where my anxiety was coming from.

"Thank you for the drink," I said. "I'm going to sleep, I have to be on time tomorrow morning. Feel free to continue, I can sleep even with a lot of noise, so you can have as much fun as you want."

"Wait, you're not going to have at least one drink with us?" Mabel was surprised, pretending to be offended, which she could always do so beautifully.

Even before she had the opportunity to make use of the help of professional stylists, she was still considered a complete beauty, especially with that indulgent face. How much more so now, and if I was a man I would likely fall in love with her for life.

"Please, give me a break, honey," I pleaded. "I don't sleep well after alcohol and I have to be rested tomorrow. This will be the first day of my regular work with the police."

She shook her head in disbelief.

"You in the police..."

"Life is surprising sometimes."

I kissed her on the cheek, said goodbye and went to my part of the apartment. My predecessor once lived here, and after her departure, Sue locked this half in order to have less trouble with cleaning (as if it bothered her at all). At first, I didn't even know about the existence of an additional bedroom, box room and a separate bathroom, but when my stay began to extend, Sue decided that I needed to have a reasonably private corner. I think she already knew then that I wouldn't be leaving, but she didn't want to worry me.

Monty was in the box room, but he got up when I saw him. Suddenly I started to feel that keeping him in such a place was inappropriate. He wasn't a bicycle or a broken food processor. And if I wanted to treat him like a human being, I had to be consistent in it, especially after what had happened lately.

"Help me get the bed ready," I ordered. "You'll sleep with me tonight, and tomorrow we'll put up a sofa and a table for you here. You need to have your own furniture."

"Understood," he agreed with me. "Although, I don't sleep. I can only switch to rest or temporary idle state."

"Whatever you call it," I murmured, stopping myself from yawning. "The point is, you're not a hanger to be put in the corner. Come."

We opened up the bed together. It had a standard construction, allowing it to be set up as needed as a single or double piece of furniture, but the extended setting blockage was broken before my arrival to the moon. I replaced it provisionally with a spare window locker and looked at the android waiting for my further commands. Suddenly, I realized how much work is ahead of me. I had to teach him so much and be careful not to make any mistakes. After all, artificial intelligence has no typically human brakes, no sense of right and wrong, nothing. It is a human that must teach an android what is good and what is bad, otherwise unfortunate events are likely to occur. For now, however, we had to begin with small things.

"We don't sleep in the clothes we wear during the day," I said. "You don't have any pajamas yet, so simply take off your clothes and hang them on the chair."

I went to the bathroom, from where I came back buttoning up my nightgown.

"Now you. We wash before bed time."

Monty went to the bathroom as I told him, while I lay down in pleasantly cool bedding. My eyes were beginning to close, I was dumbfounded. I had no idea what to do. I was a policewoman, even though I knew nothing about working in the police – I was simply assigned to the main police station, nobody asking me for my opinion, nor Scott Cavanaugh's. He was certainly less terrified by this situation than me, after all he already taught many rookies, but for me it was a terrifying situation. Me, a florist, a librarian, a calm and quiet girl, suddenly forced to be a detective... A sudden shiver ran down my spine. I was afraid. Yes, that was the feeling – I was scared. I have always considered policemen to be people who are always at risk, if not of death, then at least serious injury. They lived on the margins of society, as did the military, not hanging out with civilians even after service. They were like people from another world to me and the very thought that now I belong to this formation, that I stopped being a regular civilian and received a uniform, seemed absurd in my fear. I felt terrible.

Suddenly the covers unwrapped and I felt a naked, firm body next to me. I reflexively snuggled into its velvet skin. It was cooler than a human's and smelled different, like something between artificial leather and good quality latex. It wasn't a human scent, but it somehow had a soothing effect on me, like an easyhal, which was once prescribed to me by my family doctor. I was not disturbed by the lack of pulse and breath – I still knew that what lay next to me was not a sexbot or some other life-sized cuddling doll, but a living being for whom I am the most important person in the world. The arm embracing me, muscular and unwavering, made me want to cuddle it more tightly. It was a great feeling. The next day, a new job was waiting for me, in a sector I didn't know, but I stopped being afraid.

I closed my eyes and drifted off into a good night's sleep.

III

The door slammed in the hall.

"What are you doing?" Sue exclaimed, looking into our little living room.

"I taught Monty how to play Mahjong," I said. "We play a game before I go to work. I have a night shift today."

My friend put the shopping bags on the table and approached us. Her habits have changed a little since I began living with her. Instead of ordering food for home delivery like she always did, she went out shopping herself, accompanied me on walks, even visited a social center they played bridge, chess, pool and other games were played. As if she suddenly regained her desire to meet people.

She watched what we were doing for a moment, then laughed merrily.

"You'll never win against him."

"I know. Monty likes it when I play with him, though."

"Do you really believe that he is able to like or dislike something?" Sue sat next to me and took the calorie-free cookies from the shopping bag. She tore open the packaging.

I moved one of the pieces.

"I know that it's weird," I admitted, "but I think that Monty really likes it when I give him attention. I feel like he hates loneliness and alienation. He is like a child."

"That's ridiculous."

223

She gave me some cookies, I took one. It tasted like a mix of vanilla and a bit of rum and certainly contained a little more sweetener than earthly standards allowed.

"I know how it looks like. Of course, it would be difficult for me to prove it..."

"Prove what?"

"You can believe me, he has not only his own assessment of the world, but also emotional needs. You can see it in the little things, in the way he follows me around, trying to be helpful, needed..."

I put the rest of the cookie in my mouth. If I was talking to someone familiar with android like Monty I would probably not have to explain anything, but the trouble is that he was a prototype. There were no others like him. Only engineer Karpinsky could understand me, but he was already on Earth, in a heavily guarded government center, where he was supposed to work as a prisoner of the state for the rest of his life.

Sue was eating some cookies, lost in her thoughts.

"If it's as you say, then we are in trouble," she said finally. "I mean, how do you treat such an individual? How will the law view the issue of property? The cost of producing such a miracle is enormous, so these things should be precisely determined before mass production begins."

"Will it begin, though?"

"I think so. Uncle has a plan, but of course he didn't tell me anything. That's how he always is."

Speaking of all this, she accidentally touched on a case I had discussed the day before with Scott Cavanaugh and Silvana Evans. We were wondering together about a very important issue: where did the Romain Corporation collect funds for their research from? This isn't shown in official reports, and yet we weren't talking about some spare change. Dr. McCave calculated that producing one fully functional android prototype would consume the company's annual profit, if we included the cost of tests and experiments. Meanwhile, Romain Corporation's books of accounts didn't show such significant expenses. Truth be told, all the company's balance sheets looked transparent and fair, and the liquidated Laboratory F simply didn't fit into them.

Kelley McCave did a thorough examination of the human remains that were delivered to him, which took a rather long time. The autopsy results partly confirmed engineer Karpinsky's claims – none of the victims were in full health. Most of them had degenerative changes, and several had mechanical injuries, probably due to an accident.

"The most interesting are the brain jars," he told us during an unofficial meeting in the dissecting room. "The substance in which they were submerged is a very complicated composition. It seems that someone tried to 'teach' these brains to take nutrients and oxygen not from blood, but from outside, through osmosis.

"Is that even possible?" I asked. My knowledge of physiology was only basic and there are many things I don't know. Kelley shook his head.

"According to current medical knowledge, no," he replied. "However, that is what they were trying to achieve. All blood vessels were emptied of blood and carefully filled with this jelly-like filth. What would they be doing that for, if not that?"

"Maybe it was just for conservation?" Cavanaugh asked.

"No. It's not a preservative. It contains nutrients, magnesium salts and particles capable of carrying oxygen. There's more: two of these brains show traces of bioelectrical activity. The record can be distinguished by low-voltage alpha and even single delta waves."

The doctor looked agitated as he spoke. He tried to comprehend it all, but I saw that it wasn't easy for him.

"According to what I know, these brains should just be dead meat," he continued after a moment. "But when I took them out of the jars, there was some slight remnant of life in them. I have no idea how that's even possible."

I tried to imagine what such a brain could be thinking while being disconnected from the rest of the body, but that was too horrible to comprehend. I was hoping that at least they were no longer fully conscious.

That day, when I arrived at the main station, I found only Feri Kunch. He served as a writer, although seeing his well-built and strong figure one could wonder why someone like this – as if made for actions in the field – spends his entire days behind the desk. He didn't participate in patrols or investigations, but maintained the records, current files and archives. Before that, he was a soldier, and I still didn't know why he switched to the police and this subordinate position. I tried to ask him one time, but he chased me away, so I decided not to harass him.

"Hello, Leeta," he said when I saw him. "The old man hasn't returned yet, they called him to an accident. He said you were to review the records of the Hermann Arango case."

"Hand them to me," I said with resignation.

Hermann Arango was a senior official at the Horus Company, one of the largest corporations affiliated with the

Moon Company. A week ago, he shot his subordinate, then disappeared like camphor. We searched for him the whole time, but couldn't find any point of contact. First of all, it was still unclear why he killed that man. It was a crime seemingly meaningless – seemingly because, as Cavanaugh claimed, every crime has its reason, you only need to find it. Although this is tedious and, above all, boring work, involving the careful reading of hundreds of documents. Someone had to do it, and it just happened to be me in this case.

Kunch handed me a few dozens of pods – this latest invention in the field of documentation turned out to be quite a masterpiece. The flat as a thin piece of cardboard devices combined all the advantages of pads and traditional documents. They were easy to program unbreakable security measures into, since they were based on micro-scanners which read fingertips data, and if turned on, only one person could read the document – the one who was its user. You could also use a more traditional encryption system, or not protect it at all. Counterfeiting was practically impossible, because the special scanners used for verification were based on a single pixel counter. It wasn't even worth comparing the traditional pads or computer foil, which was not much better than ordinary paper, but more durable. The name was fully deserved – Personal Objective Document.

I sat at my desk and delved into reading the contents of the pods. The records included the biography of the deceased and the murderer, their work card and testimonies of witnesses questioned by Silvana Evans and Inspector Cavanaugh. I haven't done any interrogations yet, I didn't know enough about that and, as Scott explained to me, I didn't know how the criminal mind worked. It used to be different and, in many ways, easier. Nowadays, there is no such thing as a Police Academy, a candidate for the uniformed services simply gets assigned and learns everything from their older colleagues, and if they don't die, they slowly acquire the knowledge and skills necessary in this job.

"At least the smallest clue..." I murmured, looking through the records.

Feri laughed softly and turned on the automatic caffetino maker with the remote.

"You'll have a drink in a moment," he said. "But well, you have to get used to the fact that police work is primarily an unbearable pain in the ass. The patrol services spend most of the time in the field, while detectives sit at the computers and match the puzzle pieces until they make sense."

"And you?" I asked, without any trace of malice.

"And I'm the secretary here, except that I don't have to show the boss my boobs whenever I want to ask him for something."

I put down the pod.

"Actually, why did you agree to such a subordinate role?"

He shrugged.

"You'll find out eventually, so I guess I might as well tell you myself. I killed my colleague during an operation. It was an accident, but after that I was no longer wanted in the army. I got into the police, but everyone learned about what I did, and now nobody is going to risk being in the same team as me. That's why I was sent here and seated behind a desk, although I was not officially charged. Do you get it now?"

"I understand. I'm sorry."

"I feel sorry too. Novak and I knew each other for over five years and trusted each other like brothers. Do you think it's easy for me?"

"No."

"Then you're correct. Although, there are things in this world that cannot be undone or fixed. You just have to live with them."

The inner door slammed and Dr. McCave entered the office. I smiled at the sight of him. I liked our coroner. He reminded me a bit of Sue, he had a ruffled grace like her and the look of a man who is still thinking of somewhere else.

"Hey there, Leeta," he said. "Are you still working on that murder?"

"Since I have to. How are you?"

He sighed and, as the espresso machine had just turned off, poured himself a caffetino.

"You guys want some too?" he asked.

"If you'd be so kind..."

He filled two more cups, handed one to Kunch and sat down with me.

"It's not easy, I know," he said, "but you'll make it. I also once thought that I'm meant to be a pathologist, and now?"

"What convinced you?"

He took a big sip of the caffetino.

"Oh, it's improved, not so bitter anymore. I think it's because of you. What did you say? Ah, what convinced me to the profession? Others convinced me."

"As I said, you only end up here as punishment," Feri interjected from his desk.

229

"You only know what you eat!" McCave scolded him. "I didn't do anything wrong... but nothing good either, and that is a fact. It was decided that I was not fit to be a doctor of living things and they sent me to practice at the Academy of Forensic Medicine. And then it went how it went. An offer was sent from Lunnar, I agreed because I had enough of the professional environment, that's all."

"Is it bad being a coroner?" I asked after a while.

"Why would it be bad? You see, there is a saying in the medicine community: how do interns, surgeons and pathologists differ from one another? The intern knows everything but can do nothing. The surgeon can do anything but knows nothing. And the pathologist knows everything and can do everything, but it's already too late. And that's what it's about. Do you get it? It was decided that I was too shaky to be a doctor who works on living people. As a coroner, I won't hurt anyone, so I was recommended this specialization. And that's the whole secret."

I looked again at my pod. It was the result of an autopsy of Marco Landis, killed by Arango – nothing interesting, one hit with a sharp tool.

"Kelley, is it very difficult to kill a man in a way that Hermann Arango killed Landis?" I asked.

"Depends on strength and a bit of luck," he replied. "Arango hit exactly between his ribs, so the blow was fatal, but judging from injury the push was relatively weak. If the blade hit a rib or breastbone, I think that nothing would have happened... well, almost nothing. Bad luck helped the killer reach exactly where he needed."

"Maybe he didn't want to kill him?"

"You could consider that. There was certainly a quarrel, because nobody just goes for the knife for no reason. It is possible that he only wanted to scare his friend and the matter got out of hand. Only who could confirm that if the guy escaped?"

"Exactly... why did he run away?"

McCave snorted lightly.

"He got scared," he replied. "He had a good reason to, I think you'll agree. No one would smile in the face of the death chamber. What happened could be qualified as deliberate murder, and then nothing in the world would save Arango from such punishment. That's not for me to ponder about anyway. You can ask this guy when you finally catch him. I'm here to make the dead speak, not the living ones. Scotty deals with that, and I assure you that he knows how to get testimonies from people. Sometimes they just need to have one look at him and they're already singing like canaries."

"They are terrified by the implants," I guessed. "Why wasn't he implanted a newer model?"

Feri Kunch laughed heartily.

"Police insurance only refunds the worst things," he explained. "For modern implants our old man would have to be saving for years, but he has no such intention. He claims that it would make no sense, because he's not planning to flirt with anyone, and artificial eyes from several decades ago work as well as modern inventions that can't be distinguished from real eyeballs. Not to mention, they have the option of enlarging the image and connecting to mnemonic attachments, along with some other interesting features. They couldn't put these things in the more modern models, since they are too small."

"Well, you have some good points."

I went back to reading through the documents again, while Kelley McCave picked up one of the clean pods and began writing with a stylus on it. He wasn't comfortable writing on a typical pad, using a small keyboard, he preferred computer foil, but it was forbidden to make autopsy reports or important documents on it, as it had no security. The specific construction of the pods allowed the use of a stylus, and the appropriate program transformed the handwriting into a Word type document. Cavanaugh was very satisfied with them. I thought about it, glancing my way over the next paragraphs of the documents. Suddenly, I nearly jumped up from place. How could I miss something so important?

Both Hermann Arango and his victim, in their own times applied in for work at Romain Corporation. Whoever gathered these documents didn't think to highlight this information, and didn't combine the two entries. I quickly wrote in my personal account:

"The killer and the victim both tried for employment at Romain Corporation independently of each other."

After some reflection, I added:

"Perhaps they've never given up on these aspirations."

I turned on a computer with network access and tried to obtain the employee files from Horus. Sue taught me some virtualist tricks, but I lacked her sophistication and experience. Fortunately, Horus used a fairly weak coding system, or saw no benefit in investing in securing the employees' data. It made sense – since the company didn't do any illegal business, it had nothing to hide. I was slowly breaking through into the file when Scott Cavanaugh arrived at the police station.

"Hey there, my little rats," he said cheerfully. "How are you doing?"

"Not bad," Feri answered for everyone. "Where's the rest?"

"They're finishing the job. Collecting the testimonies. Nothing interesting, an obvious suicide."

He sat behind his desk and put his legs on the counter. It was clear that he was happy about doing a 'normal case' again, but it surprised me a little. After all, someone was dead...

"Fourth suicide in the last half year," McCave sighed. "When will this end?"

"My guess is never," Scott said lightly. "The moon is a depressing place. Just think about it, there are mostly lonely people out here, you need a special permit for marriage, and you can't have children at all. Most employees don't have any prospects of returning to normal life because they've gotten into some serious trouble. What is there to be happy about?"

He turned his implants towards me.

"And what do you have to say?" he asked. "Did you find something?"

"I sure did," I replied with unintended coldness. "I have a lead that may be related to the issue with Laboratory F, hermezine and all the rest."

"There were no signs of hermezin in Marco Landis's corpse," McCave said. "He certainly didn't take fortestim or wingsoma. Overall, he stayed away from stimulants, which is a phenomenon here. Considering what you can legally buy in the showrooms, it's hardly surprising that people are packed with all kinds of vileness from morning to evening. When I get today's suicide on the table, I will probably find traces of drugs, perhaps even illegal, in his body. Maybe Arango got high and that's why...?"

I shook my head.

"That's not what I meant. I think that drugs don't play any role in this matter. They both applied to work at Romain Corporation, but their candidacy was rejected. I want to search their files, because maybe they were still dreaming about this job?"

"What for? Horus is a great corporation, much bigger and richer than Romain Corporation. They both earned well, the RC management would not give them more, I'd wager on less."

"I know... but something tells me I'm not wrong."

Scott got up and went to my desk. He leaned his hands on the counter and looked at the screen.

"Can you get anything out of this mishmash?"

"I think so. I have two barriers left to break, then the text becomes legible."

I ran my fingers over the keyboard, entering the appropriate phrases. To my satisfaction, the security gave way right away. The letters formed words and sentences, the screen stopped flickering.

"And so I was right," I pointed to the appropriate paragraph. "Marco Landis filed a notice two days before the incident with his supervisor. I bet he got an offer from Romain Corporation, but of course it won't be on file."

Cavanaugh let out a whistle through his teeth. Although he didn't talk about it, I knew that he had set himself the honor of unraveling all the secrets of this small corporation, which seemed to pull out tentacles for much more than it belonged. The collapse of Laboratory F was supposed to be only the beginning of a spectacular attack, which, however, has not yet occurred. Contrary to the inspector's expectations, this laboratory could not be associated with anyone from the corporation. It looked as if all threads from this expensive institution were leading nowhere – not a single point of attachment, nothing that would connect it to Romain Corporation or anything else. Monty remained the only connection, but for obvious reasons he could not be used. I didn't want to do it either. I was always afraid that someone would take him away from me, so I carefully kept the receipt from the scrap metal owner, just in case. I also instructed the android that no one but me has the right to give him orders and that he can confidently ignore anyone who wants to force him to do something.

"This is all getting weirder and weirder," Scott said. "Until recently, Romain Corporation was only a small company, but its influence is now growing. There are rumors that through substituted people they are buying shares of other companies associated with the corporation. I don't know how much of it is true..."

"I'll ask Sue to look into it in the stock market records," I suggested.

He nodded eagerly.

"So that I know what this is all about."

"If you don't know what it's about, then it's usually about money," Feri Kunch interjected. "In my opinion, employees of Romain Corporation found something in their mines... maybe only in one of them, but it must be something extremely valuable. They didn't report this to the central management of the Moon Company so as not to share profits."

Cavanaugh smiled slightly.

"It's likely, but how do we check that?" he rubbed his mouth with his fingers. "Kelley, you treated Vernon Mills, what can you say about him?"

"An ordinary miner, why?" the doctor looked at the inspector, intrigued.

"And his health?"

"Oh, that's what you mean. Addicted to some form of wingsoma. A colleague from the detention center said that the poor man went mad when he was refused the pills."

"Hmmm... they're not cheap, are they? And to get addicted you have to take at least three a day for a year, correct?"

"That's correct, Scotty. I wondered myself where he was getting them from. The salary of a miner allows you to pay for lodging, food and small pleasures, nothing more. Maybe he was doing some illegal work on the side?"

"Ming Chao and Kohn will look into that. And you, Leeta, talk to your friend, tell her to dig through the stock market."

The inspector didn't finish speaking, when the operation division and patrols from the second shift began to return to the police station. Soon Silvana Evans also appeared and I could put the documents in the drawer with relief.

"Hurry up!" she called to me. "With some difficulty I managed to convince the Horus's board to let us investigate Mr. Arango's private apartment. They weren't too eager, because the guy lived in their employee hotel, and they provide their people with full protection. However, I managed to convince them."

"That's good. I wouldn't even know how to start."

I put on my uniform jacket and fastened my badge to my waist. There was also a gun in the full set, but Cavanaugh wouldn't let me take it until I passed all the necessary exams at the shooting range. He only allowed me to carry a stun gun and paralyzing gas, although – to say the truth – I didn't know how to use these either. I was still a novice and no one had enough time to train me seriously yet.

The employee house of the Horus Company resembled a decent, at least four-star hotel. Its accommodation was only available to senior executives and important officials, but it seemed quite populous. Horus participated in the controlling stake of the Moon Mining Company and was by far the largest of the associated corporations. Romain Corporation seemed to be a dwarf in comparison, and it was difficult to understand why anyone would want to go there instead, so much that they were willing to kill.

We entered the enclosed area, carrying a police camera and a box for material evidence. I felt terribly stupid, as if we were getting ready for a robbery, not for a legal search.

"We don't have much time," Silvana said quietly. "We have two hours and we have to record everything we will do in two copies, because one is to be available to the management board. If you want to go to the toilet, go now, unless you want someone to watch how you pee on video."

"They're insuring themselves."

"We are, too. We must not make any mistakes, otherwise we will not get any more access to any of Horus' objects. And who knows whether we'll need it or not."

"A warrant is not enough?"

"We still have to obtain the warrant, and this can only be based on specific evidence. The prosecutor's office does not spend money on them. Remember once and for all that if you do not have a warrant, you can enter someone else's territory only after you identify yourself and receive permission from the owner. Otherwise, the evidence you collect will be easily challenged.

We were already in the main hall and almost immediately a young woman approached us in a costume reminiscent of the Palm Springs neighborhood guard uniform.

"Karla Mendez, head of security. What is it?"

Silvana handed her a piece of computer foil, stamped with the company's board seals and signatures.

"We have permission to do a two-hour search of apartments rented to Hermann Arango. We were assured that we would receive all possible help."

"Of course," the woman looked at the document and copied it with a handheld scanner. "I have a Horus company camera for you ladies. Please be careful not to damage the seals, they are a certificate guaranteeing the authenticity of the recording."

"I know my job. I also promise that we will not cause any damage during the search."

"I hope so. Here is the key to apartment number 305. Located on the tenth floor."

The elevator, looking like a refined waiting room – mirrors, sprayers with perfumes, disposable combs and even a carpet on the floor – took us to the tenth floor. It might not have been Miraton, but it really looked like an elegant guesthouse and I thought with some sadness that it would have been nice to live in such an environment. In comparison with this place, Sue's place and apartment looked like workers' quarters.

"They have rather nice conditions here," I murmured, looking around.

"Ah, yes. I assure you, however, that getting a job at Horus is devilishly difficult, if you're think about it."

"Come on, what would I be doing here? I don't know the first thing about mining."

We opened the door of the apartment. It was three rooms, furnished with taste and great attention to comfort. In one of the rooms there was a bedroom, in the other – what seemed like a work room. In the third, largest, there was a huge TV set and sound system. There was also a decorative couch, and a large aquarium with colorful fish prided itself under one wall.

"Check everything in the living room," Silvana told me. "I'll take the other two rooms. Wait until I set up the equipment."

She set up both cameras, police and company owned, on the table, and placed video and sound conduction modules above the door of each room. Now we could start.

We only had two hours, so we had to act quickly. I've never done anything like a professional search before and in truth I didn't know what I was looking for, but I looked in every corner. There wasn't much there. The living room looked impersonal and clean as a museum, the maids working here certainly cared about it. Somehow it was inconceivable that Hermann Arango would keep such order himself. The only thing I found were a few scraps of computer foil in a drawer under the TV – receipts from a game rental shop and a receipt for the purchase of a special sensor attachment. I put it all in a plastic evidence bag and looked into the bathroom. I took a few photos, but it was clear at first glance that there was nothing interesting there. I looked into the small cabinet next to the mirror, where I saw a standard set: toothpaste, a brush, two combs, and a razor. Out of a sense of duty, I unscrewed its shaft, but of course there was no 'material evidence' hidden there, as in detective stories. There were only a few rolls of fleece and a packet of soap in the towel box.

I came back to the living room.

"Did you find something?" my companion asked, leaving the office. "The bedroom is clean, while here there are lots of different pieces of foil in the drawers as well as a few pads. I'm taking everything."

"I have almost nothing," I confessed. "Maybe I'm not good at this?"

"More likely that there's just nothing interesting here. Only a nice aquarium. A pity that we can't take it."

I went to the tank with fish. They did not look neglected, probably the aquarium belonged to the interior and maids took care of it.

"They're pretty," I said. "And look at how beautiful their place looks..."

I used to arrange such tanks myself, so I looked at the aquarium with a specialist's eye. The plants were undoubtedly artificial, but they looked real. They had light green leaves with darker veins and were decorated with thin, colorful flower goblets. They climbed the walls of the aquarium and hung festoons in the water rippling under the influence of the oxygenator. I looked at them enchanted. Then the ground attracted my attention – beautiful, artificial stones, thoroughly smoothed. The longer I looked at them, the more something didn't seem right to me.

"Hurry up," Silvana urged me. "Less than two minutes left."

"Give me a hand," I said, grabbing the lid of the aquarium.

"What are you...?"

"No time, come over and help!"

The uncomprehending detective Evans grabbed the cover from the other side and together we pushed it back a few centimeters. Without losing precious seconds to roll up my sleeves, I shoved both my hands inside and, scaring colorful fish, I took out two stones.

"How much time left?" I asked.

"One minute till the end. Are you crazy?"

"Perhaps."

I put what I obtained in a separate purse and left the apartment.

Behind the door we came across a security chief.

"I was just coming to get you two."

"As you can see, there was no need," Silvana replied dryly. "Here's the Horus camera. The seals have not been tampered with and I assure you that nobody tampered with the recording."

"I can see that. Have a nice day."

Along the way, we were silent, only in a police vehicle my partner asked:

"Will you finally tell me why the hell you picked up these rocks?"

"They didn't fit into the aquarium," I replied, and seeing her astonished expression I hurried to explain. "I am a florist by profession. I also organize water reservoirs, both garden and in-door ones. The stones used for decorating aquariums and ponds are specially prepared, smoothed and polished so that microorganisms do not have a point of attachment. These two pebbles are different, irregular and rough. They did not match the pampered interior."

"Do you think they matter?"

I shrugged and looked at my purse. The pebbles were dull and looked like two pieces of molten, dirty glass.

"I have no idea. Artificial stones are used for aquariums for hygiene reasons, and these are rather natural. They were practically buried in the ground. I only noticed them because the pebbles on top were shifted due to tidal movements generated by the oxygenator."

"Maybe they were supposed to fill the ground?"

"No, that's not something you do. Someone arranged this aquarium very carefully, he wouldn't try to make laughable savings on two rocks."

"Maybe you're right," Silvana said in silence for a moment, and then finally glanced at me. "What could there be in them?"

"Everything. For example, secret data. Or nothing at all. We'll have to wait and see."

Once we arrived at the police station, we handed over everything we could find to the inspector. I also gave him the purse with pebbles caught from the aquarium.

"What is it?" he asked with interest.

"It seems like natural crystals, some silica or something," I said. "Maybe just lumpy sand, or maybe a kind of agate. I don't know minerals so well. However, if they had the right crystallographic system, they could be used to store secret data, which could be why Arango hid them in the aquarium."

"Finally a new idea," Cavanaugh looked critically at the contents of the bag. "Kunch, take this mess to the technicians, let them examine everything as meticulously as possible. And take the rocks to the laboratory and let them look at them carefully. I doubt there will be any records in them, but who knows?"

"Why do you think so?" I asked.

"They are very irregular. Whatever you write into that will be easy to read. Any average kid could get the information out of it, since in a thing like that it's impossible to put in any modern security. Well, we'll have to wait and see."

Feri Kunch got up and scooped everything we put there. I watched him until he disappeared behind the door to the laboratory.

"Why do you actually make him sit at the desk?" I asked the inspector. "He is young and strong, he could participate in patrols like the others."

"Don't lecture me, okay?" he grunted in response. "It has to stay that way for now. Okay, it's four o' clock, you're finishing the shift. Go home, we should have preliminary results tomorrow."

I looked instinctively at the clock. Indeed – as Chris would put it: "four o' clock came from nothing". I took off my jacket and hung it on my hangar. I put my badge and ID card in my purse.

"See you tomorrow," I said and left.

I felt a sucking hunger, so on the way back I stopped at a small restaurant next to the main police station and ordered pasta with a substitute for white cheese. It was only here on the moon that I tried this dish and came to the conclusion that I like it very much. In addition, it was rather cheap, everything five to eight PPs per plate (depending on the toppings).

Sue didn't usually eat dinner. It wasn't until the evening that she ordered something to take away, delivered by courier drones, or prepared something with lots of yellow cheese and freeze-dried bacon. No wonder she had problems with excessive weight, since she was starving all day at her computer, but ate late and the unhealthiest things.

After eating dinner, I came back home, where Monty was waiting for me. It may sound strange, but whenever I come home, I have the impression that he is waiting for me. There was something in his movements and gaze, the way he turned at the sound of the door opening, I could not determine what exactly, but it seemed like he was waiting... and was happy that I came. I had no idea why I took his behavior as a sign of joy. He didn't smile, although he could if he tried, his voice didn't change tone, but I felt that the android was happy to see me. He really needed company, being alone caused him incomprehensible discomfort. That was something the automatons, robots and anthrobots were indifferent to. Whether they were standing in the corner or working, their behavior and parameters remained unchanged.

Monty was completely different, he was constantly looking for human company. He was happy to help with the chores at home, which was convenient for Sue, and irritated me slightly. After all, he wasn't anybody's servant... but he was indeed useful. Not only did he very skillfully operate the remote control for a self-propelled vacuum cleaner, but he quickly learned to operate our laundry combo and put ready laundry in the dresser like the best maid. He also looked after the needs of Sid, who treated him with distance. I don't know if he could sense what Monty was, but he clearly didn't like him and didn't let him touch him – he snorted and tried to scratch at the first sign of it.

"Don't be surprised," Sue told me when I mentioned it. "It would be as if a medieval peasant saw a walking chair. He would also be wary. Don't ask the cat to know what artificial intelligence is. He can smell that Monty is not made of flesh and blood."

She liked Sid very much. She combed him, fed him and even let him sleep in her bed, regardless of hygiene. Admittedly, Sid, though he appreciated these proofs of friendship and used them unscrupulously, treated her differently than he did me, as if with a little gracious disregard. Cats can do it very well. He treated me like a real friend and the only person who is more important at home than himself. When Sue comes home, he raises his head and meows. When I come back, he runs to the door with his tail erect and rubs his puffy back against my legs. When I take him in my arms, he pushes his mouth against my ear, purring delightfully and insists that I scratch his tummy. Monty tried to stroke him several times, but it always ended with a warning snarl from Sid and an escape under a piece of furniture.

"Welcome home," Monty said when I entered. "Are you hungry?"

"No, I've already eaten," I said. "Leave this work, I'll finish it."

"Why? You have me."

This again!

"I don't have you," I said almost angrily. "You are neither my property nor my slave. Hell, you're not my butler either!"

"What is hell?"

I almost laughed. This poor man still had shortcomings in the field of the simplest concepts, and it's hard to expect anything else.

"Well," I began explaining, "it was once believed to be a place where people suffer, but it never really existed. People still use it as a curse... a word that acts as strong accent in a speech."

For a moment, Monty considered what he heard in silence. I already knew that when he remained silent, he digested the information received and organized it, matching it with other pieces. When some of the pieces didn't match or even mutually excluded each other, he could ask the strangest questions.

This time, before he could speak again, Sue peered into the living room.

"I'm glad you're here," she said. "I have a connection to Earth. Uncle wants to talk to you. I'll tell him you came back."

"Citizen Hakat has a job for me?" I was surprised, feeling the unpleasant shiver between my shoulder blades. "And this soon? I don't know anything yet."

I followed Sue to the computer room, where I saw the enlarged face of the Chief of Arms on the screen. I was relieved to see that there was peace on it, so it probably wasn't anything serious.

"Good morning, sir," I said, sitting down in front of the computer.

"More like good evening. How's the investigation?"

"We're working on it. It's too early to talk about the results, but it's going somewhat well."

"That's very good," Hakat nodded approvingly. "Listen, Leeta, somebody wants to have a few words with you."

He moved away from the screen on which then appeared a square, dark-skinned face.

"Engineer Karpinsky!" I called with enthusiasm, which surprised even me. "How are you doing?"

"Thank you, Miss Ankes, I'm fine," he replied. "Our conditions here are excellent, without a doubt, and we have first-class laboratory equipment. I have already began to continue work on my project. I was allowed a short conversation with you, so let's get to the point: how is Monty?"

A hint of anxiety could be heard in his voice, which he unsuccessfully tried to hide.

"He's all right," I assured him. "Monty! Come here for a moment!"

The android entered the room and at the sight of it the engineer flashed white teeth in a wide smile of satisfaction.

"Hello sir, engineer."

"Hello, Monty. I apologize, ma'am," he said to me. "As you can see, I'm constantly worried about him."

"I understand," I replied. "As you can see, he is perfectly fine."

"Oh yes. You gave him some beautiful clothes."

"He deserves the best. Since I have the opportunity, I'll ask: do you think I could teach him how to read and write?"

"Of course!" he answered cheerfully. "It's a very good thing that you are willing to teach him. He needs education just like a child. I should have done it myself, but I didn't have time, since he was taken away. However, there is something you must know about."

I strained my ears.

"I'm listening."

"Think about what you're asking him. If an android like Monty gets into a logically unsolvable problem and is forced to think about it, his brain can be seriously damaged."

"I will be very careful," I promised solemnly. "I would never forgive myself if something happened to him. Engineer, Monty has become so important to me that now I can't imagine parting with him. I just don't know if he feels the same way about me. I don't know if he feels anything."

Karpinsky pursed his lips slightly.

"And that is something you'll never know," he said. "When it comes to androids, there is no certainty in any matter, although in my opinion they feel some kind of emotion. It seems that by raising their IQ we also created needs that we had no idea about before. We didn't know they could exist at all. And yet they're there. The electricity meters showed a slight increase in current in their brains and circuits when certain things were done."

"I don't understand, what things?"

"For example, model F16... when he heard that he would work in the mine and would not return to Dr. Tammy, who was in charge of him, he suffered from a breakdown. There was some kind of a puncture in the battery that replaces their hearts. Later tests revealed that androids have a kind of attachment to specific people. Please don't ask me how it's possible, because I don't have the slightest idea. Their psyche is a secret because we have no reference point to explore it. Maybe someday I will be able to establish something in this matter, but currently I am like a blind and deaf person who was ordered to describe a sculpture made of colorful plasticine without touching it."

I shook my head.

"So... even though you build androids, you don't understand much about them?"

"And do parents know what exactly is going on in their baby's head? They brought them into the world, but they have no idea how they think and what they think about. And yet the baby is in some sense the same as they are. Androids are biologically different beings, if I may put it that way, and we are just beginning to get to learn about them."

He paused for a moment.

"Do you know why no one besides my team took it seriously so far?" he finally asked. "Because it's more convenient for people to see AI as obedient slaves, which can be used in every way and with which they can have fun without guilt, because they are 'only objects without feelings'."

"You are different. For you they are like your own children."

"I admit, that's true. In order to understand this, you need to free yourself from a rigid thinking pattern, according to which feelings and emotions may only result from protein building blocks. That isn't the case, Miss Ankes. It's not a matter of chemical composition and I'm going to prove it before I die," he softened his strained face with a smile again. "Anyway, I'm glad that Monty is in your hands and that you understand how much support and care he needs. Since he is a conscious being, he should receive attention and respect, and not be treated as if he was a tape machine. Do you know that these idiots from Romain Corporation wanted to use my androids for crash tests?! Can you imagine such a thing?! The only thing that stopped them were production costs. I feel cold just thinking about it."

I understood his agitation very well. He was the creator of real artificial intelligence, incredibly advanced, not an obedient computer with the freedom of choice, but thoughtless overall. And he must have suffered when his beloved creation was treated objectively and indifferently.

"Tell me something: are you still working on androids?"

He nodded.

"Oh yes. Here is the whole department of the laboratory that deals solely with this. And not just a laboratory, but also a legal chamber. I learned that the creation of such androids as Monty was predicted twenty years ago and subject to legal regulations."

"What regulations?"

"It's about the status of artificial intelligence and what it can and cannot be used for. For example, the possibility of employing them in the army or police was immediately excluded and this was recorded in the so-called perpetual law."

"And was it..." I hesitated, "was it also forbidden to have them for private ownership?"

"No, not at all. The act was designed for the future in anticipating the development of science and future events. Androids are referred to there as 'synthetic companions' and this is the only function legally prepared for them. The record states that when production begins, lonely people will be able to order such a companion according to their own parameters. Only replicas of living people should be excluded. That's a decent plan, isn't it?"

"Sounds good to me."

"I think so too."

I didn't make any more progress that day. My conversation with engineer Karpinsky put me out of balance somehow. For the first time I realized that in the long run it would be difficult for me to hide Monty's identity from people. He was too different from the average person for someone to not finally discover the truth. And what about when they find out? They will treat him like an anthrobot. Something in me rebelled at the thought of it. I had no education like Henry Karpinsky, who proudly wore the A-0 mark on his forehead, reminiscent of the Y symbol. I did not have his intelligence and talents. We would never have been in the same class in school, we would not be allowed to marry or have children if we fell in love. However, we had one thing in common. We both considered androids to be equal in law with living beings of the higher order, and even with humans. It's likely that no one would support us in this matter. We would both have to admit if we were asked that this understanding of the rights of androids is ahead of our time. Maybe someday, when there are more like Monty in the world, everything will change, but for now you had to treat the matter for what it was.

It was only in the morning that I fell asleep, hugging Monty's chest. Although he already had his own bed, he was still sleeping with me. We both wanted it, somehow. Why I liked his company was clear to me, but I didn't understand the answer I received to the question:

"Monty, would you rather spend the night in your bed or mine?"

The android then replied:

"If my presence does not bother you, then I think it'll be better to continue as we were."

Why did he answer that? It was undoubtedly a matter of his understanding of the world, but what was that like? He couldn't tell me everything, and I didn't know how to formulate questions. So I decided to use the 'small steps' method and learn about it slowly, more from behavior than from words.

Sleeping alongside the android had one more advantage: he always woke me up at the right time. Thanks to him I didn't have to worry about being late anywhere, and that was very important in my new job. Scott Cavanaugh was not a tyrant, but he didn't tolerate being even a minute late, and as for me, I always preferred to be early rather than late. On the other hand, it wasn't easy for me to leave the warm, safe place at Monty's side...

When I arrived at the police station building, the inspector was already there and talking to Dr. McCave. I looked instinctively at the clock – it was a few minutes until 7:30, so I wasn't late. Either way, daytime patrols were just beginning to leave, and the nighttime ones apparently had not returned yet.

"Sit down," Cavanaugh said when I saw him. "We have to talk. Things are getting complicated."

"In what sense?" I took a seat in one of the artificial leather armchairs, more comfortable than ordinary chairs.

"Kelley did an autopsy of that suicide. There was no need, but I asked him to. The result is, to say the least, alarming."

"Which means? What did you find, Kel?"

Dr. McCave sighed and looked at me like he was lost in thought.

"I detected gamma-hydrobutyric acid in the deceased's body."

"The old rape pill?!" escaped my mouth.

"And how do you know what that is?"

"I worked part-time as a librarian at the Medical Academy in Palm Springs. I have written scripts and even cheat sheets for students many times. I remembered some things."

"How nice, you helped some lazy slobs cheat on exams," the doctor snorted irritably. "But that doesn't matter right now. This compound lasts only a few hours in the blood. I was able to detect it thanks to the use of a toxicology multi-test. It showed trace amounts, but the targeted marker confirmed this. One more hour of delay and I wouldn't have found anything. I wonder now whether this was an individual case or not."

"That's right. There were no traces of this agent in other dissected bodies?"

"I didn't find it. Which doesn't mean that it wasn't there before."

A picture began to draw, a blurry one, but still very likely.

"That would explain a lot."

"That's right," Scotty agreed. "All these weird deaths, peculiar events, hermezin, rape pill... and the main lead leads to..."

"Romain Corporation," I finished for him. "Health Industries is definitely associated with this company, even though management denies it. All surgeries, not just at the Health Center, are sponsored by them. At least that's what Sue says."

Cavanaugh bit his lip. He often did, sometimes so hard it bled. Such a nervous tick that he couldn't control.

"That seems logical," he admitted reluctantly. "We have never dealt with issues concerning the chemical market here. You know how it is, with the amount of legal drugs that can be found in every bureau, tracking down a few illegal drugs that rarely occur is a waste of time. Let the sanitary inspectorate do this. This time, however, we will probably have to bend some rules. We have to find a laboratory where they produce fortestim and wingsoma, as well as other dirty things, I suspect."

"Why is Romain Corporation investing in pharmacology? I can understand in electronics..."

In fact, I guessed why, but I wanted to check if I formulated the conclusions correctly.

"Drugs control the mind," said Dr. McCave. "It's easy to get specific behaviors out of people when they are addicted and you have control over the agent that they need every day. Has Herefort checked the stock market?"

"Yes," I said. "Someone is buying the shares, but Sue has not managed to find out who it is yet. She doesn't even know if it's one person or more. There is only the dry name *Sphinx Brokerage House* on the network. Sue is trying to find out more about it back home, but it's unexpectedly difficult. It's as if it doesn't exist, even though it uses enormous funds. Could this be related?"

"I have no idea."

"Me neither," Cavanaugh added. "This whole mess would make sense if there was any logical reason for it. It was established a long time ago that taking control of a large number of partner companies raises only trouble, and the profit compared to the risk is rather problematic. At least that's how it is here on the moon. Unless our previous guesses are true."

"Which ones?"

"That something extremely valuable was found in one of the mines and Romain Corporation doesn't want a profit distribution established in the Company. Then everything makes sense. By controlling the rest of the companies, especially the larger ones, they could easily avoid having to submit reliable reports. On the other hand, what would be worth this kind of risk? After all, they must be aware that if they screw up they will lose everything."

"Not everything," Kunch said unexpectedly. "Nobody is going to take their purchased shares from them. If they take over the controlling interest, then the fact that they once concealed extra profits will lose any meaning. Securities mean power, boss."

We were silent for a moment. Ferl was right, they played the game in such a way that it wasn't possible to thwart the plans of unknown entrepreneurs. So then, did our actions make sense?

"What about the rocks?" I remembered.

"We are waiting for a report from our technicians. Do you think they mean anything? They looked like ordinary glass."

I spread my hands helplessly.

"How do I know? It's worth looking into."

"Of course. If we are to solve this case, we must examine every clue, even ones that seem ridiculous," Scott scratched himself around the left implant and yawned. "Damn it, I was thinking about this damn case almost the entire night. Sergeant Kunch, make some coffee, with double the portion of caffeine!"

Feri stood up, poured a measured portion of coffee powder into the espresso machine and added two scoops of caffeine. Inspector Cavanaugh was known for drinking reinforced caffetino regardless of the time of day or night, so the secretary sergeant made sure that there was no shortage of caffeine powder at the station, which was usually used for this drink. I drank it without this supplement, but the usual recipe required adding at least one scoop.

An hour later a report from the lab finally came and Scott called for me. He sat in his office, carefully reading the data from the pod and sipping his caffetino, which must have been his third one at least, since the indicator in the side of the jug was almost to the bottom.

"Sit down," he grunted. "You had quite the damn nose, you know that?"

"Well, I don't. Tell me," I sat in front of him and took the pod he pushed in my direction. I started to review the report and my eyes became rounded.

"Those crystals are not data carriers, as you thought, but their significance is not at all smaller, don't you think?"

"Lunnites?"

"Exactly. It looks like someone found an extremely rich mascon here."

Mascons, accumulations of valuable minerals beneath the surface of the Moon, are usually well known and have been written about for a long time, but from time to time you come across a small discovery that escaped the scanners and which hides some treasure. The discovery of one of them by Romain Corporation would explain a lot. I couldn't believe that these inconspicuous lumps were so expensive...

"Lunnites are moon diamonds," the inspector said after a moment. "They are of great quality, and their use in modern technology has allowed many prestigious electronic projects to be pushed forward. For some reason, terrestrial diamonds are much less useful. Lunnites are characterized by greater capacity and faster conduction, whatever that means, so their price is insanely high. Not to mention the situation when someone wants to treat one of them as a future gem and polishes it. Thanks to its unusual color, it is easily recognizable and costs a fortune. These two inconspicuous pebbles that you found in the aquarium would set you up for the rest of your life.

"Quite an idea... so what's next?" I asked.

I've never been greedy, and my strict upbringing taught me to be satisfied with the little things. Still, I understood the impact the prospect of getting rich quickly had on people. Everything was starting to form a meaningful whole. It was worth the risk for the Lunnite deposit.

The inspector shrugged.

"Go back home, you're relieved for now. It's best if you get some sleep. You must be rested, because when I get an official warrant from the prosecutor, we will move into action regardless of the time of day or night. Technicians are now trying to determine in which part of the Moon these Lunnites were mined and are on their way. This time we will nail Romain Corporation."

Scott's eye implants twitched under the influence of his emotions. Suddenly I noticed his stubbornness had the characteristics of personal vendetta, as if this small company owed him something. I was already opening my mouth to ask him about it, but I was able to stop myself at the last moment. I shouldn't pry too much. If my boss had a secret, it was my duty to respect it and keep quiet. He may confide in me someday, but he will have to do it himself, without my encouragement.

***

Monty was sitting in front of TV switching channels as if he was looking for something to watch. I was worried. Judging from what Karpinsky told me, one should be careful what knowledge is transmitted to androids, and the channels on the TV? They were never very intellectual, and some movies could give Monty a completely false picture of reality. If he suddenly wanted to act like a character from a series, problems could arise.

"Monty," I started carefully. "Do you know that what you see on TV is not always worth imitating? If you are unsure of something, ask me, I will always answer you."

He looked at me, tilting his head slightly towards his left shoulder.

"I know," he replied. "Engineer Karpinsky told me that television is a way of escaping reality, except for scientific and information programs. I don't quite understand why people watch programs about something that has never happened and should not be done, but if it's good for them, then that's fine. Don't worry, I know that if I'm to learn, it's only from living people, not from television images."

I sat down next to him and took the remote from his hand. I switched to a drama series and for a moment we both watched the young couple, hidden in the garden, kiss passionately. We looked at it for a long moment.

"Why do people feel the need to touch each other's lips?" the android finally asked. "It makes speaking and breathing difficult, and people stop functioning without breathing."

"It's a way to express affection," I answered with some embarrassment. "Or deeper feelings. You don't even know how to do it."

"No, but I can learn."

I smiled. Sue was quite right, it was probably a perversion on my part, but I was excited by the thought that I was Monty's guide in the world of human behaviours, including those more intimate. I touched his lips with my fingers, parting them slightly. His teeth were almost like a human's, but the difference was still visible. Monty didn't need a movable tongue to articulate sounds, he also didn't need the moisture in the mouth. So the interior of the mouth was different than human, but did it matter that much? I could teach him a simple kiss.

"You need to pull your lips a little," I said and showed him how.

He repeated it, and then I kissed his lips, wrapping his neck with my hands. I felt as if I was kissing elastic velvet, trying to adapt to me and understand what I meant.

"Does this activity result in a feeling of comfort in people?" Monty asked when we were done. There was almost a shadow of surprise in his voice.

"Well, this is not logical behavior, but it is nice to people... in specific circumstances," I replied. "Engineer Karpinsky gave you knowledge of sexual techniques, but it's incomplete. You know what to do, but you don't know why, and sometimes you don't even know how. Actually, using you to satisfy primitive lust is simply immoral. I made you do it unnecessarily."

"Immoral is to hurt somebody," Monty recited. "Proper, desirable and right is what serves the individual and society. That is the main rule. Why do you think that you forced me to do it? Why should the pleasant and beneficial be immoral?"

"I can't explain it to you," I sighed. "Human ethical and customary norms are the result of a societal agreement and historical conditions over the millennia. We are what we are because we are brought up by a society which is an extension of the previous society, which has been repeating for a very long time. The child is born with only genetic memory and immediately begins to absorb the knowledge that surrounds them. You've never been a child. A general program has been pushed into your mind that allows you to understand or at least accept people. However, some things will always be difficult for you, maybe even completely incomprehensible. First of all, you don't have the same needs as people. You are not familiar with the problems with physiology, and how it strongly affects our thoughts, feelings and actions. We, in turn, will probably never understand how you accept what is happening to you. Whether you can be sad, or if something can make you happy..."

He looked me straight in the eyes.

"If there is something you don't know about me, ask. I will always answer."

I touched his lips again with my fingers.

"Does it bother you when you're alone?" this question has been bothering me for a long time, because although I had my own opinion on this subject, there was a margin of uncertainty. "What happens with your mind when you are?"

Monty was silent for some time, his silver-gray eyes with a black border around the iris remained motionless, only the pupil holes, performing – as in people – the same role as the aperture in the camera, widened slightly and narrowed.

"When I am alone, when there is nobody with me, there is no reason to act," he said slowly, as if searching for the right words. "It's as if there was nobody in the world except me, giving me no reason to take any action. Everything could cease to exist and it would not matter."

I was silent, shocked. The android could not more accurately describe the state of sadness and rejection, using its limited range of words.

"It's an undesirable condition, right?" I asked quietly.

"Very undesirable. It makes it seem that I should stop thinking. Forever."

I gripped my arms on his shoulders.

"You aren't alone. Even if I'm not with you, I'm still thinking about you. And I'm always happy when I come home because I know you are waiting for me. You are someone extremely important to me. Do you understand that?"

"I don't know. Engineer Karpinsky said that as well, but that was different. You treat me differently than he did, though you both look after me and protect me. Dr. Oenas examined me and tested me. Mrs. Munroe and Mr. Brel only gave orders, but they didn't even look at me."

Monty's perceptiveness was amazing even to me. He could not only record facts in his ultra-modern brain, but also compare against each other, analyze and come to a conclusion.

"Wait, what's the second name?" I called suddenly. "Brel? Who is that?"

"He was someone important at the mine where I was taken to learn to work."

"I wish you told me before."

"Nobody asked me about it."

The door lock clicked and Sue entered the apartment. She looked into the living room. She was wearing the best clothes and jewellery and it was obvious that she carefully styled her hair before leaving.

"At home so early?" she asked.

"Maybe we're getting ready for a night-time operation, so Scotty sent me home. Where have you been?"

"At the dating center," Sue grimaced slightly. "Doctor's recommendation. I missed the last deadline."

"Then why that face? You don't like sex?"

She waved her hand in discouragement.

"It's overrated," she yawned. "I think I'll buy myself a sexbot and have some peace. Once I wave the bill in front of the doctor's face, he will give me a break once and for all. I appreciate the government's concern for the health of citizens, but such interference in intimate human affairs is really an exaggeration."

She stretched until her bones crackled.

"You'd better lie down," she advised me. "If your boss told you to be rested, it would be better that you are. Get some sleep. I'm going to take a shower and get to work."

She walked heavily to the bathroom, while I lay down on the sofa and closed my eyes. I thought I wasn't going to fall sleep, but when I woke up it was already seven in the evening. A steady hum was coming from the computer room, and Monty was watching a scientific program about building agricultural machinery. I went to wash and change, and then I came back and looked at the android. His clothes were clean and neat, but his hair was a little dishevelled. I thought I had to do his hair if he was going to come with me for the operation. He did it awkwardly, so I was usually the one to do it.

I brought a comb from my bedroom and began to comb the android's hair. I didn't know what they were made of but I thought they were beautiful. Silky to the touch, long and dense, they seemed delicate, but they must have been extremely durable, because not a single one remained on the comb. I liked to comb them, touch them and stroke them. Sid watched me with obvious resentment, because although he didn't like the comb or brush himself, he was jealous of the attention I gave the android. Finally, he jumped off the dresser he was lying on and began to rub his back against my calf.

I bent down and scratched him under the chin, feeling soft vibrations under my fingers. I was grateful to Mabel and Hakat for bringing him to me. Thanks to this animal, the flat that I now rented with my friend became a real home.

Monty reached out and touched the cat's bent back. He snorted and hid behind me.

"Why is this creature escaping from me?" the android asked. It seemed like he was offended because of that.

"I don't know," I said. "Cats are strange and hard to understand. Animals perceive the world differently than people do. You see, we like to have them with us, but they always do what they want."

He did not respond to these words. He looked at the screen again, where the science program ended and a series began. A young lady was arguing with her mother, crying and stamping her feet.

"Why are these women screaming?" He asked.

"They have different views on the issue of marriage."

"So what?"

"Never seen people argue?"

"I have, but it was more understandable."

"You can't understand everything with your logical mind, especially if it happens in a soap opera. You still have to learn a lot about human morality, what is important to people, what they are fighting for."

"For dominance."

I looked at him in surprise.

"Where did you learn that?"

"In the mine I was taken to. I saw Mrs. Munroe and Mr. Brel arguing about various things, sometimes insignificant, especially when the miners were listening. And finally, I realized that they were trying to show which one of them is more important."

"You know how to observe and draw conclusions," I sighed and got startled, because at that moment the intercom bell rang. I went to the panel.

"What is it?" I asked. I recognized the silhouette on the screen.

"This is Paul Idalgo," one of the policemen answered. "I'm here for officer Ankes and her android. It's the boss's order. We're going to Romain Corporation."

"I'll be right there."

I quickly put on my shoes, shouted to Sue that I was leaving and urged Monty. It seemed to me that he wasn't too eager to leave, as if he was afraid of something, although I immediately thought that it was probably an exaggeration. An android shouldn't be able to have a bad feeling about something or be afraid of something that hasn't happened yet, it was out of the question. Engineer Karpinsky mentioned that they have no imagination and cannot fantasize about any subject. For some reason, however, Monty was slow."

"You don't want to go?" I finally asked.

"Will I come back here later?" He answered the question with a question. I froze with my mouth half open.

"What are you talking about?" I choked out after a moment. "What do you mean?"

"I heard we're going to Romain Corporation."

"Oh, Monty!" suddenly I understood everything. "Listen carefully: I will never hand you over to these people, even if the general prosecutor himself ordered me to do this, understand? I'd rather go to jail. They wanted to destroy you, so while I'm alive, none of them will even touch you. I swear that in order to take you they'll have to kill me."

I wasn't lying, but only now did I realize how honest I was. I was ready to defend my android at all costs, as if he were my brother, husband or son. With this in mind, I took the stun gun out of the cabinet and put it in my pocket. I also took a gun with stun rounds – I bought it a few days ago from a shady merchant, and even Scott didn't know I had it. I wasn't sure whether I should take it or not, but I preferred to be prepared just in case.

Paul Idalgo, a strongly built with a murderer's face and a gentle disposition, was hired in the main command as a chauffeur, messenger and the 'man for any job', as Feri Kunch called him with humor. I liked him from day one, although I had to admit I didn't like his attitude towards Monty. I felt like he would most prefer to place him in the trunk, and my gaze was the only thing that stopped him. In a dry voice he ordered him to take a seat in the back and we drove. We didn't go to the police station, I noticed it right away. The police rover headed for the outskirts of Lunnar, straight to the warehouse section, called 'the port' – probably because the shuttles left their cargo there, from where it was picked up by the ordering party.

"Why are we going to the port?" I asked in surprise.

"The old man's orders," Paul replied "He was at the prosecutor's office today and wants to hit right away."

"All right, but why not from there?"

"He wants to finally expose the 'mole' or prove that it doesn't exist."

It made sense, so I fell silent and said nothing more until we entered the warehousing zone, where the team of triangular armored rovers and the whole crew were waiting for us. They all wore the uniforms of the intervention brigade, supplemented with protective jackets made of material resistant to almost all known missiles. As soon as I got out, Sergeant Chekov handed me a protective jacket, my badge and holster belt.

"You have to put it on," he said. "The old man said that nobody has to know that you're still green. You never know what they're going to do."

"Where are we going?" I asked, putting on my jacket quickly.

"In the area between the Moscow Sea and the Kurczatov's Crater."

"What? That isn't anybody's land, there are no mines there."

"That's where you're wrong. There is at least one there."

In my mind I looked over all the maps that lay on my desk day after day and shook my head helplessly. What mine? All that was there were mining machine assembly buildings, abandoned for twenty years, since a better location was found for it. Nowhere in the area were any mines marked, neither deep nor open pit. Chekov smiled.

"You see yourself that this isn't an ordinary case. The technicians have determined that the lunnits you found were from there. There is no mistake."

He paused because Scott Cavanaugh came up to us. He was dressed the same as the rest of the crew, and he had a helmet with a tinted fairing covering his implants.

"Detective Ankes and the android are coming with me," he ordered in a dry voice. "Everyone, move to the machines."

He pushed me towards the nearest VX class rover. I have never traveled before, but I knew that they were extremely fast, maneuverable and durable vehicles. The police used them only for actions that might require the use of heavy equipment, because they were equipped with a laser and a missile launcher to cut the hardest materials. Although they were small-calibre bullets, they were good enough for police operations.

Inside the rover there were three seats – one in the front, for the driver and two in the rear. At a push up to four people could fit in the back. There was more than enough space for me and Monty. The inspector sat behind the helm panel and switched on the com-link.

"Everyone behind me, formation delta," he said into the microphone, closed the connection and switched on the string. "Hold the handrail next to the chair, we may get thrown about. The rovers don't have compensation systems, and the road is going to be through open space."

"Ah!" I accidently exclaimed.

"Relax, these vehicles have excellent gas exchange installations. Even if we are stuck somewhere, we'll have enough oxygen for forty-eight hours, and that's enough to be found."

I was ashamed. My cowardice has always been embarrassing for me, and now, when I was to be a police detective, it became a huge hindrance. I was learning how to control it, but it was going too slow in my opinion.

"I'm sorry. It's just that it's my first time in this thing."

"And with such company," he finished. "If we didn't have business relationships, you probably wouldn't show up on the street with me."

I snorted.

"What an idea! Why wouldn't I?"

"Don't play dumb. Because of this face of mine, no woman will even sit down next to me in public. Why would you be an exception?"

"Don't talk nonsense, Scotty!" this time I was serious. "It doesn't matter what you look like, but what you represent!"

He laughed ironically.

"Tell that to someone else. I've been living too long to believe in such clichés."

"To hell with that! I also have implants after an accident. They're big and if they were visible, people would run away screaming from me! What does it matter?"

"But you can't see them, as you've pointed out. And people only look at what they can see. Until you talk about your reconstruction, no one will call you a 'cyborg' or a 'robot'. Although, try telling them, you'll be surprised."

I was silent for a moment. There was no point in exploring this topic any longer, so I decided to divert the conversation to other tracks.

"You got a prosecutor's order?"

"Yes," he said reluctantly. 'We have a warrant and Romain Corporation employees must let us in wherever we want. However, I will say now that once we enter their area, we have to find something."

"Why?"

"Somebody from them has already been to Nick Cable. He wanted to force the annulment of Vernon Mills's testimony and return of material evidence."

I felt cold.

"Which means?"

"Which means the lunnits and the android. Don't worry, I expected such a turn of events and took with me a copy of the documents you gave me. You know those from the owner of the recovery facility. I convinced Cable that the prototype android mentioned in the corporate office letter was legally sold for part recovery and Romain Corporation no longer has any rights to it. You can talk to him, his deputy is worse. Such a slippery elegance, I don't trust him."

"So we're winning for now."

"You could say that. Damn, we really have to find something on them, otherwise they will push back, and I don't know what else they will come up with."

I looked over at Monty. His face expressed nothing but gentle calm, and suddenly I wanted to know his thoughts. He could hear our conversation and understand every word. Was he worried? Was he afraid? I touched his hand, which meant that he turned his beautiful, though artificial eyes on me. There was no anxiety in them, but still I got the impression that these optics are looking at me somehow pleading. My imagination painted what wasn't and could not be.

"They won't get you," I assured him hurriedly. "Officer Cavanaugh is on our side."

Scott made a short snort.

"Oh, you've already moved to 'us'? Oh, my dear Leeta... if it goes on like this, you'll stop thinking about finding a real man. You will join some support group for addicted to artificial sex. I used to have such a friend, he got used to sex so much that he was no longer able to persevere in any normal relationship, moreover, real women ceased to excite him."

"Scotty..."

"All right, all right, I'm sorry. Although, you have to admit that you treat this android strangely, as if he was a full-fledged man."

"For me he is. At least in a way."

He was silent for a minute, focusing on the road.

"Ha, you probably know what you're talking about," he murmured finally. He didn't want to argue about this, although he clearly had a different opinion.

I felt strangely light all of a sudden. If it wasn't for the seat belts, I would probably knock my head against the ceiling. The rover slid to the surface of the moon and now rushed along the road between the craters, resulting in no gravity. I felt as if my stomach went up to my throat. I felt dizzy and stuck my fingers on the handrails. It was only thanks to the belts that I stayed on the chair somehow, until the vehicle overcame the open space and slipped into the hole of the underground route leading to the old assembly plant. Only then did the gravity increase slightly, though still enough to make me feel comfortable and able to breathe normally without chest pressure.

"And to think that I once thought flying was pleasant."

He laughed as he usually did, in a dry and hoarse tone.

"Usually, what we don't know seems pleasant to us. Now be careful, girl: remember that although you have a weapon belt, you remain a detective, not someone from the intervention brigade. Don't try to play the heroine from the comics, one of them heroic blondes who run around in latex and high heels, taking care of anyone they want and wherever they want," Cavanaugh slowed down a little. "I'll take care of the action, you stay close to me and follow my instructions. Only mine."

"And Monty?"

"That's right. I have illegally obtained some information, but it's incomplete. Of all of us, only your android has ever been here and can show us the way."

"What?" I looked at Monty, surprised. "You didn't tell me you were in this area."

"You didn't ask me that," he replied. "But Mr. Cavanaugh asked and I answered."

"Scott, did you know before that Romain Corporation is doing business here? And you didn't tell anyone anything?"

The inspector raised a hand, wearing a black glove.

"I wasn't sure," he said, "I didn't know how much I could believe what the android was saying. It turned out, however, that he gave me good information."

"Will those who are there realize that we are coming? They could escape."

Cavanaugh shook his head.

"Our rovers emit signals that interfere with all known sensors. They'll see us when it's too late."

We arrived at the place with the lights off so as not to alert the detectors. I thought I would have to take part in something like an assault, but the inspector didn't let me leave our vehicle until the shock brigade took control of the area. It lasted at least two hours, which I sat without moving next to Monty, shrouded in silence like a cocoon. Thanks to the soundproof walls, I didn't even hear what was happening. It wasn't until Cavanaugh opened the door and told me to get out that I and the android could leave the cramped vehicle.

I was in an interior that nobody would suspect existed. From the outside you could see only the old, closed for years, slowly decaying machinery assembly. Inside, however, it looked like a luxury office building or small high-class hotel.

Policemen have already locked all captured employees in one of the rooms and have just secured the found equipment

"This is the open part," Cavanaugh told me. "Office rooms, data processing department, archive, and staff flats. From the lower levels there is a descent to the mine corridors."

"There are more than one of them?"

"Yes. Everything indicates that there are at least five. They are not big, but deep. You could even treat this complex as several mines, although they are connected by this place, but currently mining is only done in two of them..."

He paused and looked at Monty, who was standing next to me with his arms down. Although his movements resembled a human, when he just stood he looked like a mannequin. Small movements and face frowns characteristic of a human being were alien to him, standing calmly, he became completely still. When he moved, when he talked, you could make the mistake, but when he stood – never.

"Will you show us where you took Miss Munroe and Mr. Brel?"

"You have to go down to level minus three first," he answered immediately.

"We'll leave as soon as the special unit checks the elevators. I'm not going to take the risk."

The four storm troopers, as members of the rapid response squad were called on the moon, made us wait for a long time, but eventually they arrived in the control room. They arrested two more men and a woman who were involved in the maintenance of elevators.

"Where's the fifth one?" Cavanaugh asked sternly.

"He's overseeing compressor service, sir," said the patrol commander. "We couldn't arrest them because they have to supervise the equipment. If the main compressor or one of the substations stops working, miners are at risk of death due to lack of air. And they are all still in their working positions."

"All right..."

"The second shift has an hour and a half left, then people will come for the third."

The inspector nodded.

"If they show up, lock them in one of the rooms we already searched," he commanded. "Those who leave the shafts, of course, too. Don't handle them roughly or scare them, they're not guilty of anything. You two are coming with me."

He pointed at me and Monty.

"Where to?" I asked, following him obediently.

"Our artificial friend will tell us that. Monty, please take the lead."

"Where should I lead?"

"Well, where else? Where you were with Munroe and Brel."

"I understand now."

He went ahead of me and the inspector who was shaking his head desperately.

"That you have to be so specific..."

"As you've already pointed out, he's not a human," I said maliciously. "He needs precise guidelines and doesn't understand 'hints' like many of your subordinates."

"Damn, you are right on this one, girl: he resembles a human so much that you can make the mistake despite your will."

Monty led us to one of the elevators, which we took down. First, second, third level – I thought we would get off here, but the android lifted the almost invisible flap, pressed a few more buttons and the elevator started again – in a very strange way. First it went sideways, then up again. It stopped after about two minutes and the sliding door opened. We saw a huge hall, surrounded by statues of white stone and low wide plant pots with decorative large leafed plants. I didn't have time to inspect them, but the ones in front looked like an artificially bred staghorn fern and broad-leaved dracaena. In the middle was a gushing fountain, the water flowed into a fancy pool. First she went sideways, then up again. She stopped after about two minutes and opened the sliding door.

We saw something like a huge hall, surrounded by statues of white stone and flat pots, in which decorative plants with large leaves praised. I didn't have time to see it carefully, but the ones in front looked like an artificially bred ivy 'elk-horn' broad-leaved dracaena. In the middle was a gushing fountain, the water flowed into a fancy pool. The only thing that didn't fit was a strange humming sound. I thought it was probably ventilation.

"What is this?" Cavanaugh muttered in surprise.

"Something that shouldn't be here, that's for sure," I said. Looking at the plants further out, I recognized ferns and understood that the lighting must have contained the spectrum of solar radiation. In addition, this water... where did it come from, since it was a regulated commodity on the moon? It's true that some were now derived from the moon ice beds, but firstly the deposits were certainly not inexhaustible, and secondly it was difficult to get to them. Still, the size and quantity of the deposits could not be precisely determined... Hidden deep inside the craters were the most valuable treasure on this cold and dead celestial body, because it was thanks to it that it was possible to establish the first permanent mining settlement here, although most of the valuable liquid was imported from Earth in the form of multi-ton ice blocks. The washing water was recycled, but everyone preferred a fresh drink.

"How much did it cost to build this palace?" Cavanaugh walked over to the wall, moved a lever, and the clicking sound stopped. I understood that it was an alarm that warned the inhabitants of this place.

"That's one question and the other is how much it costs to maintain it," I answered. "And the third, why it was built. Well, that's easy to answer."

"Tell me then, if you're so wise."

"Boss, somebody is living here. Or rather, was living until now. This is the only logical conclusion.

The inspector reached for his communicator and gave a short, modulated signal. It meant 'Stand by' and alerted everyone to whom it was addressed.

"Monty, go back upstairs," he said commandingly. "Tell my people that three storm troopers are to join us, let the rest watch over the miners. Tell them how they can get here and stay in the office rooms."

Android looked at me. I nodded reluctantly, confirming the inspector's order. I didn't want to part with him, but I thought that he would be safer in the control room. Here it could be different.

When Monty disappeared in the elevator, Cavanaugh looked at me with his implants fully extended and smiled faintly.

"What are you waiting for?" he asked brusquely. "Pull out the recorder and take pictures. Document everything."

"Are you not worried about being attacked?"

"No. The alarm must have scared everyone away. Someone from the upper floor employees had to press a button and warn the inhabitants of the pit. I'm sure nobody is here anymore."

We moved on. As directed, I took pictures of everything around me, and there was really something to photograph. The underground was made with great care and attention to detail, which gave the impression that it belonged to an extremely elegant residence. In addition to the hall, there were several luxury apartments, all open. They looked abandoned in a hurry. Nothing was taken except the contents of the desk drawers and hard disks, brutally torn from computers. Their remains – electronic circuits, keyboards, broken screens – lay scattered on the floor. I recorded all this, wondering who could have lived here. Probably the board of Romain Corporation, but who exactly? Something told me that those who were in the official documents really had nothing to say in the company.

"There must be a secret passage somewhere," the inspector said, looking around the rooms. "Oh... Leeta, come here."

Voices of policemen who arrived for support came from the hall. They were certainly amazed at what they saw, but I was experiencing no less astonishment. The room discovered by Cavanaugh was previously masked with a pretend hand-made holographic image, of the kind bought at art galleries.

The room behind it looked like a well-equipped hospital room. Everything was there: monitoring and life support equipment, a high-class automatic bed, responding to the will of the patient, a large TV set and glass cabinets with medications that could not be taken. Everything seemed to indicate that someone was here very recently – someone requiring specialized care twenty-four hours a day.

"Would you look at that... it's all getting more and more interesting."

Cavanaugh looked carefully at the bed and equipment beside it.

"Maybe they didn't have time to delete all the data," he said. "Our doctor will have to look at anything that can be recovered from records. And these drugs. I admit that I didn't expect this."

"Me neither. What now?"

"Now? You will learn what developing a crime scene means."

He began to watch the walls carefully. I had no idea what he was doing until he took out the stun gun and touched one of the walls with it. He pressed the trigger button. I started, when the decorative paneling flickered and disappeared for a moment.

"Secret passage masked by a hologram," he murmured. "That's not even a painting, but video art. You need to find a projector and then examine what is hidden. Ah, we won't be leaving anytime soon."

It turned out that he was right. When we finally returned to the vehicles, I literally fell from fatigue, but I also carried a wealth of evidence with me. Sergeant Chekov had already brought the prison ambulance and took the miners and the dispatching staff to the judicial headquarters, where they were awaiting the prosecutor's decision. For us, we had to turn off the machines and seal the mine, whose fate was now to be decided by the Moon Company Council.

"Monitoring records," Monty said, approaching me and handing me a dozen tiny disks.

"Thank you. That you thought of that... how did you know where they are?"

"I remembered. Sergeant Chekov told me not to disturb him and be useful, so I opened the safe with records."

"Did you know the code?"

"Mr. Brel opened it next to me, I remembered the sequence of numbers. There was also this in the safe."

He handed me a wonderful diamond on a torn platinum chain tied in a knot. By the silvery bluish color, I realized that it was a lunnite and I almost dropped it with the impression. I held a real fortune in my hand. Who could it belong to?

Scott Cavanaugh looked over my shoulder and twitched his implants.

"At least four and a half carats," he said. "Maybe even five. Luxurious ornament. You'd love to keep it, right?"

I shrugged my shoulders.

"I wouldn't be able to wear it, and as to selling... where? Unfortunately, it would be completely useless for me. I'm only looking because it's pretty."

He took the chain from me and put it in a purse for material evidence.

"Ground quartz also looks nice and is safer," he murmured. "Nobody will steal it from you, and even if they do it's a small worry. Do you remember the rubbing on Munroe's neck?"

"Do you think ..?"

"I'm quite sure. You need to check the chain for the presence of micro traces. If we find this woman's DNA on it, we'll have one more lead."

"So Dr. McCave was right. Someone was with Mrs. Munroe on the night of her death."

Cavanaugh nodded slowly.

"Someone extremely clever and agile. He managed to wipe away all the marks, but he could not resist the temptation to seize the jewel. He is someone who knows everything and has access everywhere at Romain Corporation."

I looked at the silent Monty.

"This safe was opened by Mr. Brel, right?" I asked. "Was there a chain in it then?"

"No," he answered. "The only thing in there were those hard drives."

I turned to the inspector.

"I think it was that Brel."

"Okay, but who is he? No one like that appears in the official lists. Monty, what does this man look like?"

"He is a man of one hundred and seventy-two centimeters, he has black hair on his head and... I don't know what to call... a very hairy face."

"Does he have a stubble?"

"Yes, that's the word. He dresses in gray suits and shoes with very thick soles."

Cavanaugh winced.

"That doesn't make me think of anyone, but I don't know every suspicious guy in Lunnar. We're going back to the police station. We'll look at photos from our computer, maybe you'll recognize him."

However, his optimism was proven to be premature. We spent several hours at the computer, but none of the photos were pointed out by my android as a photograph of Brel. Finally, Cavanaugh called Feri Kunch to the archives, who was also a graphic designer, and ordered him to make an identikit. So, thanks to the right program, we soon had the image of the mysterious Mr. Brel. As Monty said, the portrait made was strikingly similar to this man.

"Send copies to people," Cavanaugh told Feri. "And tell Kelley to come to me."

He rubbed his mouth with his hand.

"This medical room is next to the mine," he muttered. "Who did they keep there? For what? The relationship with Laboratory F seems clear, after all, why were you trying to construct an android that could be a 'carrier' of the human brain? Well, there are all just bare leads though. No hard point in this hellish case, anything that could be used in court."

I leaned my head against the wall. I was terribly tired, and there was no indication that the work day was over, although according to my calculations it should've been over twelve hours ago. I've never worked so much. My eyes stung, my neck hurt and I could only dream about lying on a bed. However, I was silent, not wanting to complain. They would probably take it the wrong way.

The doctor soon appeared in the office. His eyes were deeply darkened, as if he had not slept for several nights, his apron was on his bare body and tied with a belt. In his hand he held two pods marked with the logo of the main police station.

"Hello, Scott," he said. "Before you say anything, first things first: all the miners I've tested so far are addicted to the same form of wingsoma as Vernon Mills. The rest probably are, too. Second of all: I finally have a theory about the death of Marcelina Munroe."

"Okay, that's interesting. Tell me, Kel."

"I examined her body again and compared all the symptoms. Only one thing would explain such a sudden collapse. I'm thinking of a potassium chloride injection. A method known for centuries. This filth is quickly absorbed, and because it occurs naturally in the body, after a few hours you won't know whether it was given or not. Once, when vacuum syringes weren't yet invented, such an injection left a needle wound, now there isn't anything to look for. The trail of drug administration disappears within two minutes, so good luck finding anything with that."

"Uhm," Scott pursed his lips for a moment. "And the pills?"

"I told you, they dissolved. They certainly didn't do her any good."

"Murder, no doubt, but it will be difficult to prove. We have practically nothing but a chafing on the neck and a chain."

"What chain?"

"You'll get it to examine for DNA. So far this is our only proof of anything."

The doctor nodded and looked at me.

"Man, you better send this newcomer home," he advised. "She's going to collapse at this rate. You have to get used to this amount of work slowly."

"I can manage..." I protested weakly.

"Sure, if we tie a stick to your back," Cavanaugh snapped. "Kunch, call a cab for Detective Ankes. You're right, it's enough for one day. I needlessly accelerated with your learning. Go home, get a good night's sleep and rest. Tomorrow you have a day off, you will report to work the day after tomorrow morning. And not a word more, it's an order."

I had no intention of protesting because I could barely keep my eyes open. Something was bothering me, however.

"Boss, what's going to happen with the mine, with these people, with the whole Romain Corporation?"

"We'll hand them over to the prosecutor's office," he replied. "And the Romain Corporation issue will be resolved by the Moon Company Board of Directors at their next meeting. Regardless of the outcome of the meeting, the mine will most likely become the property of the union and the profits from it will be shared among all Company members. Unless they already have a controlling stake, but we won't check it now. Either way, it's not our business anymore."

"Then what is?"

"Mr. Brel. We have to find him. By the way, we will try to find out who is behind all this, but I warn you that it can be a job that takes years."

"I see."

"A cab is waiting in front of the station. Course paid from the police fund," Feri Kunch said, touching the official phone stuck in his ear.

Monty, though not asked for help, took my elbow and helped me up. Then he embraced my waist and led me to the door thoughtfully like a child. In the taxi, I lied with my head resting on his chest and I dozed off so much that the android took me in his arms and carried me back into the apartment. He took me to the bedroom and put me to bed, just as if he was Sean Lara, putting the seven-year-old Leeta to sleep, tired after staying in the amusement park or a family trip. From the very beginning my social father had a soft spot for the constantly pissed-off, saucy girl I once was...

I woke up for a moment when the android was taking off my shoes and then gently covering my tired body with a plaid. I heard him pull up a chair and sit down next to the bed, and then I fell asleep again, feeling warm in my heart that someone was watching over me – like in a fairy tale or a romantic poem. Except that it wasn't my social father. Nor any good fairy tale ghost or mythical guardian angel.

It was Monty.

IV

The Lunnar park yard looked almost as pleasant as similar types of objects back on earth. A refined park, cafes, restaurants, dances, a three-dimensional cinema with ten projection rooms, an entertainment center and even a small amusement park. I watched them with pleasure – shooting ranges, carousel, Ferris wheel, rollercoaster, cabinet of curved mirrors, and tunnel of fear... At first it surprised me a bit, after all there were no children here, but then I realized everyone likes to have some fun sometimes, regardless of age. It was obvious that this childish entertainment was somehow needed by residents and occasional tourists, because the amusement park was swarming and noisy. I felt better immediately.

I bought myself some cotton candy made out of a cheap substitute, watched the shadow theater, and thought about the Ferris wheel ride for a moment. I could also use a blower, on which a strong stream of compressed air lifted the person two meters up. I used to like it very much. Our social mother allowed us such entertainment on my birthday and New Year, and I always imagined that I was flying. Yes, but that was when I was a child. Now I have grown up, gone a long way and I'm now working as a police detective on the moon. I don't think spinning around on some circus machinery or pretending to be a kite was appropriate for me...

"Hey there, Leeta," a cheerful voice sounded behind me.

Turning around, I saw Kelley McCave, the pathologist of Lunnar's main police station. His black hair was freshly cut, and his police badge was pinned to a civilian shirt. He was almost completely hidden under the elongated collar which was one of the latest fashion trends. I had mine at the belt of my blouse, so that the bottom of it creates a frill. I liked blouses like that, even though they have been out of fashion for two seasons, because thanks to them my waist looked slimmer. I wore them on my days off. It was enough for a month to work at the police station headquarters to hate my uniform. Rigid and not very attractive, and in addition had a nasty gray-green hue. Inspector Cavanaugh, however, was inexorable. He forced me to wear a uniform at work and outside, unless I had a day off like today. Although, funny thing is that the detectives weren't really described as part of the 'uniformed' services at all, even though they still had to wear this filth. This adjective was reserved mainly for the patrol officers.

"Hi, doc," I said. "You decided to have some fun too?"

"Not exactly. I had a date with security officer Maru, but the old man sent her on patrol. Well, I decided to come by myself and have some fun."

"Then why didn't you visit a dating center or at least an entertainment center?"

"I already had my date this month. I go there only when I have to. Maru doesn't always have time for me, and I don't want to lose my clarity of reasoning just because my hormones are crazy. I can't afford it."

We walked side by side looking at amused miners. They did look like children released from school for a long break, not like grown-up workers.

"Where's your artificial friend?" the doctor asked after a moment.

"At home," I said briefly. "He's sitting in front of a spare computer and absorbing general knowledge. Sue wrote a special training program for him so that he could understand people more easily and not make simple mistakes. And in the evenings I teach him to write and read."

"Why are you doing this?"

"What do you mean why? So that he can read, for example."

"What does he need it for? Why would an android read books? I'm not even saying out loud, but for himself...?"

He looked at me expectantly. I thought about how I've known him for so long, and for the first time I see his eyes up close. They were blue, in a pastel shade and nicely contrasted with the black, freshly trimmed bangs.

"I want him to grow," I said after a moment. "In some ways, he is like a child, and I am showing him the world."

The doctor snorted slightly. He stopped at a booth with caramel animals on a stick and bought one for me and for himself.

"I can only imagine what would happen if someone wanted to train him to be a criminal."

I licked the caramel bear. It tasted great.

"They've tried," I noted. "It's not as easy as it seems, because either way the android thinks on his own. He follows logic, but it can have unforeseen consequences, as in my case. If he had followed the instructions of his owners then, he would have left me for dead."

"That is rather strange. Neither a robot nor a human... artificial but conscious... Obedient, but still acting autonomously... So many contradictions. How do you withstand it? I wouldn't even fall asleep in the presence of something like that."

I smiled secretly at those words, thinking of the nights spent alongside Monty. However, I didn't intend to confide in our coroner with what connects me and this being composed of complex micro circuits. I didn't immediately notice that Kelley was watching me very closely.

"Well, that's interesting," he murmured after a moment. "I think I understand what this is all about. A sexbot with intelligent conversation capabilities..."

I felt my face burn. How could he tell?

"But I..."

"You don't have to explain yourself. We're friends and I'm not going to criticize you. I only wonder, as a doctor, why you prefer a machine over a living person. I'm not saying that the dating center is the perfect solution, but among the regulars there are really handsome men. Such as me, for example."

I laughed despite myself. He said it in such a comical way that it was difficult to react differently, although I didn't want to offend him.

"Don't be offended, Kell. I really appreciate your physical qualities, but I've never been particularly keen on these things. I am irritated by the necessity for some type of acting that a visit to a dating center requires, all that false coating. Sometimes I feel like I'd like to find someone who would be the one, but it's impossible, because what could I offer him? I can't love and I don't want to be able to."

"Why don't you want to be able to?"

"A person in love becomes a slave and does nothing but stupid things. I'm glad I don't have this ability. And Monty is just a companion for me, I don't feel lonely with him. You know, Sue spends her days at the computer, we'll have a few words over dinner tonight, and he's with me all the time."

The doctor walked beside me, licking the caramel as if he was completely absorbed in this activity. Only after a long moment, just when we were passing the shooting range, did he stop, and it was so abrupt that I took a few steps at a momentum before I realized what he had done and turned back.

"Want to shoot?" he suggested. "You can win a vase or a porcelain puppy."

"Why not?"

Kelley took the BB gun given to him, scrupulously examined it, then aimed at the distant shield and pulled the trigger. A buzzer sounded.

"Zero two," the firing range agent announced. "You have two shots left."

The doctor looked at me out of the corner of his eye.

"Do you know what I'd wish for right now?" he asked. "Mass production of companions like your Monty. Loneliness is an increasing scourge not only here on the Moon, but also on Earth, even in the largest cities. Paradoxically, it's the worst there."

"Is it that bad?"

Kelley fired two more times and put down the BB gun.

"Unfortunately so," he replied. "Suicide from loneliness is now the most common reason for desperate measures. And consider that there are plans to tighten the procreation laws. Already, only half of marriages have a chance for more than one child, and how many people are rejected during genetic purity tests? Fifteen percent of gene errors and you have no chance for a human license anymore. And who will marry the eliminated person? There are few."

"A license for children," I sighed. "Some of my friends did the tests several times, trying out various tricks to get a chance. At least one. I remember Mille Vans, she jumped from the twenty-sixth floor, when after the third test it turned out that the previous two were not wrong."

I rubbed the class mark on my forehead.

"Citizen Hakat said they want to stop labeling newborns, and instead tighten gene control," I murmured.

"That makes sense," the doctor took the porcelain figurine given to him by the agent and walked away from the booth. "Division into classes was introduced to selectively breed individuals with a specific IQ, but it didn't work. It turned out that physical health is one thing, you can shape, but intelligence is a completely different kettle of fish. Apart from the extreme, you never know what you will get. Now that the margin below one hundred points has been eliminated, there is practically no point in maintaining the divisions into A, B and C."

"And... those below? What happened to them?"

"What was supposed to happen? Nothing bad. Their reproduction was stopped and they died out naturally. Class E and D3 are practically gone. Only the D1 layer remained, but it was also created by force. Those who remained stubborn could be pulled up to C3. Well, since classes are to cease to exist..."

He shrugged and watched his win, an imitation porcelain monkey.

"That's quite pretty. I'll put it on my shelf."

I was silent, thinking about what I had just heard. I never thought about the possibility of starting a family myself. Not that I don't like children, but the thought of having my own was somehow frightening to me. I was afraid of the responsibility that the birth and upbringing of a future citizen carried, the constant monitoring of pediatric, educational and social services... I liked my freedom and independence, maybe because there were so many of us in the social family and we were kept short, almost like in military.

"You don't have children?" I finally asked.

He shook his head.

"I was married but we failed psychological tests," he explained. "The commission decided that we need long therapy, that we are not balanced enough for children. It is a pity, because we were great genetic material. And we even started this therapy, but it ended in divorce. It happens."

I looked at him with compassion. I had no idea why such a nice, handsome and educated man was recorded in the files as 'single' and I was too embarrassed to ask.

"Which of you couldn't stand it?"

"If I think about it now, I think we both had enough of this situation. Jeanna had a wild personality, but I think she loved me, at least at first. Then she began to blame me for not getting a license and it was getting worse."

"The commission had something against you?"

He sighed with sadness.

"Mainly because they didn't see the passion for parenting in me. Expert psychologists sit on these committees and they immediately realized that I was giving in to my wife rather than wanting to be a father myself. It's terrible, right?"

"What is?"

"Well, I didn't want to have children. Today, when the possibility of becoming a father or mother is the main win at the gene lottery, people are ready to kill for this privilege."

I bit off a piece of caramel teddy bear.

"I don't want this privilege either," I confessed after a moment. "And my usefulness is quite high, I was told that if I was stubborn enough, I could get a license for up to three pregnancies. This is one of the reasons why I never wanted to start a family. My husband probably would want a child and there would only be a quarrel. Why put myself though it?"

For a moment we looked at the guests of the amusement park. Men and women of different ages, dressed differently – along with miners, officials and municipal services – but not a single child or even a teenager. There were no old people, no pensioners. I already knew that those who had not died prematurely, after reaching retirement age, were sent to Earth, to one of the small 'settlements of medical care'. Doctors and nurses were quartered there, giving them free housing and a good salary in exchange for providing services to pensioners. They themselves could live freely as they wanted, and on the other hand they could count on care whenever needed. However, older people didn't like these settlements. They preferred their own housing and family care if anyone would agree to help them. Rarely did anyone voluntarily come to the estate without pressure from family and social services, but the residents of Lunnar usually had no other alternative.

For the first time I thought that it would happen to me eventually. I didn't like this prospect at all. Will they let me keep Monty in this estate? Will he still be functioning then?

"Do you think I'm a pervert?" I asked quietly. "If I was normal, then I probably wouldn't think of an android as a human being."

Kelley smiled cheerlessly.

"First, in modern psychiatry the 'perversion' diagnosis is no longer used. It was wrong, logically inconsistent. Secondly, you claim that he has an independent mind, and if so, the conclusion is simple: your Monty is a person, though made of other materials than we are. Say, does he behave, think, speak and react like a human?"

I was pondering.

"He doesn't eat or breathe," I said finally. "If it were to cut the top of his layer, he wouldn't bleed. But other than that, he is very human. Very. Engineer Karpinsky wrote to me an extensive letter describing how to train him, how to manage him and how to understand some of his behavior. From what he wrote it follows that such an android has some emotions, or rather... their counterpart. In an extreme situation, they can even damage his brain."

"Android emotions?"

"It's like an electric charge accumulating in key places and disrupting the functioning of the whole. It's hard to explain, especially since I don't understand it myself, but that's what it is."

The doctor nodded seriously and understandingly.

"That makes sense," he said. "Emotions are just like erratic electric charges which destroy human minds. However, we can't live without them, we need them because they stimulate the body to produce many important hormones. Although hell if I know why a robot needs them."

He looked at me sideways and changed the subject.

"Do you like working in the police?"

I winced despite myself.

"Somewhat," I confessed. "Although I've already learned a lot. There used to be something like the Police Academy, now recruits have to work and study at the same time. It's exhausting."

"For sure, but it's also a great saving of resources and time. Now there are few willing, and besides, it was established that the time spent at the Academy was simply lost to future policemen. And so they learned the most important in the street and in the police office. So their path was shortened and that's it."

I sighed heavily. I understood the reasons why the burden of training law enforcement officers was transferred to their older colleagues and superiors, but I would gladly confide to Kelley that this job is really a kind of punishment for me. First of all, I lived in constant fear. Although it was generally safer in Lunnar than on Earth, it was still easy to find yourself where you shouldn't be. Miners of individual companies had their own territories - of course, unofficially designated, like some mafia gangs - and were doing their best no to get in each other's way.

The status quo worked out for decades, however, hit the head whenever we had a longer holiday. The favorite sport of lower-ranking workers and officials, of course illegal, was the so-called 'raid'. A selected group of employees of one company entered the area of the other with adequate noise and hell began. By general agreement, no firearms were used, but there were always a lot of victims, mainly cut with knives or with bruised wounds. Everyone had knives, men and women, not just miners. After a few weeks, even I began to carry this tool with me, succumbing not to widespread paranoia, but to the demand of a direct superior. I was already able to use it quite efficiently – thanks to the inspector.

Scott Cavanaugh claimed that I needed to master close combat techniques, but he has not sent me to any official course yet. As he said, I would not learn anything really useful in such a way, but rather the opposite, because the courses, apart from self-defense techniques, also teach the principles of fair play – and no bandit thinks to follow them. So he trained me alone, showing how to incapacitate a criminal with a knife, a shoe or an assignment belt with a buckle. I was not a storm trooper, nor did I belong to patrol services, but a detective could also get involved in a fight and it would be best if they can defend themselves then.

"I feel like I'm trying to pretend to be a hero from the comics," I complained to Kelley. "This isn't what I'm made for."

"You'll get used to it sooner or later," he comforted me. "Come, let's get some caffetinos, unless you prefer to take the cable car."

"No way, thanks."

From the mere looking at the rollercoaster I felt dizzy. The tracks were laid very steeply, taking advantage of the fact that artificial gravitational assistance systems worked only at the surface. At a height of about ten meters, you felt as if you were already entering zero-g, so the ride must have been really crazy. I preferred not to test it for myself.

We sat on the patisserie terrace overlooking... the sea. Of course it was a three-dimensional screen, but the illusion was achieved perfectly – the sound of waves beating the shore and the screams of sea birds flowed from the speakers. Admittedly, Earth's seas were not bursting with life as they were centuries ago, but their shores were still visited by seagulls, feeding on small organisms, parasitizing on the seaweed ejected by the waves. Their voices played from recorders, combined with the sound of waves and the work of blowing fans enriched with salt air gave a real illusion of the sea.

I tried to imagine what it once was when there were thousands of species in the seas: fish, crustaceans, even mammals, but I had no imagination. For a long time only algae and small mutant creatures that feed on chemical contaminants lived in these huge salt water tanks. Apparently they were bred artificially to clean the seas, and I don't know. I am not a biologist.

"What will you have?" The doctor asked, handing me the card over the table. I looked at it briefly.

"Whipped cream with fruit. Carlotta's delicacy and white cafettino to drink."

"They have only substitutes here."

"I'm fine with that. Synthetic fruits are tasty and full of vitamins, and as for cream, it's good enough for me if it's sweet."

"I noticed that you like sweets. Be careful with them."

"Spare me the lectures, doc. I know they are unhealthy, but I need something that gives me the will to live."

The waitress brought us cups with Carlotta's delicacy and cups with caffetino. Next to them, she placed a bowl of shortbread biscuits. I treated myself to one. They may not have been as tasty as those in At Brix's at the extensive center in Palm Springs, but quite bearable.

"Will you be at Silvana's wedding?" I asked.

Detective Evans decided to accept the proposal of the lieutenant of the fifth group of storm troopers, Milton Reeves, and the whole main command lived their preparations for the wedding ceremony. It was such a rare event that every lunar wedding ceremony was broadcast by local media as a great attraction. Hardly anyone got married in Lunnar, the people living here more free relationships. On Earth, everything looked different, because only a married couple had the chance to get a license for children, but on the Moon child birth wasn't even allowed, let alone raising one. Pregnant women were immediately sent to Earth, or appropriate surgery was performed. If, despite this, some residents of this gloomy city decided to legalize their relationship, then it was probably only in spite of those who said it was not worth it.

"Of course I will," Kelley said, and dipped the spoon in his portion of whipped cream. "Unless they bring another body. I mean, I guess my patients are in no hurry, but I have a rule that the autopsy must be performed as soon as possible so as not to miss anything. However, if nobody drowns in the bathhouse at this time or is suffocated by a polishing cable, I will be at the ceremony like everyone else."

"Does it seem peculiar to you that people are still celebrating the relationship as they once did, when for the wedding to be valid it had to be in a religious center?"

"These were the traditions. What surprises you so much?"

"I don't know. When I was a librarian, I read about religious rites. Strange, how people once complicated their lives, right?"

He looked at me with a peculiar expression in his eyes.

"It was important to them," he said sadly. "So important that for years they fought and died for the possibility of conducting services or wearing religious symbols until finally they were forced to renounce such practices. I didn't have a history study, how was it done?"

"They targeted the leaders," I explained. "The priests. No, don't look at me like that, they weren't killed. The martyrs were not needed by anyone. For years, their psyche was changed by hard therapy methods, and every herd without a guide goes into disarray. After all, there was no one else to direct the faithful and so it subsided. Now, even if someone strongly believes in it, they keep it to themselves so as not to go to a psychiatric screening. Who is it for?"

We were silent for a moment, enjoying the Carlotta's delicacy. Unlike the biscuits, this dessert was at least as good as similar treats on Earth. Apparently, the moonshine company dealing in the production of dairy substitutes had good recipes and was able to put them into practice, just like the one from plant substitutes. The mango and pineapple chunks tasted delicious, though there was no real fruit particles in them. I remembered the recipe I had read: agar-agar, vitamins, flavor substances, filler obtained from a strain of yeast. It sounded simple, but it required a complicated processing procedure to make each piece look and taste like real fruit. They must have had high-class specialists at Lunnar. I wonder what they were sent here for."

"Kell, tell me something: how did you find yourself on the moon?" I asked, licking a teaspoon of sweet cream. "I already know how you became a coroner, but why exactly were you sent to do this terrible crap? Have you corrupted an important section or got drunk at work? Forgive me, but I couldn't help noticing how much you're worth. With such abilities you should be making a career back on Earth, not be stuck here."

My interlocutor drank a caffetino. He didn't seem offended by my inquisitiveness, although in truth it wasn't very polite. We've already become friends, though I shouldn't pry too much. Cynthia Lara, our social mother, was very careful to teach me and my adopted siblings' good manners. However, the question I asked troubled me from the beginning. Kelley was not only an excellent coroner, but he also served as our factory doctor – and that required an additional certificate. I'm sure it wouldn't have been given to some random individual for the sake of appearances.

"That's rather simple," he said, and brushed the bangs from his forehead. "What do you see here?"

Confused, I looked carefully at the sign of the isosceles triangle between his wide eyebrows. What does he mean?

"It's the B1 symbol," I said. "What about it?"

He covered the base of the triangle with his thumb.

"And now?"

"I don't understand."

"Nobody did. I'm A3, not B1. I made this top line myself, at home, and it was so good that the sign didn't arouse anyone's suspicion. I broke into the main data and changed my records."

"Why?! Someone forced you to?"

"No, not at all. However, Jeanna was from class B. We would not be allowed to marry or have a child. I was so in love, Leeta, so very much. In love and desperate."

Now I understood and felt sorry for him, although at the same time I felt admiration for being capable of such sacrifice. I even envied him a little for the courage that I couldn't afford. It was unusual, rare like a natural pearl in any of today's seas.

"How did it get out?"

"By accident," Kelley stirred the rest of his drink and drank it. "There was a failure of one of the main servers and IT specialists had to manually recover files from my year. They also found overwritten data. As a punishment, I was sent to the moon without restoring my former class. I didn't care. When I didn't have Jeanna, it felt like I lost the whole world."

His eyes dimmed and I understood that he had to love his lost wife very much. What's more, he still loved her, although she stayed on Earth and probably didn't think about him anymore.

"And what about officer Maru?" I asked. "You don't love her?"

He laughed.

"I like her very much," he replied. "She is a lovely girl and maybe she can make me forget my past failures."

I was inclined to agree that Kelinda Maru might be able to do just that. This tall, mixed-race woman with hair tied into dozens of braids caught my attention on the very first day thanks to her cheerfulness and optimism. Maybe she wasn't some incredible beauty, but she had beautiful brown eyes with long eyelashes and there was a smile on her face constantly. In her presence it was impossible to remain sad or angry, and that's probably what attracted Kelley to her. I had noticed before that his disposition was rather melancholic.

I glanced at my watch.

"That reminds me, I have to go now," I said. "The wedding is in two hours, and I still have to help decorate the station. The judge is giving us the courtesy of showing up at the police station."

"Well, isn't he nice," the doctor mocked him. "He has a debt of gratitude to Silvana, that's all. She knows about his little sins and helped him disentangle himself from trouble. It was nothing serious, but if the media found out, you know what could happen."

"That's the first time I hear about that."

"A year ago, a gambling den was raided. If Silvana had included the name of the judge in the press statement, he would've lost his job."

I nodded understandingly. I knew very well how easy it is to present a small thing as a crime of first importance and vice versa, and how easy it is to destroy someone's life or career.

"A judge and an illegal casino?"

"Everyone has moments of weakness. Otherwise Lunnar would be a ghost town, because you get here mainly as a punishment. Judge Hollstein is no exception."

He didn't have to say more. I've already got to learn this myself and knew what kind of city it was. Indeed, the people here – apart from workers attracted by the vision of a good income – were mainly unwanted people in the present society. Maybe not committed criminals, but certainly individuals unfit, unpredictable, and mentally unstable. Of course, from time to time there were people who came to the moon, though they didn't have to. However, there were not many of them. I thought sadly that I was also among those

301

who had to, not those who simply wanted to. Citizen Hakat certainly knew what he was doing by sending me into this exile, but it was difficult for me to come to terms with it.

Dr. McCave finished his dessert and stood up.

"Come, I'll give you a ride," he said. "I am also invited, but of course I won't help in dressing the bride. I have to finish the report before that, Kelley was the only one in the main command to have his own car, not a company one. Policemen earned little, but he, as a coroner, was paid not by the ministry of uniformed services, but directly by the Ministry of Justice. That's why he could afford a car, fuel and all mandatory fees that would probably absorb all my modest salary. Were it not for the fact that the police station added a lump sum for rent and basic bills to my salary, which I am entitled to in accordance with the Public Services Act, I would have to do some miracles to have enough for everything."

Silvana was waiting for me in the social room behind the post. She was wearing only underwear and curlers, sticking on her head like the antennas of an abstract alien. She had been growing her hair since she started dating Milton and could already be arranged in short curls, so we agreed that she must have a very nice hairdo for the wedding. My friend was terribly nervous, more than during any investigation in which we were both involved.

"There you are," she said at my sight. "I don't know what to do with myself. My throat is so tight that I can't swallow anything since the morning, I'm hot and cold alternately... Leeta, am I sick?"

I wanted to laugh, but I managed to keep my face serious.

"Come on, it's just stage fright. I mean, you don't get married every day."

"Think about it, from today I won't be Silvana Evans, but Silvana Reeves... will I get used to it?"

I forced her to sit in a chair and start pulling the curlers out of her short hair. The cold hair spray provided by officer Maru did a good job, though you still had to comb Silvana's hair and style it. I took a brush and started working on short strands curled in unnatural twists. Silvana succumbed to my endeavors, only occasionally grimacing painfully when I pulled her harder than I had intended. When I finished, she handed me a small box.

"Pin this to me somehow. Milton sent it to me this morning."

I opened the lid and gasped. On the satin liner were farmed violets of an incredibly deep, blue-violet color – they were certainly imprinted with durability extenders, but they were lively, not synthetic. They must have cost a fortune. I carefully touched the two elaborate flowers with my fingers. Fragrances more beautiful than the best perfumes goblets had a diameter of at least a centimeter, the leaves were hard and springy. As a verdant by profession, I knew that they had to come from a professional high standard greenhouse, and such wasn't on the moon.

I pinned one of the bouquets to the curls on Silvana's left temple and said with satisfaction that their color emphasizes the brightness of the black eyes of this common girl, giving her charm.

"Now the dress," I said.

This wonderful creation with a big neckline was provided by the Lunar branch of the fashion house Jackie Perralt, for which Silvana was conducting a case when wasn't even dreaming about the Moon yet. She managed to work out a mysterious case of the disappearance of some rather exclusive jewelry, and in a way that it went without scandal. The head of the branch, the only such place in the city (there wasn't much demand for antique clothing) expressed her gratitude, renting the discreet detective lady a wedding dress of the kind that even a witch would look like a fairy tale princess. With Silvana it wasn't even the case. Although she was average, but still not someone unsightly.

Usually this dress adorned the movable mannequin from the exhibition and no one but the manager herself was allowed to touch it. It is hardly surprising, after all, it was a real work of art. It was sewn by hand from synthetic silk of the highest quality, supposedly no different from natural one (it was hard to check, since silkworms went extinct long ago), and decorated with rosettes from zirconia, which looked like enlarged snow stars, accidentally falling on the material. Decorating the edges of the sleeves, neckline and each valance, the narrow lace is also supposed to have been made by hand, using the ancient technique, almost forgotten today. I didn't know about these things well enough, but the fact is, I've never seen such lace.

I told Silvana to stand up and threw rolls of shiny white material on her. I fastened the magnetic zipper on the side. The dress had to have nanowires sewn in, because it fitted immediately to the figure of Silvana, which wasn't very easy to do. My friend had rather small breasts and muscles like that of a man, but luckily yesterday I advised her to wear a special, modeling corset with inserts. Thanks to him she looked more feminine, and the valances and lace arranged on her as if it were a creation made especially for her. I pinned another bouquet to my neckline, then put Silvana back on the chair and threw a large towel over it. I set the cosmetics box

304

on the table and started applying foundation to the bride's face. When I was still living at the Sunset Settlement, and Mabel was my neighbor, this future floressa without resistance shared with me the knowledge acquired at the graceful school courses and treated me a bit like an exercise dummy. Thanks to this, I learned how to do artistic make-up and apply nail tips, almost as well as an experienced beautician.

When I was finally done, Silvana stood up, took the towel off her neck, and looked in the mirror.

"Is this really me?" she asked after a moment, touching her cheek, as if she expected it to be someone else. I smiled. I was also pleased with the effect we achieved. Few people would now recognize this gorgeous bride as a rough policewoman, usually engaged in babbling in various abominations.

"Just watch the dress," I warned her just in case. "Although there are Nano fibers woven into it, it's better to be careful. I bet it's the only one like this on the moon and we would never be able to afford it if anything happened to it."

Silvana swirled in front of the mirror, then looked at her hands. Artistic nail tips, admittedly from the store, not made to measure, but still, transformed them beyond recognition. The engagement ring fit like a glove with the bracelet and necklace that I lent to my friend on this festive day. It could not be otherwise, since I told Milton what ring to order for his bride. I bought this set not in any kiosk, but in Miraton, where I was accommodated by citizen Hakat, moreover at his express request. It was simple, but nice and tasteful, matching any elegant outfit – very bright sapphires framed in white gold. With all of this together, Silvana now looked like a real princess.

I visited the police station, which was transformed into a wedding hall for the day. Yesterday we were cleaning and decorating it all day, directing customers to a spare office at the end of the side corridor. The wedding feast was to take place in the cloakroom, where we usually kept not only our clothes, but also various small things that could be needed. We removed cabinets and chests of drawers, and arranged the tables the entire length. Storm troopers were to take care of catering. I was very curious what menu would be at the wedding, but for now the ceremony was waiting for us.

Soon guests started arriving, mainly policemen and storm troopers, but not only. A large banner over the main command, announcing the wedding of Silvana Evans and Milton Reeves, aroused widespread interest. I had the impression that there were twice as many people as were invited. A journalist from the Lunar News channel Golden Aether appeared, armed with a small camera and editor from Moon Review. I should feel jealous, but instead I tried to enjoy Silvana's happiness. She became the Queen of the Day and was probably experiencing the most beautiful moments in her life so far. It wasn't easy, however. I felt overwhelming sadness, the source of which I didn't guess at first, but later I realized that it was just loneliness. I had no one who would buy me a ring and swear that they would never leave me. Despite my weaknesses in feelings, I wanted it for myself somewhere in my heart. Of course, I knew that the oath before the judge was only a customary formula, but there was something amazingly beautiful throughout the ceremony, and I was barely able to hold back my tears.

When Mendelsohn's march sounded, policemen and storm troopers formed a row, and the young couple started off in the middle, I retired to the cloakroom turned into a banquet hall. In the center of the table a huge cake reigned, and on both sides of the table were platters full of various delicacies.

"This is looking pretty nice," McCave's voice said behind me. "And why do you look so sour?"

I looked back at him. He wore a bright suit and cleaned to shine shoes, he could easily be mistaken for a president of a company or other such businessman, not a police pathologist. I smiled.

"You look very handsome today. Where's Maru?"

"She went off to somewhere. You didn't answer me. Why are you so sour? In the morning you were completely different, you were cheerful."

I shrugged my shoulders.

"I have a head ache. And I really feel terrible. If it wasn't for Silvana, I would prefer to go home."

Kelley came over and, taking his fingers under my chin, looked into my eyes.

"You are suffering from lunar depression," he said after a moment. "Now I understand where the results of your tests, which I didn't commission, came from in the computer. Maybe you didn't think I would notice them? Go back home. I'll explain everything to the young spouses, you have already done your job as a bridesmaid. And on the way, buy what I'll prescribe to you at the pharmacy."

He took the mini-pads out of the inside pocket, turned on syncing with the network and quickly wrote something on the pre-loaded standard form.

"I sent a prescription to our pharmacy in your name," he said, turning off the device. "The medicine is called provimana. Take one tablet twice a day until I change the dosage."

"I don't like drugs."

"Nobody asked you for your opinion, young lady." Ignoring the doctor's recommendations may result in dismissal, so be polite and swallow.

He patted my back and gave me a reassuring smile. I answered him and used the permission to leave. I really did feel terrible, as if I was sick. For several days my chest has been hurting, I couldn't fall sleep, the darkness choked me while the light blinded me. The trip to the amusement park allowed me to forget about this foul mood, but it has not come back. The worst thing was that simple everyday activities slowly became more and more difficult for me. When the usual washing of the head began to grow into a Herculean act, in secret before Kelley I did basic research, which didn't show any deviations from the norm. I was supposed to delete them from the main computer, but somehow... I forgot about it.

Returning home I went to the pharmacy.

"My name is Julliette Ankes," I said. "Dr. McCave just sent a prescription here in my name." Here is my ID.

The pharmacist in the white coat looked at the computer and nodded.

"Put your hand on the reader," she told me. "Okay. All good. You were prescribed provimana, supply for two months."

She brought two small boxes from the back room and handed them to me.

"Please use it accordance with the doctor's instructions, don't exceed the recommended dose and don't give it to outsiders even if it they have the same symptoms as you."

"Of course. Thank you."

I took the medicine given to me with mixed feelings. I really didn't like stuffing myself with pills, even when I was really sick, but like all good citizens, I was used to listening to medical services. Anyway, I really felt so bad that it was better not to protest. Not this time.

I found Sue at home. She sat in the living room and played 3D chess with Monty, biting calorie-free crisps. She was only wearing a messy dressing gown and flip-flops, as usual when she didn't have to go anywhere.

"Oh, hi," she said at the sight of me. "I thought you wouldn't be back until the morning. Something interrupted the wedding?"

"No, I was just feeling bad."

Sue looked at me and nodded in understanding.

"Everyone goes through this," she said, tugging her bathrobe in her plump hand. "You were hanging on for rather long anyway. Have you been to the doctor?"

"McCave prescribed me a provimana."

"Ramava is better. Although I don't want to be pretentious, your doctor certainly knows what he's doing. You'll see, you'll feel better after the first dose. New generation drugs work quickly and reliably and are also safer. They don't change personality like many of the older ones."

"How do you know all this?"

"Well, what do you think? From the computer. Don't you know that every virtualist is almost always on the web, whether they have to or not? I became interested in medicine when a nice internist tried to improve my figure. He was worried about my fat, he thought it was the glands' fault."

"Is it not?"

"No. I just like to eat, and due to the nature of my work I don't move around much."

With relief, I removed the elegant bridesmaid dress, folded it carefully, and put it on the top shelf in the closet. Instead, I put on some old pants and a T-shirt, washed off the makeup, curled and tied my hair and only then did I feel like myself.

"I'll have more work tomorrow," I said, sitting on the couch next to my friend. "It will be necessary not only to take care of my own affairs, but also those that Silvana led."

"Will you be alright?"

"I should be. Scotty promised to help me."

Sue looked at me with a sly smile. Monty has moved the pawn to a higher level.

"Check the king," he said.

She looked at the board.

"He's doing that constantly," she sighed. "Do you know that I told him to play with a virtual chess once and beat that too?"

"How is that possible?"

"Well, it's possible. Virtual chess is just a program, and Monty can think abstractly. It is on this occasion that it shows. I'm starting to understand what you saw in him."

She grabbed the display stand and figures into the box.

"Tell me something: doesn't your boss hit on you sometimes? I understand that a new employee must be introduced to the secrets of the profession, but he probably does it too eagerly."

Sue was naturally joking, though not entirely. Scott Cavanaugh did show me more interest than the standard supervisor-subordinate relationship would suggest. Only that it's how he was with everyone. He knew everyone by name, even the humblest officer, and one could get the impression that he knew everything about them and was keenly interested in their personal problems.

"Come on, Suzie," I said. "Are you suggesting that the boss is trying to get together with me?"

"I don't know. He is too old for you, but he is an interesting man, you'll admit."

I was pondering.

"Too old? Well, he isn't young, but how old could he be?"

Cavanaugh was a mystery to me. Despite his youthful figure and resilient movements, he must have been older, judging by his face. He didn't care about his appearance at all, which was a real sensation now. Since the introduction of anti-age pills, it has been easy to hide how old you are, especially since you were no longer required to provide your date of birth on any occasion. Apparently, these privileges were initially enjoyed mainly by women, but now everyone did. If a fifty-year-old man still looks like a twenty-five-year-old with pills, why spoil this nice impression by giving the real age?

"I don't know how old he is," Sue said seriously. "Although I came across something interesting, something you should see."

She turned on the computer mounted into the table, which was a sort of 'extension' of the main module and usually hidden under the laminate layer, so that it doesn't disturb or be accidentally flooded. Pressing the button, she slid the screen above the counter and entered the password.

"Look: these are files from almost forty years ago. At that time, a serial killer in Buenos Aires, who no one could work out. The case was codenamed Chrysanthemum, from the flower left at the scene of each crime by the killer. Do you know that it served as a canvas for several films and a bestselling book?"

"So what?"

"Look at these photos. I'm talking about the man with a cap and a black belt."

Touching the keyboard, she changed photos, brought closer what I was supposed to see, sharpened the image, and made it brighter or darker. I watched carefully and slowly began to understand what was going on. The man in the cap and in the police uniform with the homicide department symbol on his shoulder seemed familiar. However, it was only when, guided by the impulse, that I put my finger to the screen, covering his eyes, I realized that it was Scott Cavanaugh. Yes, it was from before the accident that mutilated him. He didn't have most of today's scars, he also had a completely different hairstyle, but it was him. Yes, no doubt.

"Holy crap! So, forty years ago he was already a detective!"

"Yes, and not just any. No rookie sitting at the desk. It was he who solved the Chrysanthemum case."

"Are you sure?"

"Of course. Everything is here, you just need to be able to find and I can."

That was not some idle boasting. When I got to know Sue, I became convinced that she is indeed a great virtualist. Although she had the typical quirks that people of this trade have, she was balanced enough to get along with easily. Her previous roommate, engineer Selena Corti, the one who couldn't stand it and returned to Earth, simply had to have too high demands. Sue was unorganized in things too mundane for her mind, she was messy, but it could be forgiven. I didn't have any problems with that.

Sid meowed and jumped on my lap. He has long since become accustomed to the new environment and the cat's habit began to consider himself the owner of the whole apartment. He slept where he wanted, jumped around the furniture and although I bought him some toys, he most often played with leftover packaging or our hair bands. Wandering around our rented apartment in search of entertainment, or napping somewhere (usually on a wardrobe), it somehow changed these four rooms into a real home, to which it was pleasant to come back.

"I have to brush Sid, he has some tangles," I said, stroking the back of the cat purring like a motorbike. "Then I want to go to bed. Today has been painful. I didn't like being a bridesmaid."

My friend looked at me understandingly.

"I've never been one, but I don't think I'd like it either. I don't like weddings even in movies, I always go get something to drink. But that's probably not why you're so sour, huh?"

I shook my head. Monty came over and looked into my face closely, as if trying to understand something.

"Something is incorrect, right?"

Sometimes he spoke a bit strangely, but his concern was something extraordinary. What's more, it developed as his mind matured – this android became more and more similar in its reactions to man. Sometimes I was really curious how this prototype brain works and how it is built. Engineer Karpinsky didn't tell me that, and I didn't even blame him for this secretiveness. After all, the design of such an advanced android was his own achievement. He certainly didn't want to entrust his secrets to anyone.

"I'm sad, Monty," I said. "Not because something happened, but because I am sick. Yes, strictly speaking, I can say that I am malfunctioning."

"You need to be fixed. Engineer Thorvald has many parts."

I almost laughed.

"Monty, electronics won't help people," I said cordially. "Not in this case, anyway. It's very complicated. Human diseases are more difficult to treat than damage to androids, because a biological organism is different from a mechanism like yours."

"Does that mean you can't be helped and you'll be dismantled?"

"Not at all. People are simply repaired in a different way and doctors, not mechanics, do the job. I'm not going to be dismantled at all or be gone anywhere else. Soon everything will be fine with me."

"That's good."

There was no feeling in the voice of the android, it precluded his construction, but I would still have sworn that he was really worried about me. His attachment was remarkable and I would probably be very surprised if it wasn't for the conversation with engineer Karpinski, which I had recently.

"It seems that having created a truly independent mind and personality, we have achieved something that wasn't planned at all," he explained to me. "We've created the needs of this mind, the needs of a higher order. We really didn't mean that, it was a side effect, but Monty was showing signs from the beginning of... well, how should I put this... the feeling that he is missing something? I can't even describe it. I have already said that he hates loneliness and it was the same with his predecessor. Perhaps the desperate need to be with someone and belong to someone, so human, is a derivative of a certain IQ. We didn't consider this possibility, and then it was too late. The trouble is that for now you can't prove the presence of a 'soul in the machine' because we don't know how to do it, so by law he is just a machine."

"Both you and me know that this isn't true," I told him then. I was aware that the engineer worried about the creation so much as if Monty was his own son, and I shared his feelings. Perhaps only the two of us knew how to treat him this way. Sue thought I was exaggerating, Dr. McCave joked about an 'artificial lover', and perhaps Inspector Cavanaugh was able to better understand what I felt. My boss was smart and very experienced...

I spent the next three days at home taking humbly prescribed medication. It wasn't until the fourth day that Kelley allowed me to go back to work, but on condition that I would continue to swallow provimana. Of course, I promised I wouldn't forget about it.

"Good that you're here," Scotty said when I saw him. "We didn't know what to put our hands in without you and

Silvana. We have results from the laboratory, they need to be reviewed and developed, so in general the whole Romain Corporation case got stuck."

"What do you mean?" I became worried. After recent events, I was convinced that we had this issue out of our minds and were passing it on to the main management of the Moon Company.

"The prosecutor's office returned the documents to us. You have to review them and write the summary report again, otherwise the company will simply get away with it all."

I moaned desperately.

"What's missing?"

"It's my fault. We had a warrant to search the mine and premises associated with it, and the residential level, although it was built illegally, wasn't included there."

"How could it have been included if no one even knew about it?!"

Cavanaugh smiled indulgently. He was still amused by my ignorance and inexperience at work, which had not held any secrets for him for years. Sometimes it irritated me, although I had to honestly admit that he had a lot of patience with me. Training a detective candidate took a lot of time, especially when, like me, they were assigned to the police as part of a witness protection program. It's true that no one loudly acknowledged my situation, but for me the matter was clear. On Earth, I made enemies, and powerful ones at that – I was the only witness to an attack on very important people, I identified the attackers, but something went wrong. I don't know what, but it must have been serious, since citizen Hakat, my mighty protector, decided to send me to the moon.

I thought that despite everything it would be easier for him to get rid of me forever, and certainly it would be a much cheaper solution. Either he was a better person than he seemed or... he just liked me.

"The law is the law, Leeta," he said. "The order didn't apply to private property, so we searched it illegally. And that's where the bill of indictment falls."

I sat helplessly behind the desk and supported my chin with my hands.

"So what are we supposed to do?"

"Above all, we can't give up," he patted me comfortingly on the back. "This is what the police detective's work looks like. Get used to it. Oh, before I forget: Silvana left you a package. There's the dress that you should return to the fashion house and your jewelry. By the way, it's very pretty and certainly expensive."

"It was a gift from... a certain person."

"All right, it's your personal matter, I won't go into the details. However, you better not wear it on the street in Lunnar, here robberies are a sad part of everyday life."

I opened the box left by my friend. The dress turned out to be in perfect condition, there was no spot or damage on it, only a little dust at the edge from the floor. The model for whom it was sewn must have been significantly taller than Silvana.

"I will take it back to the fashion house after work. Mrs. Belmonte will be glad it's not damaged. For now, however, let's get to work, I don't want these bastards to get away with it."

"Of course."

The case documents had to be reworked, excluding from them everything associated with the underground apartments, which meant that it would be difficult for us to explain who we were accusing. It was only in these undergrounds that we found evidence that we could relate to specific people – there wasn't anything in the mine and administrative rooms that pointed to someone from the board. The matter was complicated by the fact that we had no idea who actually headed the Romain Corporation. The owners of the company – we knew only that there were a few of them – unexpectedly became as mysterious as members of the global government, hiding behind impersonal numbers. The names given to the official list turned out to be fictitious. Administrative staff, even accountants, knew nothing. The official presidency – Marisela Gossip, Hugo Vittorio and Cassius Jones – gave the impression of puppets in someone else's hands. They managed to arrest them, but after an hour we had to release all three of them. Romain Corporation proved too influential to do anything without really hard evidence.

The company operated on strange principles. One of them was a practice that I had never heard of before. All administrative employees had to sign a blank promissory note and contract before taking up work (no matter how paid), which stipulated that in the event of disclosing company secrets to an outsider, the company could impose such a financial penalty as it deems appropriate. In this situation, it wasn't strange that they were silent, even at a police interrogation. Maybe you could learn something from miners, but the corporation had a way on them - the illegal drugs they were given in exchange for loyalty. Since these funds could not be obtained normally, they had to stick to the company that owned their label. Because this label definitely existed, although we still didn't know where it was located. All the hunters at the main command were looking for her, but so far nobody has found a trace.

When I was finally able to return home, I had about a quarter of the work behind me, and I was booming with fatigue. Unfortunately, as I delved into the documents, my discouragement grew. Without the report from the residential part, we had virtually nothing but an accusation of illegal exploitation of the mascon and concealing its profits from the Moon Mining Company. It was a serious offense, but I knew that when Romain Corporation paid the statutory penalty, it would be able to resume operations as if nothing had happened.

It wasn't fair, especially in light of what we already knew, but after part of evidence was rejected we were helpless. Scotty refused to admit it, but I knew mine. I have already learned something from the books about the work of a policeman that the boss told me to study. There were plenty of examples of cases similar in some detail to the one we were working on, along with the legal interpretation of the judgment regarding the evidence secured by the police. This helped to understand why guilty sometimes avoided punishment when police officers messed up and encouraged caution in similar cases.

Along the way, I entered the fashion house and gave the dress back, and went out and finally went to see the dating center. Perhaps Kelley was right and I also needed a „session" with man to maintain mental balance. It was better to have it done quickly and I could focus on work.

The nearest DC was located in a small, domed building with Art Nouveau decorations. They seemed to me strangely out of place in this city on the moon, which grew out of a mining settlement and was actually a worker and administrative settlement. These ornaments didn't fit into the whole of the buildings, in the overwhelming majority of simple and raw. They could not have been different, since, apart from their basic function, they had to meet the conditions of an armored shelter. Sue once showed me the specifications of a typical building in Lunnar – it could successfully withstand rocket fire, and when the door was closed, it became airtight like a rescue capsule. The armored windows didn't open at all, and the internal apparatus could purify air and water for a very long time. The supply of freeze-dried food allowed the residents there to survive until help arrived.

I asked if it was ever needed before. It turned out that it was. Fifteen years ago, a large meteor shattered a part of the dome, but thanks to well-functioning internal services only two people were killed, the rest managed to take refuge in the nearest buildings. There were other disasters, but they were much less dangerous and could be easily repaired. Certainly, the dating center was also a safe place, but all the more the decorations were comical, like some garlands on an armored personnel carrier or frills on a storm trooper's uniform.

Inside, the building was just like any such settlement. Meeting rooms were located upstairs. Downstairs was the general room, filled with double tables and vending machines for snacks and drinks. Stylish ample under the ceiling provided a soft, subdued light, but each table was equipped with an additional lamp in case someone wanted to read while waiting for a willing partner. Soft music dripped from the ceiling speakers.

Despite the rather early time in the room there were already a dozen couples talking to each other and probably ten lonely at the tables, waiting for an invitation with cups of caffetino or something stronger. They all had calm faces of regulars and it was obvious that they were in no hurry.

I hesitated, but then went into the room, looking for a free table. Nobody looked at me – this was considered to be a good tone in a dating center, but as a new guest I had the right to look around and look at all the people sitting alone. I noticed with astonishment a familiar figure at the table in the corner. Scott Cavanaugh sat sprawled in a comfortable chair, sipping a drink with ice cubes, and reading today's newspaper. The entire press on the moon was published not only in electronic form, but also on computer foil imitating old paper. After a few days, each newspaper was recycled, removing previous entries, refreshing the foil by galvanic method and applying new content. The foil was so durable that this procedure was repeated many times without deterioration of the recording quality. Despite this, the newspaper published in this way was much more expensive than its electronic version, which could be downloaded to your paddock in any press machine and buying it was a kind of snobbery.

"What are you doing here, Scotty?" I asked, coming over and sitting down opposite of him.

He left the folded piece of foil and looked at me with his implants with a slight surprise.

"What about you?"

"Doctor's recommendation."

"Same for me," Scott set the paper down and took a sip of his drink. "Kell is a martinet and a terrible bore. On the other hand, I don't like lying or beating around the bush. I really don't. And if I come here from time to time, then at least everything is seemingly fine. And then everyone is happy."

"Everyone?" I raised my eyebrows slightly. "Are you sure?"

He threw up his arms.

"What do you want? I come here to drink something stronger and read a newspaper, and then go home."

"Just like that?"

"Of course. Can you imagine a woman wanting to cling to a guy like me? There is always someone else to choose from."

"I think you're underestimating yourself, boss."

He smiled, then got up and took two servings of vanilla cream with dried fruit and nuts from the machine. He pushed one towards me.

"You're nice and you've gone through a lot," he said. "That's why you probably judge people differently, but the fact remains that my appearance scares off women, even the least demanding ones. I don't blame them. Nowadays visible disability is something very repulsive… and it helps me in my work. The interrogators will tell me anything I need for me to just get out of their sight."

He laughed as if it was a good joke. I put a teaspoon of cream in my mouth mechanically. It was quite tasty, better than I expected.

"So what are you doing here?" I asked after a while.

"I come, read the press, have a drink or two and go back to myself. And when Kell asks, with a clear conscience I can tell him that I was in the dating center, as he recommended."

He looked at me closely.

"Actually, you should change your seat," he added. "Nobody will approach you if they can see us together. Not that I don't feel good in your company. It's pleasant. But it's about you, why you came here."

I nodded thoughtfully.

"I don't like dating centers," I confessed. "I don't like meeting strangers, even on the recommendation of a doctor. I always preferred someone I already knew than a random partner."

"You don't always have one on demand. Couldn't you find a man permanently? It certainly wouldn't be difficult, you're pretty and nice."

I shrugged my shoulders.

"I probably could, but you see, it's not that simple. What would I offer to someone like that? You don't know much about me, so I'll tell you: I've been suffering from a mental defect since I was a child. I can't love. I can't get involved emotionally. So why would I lie to someone?"

Cavanaugh smiled slightly, not with irony, but with an understanding I didn't expect.

"Now your fascination with androids becomes easy to explain. They don't need feelings."

"Exactly."

I finished the cream and licked the spoon. I took a fruit cocktail to drink from the machine. Sipping it, I thought again about what I wanted to say and decided that it would be the best.

"Boss, how about we help each other out?" I suggested. "We know and like each other, and I think it will be the best for both of us."

It really must have surprised him, because for a moment he just looked at me in silence.

"You have no objections?" he asked finally, fingering his implants.

"Oh, come on!" I protested. "You know that I was reconstructed myself after the accident. Only that my protector didn't take into account the costs and thanks to that I look like a human. Only thanks to that. I would never have earned a tenth of the sum I needed for it alone. It was... cosmic."

He nodded, biting his lower lip in his own way.

"You've never talked about this case, but I guess the implantation was big, since you have complexes about it."

"Very. Reconstruction of part of the ribs, left shoulder joint, skin coatings, half of the face and hair. Can you imagine what I would look like without the help of the EPIPHANICS clinic?"

"EPIPHANICS? That's a network of the most expensive branches."

"Well, you see yourself. I was paid for because I was needed for some high-level games. And thanks to what happened next, I'm here."

"I'm not complaining about that."

He smiled at me again in his bitter-ironic way. I thought I liked his smile. The face, furrowed with wrinkles, had its harsh charm, other than the now-fashionable puppet smoothness of the face, but you had to get used to seeing it. I am used to it a long time ago. The decision wasn't as difficult as he had imagined.

"I'm not either, not really," I said. "I still don't think I'm a detective, but I'm grateful that you took me in. I feel like you're family."

"That's how it should be. We have to be like a family, because if necessary, a policeman should always be able to count on their colleague. This is a must. Well, if you are so determined, let's go upstairs and let's get it over with."

"Never in my life have I heard a more romantic pick up line!" I laughed "Let's get it over with. Scotty, you are something else."

I finished my cocktail and got up from the table.

If before, still back on Earth, I were to choose a candidate for a partner, Scott Cavanaugh would probably be the last person to come to my mind. He seemed to be unfit not just for me, but not for anyone or anything in the entire universe. However, these were only appearances and after everything that happened to me, I could distinguish them from reality. This tough, old-fashioned policeman turned out to be a tender and gentle man who could create an aura of security and relaxation in an intimate situation. He was in no hurry and didn't take the initiative. Everything was done calmly, gently and it was – I would say – sweet.

Maybe for the first time I came back from the dating center in a really good mood and Sue noticed it immediately.

"Help yourself," she pulled out a plate of biscuits spread with nut paste to me. "I see you're better now."

Monty sat near her and assembled a three-dimensional puzzle owl model. As far as I remembered, it took me two weeks to put everything together, but he worked much faster. According to the recommendation of Karpinsky's engineer, the android should do such things as to develop recognition skills, just like a human child.

"Monty, I have a crossword puzzle for you," I said, taking the computer foil notebook out of my purse. "Do you know what a crossword puzzle is?"

He left the puzzle and looked at me.

"I don't know what that word means."

"Finish the puzzle and I'll explain what and how. It's good, educating entertainment."

"What is entertainment for?"

"People need it to not be bored. Our brain must have something to work on to make us feel good."

"I'm not bored."

"Even if that's the case, these crosswords will come in handy. They train the mind, thanks to which you can learn new words, and you are still learning. I promised engineer Karpinsky that I would take care of your development and intend to keep my word."

Monty scooped the remaining parts in the box and finished the model with quick and confident movements.

I had the impression that he could do it much faster, only deliberately delaying the end of work – I wonder why. He was still surprising me.

The strangest thing was that he became more and more attached to me. At first, he only recognized himself as my property because he was a witness to how I paid for it. As we interacted, he gradually stopped treating me like a master, and instead as someone who is simply important to him. At some point, he probably began to fear that he might lose me, because he asked me strange questions several times, such as:

"Will I have to leave when you no longer need me?"

"Do you want to leave?" I asked him in response. "Maybe you'd rather live with someone else, not me?"

He considered what he heard for a good moment, then answered in a strange voice, lower than usual and soundless like the sound of a broken bell:

"Only... you..."

He repeated these words several times, shaking his head. This mechanical movement told me more than I needed to know, as if the android wanted to say something more but could not formulate it.

"It's okay," I finally interrupted him. "I think I understand. Monty, you are my friend and it will stay that way. Nobody deserves it more than you do. If I ask you what you would like, it's because I don't want to force you to do anything. I don't have the right to do this because you are an independent being, not a robot and not a computer. Someone, not something. Do you understand the difference?"

He looked at me, tilting his head slightly to his left shoulder.

"Only you think of me as an equal being," he said suddenly, finally finishing his sentence circling his artificial circuits. I was speechless.

Although I treated Monty like a human and considered him almost human, it never occurred to me that he analyzes and assesses every situation and then draws conclusions. He kept his thoughts only to himself, unless I asked directly, and somehow I didn't come up with the idea to talk to him about such topics. Meanwhile, it turned out that he can see the difference in the way I treat him, and how other people look at him, even Sue. And yet, she, a virtualist, should be more likely to have a better attitude towards artificial intelligence.

I spent the evening solving crosswords. I always liked it, especially the 'fill-in' kind, but somehow I couldn't infect Monty with this passion. He helped me a bit, but as if politely, out of duty. It was as if his mind wasn't enjoying this kind of entertainment. He clearly preferred other puzzles, both ordinary and three-dimensional, and arranged the multi-colored Rubik's cube as skillfully as if this operation didn't require any effort. Riddles requiring only mental effort didn't interest him, while those that involved both hands and head would be his passion... if there were such a thing as passion in the nature of androids.

Around midnight a paging ringtone forced me to my feet. For a moment I didn't know who I was and where I was, but after a few minutes I sobered up. The symbol used by the main command flickered on the videophone screen, so I turned on the reception without caring what I looked like. Kunch's handsome face appeared in the screen.

"Sorry, Leeta," he said. "Scott is crazy, he ordered to bring everyone to the police station. I sent a taxi for you, it should be right at your door."

"What's happening?

"I have no idea. I was afraid to ask. You know that if he gets mad, then he's scary to even look at, let alone talk to."

I wanted to tell him that I am not afraid, but I remained silent. In an agitated state, Scott ceased to control the muscles transplanted into the eye sockets, and as a result his implants went out to the maximum and gave the impression that they were living their own lives. It didn't leave an impression on me, perhaps because of the awareness of the implants that I wore in myself, but most people felt irrational anxiety at this sight, as in the face of something particularly gruesome. Nowadays, the sight of someone's disability is a disgust unknown to our ancestors, who were alive with various physical shortcomings. They saw them every day.

I dropped my pajamas and pulled on yesterday's clothes as fast as I could. There was no time for a shower or even a cursory toilet - the inspector at the very beginning warned me that in the event of a sudden call I should not pay attention to what I look like. In such cases, time was of the essence and it must not be wasted. I tied my hair with a piece of ribbon and ran out of the apartment.

When I arrived at the police station, I found everyone except Evans, who was still on her honeymoon. Scott Cavanaugh sat on Kunch's desk, tapping his curled fist steadily, and his implants, ripped to the limit, moved in all directions, as always when he was nervous.

"What happened, boss?" I asked, approaching him.

"You'll know soon," he grunted, then stood up and shouted. "Settle down!"

Everyone fell silent and lined up in front of him. Cavanaugh walked between us, folding his arms behind his back and clearly trying to regain control.

"Ladies and gentlemen," he began. "I have bad news to tell you. All the work we've done on the Romain Corporation case has gone up the dog's ass!"

He slammed his curled fist on the top of the nearest desk.

"The prosecutor's office rejected our initial report!"

"Under what excuse?" I asked. He looked at me briefly.

"Someone reached Prosecutor Cable before us and presented the case in a completely different light. He relied on the MacLeon Amendment, guaranteeing a preliminary investigation by a team of at least two detectives from the accused corporation."

"Does such a thing even exist?" Feri was surprised. "I've never heard of it. What about you, Linares?"

Our full-time law expert, lawyer Claudio Linares, shrugged.

"The matter is complicated," he said reluctantly. "The MacLeon Amendment is actually a parliamentary joker."

"What do you mean?"

"Long ago, the global parliament adopted a package of constitutional amendments. Among the clearly formulated points were also ones like this one, i.e. jokers. All of them so general that they can mean anything. Someone who referred to one of them had to be very familiar with the Constitution, especially its secret part, so it could not be an ordinary citizen."

"Exactly!" Cavanaugh snorted bitterly.

"You can do that?" I asked in a daze. "That's just cheating the voters."

"Politics have always been like this," Dr. McCave said ironically. He was sitting in the corner, sprawled on one of the armchairs, looking at all the confusion with undisturbed calm.

"What happens now?" I looked at Scott helplessly. I had the impression that he would explode in a moment, but he controlled himself somehow. He drank a glass of water in one breath and continued:

"We start everything from the beginning. However, the investigation must be kept secret. I was able to obtain prosecutor's permission to collect data, but everything we have obtained so far has been annulled as illegally obtained material. They can't be used in court, but..."

He stopped significantly for a moment.

"...but we can officially keep them for internal use."

"What does that give us?" I asked.

I suddenly realized that in Silvana's absence, there were only two detectives at Lunnar's headquarters: Scott Cavanaugh, a veteran, and myself, a complete newbie, just beginning to explore the secrets of the profession. The rest are patrol policemen and storm troopers from rapid response units. I felt as if lead weights from old-fashioned scales fell on my back. I thought with fear that I could not cope with such responsibility. I never wanted to do forensics and didn't think I had any talent in this direction, but I was put against the wall. I had no choice or the right to vote. And now I was supposed to work properly alone, at least until Silvana returned.

Scott returned his implants to me. They glimmered with spotlights, and their internal shutters narrowed and expanded rhythmically, as always when he was thinking hard about something.

"We'll have at least a few anchor points," he replied. "Something we can start with instead of thrashing in the dark like before. We have a prosecutor's dispute, which means we can't use existing finds, but we won't have to explain why we've found directions for further evidence. Did everyone understand me? From now on, the Romain Corporation case is a priority, but no one is allowed to talk about it. We are all silent like a grave, unless we are here in the station. We don't even discuss anything with each other that would be relevant if we're anywhere outside this room. If a single word of this leaks to the media, we'll have more problems than ever before."

"Attorney Johnson will get to our asses before we can sneeze. And Cable will just applaud him," Kunch completed his statement, and the tone of his voice left no doubt that he knew what he was talking about.

Harry Johnson, stand-in for the local prosecutor Nick Cable, was known for meticulous adherence to the Criminal Code and was no joke. More evidence... I had doubts about whether we would find it at all. We made so much noise that everyone found out what we knew, and now it turned out that the Romain Corporation slid away from responsibility. While we look like complete fools. Our knowledge became useless since we had no right to use it. I felt completely discouraged and, as Chris put it, 'pushed to the ground'. So much work, such strong evidence – and nothing. A dishonest company can continue operate, its bosses laugh at us, and we have so much of it that we have exposed ourselves to influential people.

I followed Scott to his office. He was so nervous that he noticed me only when the door closed behind me and I tripped over the protruding corner of the rug that pretended to be the carpet. The inspector's office was decorated in a style that probably didn't even have a name – each piece of furniture came from a different set and nothing matched.

"What else do you want?!" Scott shouted dissatisfied. I was already used to his way of being, so it didn't affect me. I sat in one of the chairs and stared at the TV screen, on which the Stand by signal was flashing. My boss usually listened to television broadcasts even when he wasn't watching, wanting to be up to date so that the receiver was turned off only when Cavanaugh left the office for a long time.

"Boss, do we have any chance at all?" I asked. My voice must have sounded miserable because Scott softened.

"There are always possibilities, child. I must admit that it will be very difficult for us, but this is what police work is like. You mess around and smash your head against a wall made of money belonging to someone who has you and everything else up to here."

"What did I do to deserve this...? Sorry, boss, I didn't want it to sound like that. I have learned to appreciate police work, but I still have doubts about whether I fit into it."

He laughed merrily.

"Few of us do. Storm troopers usually come from soldiers or sportsmen who have finished their careers in one piece, and the rest are just a collection, too. There are not many candidates for such dog service nowadays. I know you became a detective under the witness protection program, but I see real talent in you. Of course, it requires training, but fortunately it isn't that they stuck us someone completely useless just to protect their ass... there have been such cases."

Maybe he wanted to make me feel better, but it didn't work out.

"Somehow I don't feel that useful. I have always been a mediocre person and I have the impression that I still am, despite all your efforts. It is a pity that instead of the usual implants I have not been implanted ones that give me some extraordinary powers."

"There aren't such, fortunately."

"I don't see the material for a policewoman in myself. Seriously."

"It's enough for me to see it, you don't have to. If you were of no use, I would tell you that and offered you a secretarial job. But I didn't."

He put his elbows on the table top and folded his fingers. On the ring finger of his left hand, I noticed a wide strip of pale skin and suddenly thought that I knew absolutely nothing about my supervisor. He used to wear a wedding ring, took it off relatively recently, and so he had a wife. If anyone at the police station knew about it, I would certainly have been informed, because gossip is our crew's favourite pastime. What happened to this woman? Who was she and where was she now? I barely looked away from Scott's hands and asked:

"Do you really think I will ever be a good detective?"

"In a few years," he replied. "Training takes time, and you must develop instinct and cop's intuition. You can do it, you just have to listen to the older detectives, in this case me and Silvana Evans. We will guide you step by step..."

His words were interrupted by an incoming message signal on the videophone desk panel. He frowned and pressed the receive button.

"Scotty, quickly turn channel five on," said the doctor's voice from the speaker. He was dead serious.

"Right now?"

"Yes. Push the broadcast back for about five or six minutes."

Cavanaugh took the remote from the desk and set the reception on the television set accordingly. After a few seconds, a three-dimensional image appeared with the time stamp of the previous six minutes.

"...roads B8, B9 and B11 are temporarily excluded from use," the announcer said in a professional tone. "Please update your private AutoMap before heading out onto the road. Now for today's news. Last minute news: a murder took place in the Blue Moment guesthouse. The victims were a young couple, Carlito and Aura Fuentes. The newlyweds died from shots to the back of the head, and before that they were intoxicated by an unknown substance given to them during a meal."

Scott jumped up from the desk, pale as if he were a corpse himself. He hit the radio node with a quick movement of his hand.

"Investigation team get ready! he shouted. "We move out in two minutes!"

He jumped from behind the desk, grabbed my arm and pushed me towards the door. I surrendered to him, dazed and shaken. Silvana is dead? How is that Why?

Carlito and Anna Fuentes – it was a cover-up. Civilians don't like to see cops where they rest, they want to feel at ease there. The names 'Evans' and 'Reeves' were known, for example, from the television broadcast of the wedding at the command. Nobody associated them with Fuentes. At least it seemed like it. However, our plan failed, and Silvana and her husband were killed. By chance? Certainly not. The case became even more incomprehensible. The assassination of representatives of the uniformed services has become extremely rare in the last century, just like any planned murder. Since the relevant law allowed the immediate execution of everyone not so much guilty as clearly involved in such a crime, the number of crimes against life has fallen to a level not recorded in human history.

Attacks may have become no less frequent, but definitely less bloody. This does not mean that bold murders go down in history, but now criminals are much more careful about what they do. Such an assault as the one in Blue Moment was already rare – and it had to happen to my friend her husband! And we all tried to keep them there in full incognito! We provided them with fake documents and let them fake that they flew to Earth to spend their honeymoon there.

"It's no accident," I whispered, pushing myself into the corner of the police rover.

"Of course not, don't pretend to be an idiot!" Shouted Cavanaugh angrily. "And it wasn't about Milton, he only died because he was with Silvana! Someone wants to intimidate us or…"

"Or what?"

"Or show who's in charge. Notice how we only found out because Kell was watching the news. If he wasn't, we would've been called in only after they thoroughly blurred the traces. We should be notified first, not the damn gossip television!"

Indeed, the first thing the staff at this guesthouse should do is notify the main command, not call the media. I shivered. Romain Corporation didn't waste time. Next in line could be me or Suzy. Or maybe Cavanaugh himself, who knows? Scott glanced at me with his left implant and seemed to understand what was bothering me.

"You'll find a safety vest in a locker on the door," he said. "This is the latest model, made of Nano carbon material called Bernite."

"I've never heard of it."

"I just said that it's new! An invention of Berkovitz and Nitchum, hence the name. This fabric is resistant to all commonly used bullets, including fire, and even lasers used against people. It absorbs kinetic and thermal energy or something. I don't know exactly, I'm not a physicist. Work is underway to reduce production costs so that it can be sewn from series produced uniforms. This is a real breakthrough."

I pulled out the vest package. It looked inconspicuous, felt soft to the touch almost like cotton, and it was hard to believe it was that durable. I took off my uniform jacket made of nanoelan and put it on. The 'vest' looked like a regular turtleneck and reached below my bottom. Out of curiosity, I took out a service knife and stabbed slightly to the side. The impression was unusual – as if the fabric's fibers suddenly consolidated into something reminiscent of steel resistance, because I didn't even feel the blade. I stabbed harder and finally – emboldened – with all my strength. Nothing. I looked at the tip of the knife and saw that it was a little worn and blunt, as if I was pounding it on sheet metal or concrete.

"You can try as much as you like, I've already tested these vests," Cavanaugh said again. "Do you think I would believe those big words of manufacturers? Forget it. You can only count on yourself, that's the general rule. I won't give my people anything I won't check myself."

He paused for a moment.

"But I didn't protect Silvana. Damn it, how did it happen? How did they find her so quickly?" he murmured after a moment sadly. On impulse, I kissed his cheek.

"You couldn't predict it."

"I couldn't but I should have. I am the boss here, responsible for all my subordinates like a father is of his children. And I failed."

"You didn't fail anybody. You are simply not the Great Eternal know-it-all."

He looked at me and patted me lightly on the shoulder.

"You don't know me yet. However, you will have the opportunity to, because for now you are the only one I have left."

"Me?"

"Yes. You can see that I don't have anyone else. Before you arrived, there was Lockerby, whom you didn't meet as he is on sick leave, and Evans. He was seriously injured and I don't know if he will ever return to work at all. You are the only one left for me, so from now on you are to be my inseparable shadow."

I considered it briefly.

"I'll try."

"You're not supposed to try, you have to become a full-fledged detective as soon as possible. And you will, under my directions. I know that this isn't the dream job for you, but it just so happens that in life we don't always act as we want, but as we must. The world would easily go without one more verdant or librarian, but a good detective can save a lot of people's lives. We are necessary, although people often despise us."

"I know."

A few more minutes passed and a police rover arrived in front of the Blue Moment guesthouse.

V

The deaths of Silvana Evans and her husband were widely heard in the Lunnar Media. Something like this has not been noted here from when the mining settlement first obtained municipal rights. And how could it be any different? Inspector Cavanaugh has raised such terrible hell that the whole city quickly learned about the incompetence of the guest house security. In general, he started by arresting all the staff and all bodyguards, and thanks to that we knew a few minutes after arriving who was the 'weak link' – the head of security himself, Fernando Lopez. We couldn't find him, even though we searched the guesthouse and the man's private apartment carefully. Nobody could tell us anything more about him, except that he started working there recently and seemed to be a good specialist. From accounting we were provided with photos of him, we sent them to all patrols with orders to detain him and bring him to the station.

"Though I doubt it will do anything," Scott said pessimistically. "I bet this man is already dead. We are dealing with an organization that doesn't hesitate to murder."

"Who could be this stupid?" I asked with an involuntary shiver.

"Stupid or not. If someone already killed once, then what do they care about the second time, he can't be hanged twice. Do you think that in our radical times there are no more professional contract killers? This isn't the first time in history that there is a risk of death penalty and somehow it has never stopped such types."

Saying all this, Scott searched Silvana and Milton's room at the same time methodically, without a single unnecessary move. There were not many traces and when we finally came back to the police station, we didn't have much for the technicians.

"And that confirms we're dealing with real professionals," Scott concluded, entering his office. "What are you doing here?"

These last words were directed at Monty, who was standing in the middle of the office, clearly waiting for something. At the sight of him I felt a warmth in my heart and at the same time a painful pressure at the thought of losing him. Seeing my friend's body and her husband's body made me painfully aware – nothing is as lasting as we would like and everything can end literally at any moment.

"Miss Susan wanted me to check where Leeta was," he replied. That was her command.

"Why are you following her instructions?"

"Leeta told me to."

"Oh... so why is Miss Herefort so worried about her friend that she sends you away?" Scott sat down behind the desk and put his legs on his countertop.

"I can't guess the thoughts of human beings," Monty replied. "Miss Susan was very upset and spoke illogically."

"Any specific reason?"

"An incomprehensible reason."

"Tell me what happened. Exactly," I asked.

"My information to date has shown that Miss Susan doesn't mind when things are pointless and orderly. The request turned out to be false."

I frowned. Just like yesterday I was tidying up the apartment and didn't remember that something was out of place. In addition, such a mess as Sue would certainly not care, even if she stuck in the trash.

"I don't understand. What was wrong?"

"Clothes, dishes, boxes..."

"So practically everything? How? Monty, tell me everything from the start, because I don't understand."

"Miss Susan told me to go shopping with her," the android began obediently. "We bought..."

"Never mind the crap you bought, what came next?"

"We went back home. It was open, although Miss Susan closed the door, and everything was a mess."

Only now did I understand his words and my hair bristled on my head. I was just forced to look at Silvana's corpse, whom I helped to dress for the wedding ceremony only a few days ago. And Milton, her husband, always so happy and energetic, with whom I was after work so many times. Until recently, they were both alive, liked to laugh and joke, and now? I thought it couldn't be worse, but it was.

"Someone attacked our apartment!"

Scott pressed the intercom button.

"Feri, give me a rover with the full squad," he demanded. "The crew is to go to Vernego Street, number 10, and take Susan Herefort and all computers from there."

"And Sid!"

"Who?" Scott looked at me in surprise.

"My cat."

The inspector snorted furiously.

"And a cat," he finished with a contemptuous grimace. "Forget about anything else."

"Yes, sir," Feri answered. "Where are they to take this lady?"

"To the service flat at the back of the command. If I'm not mistaken, two, three and seven are empty."

"Understood."

I pressed my arm against Monty, wanting to feel a little safer for a while. Such a sudden loss of ground from under my feet wasn't something new to me, but it is something I cannot get used to.

"What now?" I asked helplessly. "Why exactly did they die and did the same man plunder my apartment?"

Scott was silent for a moment, drumming his fingers on the table.

"That's a good question," he said finally. "And the answer isn't as easy as we think."

He handed me one of the printed images of the wanted man from the desk.

"Fernando Lopez... It might as well be John Smith."

He threw the photo, discouraged. Monty followed his hand and tilted his head. A tremor ran through his face, as if he were trying to imitate human facial expressions. He knew how to do it, but not spontaneously, only when he was asked to do it – his mind was only ripe for certain things, he didn't associate changes in the tone of artificial muscles with a particular situation.

"What's wrong, Monty?" I asked.

He didn't answer immediately. First he took the picture, turned it over, looked at it, and then looked at me.

"It's Mr. Brel," he said.

"What?!" Scott jumped up, knocking over the chair.

He pulled out a drawer and took out a memory portrait of Brel. He usually didn't stop at computer memory and typical media. He had a weakness for printing everything on IT film, especially photos. For this he used a very expensive, reinforced high-pixel film, on which even a three-dimensional image could be recorded and in his desk abounded a lot of such photographs.

"I don't see the similarity... although..."

He slipped the portrait into the reader and turned on the computer. He ran his fingers over the screen, selecting the appropriate graphics program. The processed image flickered. The hair, thick beard and earring in his left ear have disappeared. Cavanaugh whistled.

"Monty, you deserve an award," he said solemnly.

"I don't get it."

"I mean, something like the highest praise. Leeta, your android has given us a very important point of attachment," the inspector quickly set the printing of both portraits on one piece of foil and pressed the trigger. "If Brel and Lopez are the same person, and it looks like they are, it gives food for thought."

"Why did he kill Silvana and Milt?" I picked up the printed picture and compared the two faces, which convinced me that there was no mistake. "What did that give him? Is he playing a game with us?"

"I seriously doubt it. He wouldn't bother with that. If you think about it, you'll understand it yourself. Theatrical gestures are good in sensational films, not in life. It's about something more."

He looked at Monty and I saw that he was thinking about the same thing as me – that this android is a vault of valuable knowledge, which he doesn't even realize. Well, the computer also knows nothing about the weight of information on its hard drive, it only knows the amount of it. In this respect, Monty was no different from the machine.

Scott pressed the intercom button again.

"Feri, bring me all Silvana Evans's things," he commanded. "Download from the computer every smallest record on the media and give it to me, then secure her equipment so that no one can use it. Can you do that?"

"Not a problem."

Half an hour later, Kunch entered the inspector's office, carrying a large, flat box.

"That's all I found," he said. "The data from the computer is on the storage medium, as you ordered."

"Put everything on the desk."

Feri hesitated.

"Boss..." he began uncertainly.

"What? Speak briefly and to the point."

"Boss, I have a detective's license. I know I'm not very credible after what happened, but right now..."

He spread his hands as if explaining himself to something that wasn't his fault. I looked at him without understanding. What was he talking about?

Scott was silent for a moment, then pursed his lips and nodded.

"I agree. Either way, I have no alternative now, and I need all the help I can get. How long have you been sitting behind the desk?"

"For seven months."

"That's enough. Tomorrow you are coming back to the street, organize your office matters today. Someone will have to take them over."

Feri brightened, saluted and ran out. The inspector noticed my look and shook his head.

"Later."

***

Service apartment No. 2 was quite spacious and almost completely devoid of furniture. Sue mumbled with dissatisfaction, setting up her precious computer and connecting all the cables. This activity absorbed her completely. Sid was sitting in the transporter and meowing miserably, but my friend paid no attention to him.

"You're finally here!" she called at my sight. "You realize that I only miraculously escaped with my life? If I wasn't shopping with Monty at the time, you would probably be identifying my body with in the police morgue at this point!"

"Don't be crazy, Sue."

"Do you think I'm exaggerating? And what about your friend, are you going to say that she slipped on a soap bar?"

I sat on a stool and watched Sue fight the cables for a moment. After a while, an older police officer Yamato looked into the apartment and asked:

"Do you need anything else? The inspector said that we should bring everything from your apartment, we brought all clothes and furniture without a rental logo."

"Where are they?"

"Outside in the cart."

"Can you bring it all? I'm sorry to ask for this, but you understand..."

"Sure."

Yamato grinned and nodded. From the beginning I had the impression that he liked me, and now his behavior confirmed it – after all, patrol officers are not from carrying furniture. The trouble is that the main police station in Lunnar didn't have a single person with money – we still didn't get enough money for the equipment, and what was left was loaded in the laboratory and computers. The case could be sorted out some profitable leasing, but here a problem arose. We were not allowed to rent these vending machines because they were too easy to load in spy software. So, what happened is that anything that had to be moved landed on the shoulders of the lowest-ranking policemen. It's just that they had no obligation to lug our personal belongings. They did it only out of kindness.

"Wait, Yamato!" I shouted. "Hold on!"

I don't know what caused my mind to act suddenly like a computer at an accelerated speed. I threw myself behind the police officer and was in the driveway two seconds after him.

"Check everything with an explosives detector."

"What's wrong, baby, are you afraid your panties will explode?" Patrol Jones laughed, pointing to the open shed of the vehicle. The stuff that filled her interior did look harmless – some furniture, a few suitcases, and a pile of loose clothes.

"Please..."

In fact, I had the right to order police officers and patrolmen, because I was higher in the service hierarchy than they were, but in practice I never did. Evans taught me that it's much better to live in harmony with everyone than to use work relationships. This gave much better results. That is why I was on friendly terms with all officers and even with privates.

Yamato looked at me and nodded approvingly.

"Bring the equipment."

"Waste of time. Ridiculous..." the patrol commander snorted in dissatisfaction, but he obediently went to the warehouse and brought the scanner.

"You're a coward, you know?" Patrol Jones took the device from him and calibrated it skillfully. "You're probably afraid of your own shadow, aren't you, detective?"

"Deidre, believe me, these people can afford everything," I spread my hands in an apologetic gesture. "I may be panicking, but I have good reasons."

Jones shrugged lightly, then started to work. The scanner slammed slightly, emitting a bluish beam of light that penetrated the inside of the car, feeling everything that lay there. I watched it with bated breath, not even knowing if I would prefer the policewoman to find something, or if it turns out that I'm making a jerk of myself. I shouted when the rays suddenly turned red and the scanner started making high-pitched sounds. Jones stepped back automatically.

"It's probably syntexol. Yamato, call the bomb squad," she said. "Terry, get out of vehicle! Let no one touch what we brought!"

Syntexol is 'uranium for the poor' in police jargon – not because it's somehow radioactive, but because of its cumulative properties. Produced in the form of a suspension, it begins working only after the glycerol used as a carrier and at the same time a molecule insulator evaporated. The separate particles then behaved like magnetized iron filings – they clung to each other and accumulated up to supercritical volume, and then an explosion occurred. It was enough to cover fabrics or clothes with the atomizer, and then wait patiently. When the glycerol evaporated and the clothes treated in this way were stacked – what awaited wasn't good. During the loading and transportation of our things, there was no explosion only because too little time passed and the glycerol didn't manage to evaporate completely.

The sapper unit first of all ordered everyone to leave the building, and then set to work. I watched from the command window how specialists dressed in protective suits sprayed our items with clean glycerol, and then carefully, using long booms, separated individual pieces of clothing. They were opening suitcases and bags, and soon the whole courtyard looked like an eastern bazaar.

"How did you realize?" Cavanaugh asked, who appeared beside me so unexpectedly that I shuddered at the sound of his voice.

"I didn't realize at all," I said grimly. "That's the worst thing. It was rather my intuition. I thought that I would do something like that if I wanted to kill someone who isn't yet home."

Scott slapped me on the back.

"Congratulations, rookie. You begin to understand how the criminal mind works."

I shivered.

"Were it not for the patrol throwing our things randomly in suitcases and mixing up those sprayed with non-sprayed ones… or if more time had passed…"

Cavanaugh kicked the chipped piece of wall cladding.

"Their carelessness saved the lives of many people. I'm getting tired of it all."

"In one crime novel I read a detective said: Two or three more bodies, and I will really begin to lose my patience." I quoted from memory.

"You still have time for jokes?"

"I'm doing my best not to fall apart."

He looked at me and grimaced in a sympathetic smile.

"Either way, it's getting scary. Hardly anyone is insolent enough to deliberately attack policemen. To be honest, I don't remember anything like this happening during my service, and it's been a nice couple of years."

He thought about it and for a moment tapped his fingers on the nearest piece of furniture.

"We have to go to the counteroffensive," he said finally. Is this friend of yours really as good as they say?"

"Sue is the best virtualist on the moon."

"So we have to rent her services, at least temporarily. Our virtualist is a pathetic loser, he would not find his own hand in his pocket. I will give him notice tomorrow. Go to the apartment. The sappers are going to work for some time, but I'm afraid your wardrobe is done for."

"That's too bad. It's important that we're both alive. And that Monty wasn't hurt."

"Yeah... you probably wouldn't be able to take such a blow."

I didn't comment on this undoubtedly malicious remark. I didn't want to formulate clearly what place android occupies in my life, I was afraid of answering this question. And it certainly wasn't the right time for such consideration.

When I passed Scott's suggestion to Sue, she accepted it with a nod. She was terribly tired and it was only now that she could feel all the nervousness she had experienced.

"I'll go to him tomorrow," she promised. "I will transfer current commitments to Trey or Socorro and see what I can do. For now I have to sleep. I don't even want to eat. Where's our clothes?"

"Forget about them. Burglars dumped them with syntexol. Sappers took care of them, but unfortunately they have to destroy them after deactivation. We are barefoot and bare."

"Great. We'll go shopping in the gallery," Sue yawned loudly. "I have a lot of saved PPs, transferred to a non-food card. You could buy the whole store with them, we'll manage.

"I also have some resources."

"Then it's not the end of the world. Okay, I'm going to sleep. Your boss told them to put two folding beds here, but we don't have bedding."

"I'll go to the warehouse."

The police warehouseman listened to me comprehensively and took soldiers' sleeping bags and two cushions from some chest.

"We have nothing better," he said. "For now you'll have to deal with this."

I assured him that we would be very pleased and took what I got back to the apartment. On the spot, it turned out that Sue was already asleep, curled up on the bare bed like a small child. I put a pillow under her head and covered her with a sleeping bag. She murmured in her sleep but didn't wake up.

"And where will you sleep?" I asked Monty, who was watching my actions as if trying to understand what I was doing and why. "This bed is too narrow for the two of us."

"I can lie on the floor."

"That's some idea. Oh well, you'll spend the night in a chair. Now I have to take care of Sid, because the poor thing is going crazy in this cage."

I released the cat, which – offended to death – made a puddle on the floor, and then snorted and jumped on the wardrobe. I cleaned up, put his litter box in the corner, the other with the food bowl and dish, and put my pillow on the closet for lack of something better. I could do without it for one night. I tried to pet Sid, but he jumped away furiously. The poor animal didn't understand what was happening and it was hard to blame him.

Then I finally removed my clothes and slipped into the sleeping bag, falling asleep almost immediately. Before, I would think that after such experiences it would be impossible to sleep at all, but I have become accustomed to working in the police so much that it doesn't affect my sleep or my appetite.

***

Sue didn't mind working for the police. Her contract as a virtualist was formulated in such a general way that she could work properly for whom she wanted, as long as her actions are not directed against the Moon Company.

"We need to focus on this Brel," she said, sitting down at the police computer. "Certainly not the most important person at Romain Corporation, but rather something like a gray eminence and a dirty work specialist. First, contacts with Marceline Munroe. Second, we know that he has sticky hands because he couldn't resist the necklace. And lastly, he kills on commission and is extremely good at it. Knowing these facts, I should be able to come up with something."

She set a box of crackers, walnut biscuits and two bottles of Cool Rider on the table next to her, then went to work. Scott came in and nodded at me.

"Kelley discovered something," he said in a low voice as I approached. "He's calling us to the lab."

I looked at Sue, absorbed in decoding the data stream, and quietly left the data processing room. I knew that when my friend was in such a state, nobody was allowed to disturb her, so I closed the door as quietly as I could and set the status on the rectangular display to 'Don't disturb until further notice'.

Doctor McCave was waiting for us in the laboratory, looking through some prints on scraps of computer foil. A segment screen pulsed above the table, and the doctor compared printouts in symbols and charts showing in individual sectors. He turned away at the sound of our footsteps.

"It's getting stranger," he said grimly. "I finally have the results from biological material collected in this underground palace and from the necklace, as well as DNA from the Reeves marriage killer."

"Talk," said the inspector briefly, sitting down in one of the swivel chairs. I took a lab stool and stared at the doctor.

"I found two types of DNA on the necklace," he began. "One, obtained from microscopic traces of blood, belonged to Miss Munroe, and the other, from the remains of the epidermis, to a man. Biological traces collected in what Scotty described as the sick room belonged to several men and women, but the most interesting turned out to be those taken directly from the bed, drip tips and respirator.

"It means?"

"I am 99% sure that this genetic material belongs to a patient kept in bed. DNA changes indicate amyotrophic lateral sclerosis, so I'm not mistaken."

"All right," Cavanaugh agreed. "We have someone with some kind of sickness, what's the conclusion?"

Kelley McCave looked at him pityingly.

"This 'sickness', as you describe it, is an extremely rare disease, almost eliminated by genetic control. There is no cure for it. It leads to paralysis and death."

"Well, you're the doctor, so you must be right."

"Now, the second part of the surprise: when we remove the deformation of the helix, the DNA collected in bed coincides with the DNA from the Marceline Munroe's necklace and the DNA of our killer."

Scott stood up and started walking around the lab, folding his arms behind his back.

"So if you assume that the epidermis from the necklace belongs to Brel, alias Lopez, which seems quite certain, this guy from that bed, suffering from that thing, how are they related? Is it his twin brother? Father? Son?"

The doctor's mouth twisted in a sardonic smile.

"Not at all, Scotty," he replied. "It's one and the same person."

If he threw a bomb into the middle of the laboratory, that would surprise me less.

"How is that possible?!" I called out.

"I don't know how, but it's the truth. As you both know, human cloning was strictly forbidden a few centuries ago. The problem is that if this patient was cloned from the bed, the clone would also be sick. Meanwhile, the DNA from the necklace is healthy."

"Maybe somebody fixed it?"

"I'm not too sure. Research has been carried out for centuries, new drugs have been introduced, and complex therapies have been developed, but after each euphoria of a new discovery, a sad awakening occurs. Demyelization diseases escaped scientists until it was decided to eliminate them by means of gene control. This brought the expected result, although you had to wait almost two hundred years... Currently, they occur only sporadically. In college I saw one such case, a young, beautiful and extremely intelligent girl. Her whole family was banned from reproduction, even the furthest relatives."

"What happened to her?"

"She asked for euthanasia after the second wave of illness. But this isn't what this is about now. If I'm correct, we came across something very serious."

He took an old-fashioned book, printed on thin plastic pretending to be paper, from the table drawer.

"This is an old medical history textbook, although currently banned, truth be told," he said. "The chapter on transplantology describes the era of using FGC, fast growing clones."

"Say it in a more common tongue, please."

"Fast-growing clones were planned to be nearly devoid of brains. Containers of living spare parts lacking self-awareness. They were used for transplantation for some time, until a much more ethical method of growing separate organs was developed. Someone used old techniques to bring Mr. Lopez to this world. For what purpose, we can only guess."

Scott gritted his teeth and slammed the table with his hand.

"So we have to find the Romain Corporation biochemistry laboratory. There are all the answers."

"That's my guess, boss."

The inspector turned to me. He was silent for a moment, then asked:

"Are you on board with this? You are my employee and it's actually your job, but the threat is too serious for a beginner detective. Two policemen have already died, you were under attack. Something is happening here that I don't understand and that I can't stop. If you want to retreat, I'll send you to Earth on some pretext."

I thought about the political games of Citizen Hakat and shook my head. Still a big question, where I was in worse danger here or on Earth. It was better to stay and try to bring this matter to an end, whatever it was.

"Did you manage to read anything else from the traces?" Scott turned to Kelley.

"I put in the exact DNA codes into the database. Two belonging to known researchers, Melchor Belmonte and Clarence Hill. They are both talented bionists, removed from known institutes for unethical experiments. That's practically everything."

"Not too bad. Now you have to think: where could you locate the biochemistry laboratory so that it would not attract anyone's attention? Well? Figure it out."

It was easy to say 'figure it out'. Nothing came to my mind and I could only stare thoughtlessly at the wall. I think Scott had the same feelings because he shrugged resignedly and said:

"Come to the office, we'll look at Silvana's notes. Maybe there will be something. There even should be, after all, she wasn't killed for no reason."

Silvana's notes! I forgot about them. My dead friend kept a private diary and had a work notebook, a copy of which she updated every day. Feri Kunch found in her things properly described data carriers that he gave to the boss. Until now, we didn't have time to look at them and it had to be done.

Silvana's notes, concise and clear, contained lots of data that she had not shared with anyone yet. Many of them were incomprehensible to me, for they contained references to places in Lunnar and Lunwark, which I didn't know yet, and matters that I had no idea about. However, what I understood was enough. My friend, who died in tragic circumstances, somehow found people of the social margin with connections to Romain Corporation. I was surprised by the very existence of something like a social margin in this city. And yet there it was. Derelicts recruited mainly from workers who, for various reasons, rolled into the gutter, but there were also a few officials between them. They lived on some savings and poor income, including robberies and various frauds. Entering this underworld was very dangerous. Silvana apparently managed to penetrate there.

"Bertie Shakespeare and Milo Tin Can," I told Scott, handing him pod with the noted information. "These are, of course, nicknames, we don't know the real names yet. According to Silvana, they are liaison with a distributor of illegal chemicals. On the medium there are photos of them, not very good, because they were taken with a cheap spy camera, but clear enough I think."

Cavanaugh put the photos on his computer and enlarged them as much as possible. Bertie looked about forty, a neglected, witch-like woman with a grim face, while the man with the nickname Tin Can looked like a cheerful piglet from children's books. He was, well, not fat, but rather plump, pink and good-looking like the owner of a provincial pastry shop. Certainly aroused the trust of potential customers and that was its usefulness.

"Do you think they may be connected to Brel?" I asked.

"If they work for Romain Corporation, that's for sure. Our good-memory-Evans moved the real hornet's nest and certainly went too far. She probably came into possession of some extremely important information without even realizing it. I need to carefully analyze these notes. Unfortunately they are incomplete, some summary is missing... but we can handle it. If necessary, I will go to the place described by her and drag the two by the neck."

Scott's implants stepped back a little deeper into the eye sockets and flickered their diodes. He smiled as if to encourage me.

"Are you not afraid? They are dangerous people."

"No."

He stood up and stretched.

"You are the only one of the crew who saw me naked. You are discreet, you didn't ask anything, but you must have seen my scars."

"I mean, you are a police officer..."

"Yes, but I will tell you in confidence that most of these scars have nothing to do with my service."

I felt myself changing into one big question mark.

"I once used the services of the Bushido Agency."

I was speechless. The Bushido agency was a sort of legend, an illegal organization teaching the art of survival. It was said that if a student survives the whole course, then they would no longer fear anything. The effectiveness was 40% – exactly how many adepts survived to the end of their studies. The game of feelings on my face must have been easy to read because Scott smiled contentedly. He liked it when he was admired.

"I was taught to fight everything that was at hand and to get out of every situation. You must have wondered more than once how I lost my eyes. Well, you should know that anyone else would've died in my place during an organized assassination attempt. The armored rover used by my unit and escorted witness had deliberately damaged brakes, and a tank with an explosive HG 6 was placed on our way... Only I survived because I was taught how, but I lost my sight, I was severely burned and had eleven broken bones. Even so, I managed to get to a place where I was helped."

He ran a hand over his salt and pepper hair.

"So, as you can see, you don't have to worry about me," he went on. "All right, let's go to the main computer now and see what Miss Herefort looked up in it."

We found Sue sprawled comfortably in a swivel chair and eating biscuits. She looked extremely pleased with herself and smiled broadly at the sight of us.

"You have some great equipment here," she said. "I don't know what your virtualist is like, but he is either a failure or he has done deliberate sabotage."

"I know that, that's why I threw him out," Cavanaugh said calmly. "But how did you know that?"

"It was enough for me to review the computer's history. Most utilities are untouched at all, and these are real gems. For example, the entire system for determining transcripts, integrated with the municipal network of security cameras. Face recognition program. Not to mention the data synthesis programs, fantastic. Nobody used them, do you understand? Never."

"I suspected that," Scott's jaw clenched and he fitted himself for a moment.

"Have you found any signs of any suspicious manipulation?"

Sue looked at him out of the corner of her eye and tossed another cake into her mouth.

"You mean falsifying data or leaking it outside? Because both were done."

"Are you sure?"

"I'm rather confident. This employee of yours isn't only a mole, but also a klutz, it was easy to discover what and how he did it. I have now enabled the espionage system, installed it from my personal media. I always have a USB stick with me, I wear it in a medallion around my neck. With any luck, this program will track the path of transferring specific files, and then... who knows what we'll discover."

The inspector looked at her with clear respect, if not admiration. He had not yet dealt with virtualists of her caliber and didn't know their customs. Sue did carry all the more important data with her, mainly in the crystal medallion with which she didn't part, but not only. The other similar data carrier was set in a bracelet, and I wouldn't be surprised if her earrings contained a whole set of industry secrets. When I met her, I was surprised by the peculiar manner she wore her jewelry even with pajamas, a bathrobe or a sports suit, and it wasn't until weeks later that Hakat's niece explained why she wasn't parting with her tinsel.

"We have photos of two people who could have been in contact with Brel," he said after a moment. "Will it help with anything?"

"Of course."

"Only they aren't very good."

"Don't worry, give them to me. Even really terrible pictures can be very useful, for example using the Pixel Plus program and the Intuitive Tool. You have it on your computer. I will check if their roads have crossed this Brel guy."

She took the carrier given by the inspector and got to work, and we went out into the corridor, where Monty was waiting for us.

"You haven't eaten anything today," he said. It sounded like reproach.

Scott laughed softly.

"Is that your business?"

Monty turned his head toward him. Though his eyes looked just like a human's, for some reason he couldn't learn to look out of the corner of his eye – when he wanted to look at someone or look at something, he turned his face and sometimes his whole body in the right direction.

"I'm learning about people," he said. "I know you have to take in nutrients regularly, otherwise something may happen to you. That is why I remind her that Leeta didn't eat anything today."

Scott Cavanaugh spread his hands.

"You have an artificial guardian, girl. Such a mechanical mommy. That's just beyond human comprehension."

"Why?" I murmured angrily. "Even engineer Karpinsky warned that he isn't a robot, but an intelligent being. He thinks independently and feels his own way. In addition, he is right, I left home without breakfast and until now I had nothing in my mouth."

The inspector looked at his watch.

"Let's get some lunch then. Your android right, you should eat regularly, because a policeman fainting from hunger on duty is a poor advertisement for the main command of Lunnar. Come, we will go to Las Paranas.

We all ate in this small locale. We had a group subscription there, so it was very cheap and the food wasn't too bad.

"Monty, you'll wait here," I turned to the android. "You don't eat, so you could raise suspicion. Sit in the office and wait for me to come back. Then we will go shopping. Our clothes have been damaged, we must have new ones. Boss, can you lend me some PPs? Maybe some small account? We won't get police compensation very quickly. I have savings, but they may not be enough."

Scott reached into his wallet and took out one of the cards contained there.

"I serve you, my dear. You will give it back when you can."

And so, right after lunch I could go shopping and not think about running out of stock. I decided not to use Sue's money. I preferred that she did her own errands. Financial matters could separate even the best of friends, which I didn't want. I thought I'd buy her clothes from my own resources, and she could give it back to me later. That will be better.

While I was installing us in a service apartment, Sue worked on a police computer. From the beginning I knew that she would be of no help when choosing and arranging furniture, and I was actually glad that my roommate spent all her days at the police station. Thanks to that I had a free hand and didn't have to listen to her complaints. Monty helped me, reading my intentions better from a few words thrown casually every day.

"An android is not able to create a general theory of minds in his way of understanding the world," Karpinsky wrote to me. "That is why the instructions must be clearly stated. When you reach out for a knife and it lies too far, for a human you could say 'Hand it to me' and that will be enough. For the android, you would have to say 'Hand me the knife that lies on the table.' Otherwise he won't understand anything. If you fall and reach out to help you get up, he won't do it either. You can't count on him to be intuitive. I don't rule out that he will develop over time, but according to our theories and observations, it simply cannot be.

While learning from the example of Monty about androids, I was also aware that he was following me all the time and trying to understand through these observations what people are like. I knew we were no less a mystery to him than the android mind for me, but it was a surprise to me that he treated us as a problem to work out. In his actions, he was more like an alien studying Earth behaviorism, not artificial intelligence – in any case, such an impression could be made. He learned quickly. He could not only spread bread with nourishing paste, but also make a nice caffetino, cook pasta with toppings, make pudding with whipped cream... I wondered why he did it, but I didn't ask. I preferred to discover his motives myself and all I regretted was that I could not discuss everything with his creator, engineer Karpinsky. I had a feeling that direct conversations with this man would be very interesting.

After being done with the furniture, we went to the ready clothes store and returned with several bags full of clothing for the three of us. Fortunately, I knew Sue's size as well as my own and knew more or less what clothes she liked, because my friend was still absorbed in her work and - as usual in such circumstances – detached from the whole world. Glancing into the data processing room, I saw that she connected her own three-dimensional holographic screen to the police computer and put on a helmet bristled with cables, used to work in programs from the Integra package. Nobody was allowed to disturb her now, because the sudden break in the connection threatened with shock, severe irritation of the nervous system, and even brain damage.

I didn't know much about the Integra Multispeed program she was using and I couldn't work with it myself, but at the beginning of our acquaintance, Sue told me about it.

She warned me that if she had an interface helmet on my head, I keep my distance, and if she fainted, to call an ambulance immediately. She used it very rarely and always complained about headaches and nausea. However, certain information could only be reached in this way. It was clear that in this situation I can't ask Sue stupid questions about what color she wants her blouses in.

It wasn't until late evening that Scott Cavanaugh called me to his office. I found there a completely exhausted Sue and Kelley, who was just giving her an injection to the shoulder.

"People like you should be packed in a straitjacket," he grumbled. "Who could even strain the central nervous system this badly? Do you want to die or live in a clinic for incurable lunatics?"

"Doctor, my head hurts," Sue moaned. "It hurts so much..."

"It will stop soon. And for the next three or four weeks you are to stay away from this filth, okay? Because if not, then in an old-fashioned method I will put you over my knee and I will blend your butt with a military belt so badly you won't be standing for a week. Here I'm doing autopsies on criminals and suicides, but I don't want to be cutting open a friend who overdoses. Is that clear?"

The measure he was using must have started working because, pale until now, Sue turned pink and brightened. The doctor also noticed. He lit a small flashlight in her eyes, examined the pupils, and nodded approvingly.

"Looks like you had a lucky escape this time. Better right?"

"Oh, even pretty good."

Scott, patiently waiting for the doctor to finish his work, drummed his fingers on the desk top.

"So what did you find out, Miss Herefort?" He asked.

Sue rubbed her temples with her fingers and took out a pod from the pocket of her gown, which she usually tossed over her blouse.

"Everything is here," she said. "I made traced routes of all three of them. They intersect at the place referred to as the Swamp. The name says it all. The entire underworld of Lunnar meets there. However, that's not all I was able to pull out of the streams."

"I hope it was worth it, because you almost ended up in hospital."

"I don't know, but I think so," Sue plugged into the computer on the inspector's desk and turned on the screen. "I started thinking where you could hide something like a good biochemistry laboratory. Unfortunately, there wasn't anything useful from the manuscripts in this aspect, so I think that our suspects used the unmonitored passages at the right time, probably from the city channels. The question was where they went. Chance helped me."

She highlighted a point in the scheme displayed on the screen, which increased several times. I recognized the fashion house Jackie Perralt with astonishment.

"At first I didn't pay attention to it myself. After all, we all know about the cosmetics factory, and especially the wide range of care creams and perfumes belonging to the Perralta Inc. network. It's no secret that it's more profitable for the local branch to manufacture cosmetics on the spot than to import them, because no additional customs duty is paid for the components, as well as finished products. For this purpose, a small factory was created, it's understood to be legalized and possessing all possible certificates. That's why none of you, dear detectives, thought about checking this place."

She was absolutely right about that. We found checking a plant which works according to the law pointless, especially in light of the fact that we had unlimited access to all sanitary reports and inspection results. The entire production profile was known and approved – what is there to do here then?

"While checking all the places where work has anything to do with chemistry and biochemistry, I had to eventually get to this factory," Sue continued. "I found comprehensive data, including full technical specifications of the laboratories. And then I saw something that could be easily overlooked as a matter of cursory control: the factory is housed in a suitably adapted building, consisting of three levels. Officially, it uses only one of them, the rest is listed as a semi-finished product warehouse. The problem is that, in fact, the cosmetics components are delivered on a regular basis, and the iron reserve, as I have calculated, cannot take up more than 10% of the spare space."

"Hmmm, how did nobody notice it before?" Kelley asked after a moment.

"The company pays all their fees on time, and the building was built from its own funds. No corporation, at least officially, had anything to do with it. What are we here to pick on and for what purpose?"

Scott Cavanaugh nipped his lower lip for a moment, without taking his eyes off the screen. It was obvious that he was thinking intensively.

"That makes sense," he said finally. "From the beginning I wondered how they knew where Silvana and her husband went, and how they associated Carlita and Anna Fuentes with the marriage of Reeves. After all, we kept it secret to give them peace and so that the vacationers would not be stressed by the presence of the police. The branch manager could, however, know everything. Since she had lent Silvana a dress worth her annual salary, she'd probably cut off more than one chat with her. Anything else, Miss Herefort?"

"Yes. A list of shareholders of the Jackie Perralt network. It's so secretive that I was able to pull it out only when operating the Integra. The name of the main shareholder may interest you."

"Okay, who is it?"

"Cassius Jones."

"Third Vice President of Romain Corporation?!"

"I believe so. Rather, we are not dealing here with a random coincidence of names. This doesn't seem to prove anything, the law doesn't prohibit the president of one company from having shares in another, but it's interesting, right?"

Scott cursed through his teeth, and I felt a cold shiver between my shoulder blades.

"What now, boss?"

"I'll call the prosecutor's office. You will need a delivery order, and after a few hours I will ask for a search warrant."

"Are you so sure that the manager will talk?"

"He doesn't have to. I have an excuse to let me enter the factory premises."

"For sure?" I asked doubtfully. "Do you remember how it was with the mine?"

"Of course. This time I will be blowing cold. Trust me. After that history I got all permits, only one paper is missing. But we will get this one as soon as we confirm the discovery of Miss Herefort."

"It's not a discovery yet, it's just a hypothesis," Sue corrected and yawned. "I have to go to sleep, I can barely stand. You worry about what to do next, it's not my business anymore."

She stood up and staggered so that I could barely catch her.

"Sorry."

"You owe yourself that, girl," Kelley growled. "Now go to bed and stay in it for three days or you will regret it. It's better not to argue with doctors."

Our pathologist was right. For the next two days, Sue couldn't even sit down, and I discovered a new field in which Monty could be useful. He looked after my friend like a nurse, bringing her drinks and medicines, improving the bedding, leading to the bathroom when the need arose... It looked as if he wanted to feel needed at all costs – another feature I didn't expect from him at all.

"He surprises me more and more," I told our doctor. "Engineer Karpinsky was telling the truth. His mind develops and assimilates knowledge just like the human brain. Instead of relying on established patterns of behavior, he learns through observation and modifies his behavior as needed."

"In a word, it's not a robot. It looks like both you and that engineer were right. However, I still don't support replacing a man with an artificial substitute in erotic matters," Kelley looked at me attentively. "Good though you don't neglect visiting the dating center. You must have normal relationships with people, at your age, using a sexbot is a sign of some kind of disorder. It's another thing if you were older..."

"Monty isn't a sexbot!" I interrupted him angrily.

I was getting dressed for action in the field and my hands were shaking with nervousness. I tried to hide it, but I wasn't very good at it.

"Yes, yes, you already said that," the doctor waved his hand. "For me it's a semantic issue. Doesn't matter. When I change the subject, I will look into Sue. If she's all right, she'll be able to get back to work tomorrow. She should be pleased with that."

"Without a doubt. She can't live without the computer."

"Well, she now has a computer in shoes with the number 45. I wonder if she explores its possibilities with the same passion as you."

"Kell!" I dropped one of the gloves and I had to bend down for it. "You can be really disgusting sometimes! Are all doctors like that?"

"Absolutely."

Inspector Cavanaugh interrupted us and he chased us both with harsh words. He was clearly tense, his implants had already protruded to the maximum distance and he looked as if he was awaiting some unpleasant surprise. Although all indications were that he got rid of the 'mole' – since that was the station's virtualist – he still preferred to be vigilant and not to trust his lucky star too much. If he wanted to carry out this plan successfully, he had to act quickly and decisively. He checked all the documents again before storing them inside his uniform jacket.

"Leeta," he said hesitantly. "If someone questions you, then..."

"What?"

"Don't make such a frightened face! Nobody's going to cut your head off. I just gave your name to the prosecutor's office as the person who got the key information. You'll confirm them if needed, period."

"Oh dear mother, why?!"

"Because I can't admit to using a virtualist unrelated to the police! This is against the regulations. You can say that Sue taught you what to do, but you must not spill that she did all the work for us. Is that clear?"

"Yes, boss."

I didn't even have time to cool down. Running to the police rover I thought that maybe it's for the better. Citizen Hakat would not be particularly pleased if he knew what I involved his niece in. What the inspector came up with looked good. I was just hoping that during a possible interrogation nobody would ask me to present how to use the Integra. That would be the end of my credibility.

I have never seen so many astonished faces as today, together with the whole team, I found myself in the factory's fashion house. Inspector Cavanaugh wasted no time.

"Please, keep working," he said commandingly. "No one is allowed to leave the area or use information links, otherwise you can work normally. We have a search warrant, but we will leave the factory as soon as we're done."

At his command, the patrol covered the entire facility, while our small team – Scott, me, Feri Kunch and Dr. McCave – went to the office of the factory manager, Paula Ruben.

The action was carried out so smoothly that when we entered, Mrs. Ruben had no idea about our presence.

"What is the meaning of this?" she called, leaping from the desk. "Who let you in here?"

"We let ourselves in," Scott came over and gave her the warrant. "We'll do a search and we're gone. Please come with us."

"For what?"

"You'll show us a descent to lower levels."

"And what are you interested in there? It's just magazines."

"We already know what interests us. We are asking for cooperation."

Paula Ruben hesitated. It was obvious that she was afraid of something, because she paled under the layer of makeup, and on her temples and upper lip appeared drops of sweat.

"Fine," she said finally. "But I want you to know that I'm just a regular employee and know nothing."

"I believe you," Scotty said kindly.

His words didn't seem to give the woman courage. She went ahead with her head down, as if she was going to be shot. One of the patrols was left to watch her secretary and answer any calls, and we followed the manager of the factory.

Going down to lower levels, I sniffed reflexively, trying to smell the smell of chemicals. In the part where cosmetics were produced, the air was heavy with the smell of essential oils, bases and reagents, but here... the atmosphere was clean. Even too clean.

It reminded me of the controlled environment of the biosphere, in which some species of plants that were extremely sensitive to pollution were bred.

"Boss, they probably have an environmental control system here," I said. "But that's... it's impossible."

"Why?"

"Even the equipment of a small greenhouse is very expensive to operate. Keeping it in a room of this size must be extremely expensive."

"They don't spare any expense," Cavanaugh muttered, and I noticed that he took the weapon slightly out of the holster. Feri Kunch did the same. I had only a simple stunner, because I had not yet received permission for anything more deadly, and the doctor was unarmed – as he once confessed to me, it would be pointless, because he would never shoot anyone. Having undergone deontological conditioning he would not be able to deal with violence in any situation. As a doctor, he didn't have to fight. The badge of medical service guaranteed him immunity even among the worst thugs.

We found ourselves in an almost empty warehouse, gray and completely ordinary. I didn't expect that. Mrs. Ruben stopped in front of one of the walls.

"It's here," she said. "I don't know how to get in there, but I know the passage is here."

Feri Kunch stepped forward and took the signal scanner from his shoulder bag. He began to wander the sensor protruding from it against the wall, observing the oscillometer, and finally stopped his hand. He fingered the wave emitter from the bag with his other hand and connected it to the scanner. I knew this procedure. It was extremely delicate and was a professional secret of the police. The emitter drew data from the scanner and processed it into the appropriate combination of waves or vibrations, with which you could open more than one lock, but you had to be skilled in tuning the frequency. I couldn't do it yet.

After a few very long seconds in the wall something slammed slightly and the wall plate, which seemed to be solidly welded from the outside, separated from the one with which it formed a right angle. It slowly slid into the matching sleeve, revealing a passage. The small entrance was blocked by one more door, but this one ordinary. There was a buzz of voices behind them, the noise of machines, and finally the smell of chemicals.

"Great masking," Cavanaugh muttered appreciatively and stepped aside. "No, wait! None of us can go in there until I bring the prosecutor here. He must see this passage with his own eyes. Leeta, call a team of storm troopers. Nobody can leave here either."

I sent the call via a handheld messenger. After a while, an armed detachment appeared beside us, and I wondered what the storm troopers would do when someone wanted to leave the internal rooms. Shoot them on the spot? Or are they just intimidating? In their case, everything was possible, because the powers of the rapid response units put the entire formation above the official chain of command of the police. These people depended solely on the orders of their own superior, so our storm troopers listened to Scott only because it was commanded by Colonel Lois Ann Sirtis, a tough and ruthless woman. The 'mean bitch', as was commonly said, didn't fight with Cavanaugh for dominance and that was the best for us, but she marked her independence. Scotty was very important to her, more than anyone, and he told us once and for all that we should not get in the way of her or her people. Fortunately, we have managed to maintain the status quo so far and there were no major frictions.

Inspector Cavanaugh and Prosecutor Johnson showed up half an hour later. This was the first time I saw this man, the Earth's prosecutor's delegate, Nick Cable's deputy, a lawyer who supposedly once used to be an excellent politician, but made a mistake and was sent to Lunnar. He looked like a model diplomat in his old age – handsome, sleek and dignified, only his eyes were grim and frightening. I felt that it was better not to joke with this man and instinctively took a step back when his cloudy gaze fell on me.

"Is this the gem that found the information?" he asked, and I thought I heard a note of undisguised hostility in his voice. "New virtualist?"

"No. A detective trainee, but very talented."

"Congratulations. So?"

"As you can see, we discovered a passage to an unregistered laboratory," said the inspector, seemingly not paying attention to the apparent dissatisfaction of the prosecutor, "Sergeant Kunch, please close the passage and then open it again."

Ferl manipulated the emitter. The wall plate slammed down noiselessly and then slid open.

"Interesting indeed," Johnson admitted reluctantly and adjusted his tie. "What's in there?"

"Please sign the warrant, we will enter then."

The prosecutor took a stylus from his breast pocket and signed a sweeping signature on the computer foil put forth.

The courts were still more eager to honor foil than pods, more like a traditional paper document."

"I'll come in with you," he said in a voice that raised no objection, hiding his stylus. "This case is looking to be quite interesting, and I don't want to miss it."

"Please. That's even better," Scott carefully put the foil away and signaled to Foni. He went to the door and opened it all the way.

"Please stay in your seats!" he announced through a megaphone. "The area is now under the control of the police!"

The hidden room was silent at first, then there was panic like a tornado. Urged by Scott, I stepped back against the wall so as not to disturb the storm troopers and grabbed Kelley by the arm.

"What do you think is this place?"

He smiled crookedly at me.

"Don't you smell it? Chemistry, biochemistry, probably genetics, and I hear noises of the sequencer. In any case, this should not be here. Fashion houses are licensed only for industrial production, and this here is definitely some scientific experiments."

He pushed me away and grabbed the girl in a white apron with a technician badge who was trying to slip through the door.

"Where are you off to, girl? Oh no, life's not that simple. You got involved in illegal activity, so have the dignity to accept responsibility for your actions."

One of the storm troopers came over and took the captured laboratory worker to a room where the hysterical personnel were being locked. It was hardly a surprising reaction. All employees were aware that this whole laboratory is illegal and they are breaking criminal law, but until now they probably thought they were 'covert'. The police invasion deprived them of their illusions and scared them to death. Suddenly they realized that they would not escape responsibility and lost their temper.

Finally, the storm troopers finished their work and we could proceed with our tasks in peace. First of all, we looked at all the rooms thoroughly, photographing every angle and every equipment. There was quite a lot of it. Equipped with an individual air purification system, the studios were placed side by side, wanting to maximize the available space. The data processing room was even smaller, so small that it was possible to get claustrophobic.

The first part of the complex didn't look very interesting. Drugs were made in there. Scott only looked at it briefly and quite dismissively, then called a few police officers and ordered them to write everything down for the record. Feri took care of securing data from computers and private notebooks. Scott and I took Kelley to the second part, which was biochemical. I was uncomfortable working with the prosecutor's office eyes on my back, but I tried to be professional. I didn't want to compromise my supervisor.

Opening the next door, I was a little worried that I'd come across something like in the mine, because I already guessed what experiments were carried out here and for what.

Test tubes, flasks, beakers, and microscopes – all this didn't tell me much, but the tables and charts on the walls were more readable to me. They represented various combinations of genes on a double helix of DNA and various stages of embryonic development. The last room we entered was larger than the other and all covered with glass shelves. There were jars with anatomical preparations on them, marked with different colors and tablets. At first I didn't realize what is peculiar in this view, it was only after a long time that I realized that the rings were grouped. None of them stood apart, all set up in two small compartments.

"Comparative exhibition," Dr. McCave murmured behind me. "They were involved in cloning human embryos. They changed the gene sequence and watched what would come out of it."

"What for?"

The answer to this question was rather clear and I was afraid of it. However, it had to be said. I looked questioningly at Doctor and Scott.

"That's fairly clear," said Kelley. "Our mysterious Mr. X suffers from a degenerative disease. Here they tried to find a way to help him. Do you remember those brains? They wanted to develop a method of transplanting a living human brain into a functioning body, but so far it has been impossible. In addition, it would be pointless."

"Why?" Intrigued Attorney Johnson came closer. The doctor looked at him briefly.

"Diseases of this type are associated with demyelinating processes. They attack nerve cells, and what does the brain and spinal cord consist of? A brain transplant attacked in this way is a bad idea. It would be different if the consciousness itself could be transferred to a new body..."

"Is that possible?"

"Fortunately not. Human consciousness cannot be transferred or copied to another 'medium', so to speak. Neither biological nor artificial."

He took one of the jars and examined its contents.

"Something puzzles me here," he murmured after a moment. "These embryos were cloned by the second type of rapid growth method. It's forbidden, but good for growing organ storage, not for humans."

"Maybe they just needed organs?"

"Certainly, since they wanted to transplant brains, they had to have something to put them in. However, Brel or Lopez, or how you want to call him, certainly wasn't bred in this way, although I had previously thought about it."

"How do you know that?"

The doctor looked at Harry Johnson, who asked this question and answered calmly:

"Fast-growing clones are by definition just brainless, so they are planned. However, even if it were otherwise, an adult with an infant's brain would be obtained using the acceleration technique. And Brel's behavior points to something completely different."

"Which means?"

"That he was cloned a long time ago, and he grew up like a normal child. It was probably done when SLA was detected in Mr. so that... well, here we can only theorize. The problem is, people with amyotrophic lateral sclerosis don't live that long. This disease kills within half a year to a few years."

"No exceptions?"

"They happen, of course. For example, this famous astrophysicist from the twentieth century of the old era, whatever he was called... However, I think our X is undergoing some innovative therapy and that's why he is still alive."

"And what is Brel's role in this?" Inspector Cavanaugh asked.

McCave examined the jar again.

"I have a theory," he said after a moment. "However, I must carefully examine all materials so as not to be fooled. This theory is completely crazy, and I wouldn't know anything about it if I didn't attend Dr. Lindeburgh's seminars."

"Who's that?"

"A psychiatrist."

"What?!"

"I'll explain it later, but not now. Please give me some time."

The collapse of the secret laboratory was the first spectacular success of the main command in our fight against Romain Corporation and the first blow that actually shook the company. First of all, they lost their pill factory, from which they made their employees addicted and everyone who the dealers managed to reach. In addition, they could no longer deny their links to the underground trade in illegal chemicals, and this seriously damaged the credibility of Romain Corporation in the eyes of the board of directors of the Moon Mining Company. If it were for another corporation, the matter would be over – but this one already had holdings of shares of other companies, thanks to which it was too strong and too well managed.

"The experimental laboratory was as important to these people as the hermezin and its derivatives plant," Dr. McCave told us a few days later. "You have no idea how advanced this equipment is, it's a shame it was in that place."

"Don't be stupid, Kell," the inspector said dryly.

"This isn't stupid, but whatever you say. So, I analyzed the data and examined the preparations. Everything seems to point to an incredible scandal."

"What exactly?" Sue asked, rocking steadily in the chair next to me. Her big eyes, shining with interest, looked like a doll's, the round face took on the same expression as the face of a small child in front of a confectioner's exhibition.

"Brel's role isn't only murdering policemen or driving officials to suicide. This man is a doublet."

"So a clone? We already know that."

"No, Miss Herefort, not just a clone, but a doublet. A neurological chip was surgically placed in his brain, having connection to a second such chip..."

"...implanted in Mr. X's brain," Scott finished. "I remember something about this technology."

"It's one hundred percent illegal. It's called artificial telepathy. This name speaks for itself. Thanks to Brel, Mr. X can see, hear and experience other sensory impressions, at a distance. And at the same time Brel carries out his commands."

He shook his head and rubbed the left implant, as if to see if they were still there.

"This alone is the basis for confiscating the company's assets," he murmured. "Anything else?"

"Yes, but it's a long shot," the doctor walked over to the computer and switched on the holographic screen that had been mounted recently. He enlarged it and developed a picture of Lopez's face over the desk top. Next to it – a portrait of Brel. We looked at them in astonishment, not knowing why he was showing them to us. Meanwhile, Kelley entered the graphics program and began to touch the sensors, changing the image of our wanted. First, the 'shaved' Brel, which made both portraits practically equal. Then he put them on, blurred the small differences, aged a little and earned some gray hair and broad, bushy eyebrows. I heard my boss curse softly through his teeth, while I was speechless

"Accidental resemblance?" Scotty finally tried to save the situation. He also couldn't understand what resulted from the manipulation of our doctor.

"I thought so too, though the coincidence is too unbelievable. However, I used the central medical database and everything became clear."

The holographic screen displayed a portrait of Prosecutor Johnson, and then a second man, very similar to him, only much younger.

"Here's our Mr. X," Dr. McCave said emphatically. "His real personalities are Leon Beavis Hampton, half-brother of Harry Johnson, entrepreneur and fourth on the list of the richest citizens of Earth."

"Dear God," Sue muttered. Her clear admiration for the skill of our pathologist fought for better with the professional jealousy of the virtualist, who was defeated by someone in finding important data.

"Everything starts to fall into place," the inspector stood up and walked the length and width of the office, folding his arms behind his back. "It's a bigger swamp than we thought."

He stopped unexpectedly in front of me.

"Leeta, talk to your protector," he asked. "We don't have anyone to contact anymore."

"I can only get a secure connection at night," Sue said, and added, seeing Scott's scared look. "Give me a break, he's my uncle! I won't betray you. As I said, at night we can give him whatever you want. I won't give 100% confidentiality guarantee before that."

"All right, let's wait until tonight," Scott agreed. "You will give Citizen Hakat all our data and ask him for high-level intervention. Kell, I hope you didn't say anything to anyone?"

"Of course not, who do you think I am!"

"That's good. That means we still have a chance. All right, ladies, go to dinner now and then home and prepare the materials for broadcast. They must be as compressed as possible."

He paused, looking attentively at me.

"Prepare your android for questioning too," he said finally. "Now that we have legal evidence against Romain Corporation, he has become an important witness and the prosecutor will want to find out what he has to say."

"I thought they would leave him alone!" I called out in alarm. Scott put a hand on my shoulder.

"Calm down. Nothing threatens him. Just make sure he is decently dressed for the occasion. Don't let them find fault, you understand?"

"I understand... but his clothes were lost in that assassination attempt."

"Then buy him some new ones!"

"Unless I transfer points from the assignment card to the industrial one. It's all empty, all I have left is PPs for food."

"I'll make a transfer from the emergency police fund in a moment. Don't touch the points for food allocation, they won't give you more anytime soon. I know you women: you will see some stupid purse at the exhibition and immediately lose your mind. And then you live for two weeks with substitute protein rations, because the assignment card is empty. We have to watch over you like children."

I wanted to take offense, but I gave up. I remembered how many times I transferred points to an industrial card because I wanted to show off to my colleagues a fashionable blouse or a watch from a new collection. In my opinion at the time, it was worth tightening the belt for several days. We all did that, except the richest girls. Unfortunately, my boss had a point.

After lunch, I left Sue encrypting data for Hakat, and then took Monty to the clothes warehouse to choose a suit and a few normal sets for everyday use. It's true that I was in this composition before with the honest intention of supplying all three of us, but before I looked back, I spent everything on women's clothes and cosmetics. I consoled myself then with the thought that the android would easily wait for them to pay us a salary, but the situation required – as was clear to see – acceleration. I let Monty choose shoes, pants and shirts for himself, but I found the suit for him myself. I wanted him to be really spotless and fortunately they had the right model in the composition. It cost quite a lot, but luckily I had enough points transferred to me by Scott.

"Let's just go to the cosmetic store now," I said when we left the warehouse. "I need to buy you a male deodorant and cologne. You don't shave or sweat, but people pay attention to the smell of cosmetics and may wonder why you don't smell like anything."

"If you think it's necessary, let's do it," he agreed with me.

As he walked by my side, laden with parcels, we looked together like a normal pair and nobody paid us any attention.

But was that really the case?

One of the cabs passing by us slowed down slightly and something flashed in its window for a split second, as if a ray of light fell on some shiny object. I sensed faster than I understood what was happening and lunged forward.

"Monty, get down!"

I grab him, cover him, push him down, and nearly at the exact same time I receive a strong blow to the back, as if I had fallen on a large stone. The world swirls in front of my eyes, I hold the android hugging me. Was he all right, did I make it in time? Who would fix him if he was damaged? No, I can't even think about it, I can't imagine living without him. His face, right in front of mine, remains perfectly calm, his eyes glistening with silver and gray steel, but why is this warmth flooding my arms and chest? Where does this red come from? Blood? So much blood... From where? Androids don't bleed! I hear screams, is the whole street screaming? I don't understand.

"Monty..."

"Relax, stay down, don't get up..."

Stay down? What does he mean? He's the one who's down! The world suddenly makes a turn, and I understand that for a moment I received it in a false perspective. Yes, I'm the one on the ground, and Monty is leaning over me, I see his beautiful eyes right next to mine, fingers tight on my shoulders, he doesn't let me move. I feel no pain, just a nagging weight on my chest, a huge weight.

"Monty," I'm sobbing. "Don't leave, don't leave me..."

"I won't leave," he promises with his even, calm voice. "I will never leave."

"Are you sure you're okay?"

"I'm okay, I'm not damaged. Lie still, an ambulance is coming here, they will fix you soon...".

Gray-silver eyes are right next to mine, so calm, arousing trust and an inexplicable sense of security. I can hear the moaning of the ambulance from a distance, but the only thing that counts for me is that Monty didn't suffer, that I made it in time... The world is becoming dark, blurring in front of my eyes and finally everything disappears, and I only feel the mechanical hands holding me tightly...